THE FIRE INSIDE

B. A. Colella

For all our first responders—men and women who rush in when others step back, who bring hope in the darkest moments, and whose sacrifices often go unseen.

A Glossary of Fire Service Terms and Map of the
MAFA Fire District can be found at the back of this book.

Part I

New Horizons

1

Friday, August 15

Tony Moretti released his grip on the Pulaski hand tool and eyed the low-rising flames dancing along the wooded ridgeline while the *brrrr-brrrr* of a chainsaw reverberated in his ears. Despite the danger, his hands were perfectly still. There was no trace of the anxiety that had dogged him for so long. Proof that the summer had exorcised his mental demons.

The wildfire had topped the jagged hillside and now inched into the ravine, devouring the dry brown vegetation in its path. Soon it would lay waste to the green leaves and branches of the majestic Douglas fir, bigleaf maple, and western hemlock trees as it marched inexorably toward the containment line and the exhausted crew.

With dusk approaching, the temperature hovered in the low nineties, and the wind velocity had increased during the past half hour. Glowing embers swirled among the crew like thousands of swarming fireflies. High heat, low humidity, and gusting winds were the deadliest enemies of wildland firefighters.

It was Tony's last day on this Oregon fire line. *How did three months pass so quickly?* he wondered.

The crew had been at it with saws and hand tools all afternoon, stripping all organic material from a forty-foot-wide swath of ground. The fire, when it arrived, would meet nothing but bare earth—a defensive barrier Tony and his colleagues hoped would be impassable.

"Hey, Airport, you takin' a break already?" asked Jimmy Morris, working the line to Tony's right. "Maybe this ain't the work for you."

Tony laughed as sweat dripped from his forehead in a steady stream. "Don't worry about me, Jimbo. I'm twice the man you are." His eyes stung, but he knew better than to rub them. He reached into his pack, pulled out a quart bottle, downed a gulp of warm water, and poured the rest over his face.

"Twice the man? Nah. Twice the sweating pig, maybe. That beard is so wet you could wring it out and use the water to extinguish the whole hillside." Jimmy poked Tony with the handle of his chingadera—a wide-bladed scraping and chopping tool—and broke out into a wide grin. "I know you want to go back home and be the big-time East Coast firefighter, but you know you're gonna miss us."

"Oh, he knows it. He just won't admit it," Lauren Baxter, working to Tony's right, chimed in.

"Miss your ugly mugs?" Tony scoffed playfully. "Miss hiking into the wilderness on ninety-degree days with forty pounds of gear on my back? Miss inhaling all this smoke with no respirator? Miss the constant threat of being overrun by fire? Miss putting my life on the line for a measly fifteen bucks an hour? No chance."

But Tony *would* miss it, despite the aches and pains, the unrelenting physical struggle, and the wheezing cough. He'd miss Jimmy and the rest of the twenty-person hand crew he'd come to know during his stint as a seasonal firefighter for the US Forest Service. He'd built an unbreakable bond with these men and women. They'd helped him put the past behind, and he wasn't eager for their association to end.

Hector Torres, the crew boss—a man even taller and more powerfully built than Tony—interjected. "Okay, amigos, everyone knows you two have some twisted love for each other, but we've got a fire line to finish cutting before nightfall."

Jimmy, dwarfed by his two colleagues, cranked a thumb toward Hector and shot a wry look at Tony. "And you called *me* the asshole?"

Lauren spit out the water she'd been drinking and hooted with laughter.

Tony laughed too, then stowed the empty plastic bottle in his pack and resumed his work. Using the axe end of the Pulaski—a tool with a thirty-six-inch handle and dual cutting and scraping heads—he hacked at the brush, grass, and roots before scraping the fallen vegetation away from the advancing flames. His muscles strained with each swing, but he didn't relent. Dust, mixed with sweat, clung to his face like paste while the scent of freshly turned earth mingled with the approaching smoke, steeling him for what had to be done.

Two air drops of fire-retardant slurry had slowed the fire's progress, but the steep, rugged terrain meant no access for heavy equipment, so the work had to be done by hand. *Cutting lines, that's what stops wildfires,* Tony thought.

Although he'd met the physical standards necessary for the job, nothing could prepare a new wildland firefighter for the extreme endurance required to cut fire breaks through old-growth forests. Tony had done so much physical labor this summer that, at forty, he was in the best shape of his life.

The team's current assignment was a stubborn blaze in the jagged topography of the Columbia River Gorge, between Portland to the west and Mount Hood to the east. Tony's crew had arrived in Oregon three weeks ago after completing their last job in the Colorado Rockies. Before that, they'd plied their trade in the Wasatch Mountains of Utah.

He'd miss the beauty of the American West, with its spectacular and seemingly endless scenery. And the night skies were unbelievably clear. Without a city's light pollution, the Milky Way was so much brighter and more visible to the naked eye. *I could make myself a home out here someday,* he thought.

Another glance at the ridge confirmed the flames were growing higher and moving faster. Was the crew far enough ahead of it? Was it too late to start a backburn to further increase the width of the barrier? Fire conditions could change drastically in minutes, and he redoubled his efforts to clear the thick vegetation on the moderately sloping hillside.

While he worked, he studied the surrounding terrain for an avenue of retreat. The planned area of refuge was a hundred and fifty yards below them, next to a nearly dry stream at the bottom of the ravine.

Tony spotted what looked like the clearest path to the stream and made a mental note. *I should be scared to death, but I'm not.* In fact, he'd been fatalistic during his entire stint with the Forest Service, and he knew the source of that mindset lay not in the dangers of wildland firefighting but in a very different scenario that had played out on a frigid February night three years ago at the Reynolds International Airport in central Pennsylvania.

"Save some strength, Airport," Jimmy said. "I know you're a he-man, but we could be on this line a while."

"Just focused on the job, Jimbo, thinking about the delicious meal we're going to devour at base camp. Can't take another MRE."

"I'm with you there, brother. I can't wait for a big juicy steak with—"

Tony's radio, strapped to the front of his long-sleeved bright yellow brush shirt, squawked. "All units from Operations, the fire is picking up speed. Redeploy to your safe zones immediately."

"Holy shit," Jimmy said as he scanned the ridgeline. "Look how fast it's moving. I didn't see that coming."

Tony had, but he didn't say so as he flipped the Pulaski over his shoulder.

"Everyone, listen up. We're getting out of here," Hector shouted as he moved behind the line. "Our safe spot is next to the streambed. Let's move!"

With that order, twenty men and women hefted their hand tools and chainsaws, backed away from the line they'd been cutting, and began picking their way down the slope as quickly as possible.

"Follow me, Jimbo," Tony said. "I know the best route to the stream."

"I'm with you, buddy," Jimmy replied.

For the first time all summer, Tony noticed fear in his friend's eyes.

It's said by experienced firefighters that wildfires, like mountains, make their own weather. That phenomenon revealed itself in dramatic fashion as the wind picked up and sent hot gusts into the retreating crew. Stomping feet, howls of pain, and curses filled the air as they navigated the tangled brush.

Halfway down the slope, the ravine grew darker while the rapidly multiplying embers glowed brighter. Spot fires appeared on the opposite side of the stream. *Not good.*

Hector saw it too. "It's crossed the stream. Drop your packs, grab your shelters, and run!"

It was the wildland firefighter's worst fear—entrapment. Yet, even as he felt the heat on his back, Tony remained calm.

He immediately stopped, dropping the Pulaski. He released the straps of his field pack and let it fall to the ground as a blistering gust hit him in the face. Ignoring the assault, he reached for the blue fire shelter at the bottom of the pack. Jimmy was ten yards behind and doing the same.

Tony yanked the yellow strap, pulling the aluminized shelter kit out of its case. "Run, Jimbo!" he called as he retrieved the Pulaski. Summoning all his strength, he turned and sprinted for the stream, now less than fifty yards away. *This is going to be close.*

"Oh shit!" Jimmy yelled.

Tony glanced over his shoulder; Jimmy was sprawled on his back. Without hesitation, he skidded to a stop, reversed direction, and took off for his friend.

Jimmy tried getting to his feet but collapsed onto one knee. "I tripped over a fucking rock," he said as Tony approached. "I think I broke my ankle."

"I've got you," Tony said. "Where's your shelter?"

"I don't know. It flew out of my hand when I fell." Jimmy's eyes reflected terror and hopelessness.

Tony scanned the ground, but the brush was too thick. "Forget it. We can double up." He dropped his tool and hoisted Jimmy to his feet.

Hector, who must have seen what had happened, sprinted to Tony's side. "We've got to go!"

Together, holding fast to their shelter packs while Jimmy draped his arms over their shoulders, they hustled over the rocks and through the thick undergrowth.

Lauren came up behind them. "I've got Jimmy's shelter. Let's go!"

That solves one problem, Tony thought as the little group crashed through the brush toward the previously cleared spot at the edge of the stream. *But it'll still be a miracle if we survive.* As before, he felt no fear, only concern for his colleagues.

"Let's get him in his shelter!" Hector ordered.

"I can do it myself," Jimmy said. "Just set me down."

They did, and Lauren tossed him the shelter pack.

During the next frantic seconds, Tony executed procedures he'd practiced many times. He didn't need to think. It was pure muscle memory. He knelt, tugged the red ring tab to remove the vinyl overwrap, grasped the left- and right-hand tabs, and shook the aluminized folds of the shelter open. Then he stepped into the base of the shelter and, with his feet toward the advancing flames, dropped onto his butt. He eyed his friend. "You okay, Jimbo?"

"Oh, damn . . . yeah, I'm good," Jimmy replied as he pulled up his Nomex shroud to protect his face and neck.

Tony did the same, pausing only in response to his friend's howl of pain as Jimmy lifted the injured leg into the shelter.

Driven by the wind, the flames raced down the slope. The heat on Tony's face and upper body was unbearable, but he waited for Jimmy to pull the top of the shelter over his head.

"Damn, that hurts," Jimmy cried.

Hector and Lauren also kept watch over Jimmy before nestling into their own shelters. The entire crew—except for Tony—was ensconced in their last-chance cocoons, grouped in an uneven line along the edge of the stream. The scene was akin to some surreal campground where the sleeping bags were made of aluminum and the campers slept face down.

"Looks good, Jimbo," Tony shouted and pulled the folds of his shelter over his hard hat, lay back, and rolled onto his belly. To protect his airway, he scraped a little hole in the dirt with his gloved hands and pressed his face to the ground. Next, he pushed the top and sides of the aluminized material outward to create maximum air space. Using his arms and legs, he pushed down to anchor the shelter to the ground.

Emergency fire shelters, which were designed to deflect radiant heat of up to 2,000 degrees Fahrenheit for short periods and provide protection against convected heat, were ineffective against direct flame contact. The crew's only hope was that the fire would pass safely overhead.

"Are you anchored, Jimbo?" Tony asked.

"Pretty much, but I can't push down with this damn ankle."

"Do the best you can. I'm right next to you." Not that it mattered. Leaving the shelter to help someone would result in almost certain death. There was nothing to be done but lie still, and the wait wasn't long.

The storm burst upon them like a tornado. Tony likened it to the roar of jet engines at takeoff—but more personal. The noise rose high and shrill, as if Mother Nature herself were screaming.

Smoke infiltrated the space as wind buffeted the little shelter, and Tony began to cough. He wanted to scrape more dirt but needed his hands to keep the shelter anchored. He dug his nose into the ground until it hurt. Pain fired his airway as he tried to hold his breath. Debris pelted the top of the shelter. If a tree fell now, it would most likely be the end for him and many of his friends.

While he willed the danger to pass, he thought not of his survival but of the changes he'd undergone during the past three years. He also thought about his ex-wife, Lisa, and Allie and their unresolved relationship. A twisted path had brought him to this point, and although he didn't fear for his life, he wasn't ready for it to end. Despite his psychological turmoil, he had people he loved and things he wanted to do. *This fire will not kill me!*

"You still with me, Jimbo?" Tony called out. He thought he heard an "okay" in response, but the howling wind muffled all other sound. He said a brief prayer for his friend.

In what felt like hours but was actually less than a minute, the gusts eased. Unfortunately, the heat only increased. The familiar burning sensation in his ears—damaged long ago—returned with a vengeance as heat penetrated his shroud and overwhelmed his lightweight brush shirt and pants. What he wouldn't have given for the heavy turnout gear and self-contained breathing apparatus of his structural firefighting days. *I'm stuck in an oven, and there's nothing I can do about it.*

"I'm burning up!" a voice called out.

"It's on top of me!" cried another.

Moments later, someone shrieked. Unintelligible shouts mixed with unmistakable howls of pain.

It was then that Tony's worst symptoms returned. Within seconds, violent tremors rocked his muscles, and he became lightheaded. Panic rose. He couldn't let his friend roast alive. Against all logic, he prepared to exit the shelter.

"You still alive in there, Tony?"

Jimmy's words brought Tony back to his senses. The fire must have passed. *Jimbo's okay.*

He chanced lifting the front corner of the aluminized fabric an inch. "I'm good, Jimbo. How about you?"

"I'll live. I couldn't hold down the corner near my bad ankle, so I think it's burned *and* broken. At least I'll get some paid time off. Not a bad deal." The pain in Jimbo's voice betrayed his false bravado.

Tony raised the edge a little higher. "Not bad at all, buddy," he lied.

Five minutes later, Hector gave the all clear and the crew shed their protective covers. Most were unhurt, while a few had suffered minor burns. A four-foot tree limb had fallen onto Lauren's shelter but hadn't penetrated it. She'd have a hell of a backache but was otherwise okay.

The youngest member of the crew, a nineteen-year-old kid named Archie Daniels, wasn't as fortunate. He'd gotten out of his shelter, trying to escape into the stream, but the water was too shallow, and he'd inhaled superheated air while suffering burns to his face, back, and legs. The others knew he'd have to be airlifted by helicopter and faced a long recovery of burn treatment and pulmonary therapy—assuming he survived the night.

As for Jimmy, the crew carried him on a stretcher to an access road, where he was evacuated to base camp.

Tony sat in quiet reflection as he and his colleagues waited to be driven back to camp. Until this point, he'd thought that his time in the wilderness had silenced the mental demons he'd battled for three long years, but today's events had shattered that illusion. The familiar torment had resurfaced with a cruel intensity, and his reaction had almost caused him to make the same tragic error as poor Archie.

Oddly, his psychological turmoil hadn't been caused by his close encounter with death. In fact, he'd remained perfectly calm and cogent—almost unnaturally so—as the firestorm tried to take his life. Things hadn't turned until he'd heard Archie cry out in pain. The sound of *human suffering* had triggered the return of his dormant symptoms: anxiety, shakes, and mind-muddling panic.

He held his head in his hands, trying to fend off the ghosts: the dead copilot with her hand still on the throttles, the teen boy in coach whose terror-ridden face stared at the cabin ceiling, the mutilated torso entangled in the wreckage. He could see them all, each image more unsettling than the last.

It was going to be a long night.

***

The next morning, Tony woke at dawn, packed up, and said an emotional goodbye to Hector, Lauren, and the rest of the crew. Before catching his ride to the airport, he had time for one last stop.

"Hi, buddy," Jimmy said as Tony ducked into the inflatable medical tent. "Come to sign my cast?"

"I came to make sure you weren't trying to escape."

"If only," Jimmy said and shook his head. "It's not so bad. Great food, air conditioning, no flames trying to burn me alive. You know?"

Tony saw something in Jimmy's eyes that evoked a chill. "Yeah, I do know."

"Thanks for saving my ass, by the way. If it wasn't for you, I'd be a well-done corpse in some half-ass portable morgue."

"It was a team effort," Tony said as a tear welled up in his eye. He brushed it away quickly.

"Bullshit, and don't go soft on me now, buddy. I want to remember you as the badass you are."

"Okay," Tony said and forced a smile. "But you've got to promise me you'll take care of yourself. There's lots of fire out there."

"Don't worry, Airport, I've got no desire to meet my maker. Not yet anyway."

At that moment, both men shared a knowing look, the kind only those who've been to the edge could possibly know. Jimmy opened his mouth but closed it quickly.

"What?" Tony asked.

"You know what?" Jimmy's expression turned deadly serious. "I was scared shitless yesterday. So were Hector and Lauren, and everybody else. But not you. Uh-uh. You have no fear." Jimmy shook his head. "Christ, that fire almost killed us, but for you it was like we were having a walk in the park. Like you were waiting to get killed."

"I can assure you I was not," Tony said and looked closely at his friend. "Where are you getting this from?"

"I've seen it before. Usually in guys who stayed on the line year after year. It ain't no big surprise. The job gets to you after you've done it too long. Hell, I'm probably going to get it myself someday. But you . . ."

"Spit it out."

"You've been out here three *months*, not three years. And I seen it in you from day one. No fear, and that ain't normal."

Jimmy was wrong about that. Tony had plenty of fear, just not for himself.

"I don't know what happened to you at that plane crash, but you still ain't over it and you need some help. I don't mean chewin' the fat with some buddies at a bar. I'm talking *professional* help. There, that's all I got to say."

Tony took a deep breath and considered. "I hear you, Jimbo. That couldn't have been easy for you to say. You're right, I had some issues after the crash. I *did* get help, and maybe I should have sought help from the counselors they make available to us out here, but . . ."

"But you thought three months of sweatin' your ass off in the forest would chase it away."

"I guess I did," Tony said. "I promise I'll get some help when I start my new job."

"You're probably feedin' me a load of crap, but I hope you do."

Jimmy was right. Tony's plan to sweat himself into a better state of mind had failed. The carnage resulting from the crash of Leisure Air Flight 741 was still with him and might be forever. In two weeks, he would embark on a new journey, one in which he was no longer sure he could pass muster.

2

Thursday, August 28

Born *to Run* blared through the Cherokee's speakers as Tony cruised along Main Street. Springsteen's soulful rock was an acquired taste, inherited from his father's music collection. The irony of the iconic anthem wasn't lost on the former small-town boy who'd long dreamt of escaping to the big city.

Tony hadn't made the decision to change jobs lightly. At forty, he saw twenty solid years ahead to make an impact in his profession, and he'd already pushed the limits of what he could accomplish at an airport. It was time for a new challenge—municipal firefighting.

The year-old two-story red brick headquarters of the Monongahela Area Fire Authority, with its five glass-and-steel-paneled garage doors, stood in stark contrast to the aging buildings that lined Main Street in the central business district of River Bend, a city of twenty-six thousand at the southeast corner of Allegheny County, Pennsylvania, along a meandering stretch of the Monongahela River, seventeen miles southeast of Pittsburgh.

Headquarters staff occupied the second floor, while Tony's new workplace, Fire Station-300, utilized the first.

During his interviews, it was explained that the headquarters were built to blend in with the "flavor of the neighborhood." Nice try, but it didn't work. Main Street, making a valiant effort to come back, was dotted with dilapidated buildings, boarded-up storefronts, and vacant lots—ghosts of a once-thriving business district.

Tony drove up to the fenced gate behind the building and hit the buzzer. "Tony Moretti reporting for duty." He regretted the statement as soon as the words left his lips. He must sound like an actor in a corny war movie. It reminded him how he and Robbie had announced their arrival on their first day at Reynolds International. *Could that have been three years ago?*

The gate slid aside, and he found a spot against a chain link fence topped with barbed wire, another feature that reminded him of Reynolds. Exiting his SUV, he whiffed a recent application of sealant emanating from the shiny black asphalt.

Two glass-paneled entry doors, set into the back wall, were spaced ten feet apart. A Maltese Cross, etched on the right door, read ***River Bend – Station 300*** on its top and bottom leaves, while ***Courage*** and ***Honor*** marked the left and right leaves. The door on the left—the one Tony entered—featured an identical Maltese Cross inscribed with ***Monongahela Area Fire Authority***. Under it, white vinyl letters read: ***MAFA Administrative Offices – 2nd Floor***.

The lobby featured a sturdy metal table flanked by a stairwell and an elevator, while a row of padded metal chairs lined the back wall. The table supported a telephone and logbook. A sign above it read:

Monongahela Area Fire Authority
Serving the Communities of:
Buchanan
East Forge
Furnace
Hillcrest Acres
Mill Town
Penn's Grove
River Bend
Rocky Shore
Union Center
Washington Heights
West Forge

A painted scene on the left side wall depicted firefighters in action. Bright red letters above it proclaimed:

HOME OF THE BRAVEST

A mural on the opposite wall featured scenes of steel mills and steelworkers in action. A tribute to the area's industrial heritage. A classy touch.

Tony scribbled his name in the log, picked up the phone, and waited for the buzz granting him access to the stairwell. Iris Ludlow, the chief's administrative assistant, met him on the second floor, informed him that Chief Ramsey was downstairs in the fire station, and escorted him to a seat in the chief's office.

The office smelled of fresh latex paint and new cherry furniture. A desktop computer sat atop an L-shaped desk, its keyboard covered with papers. A nameplate engraved with ***Chief Louis Ramsey*** faced two padded chairs. A few family photos topped the credenza, and a stack of boxes was crammed into a corner. Strangely austere, considering MAFA had been in business for almost a year. Memories of his meetings with Chief Archer at Reynolds International flooded back, although that office was much less spartan. *I've come pretty far since those days as a rookie.* He ran a hand over his cheeks, freshly shaved for the first time in three months. *Back to reality.*

"There's our new lieutenant!" the chief said as he strode in carrying two coffee cups.

Tony stood. A stout, energetic man, Chief Ramsey had thick gray hair and stood almost a head shorter than Tony's six-foot-four frame.

"Sit, please," Ramsey said. "Sorry about the delay, but we have a problem with our new air compressor, which I was explaining to our vendor. It's not anchored according to our specifications, and if we let it go, it will vibrate itself loose, not to mention damaging the new floor." The chief swept a hand across the desk. "And don't mind the mess. We've been using this office to store records from the consolidated volunteer departments, and I just moved in."

That explains the no-frills look, Tony thought.

The chief set one cup in front of Tony, took a sip from the other, and plopped it onto his desk chair. Coffee splashed from the cup and landed in a puddle in front of a stack of papers. The chief took no notice. "I can get you some cream and sugar if you like."

"No need, Chief. This will be fine." Tony hated black, unsweetened coffee, but it was a harmless fib.

"Ahh, first cup of the day," Ramsey said after taking another sip as the spilled brew crept toward the papers.

Tony raised a hand to warn the chief of the impending mess but couldn't get a word in as Ramsey plowed ahead.

"Anyway, the compressor is just one of the many growing pains we have here at MAFA," he said, emphasizing *maa-fa*. "The troops have taken to calling it the mafia, by the way."

"That's creative, kind of," Tony said.

"They think I don't know." Ramsey tilted his head and smiled. "But I think it's a hoot. Better than the name the neighborhood kids thought up. They've taken to calling us the 'Effin' A-Holes.'"

Tony nearly spit out the coffee. "Wow."

"I know," Davis said and shook his head. "The kids around here are mostly underprivileged, but they're not dumb. One of my goals is to engage with the local youth, get them on our side. Wouldn't it be great if some of them joined our department one day?"

"It would," Tony said, and he meant it. The chief's plans to assist the people of this area had helped convince him to take the job.

"As you know, we've been in business for over eleven months. In fact, our one-year anniversary is next Monday, which happens to be your first day on the job, if your personal arrangements are squared away."

"They are, and I can't wait to get started."

"Good, good. I've got to hand it to the volunteers. They continued to man their stations until we initiated our service, knowing full well they were about to be replaced. A showing of wonderful community spirit, and I applaud them for it. Oh, and sorry for the delay in getting you hired. The paperwork got snagged. We're a semi-independent authority, but we still have a maddening bureaucracy."

"That's okay, it gave me a chance to finish my tour out west and settle into a new place."

"Oh yes, you just got in from . . . Washington?"

"Two weeks ago, from Oregon. The Columbia River Valley."

"Right. Beautiful country, but those wildfires looked uncontrollable, at least from the news footage."

The intercom buzzed. "Chief, I've got someone named Mark from Coulton Safety on the phone. Says you're expecting his call."

"Tell him I'll call him back, Iris." The chief rolled his eyes. "I've been trying to finagle one of those high-tech electronic accountability systems, but that guy's system is out of our price range, at least for now. We've just about exhausted our annual fire equipment budget, but I've got my eye on a chunk of federal money from the Assistance to Firefighters Grant Program, and I've set Iris on it. She's a bloodhound." He took another sip. "But in the meantime, we still use accountability tags and check-in boards. Very twentieth century, and it means you'll have to keep close watch on your people, which I'm sure you're going to do anyway. Use the tags on *every* call, even automatic alarms and garbage fires. It must become second nature."

Tony nodded but couldn't suppress a grin as the chief barreled on and the coffee soaked into the unfortunate papers.

The chief paused. "Hmm, did I say something funny?"

"Oh, no, Chief. I'm excited about my new job, and your enthusiasm cranked it up a few notches."

"Ahh, very good," Ramsey said with a suspicious smile. "We have a young department, and we're serious about the health of everyone in it. Physical fitness is a big priority of mine, and each of our stations is equipped with free weights, treadmills, stationary bikes, and rowers. With a few exceptions, most of our people are in pretty good shape. Not only is our workplace smoke-free, but, like you, each firefighter has signed an agreement to abstain from smoking, on or off the job, during their employment. The firefighter's union, IAFF Local 5631, is in full support."

"Impressive," Tony said.

"We think so," Ramsey agreed. "Anyway, while most of our little melting pot of firefighters have experience, they hail from different departments, and some of those outfits were weak on firefighter accountability. That's not the case here. The same goes for personal accountability reports. Call for a PAR often. Get everyone used to the system until it's routine. If we can keep an eye on each other at all times, it'll go a long way toward ensuring everyone goes home after their shift."

"I consider crew safety my top responsibility," Tony said.

"I have no doubt, but there's something you need to be aware of." The chief's demeanor darkened. "Not everyone is going to accept you as an officer. First, you don't have a lot of experience, and second, although I know better, there's a natural inclination to look down on airport firefighting as something guys bid into when they're a couple years out from retirement."

"Thanks for the kind words, Chief, but don't worry. I anticipated that kind of welcome. It was a factor I considered before accepting the lieutenant's position. I can deal with it, and I'm anxious to show my new colleagues what I can do."

The chief smiled. "That's what I want to hear, and there's one last thing," he said as his face lit up. "You, Tony, are my great experiment."

Tony leaned forward and shot his best deer-in-the-headlights expression.

Ramsey chuckled. "We're building a brand-new fire department from the ground up, and it's an exciting time. But we've got to do it the right way, from the very beginning. That's why I wanted you."

I hope he doesn't plan to use me as some kind of example.

"Have you heard the old saying that the fire service reflects a hundred years of tradition, unimpeded by progress?"

"Hah, yes, I've heard that joke many times."

"All too often, especially in western Pennsylvania, it isn't a joke." Ramsey paused. "As I said, most of our new employees are veterans of the fire service, like yourself. They're all good people with excellent records of firefighting, but many of them have come to us from traditional departments where change came slowly, if at all.

"Despite that, it is a very young department, with a few old hands sprinkled in. I had to do a lot of convincing before the Authority Board, and my deputy chiefs agreed to take a chance hiring so many new or relatively inexperienced firefighters. That extended to hiring you as a lieutenant. It's a big leap, but I like what you bring to the table. You have a master's degree, you're physically fit, and from what I've gathered, an excellent decision-maker in stressful circumstances. Chief Archer raved about your technical and leadership skills, and Captain Schrum couldn't say enough about your actions on the night of that tragic plane crash."

Tony's ears perked up. The chief had spoken to Captain Schrum? *Wow.*

"Those qualities are hard to find, and I couldn't pass up the opportunity to hire you. Sort of like an NFL team that spots a gem of an undrafted free agent."

Tony wasn't sure he liked the analogy.

"So, Tony, I want you to set a standard of excellence. Not only for our raw recruits, but for everyone. I believe you represent the future, and that's what we need. We're going to build something special here, and I know you're going to be a big part of it."

Yep, I'm going to be an example. "Thanks, Chief, I won't let you down."

"I know you won't." He stood and squeezed Tony's hand. "Your crew, B-Platoon, is off today or else I'd take you downstairs to meet the troops. We'll let Captain Dudek do the honors on Monday. In the meantime, Iris will set you up with your ID and password. Have a great weekend, and we'll see you soon."

Tony hadn't expected this. He'd hoped to ease into his new role as he learned the ropes of crew leadership, but the chief had other ideas. *Well, Tony, I hope you're up for the challenge.*

3

Sunday, August 31

Benjamin Fitzpatrick stomped the crown of the black helmet as he tried to stuff it into the oversized red bag, which still bore the name **RIVER BEND VFD** in gold lettering. Useless. No matter how much he shoved and repositioned, he couldn't get the damned thing to fit inside with his bunker pants and coat. With a sigh, he pulled the zipper shut, stuck the helmet under the bag's thick black carrying straps, and tossed it into the corner.

Until one year ago, Benjamin, known to everyone as Fitz, had worn a *white* helmet that identified him as the deputy chief of the River Bend Volunteer Fire Department, one of the busiest of the many volunteer departments that lined both shores of the Monongahela River southeast of Pittsburgh. Hell, one of the busiest anywhere in the metro area. His chief had trusted—no, depended on—him to lead the guys into the worst situations imaginable. Now it was all a memory.

He'd been with the River Bend VFD ever since his dad, a deputy chief, had sworn him in as a junior explorer at age fifteen. Twenty-two years later, Fitz was ready to take over the top spot when the chief, a brilliant but aging strategist, announced his retirement.

Most area fire departments elected their line officers, but not River Bend, where only the chief was selected by vote. The deputy chiefs, captains, and lieutenants were appointed, but only after meeting strict criteria for training, emergency call attendance, and firefighter certification. Chiefs of surrounding departments said such requirements were crazy and would deter volunteerism. But those inside-the-box thinkers, as Fitz liked to call them, were wrong. Volunteers flocked to River Bend, drawn by the challenge and the opportunity to be the best.

Fitz's plan was thwarted when River Bend was swallowed up in the MAFA consolidation of six fire departments on the south side of the river and five to the north. Eleven proud organizations, staffed entirely by volunteers and tracing their histories back a hundred years, unceremoniously closed and replaced by the four centrally located stations of the Monongahela Area Fire Authority. Now he served as a *Supplemental, Paid-on-Call Volunteer.* An afterthought.

As a certified public accountant, he had the potential to earn substantial income with one of the prestigious firms in downtown Pittsburgh, but his roots were in River Bend, and he was deeply invested in the community. Instead, he'd chosen a boutique accounting firm that allowed him to work from home so that he could respond to fire calls at any time of the day or night. That decision was a constant source of irritation for his ex-wife, who had visions of a big house in an upscale suburb, far from the Mon Valley. Should he have done things differently?

The consolidation agreement specified an opportunity for volunteers to serve as paid-on-call staff at a rate of twenty dollars per hour, provided they had achieved Pennsylvania Firefighter II certification, signed up for a twelve-hour shift every three weeks, and attended at least two training sessions per month. They also had to meet the physical requirements, which included a comprehensive medical examination and passing a standard firefighting physical agility test. Fitz had estimated that at least thirty former volunteers from the closed stations could meet those requirements, but only twelve had chosen to pursue the opportunity, and a year later, the number was down to five.

Working shifts for B-Platoon at Station-300, in the heart of River Bend, three blocks from his now-closed volunteer station, became the new reality. MAFA's standard operating procedures barred volunteers from storing turnout gear in their personal vehicles or responding directly to emergencies, but he hadn't been called on either infraction. Intimate knowledge of the area earned respect from the officers, who turned a blind eye whenever he arrived at a scene and pulled his bag from the bed of his pickup.

Since the accounting gig provided a flexible schedule, he typically signed up for one twelve-hour and one twenty-four-hour shift each week, far above the minimum required for paid-on-call volunteers. He'd chosen the next day because B-Platoon was due to get some new, supposedly hotshot lieutenant.

What would his dad, deceased five years, think about the travesty? He pushed the thought away.

4

Monday, September 1

Decked out in a crisp navy-blue short-sleeved shirt adorned with MAFA arm patches on either arm, shiny single gold bugles affixed to the lapels, and **LT MORETTI** stitched in matching gold lettering above his left breast pocket, Tony approached the employee entrance of Station-300.

He touched his ID to the security card reader and punched in the personal code he'd selected when Iris had set up his access—19779, the same number from his airport days. The device buzzed as the magnetic lock released. *Door number two today, Tony. Let's see what you can do.*

Captain Barney Dudek met him at the door. Dudek, whom he'd met and taken a liking to during the interview process, was a big-boned, totally bald fiftysomething who stood a few inches shorter than Tony.

"Good to see you, Tony," Dudek said. "God knows we need your help with this flock of children."

"Great to be here. Sorry about the two-week delay."

Dudek waved off the concern. "Not your fault. Let's talk for a few minutes in our office."

As Dudek led the way, Tony noticed the captain's love handles overlapping his wide uniform belt. He seemed to waddle as he walked. Bad knee or hip, perhaps? Not the picture of the young, vibrant personnel painted by the chief. They passed through a hallway lined with a large glass case displaying memorabilia of the defunct volunteer departments that Station-300 had replaced. He'd have to learn those names.

The office contained two modern beige metal desks, but it lacked departmental or personal photos or memorabilia. The only item on the wall was an oddly retro corkboard with September's schedule for all three platoons pinned to it. The captain took a seat while Tony stood inside the doorway.

"I know," the captain said, "it's sterile. But we never had much of a chance to spruce it up, and the last year has been so busy we never bothered. Anyway, here we are."

"No worries, Cap."

"Please, Tony, call me Barney. We're partners. The troops call me Cap, at least to my face, but I've heard they call me the *relic* when I'm not around." Dudek took a breath. "They're right. I have no business here. I'm fifty-seven years old and I should be enjoying my retirement after thirty-two years with the Pittsburgh Bureau of Fire. But Lou, Chief Ramsey, and I go way back. He cajoled me out of my leisure time to be a part of something new. He's a passionate man, and a hard guy to turn down."

Tony could relate to Ramsey's charisma. Dudek must be one of the old hands the chief had mentioned.

"Don't worry, I won't die on you, at least not for a while." Dudek winked but offered a sad grin. "I'm here to do a job, and I'm not going to let Lou down." He handed Tony a copy of the master duty roster. "Now that you're here, the department is at its full authorized strength of ninety-nine, but this station, and this shift, is our world. You and I, Engine-301, Ladder-302, Rescue-303, Foam-304, and our ten firefighters populate that world. It's our job to make sure we give our people the leadership and training they need to do the job safely and go home at the end of their shift."

Dudek's words were music to Tony's ears. *I think we're going to make a great team.*

"Ritchie McMahon, Battalion Chief-1, is upstairs meeting with the chief. His responsibilities include Stations-300 and 400, and all the territory south of the Mon. He's a real character, and you'll meet him later."

"I look forward to it," Tony said.

"He's a great guy," Dudek said. "There's a lot to learn about our routine, but you'll pick it up in no time. For now, remember that Main Street parallels South Shore Boulevard, part of PA Route 837, the main east–west corridor south of the river. It's a little confusing, but South Shore Boulevard changes names depending on which municipality you're in. East of us, it becomes Duquesne Boulevard. West of us, it's known as the Clairton-Dravosburg Road."

"Of course it does," Tony said. "I lived in Pittsburgh long enough to understand the convoluted road system. I made a point of driving the area several times since I moved in, so I'm a little familiar."

"Very good. Speaking of convoluted systems, law enforcement coverage in our eleven municipalities is a tangled web of agencies. Here in River Bend, we have the only independent police force south of the river. On the north side, Union Center and Washington Heights each have their own departments. The remaining towns rely on either the Allegheny County Police or the PA State Police—there's no rhyme or reason to it." Dudek shrugged. "Just something to keep in mind, considering how often we work with law enforcement."

"I will. Thanks, Barney."

"I've got much more to tell you," Dudek said, "but right now it's time for morning briefing." He led Tony into the hallway and stopped. "So you don't get caught unaware, each of our four stations is assigned a set of hi-low electronic tones that County Dispatch uses to alert us. They set off our klaxon, bring the lights up at night, and between 7:00 a.m. and 5:00 p.m., they trigger the garage doors for the pumper, ladder truck, and heavy rescue."

"That's good information. Thanks, Barney."

"My pleasure. Let's go meet the troops."

***

Fitz descended the musty stairwell from his second-floor apartment. Outside, he inhaled the steamy morning air. Too hot for this hour, but typical of western Pennsylvania, at least until mid-September. He didn't mind. What he did mind was the situation he'd been dealt. Dropping his gear bag into the bed of his Ford pickup, he climbed behind the wheel and checked his watch—5:57. The station was five minutes away, and he didn't want to get there too early, so he sat and pondered.

He understood the reason for the consolidation, and grudgingly supported it, because things had fallen too far to be salvaged. The other ten stations were teetering on the brink of extinction. The tax base had fallen as residents left for opportunities elsewhere, leaving the old and underprivileged behind.

Although River Bend was holding its own, the area had not experienced the resurgence of other communities in the Pittsburgh Metro Area after the steel industry's collapse. As a result, there was little money for apparatus, equipment, or station upkeep. And a once-deep pool of potential volunteers had evaporated.

Fitz the CPA knew a shrewd use of state and federal grants, in combination with strategic loans, could've alleviated the funding problems. But the chiefs of those other ten departments, some in their seventies and others barely out of their teens, had ignored the proposals he'd presented at regional meetings. Refused to explore new sources of revenue. Refused to loosen their residency requirements to broaden the base of recruits. And above all, refused to even *consider* consolidation to pool resources and survive.

Eleven stations in a roughly twenty-five-square-mile area with a shrunken population was overkill, but the demographics might have supported up to *six* stations with a central administrative hub. Fitz preached the potential benefits of consolidation and cited examples where similar strategies had worked, but none of the other volunteer departments had acted on his proposals. *They couldn't give up their little fiefdoms.*

Eventually, and predictably, the region ended up with inadequate fire protection. Too few personnel to operate a fleet of antiquated equipment. Yet the outrage these same chiefs vented after each community approved the referenda of consolidation was something to behold. *Too late, fellas, you screwed the pooch.* They had been dinosaurs, and now they were extinct.

Thoroughly disgusted, he considered calling off. *It's not like anyone would miss me.* But he couldn't. He'd made a commitment. Thinking of his father, he fired up the engine.

Taking orders from the captain was one thing. A thirty-year decorated veteran of the Pittsburgh Bureau of Fire, Dudek commanded respect. But this new lieutenant? Yes, he knew the guy was a big hero in that plane crash a few years back, but that was one incident, and an airport environment couldn't compare to the gritty streets of the Mon Valley.

In a foul mood when he arrived at the station, he paused at the display case holding the group photo of the old River Bend VFD and touched the glass in front of his father's picture.

"Thanks, Dad," he whispered. "For everything."

✳✳✳

Tony preferred the twenty-four-hour shifts—with two days off in between—he'd worked at the airport, and during his interview, he was pleased to learn that MAFA used the same scheduling system. With one Kelly day—a twelve-hour shift in lieu of the normal twenty-four—mixed in every month, the workweek averaged fifty-two hours.

Unlike at the airport, briefings at Station-300 were held in the classroom, a large space with long, narrow bingo hall–style tables and metal chairs with blue padded seats and backs. The eleven firefighters who greeted him and the captain looked lost in a room that could hold three times their number. Crew members, filling the first three rows, ended their conversations and sat bolt upright as Dudek positioned himself in front of a massive display screen. A relic, maybe, but the captain commanded respect. *Will they respond to me that way?* Tony wondered.

"Okay, boys and girls," the captain began, "today you meet Engine-301's new lieutenant, Tony Moretti. He joins us from the Reynolds International Airport."

Tony noted a handful of sighs and some hushed chatter as he offered an upbeat "Good morning, everyone." A few firefighters nodded, some whispered to their colleagues, but no one uttered a greeting. Taking the measure of this new, unknown officer, no doubt. Moisture tinged the back of his neck. *They think they're looking at a fraud.*

The captain, who must have sensed the awkwardness, added: "But he's spent the past three months baking in the forests of the west, fighting some of this year's biggest and toughest wildfires."

The mumbling stopped and eyebrows raised as the crew examined him in an unexpected light. *The best three months I could have spent.*

"We all know the drill when someone new joins the platoon, so let's stand and tell Tony a little about yourselves."

Groans, eye rolls, and one "Oh, come on, Cap," rose from the crew.

"Yeah, yeah, I know," Dudek said. "You're all a bunch of shrinking violets. Engine-301, Lieutenant Moretti's crew, you're up."

A short, dark-complected older man with a wavy gray mane and a crooked nose got to his feet. "Elias Papadopoulos, driver-operator," he announced in a booming voice. With a broad chest and thick arms, he looked like the kind of man who didn't need to work out at a gym.

"Ease up, Big Pappy," a young black firefighter with tight, uniform cornrows commented.

The assembly laughed. Big Pappy, who looked to be in his fifties, did not. Obviously not a man to be trifled with. "I've been a firefighter for twenty-three years. I came here after retiring from Pittsburgh."

"Double-dipper," the black firefighter said as he rose. "Warren Jones. Seven years of firefighting experience." His tone had an edge to it.

"As a vollie," noted a pale-skinned man with thinning red hair. Warren ignored the comment and sat.

"That's enough, Danny," the captain admonished. "Everyone in here is a state-certified Firefighter II, at least."

The red-haired man seemed unconvinced.

"Madeline Foster, Probationary firefighter," a diminutive early-twenties blonde reported in a small voice. Sweet-faced with an upturned nose, she reminded Tony of his kid sister at that age. "I don't have any firefighting experience," she added. Her slight frame and the butterfly tattoo on her left wrist contrasted with arms that had seen some serious weight training.

"Not true, Maddie," someone added. "You have three and a half weeks in already."

"Mostly fighting Romeo off," a firefighter behind her said.

More laughter ensued as the poor girl's freckles burned bright orange.

Heat rose in Tony's face. Sexual harassment was no joke to him, and the situation would bear watching. He suppressed the anger but suffered a moment of trepidation. *This is my crew?*

"Okay," Dudek said. "Ladder-302."

"Danny O'Reilly, driver-operator," the red-haired man said. "Retired after twenty years with the Youngstown Fire Department. I seen it all."

"Why didn't you tell him how you hate the big city, Danny?" the other woman in the room added in a husky voice. A tall, solidly built thirtysomething with dark brown hair pulled back in a severe bun, she resembled the archetypal firefighter. "Sarah Petruska. I served ten years with the Mount Lebanon Fire Department before coming here."

"Pet took a pay cut to see how we fight fire in a seedier part of the county," Warren said. Sarah sat without acknowledging the comment.

"Mike Green, twelve years of vol-un-teer firefighting, right here in River Bend," a young, short wall of a black man said with slow, deliberate sarcasm as he eyed Danny.

"Muscles," chimed the truck crew in unison. Muscles, indeed. Tony had been working out with weights for three years, but there was no comparison between their physiques. Green's large and well-defined biceps complemented his sculpted triceps—the muscles that really did the work. He wore his shirt a size too small, and he'd cut V-shaped slits into the short sleeves. Not exactly regulation, but who'd quibble with him?

"Randy Pellegrino, five years as a paid, part-time firefighter in West Virginia," another twentysomething, with carefully styled but prematurely receding black hair, said.

"You tell 'em, Romeo, if you can't find the girl of your dreams, at least the hookers are better up here," Petruska said. Randy blushed beet red.

The final member of the ladder truck crew was a solid, clean-cut kid. "Ahh, hi, Lieutenant. My name is Lucas Bennett, but everyone calls me Luke. I'm a probationary firefighter, four months out of the fire academy. I want to learn from all of you."

Tony noted a few eye rolls, but no comments as Luke resumed his seat.

"Rescue-303, you're up," Dudek said.

"Ooh, the *hard* men," Warren said. He seemed to have a comment for everyone.

"Got that right," a stocky man in his late thirties with salt-and-pepper hair said. "Corey Adamski, eight years with the DCFD. That's *Washington, D.C.*," he added. More oohs and scattered laughter. Adamski's left arm sported a tattoo of an axe, while interlacing flames adorned his right. A bit much, in Tony's opinion.

The other member of the rescue squad was a tall, thin black man who looked like he was pushing fifty. "Dontrell Carter. Eighteen years with six different paid-on-call and volunteer departments," he said in a matter-of-fact tone. A serious man whose gray mustache only added to his persona.

"Donny moves around a lot," Warren added as he received a death stare from the object of his humor.

"More than you'll ever see, sonny, and you know the name is Dontrell, *not* Donny."

The captain waved his arms in a referee's incomplete pass gesture. "You're the man, Dontrell," he said.

Turning to Tony, Dudek said, "As you know, we currently have five paid-on-call volunteers supplementing our department, but only one on B-Platoon, and he's the best. A former deputy chief of the old River Bend VFD, and a personal friend of mine, Benjamin Fitzpatrick."

Fitzpatrick, a man about Tony's age and of average height and build, stood but said nothing. Tony noted the contrast between his closely cropped brown hair and the traditional handlebar-style firefighter's mustache that extended below his upper lip and the edges of his mouth.

"Fitz knows more about this station's district, and the entire MAFA service area, than anyone else in this room," Dudek said, apparently trying to fill in the gaps for his silent friend. "He's a tremendous asset, and you'll be wise to solicit his advice."

"I'll be sure to do that," Tony said with a nod to the unsmiling Fitzpatrick.

Curiously, no one commented. Were they intimidated? Tony had to admit he was.

"All right, all right, you've shown Lieutenant Moretti your worst, now I want you to show him your best as he works to earn your respect. Now get *outside* and check your rigs."

Tony spent the bulk of his first twenty-four-hour shift meeting with each crew member briefly, familiarizing himself with the apparatus and portable equipment, and learning the basics of the department's paperwork, computer reporting system, standard operating procedures, and daily routine. Before he hit the rack in the lieutenant's bunk room, Dudek caught him in the hallway.

"Some of them are new and pretty raw," Dudek said, "and we've had a lot of changes during our first year. They're still feeling each other out and trying to find their footing. It's going to be a process, but our goal is to meld them into a close-knit team. Their lives will depend on it."

"Got you, Cap . . . er, Barney. I'm sure we can do it."

Dudek smiled.

Tony had no doubts, but he wondered how long the process would take, and how torturous it would be.

***

Dudek's comments about volunteers struck a nerve in Fitz. All four of MAFA's stations—a pair north of the river and another two south— were staffed by paid, *professional* firefighters, as they called themselves. Fitz refused to use the term, preferring instead *career* firefighters. In his experience, volunteers could be just as professional, and the River Bend VFD had proven it many times over the years.

He spent the shift in a state of controlled anger. This situation would never be easy, but Fitz hadn't anticipated the raw anger and resentment consuming him.

5

Saturday, September 6

Tony's camera clicked, capturing the easy swagger of teenagers parading down Main Street against the backdrop of crumbling brick facades and faded shop signs. The laughter and playful jabs of friends enjoying a day off from school. For a moment, he envied their blissful ignorance.

An avid amateur photographer since his college days, he'd received the camera as an anniversary gift from Lisa. Their fifth? Sixth? He couldn't recall, but the memory of his ex-wife tugged at his heart. *Will I ever stop thinking of her?*

At the corner of Elm, his lens zeroed in on an elderly woman wrapped in a colorful babushka. She lingered at the curb, scanning for traffic before venturing into the street. Tony adjusted his focus, marveling at the story her lined face seemed to tell.

After an uneventful first week on the job filled with paperwork, preplanning inspections, training, and policy reviews, he was eager to explore the area, and maybe reawaken his love for photography in the process. But the heat and humidity were suffocating. The electronic marquee above the Mon Valley Savings Bank flashed the time and temperature—8:33 a.m. and ninety-two degrees. *Way too hot for September.* He wiped sweat from his dripping brow and drained half his water bottle, longing for the crisp, dry air of the West.

At Main and Wydott Streets, he spotted a middle-aged man, shirtsleeves rolled up, hosing down the sidewalk in front of Ellison's

Notary and Public Services. He snapped a series of shots, garnering a suspicious look from the man. Tony offered a friendly wave, but the gesture went unanswered.

Once too self-conscious to capture people on the street, but determined to push himself beyond old boundaries, Tony now embraced his college photography professor's advice: "Photograph people as they live their lives."

Next door to the notary office, a faded advertisement stretched across the side of a boarded-up three-story relic. Peeling white letters proclaimed:

Pulaski's Dry Goods – 5,000 Items in Stock

He framed the shot and captured the vestige of days gone by.

Of the eleven communities within MAFA's jurisdiction, River Bend boasted the most active business district, but it couldn't be described as vibrant. Signs of neglect abounded: cracked sidewalks, missing street signs, broken lamps, vandalized parking meters, and torn awnings that sagged above boarded-up windows. Tony estimated that at least a third of Main Street's storefronts—tagged with hastily scrawled graffiti—were vacant. And there was something about the air—he couldn't describe it exactly, but it carried the unmistakable odor of decay.

Yet all was not lost. Long-standing businesses like hardware stores, bakeries, and financial service institutions continued to thrive. Meanwhile, a handful of innovative start-ups infused the town with a sense of renewal: A farm-to-table restaurant had taken over an old bookstore, a brightly lit tech service company occupied an otherwise empty strip of shops, and an eco-friendly clothing store stood its ground between two vacant lots. The juxtaposition of decay and resilience was palpable, painting a vivid picture of a business district caught between despair and hope.

Tony's walk brought him to River Bend's main square, where a Civil War monument surrounded by the greenest patch of ground he'd seen yet stood tall against the sky. Two cannons, coated with the green patina of age, flanked the monument's base. A longtime Civil War buff, he recognized the design—bronze Napoleon smoothbores, twelve-pounders. He focused on the soldier atop the monument and adjusted the camera's depth of field while a puffy cloud passed overhead. *Yes! The perfect contrast.*

In front of a shuttered department store on the north side of the square, an elderly man stood behind a fruit stand, arranging apples, oranges, and bananas in neat pyramids. He gave a friendly wave and smiled as his photo was taken. Tony rewarded the man's warmth by purchasing three apples, learning that he was a Ukrainian national, recently arrived and deeply concerned about relatives in that war-torn country.

This town, like most of western Pennsylvania, bore the DNA of generations of immigrants—a melting pot of strength and tenacity. A block beyond the square, a Thai restaurant gave further evidence of the evolving nature of that cultural mix.

Thunder cracked in the distance as the wind picked up, blowing a discarded shopping bag into the street. A rainstorm couldn't be far behind. *Time to call it a morning.* What he wouldn't give for an air-conditioned coffee shop where he could cool off with an iced Americano. But since no such luxury existed in River Bend, he'd have to settle for a cold shower and a pot of drip coffee at the apartment.

On his way home, Tony paused to take a few photos of Mario, the seventysomething co-owner of Olivero's Market, as he rolled up the storefront security grill, another unfortunate but common sight along Main Street.

Mario Olivero and his wife, Rose, operated the store from 9:00 a.m. to 5:00 p.m., six days a week, without any help. Tony had gotten to know the couple during grocery runs to stock up his new kitchen. Until fifteen years ago, as Mario had once explained, the store had operated from 7 a.m. to 9 p.m., but reliable help had become scarce, and the neighborhood had grown unsafe at night.

As Mario slipped back into the store, Tony waved goodbye and started for home.

"You planning a heist?"

Tony spun around. Across the street, a skinny black kid, probably in his midteens, dismounted a beat-up red bicycle, leaned it against a telephone pole, and pulled three old-fashioned milk bottles from a metal basket attached to the handlebars. The youth, whose height belied his baby face, wore a T-shirt with *No Limits* written across the front.

Eyeing Tony, he said, "The old man don't keep much cash in there."

Tony slung the camera over his shoulder. *Okay, I'll play your game.* "How do you know that? I hear he's loaded."

"Loaded Glock, maybe," the kid said without a hint of humor. "You better get your ass back up to the heights where you belong."

"I'm not from Washington Heights. I live here in River Bend, five blocks, that way," Tony said as he pointed toward the western edge of the business district.

"Bullshit. There ain't a white guy lives around here not got eighty years on him."

"I guess I'm the exception."

"You're the dumbass. Just waitin' for somebody to whack you over the head and lift that fancy camera."

"It's not that fancy. I'll show you," Tony said and stepped into the street.

The kid backpedaled. "I don't care about your camera, so you can stay right there." He pulled a cell phone from his back pocket and aimed it at Tony. "I'm sending your face to my boys. If you try anything, they'll mess you up."

Tony suppressed a smile and stopped in the middle of the street, palms raised. "Okay, I hear you. I moved in three weeks ago and I haven't met many people yet. I thought—"

"I don't care who you met or what you thought. I got no need to know you."

Tony considered. Despite his bravado, the kid looked uncertain. Scared and trying to hold his ground? Maybe. With a shrug, he turned and crossed back to his original position.

A Port Authority bus stopped at the corner, its doors hissing open to unload a small stream of passengers. By the time it moved down the block, the kid was back on the bike, a grocery bag snugged into the basket. He flicked a brief, unreadable glance at Tony before pushing off and pedaling away.

Tony smiled. The kid had stood his ground and achieved his victory. *Tough little sucker.*

6

Sunday, September 7

Dylan Ross scanned the interior of the old beauty shop as the last of the lighter fluid dribbled from the can. Empty for years, the shop contained nothing but three tattered salon chairs and a couple of dust-covered mirrors. Soaked rags lined the walls, and three branch lines ran to the base of the chairs, but it wasn't enough to get the place going. Not the way he wanted to, anyway. He'd hoped for stacks of papers, boxes, anything. These empty buildings *always* had a pile of some combustible shit lying around.

Damn. He shouldn't have squirted so much fluid on the stupid chairs. Should've saved it for the walls. That was what happened when he didn't take the time to think. *It's been too long since the last one.*

Too late now. He had to get out of there before someone on the sidewalk noticed something. But that was a joke. Nothing but junkies and whores around here. Time for a little urban renewal.

He dug the butane lighter from his pocket, bent down, and lit the nearest rag. He exhaled as it caught and edged to the door. Never turn your back on a fire—a lesson learned the hard way. The scar on his neck was a reminder.

Slowly, the flames took hold, jumping from one rag to the next and reflecting across the soaped-up storefront windows. He lifted the backpack, slid his arms into the straps, and smiled. Lighter fluid was the ticket. Anything stronger, like gasoline, and you risked frying yourself; anything less volatile and it was too damn hard to get a fire going. And the smell of lighter fluid didn't soak into his clothing the way kerosene did. More lessons he'd learned in the years since he'd first tried his hand at *weeding*, as he called it.

The flames took hold quickly along the perimeter, but the branch lines died at the base of the chairs.

"Dammit to hell," he shouted and darted to the first chair with the lighter in hand. The fluid-soaked padding caught fire immediately. He lit the second chair and backed away as black smoke began to fill the space. After a final glance, he pushed the door open and entered the alley.

Deserted, just as he'd known it would be. He donned his sunglasses, pulled the baseball cap down low over his forehead, and stuck his hands in the pockets of his jeans. Just another loser on his way to nowhere. Two blocks away and still strolling the alleyways, he heard the wail of the first sirens. He smiled.

***

Tony watched from the alarm room as a group of neighborhood kids dribbled, passed, and shot circles around the five players from B-Platoon while three firefighter spectators howled with laughter. One kid blew through defenders Romeo Pellegrino and Warren Jones, then faked a pass that froze Muscles Green in place. He juked Luke Bennett so effectively that the young probie lost his balance and collided with Pet Petruska. Both firefighters landed on their butts as the teen banked an easy layup.

"Doesn't look good for the home team," Tony said.

"Never does," Danny O'Reilly, staffing the alarm room, replied. "River Bend's bravest get regular ass kickings from those kids."

"Whose idea was it to put up that portable hoop?"

"The chief. Said it would help us gain respect with the neighborhood kids."

"Not with those basketball skills," Tony said. As the slaughter continued, he spotted another teen, standing off to the side. Squinting into the sun, he recognized him as the one he'd encountered during his photographic excursion. The youth made no attempt to join the game.

"Who's that kid? The one in front of Ladder-302's bay."

"Don't know," Danny said. "Seen him a few times but never got his name. Why?"

"Just wondered why he wasn't playing."

"He's got a bum leg or something. *Tries* to play sometimes. He's a good shooter, but those other guys are too quick for him. No mercy, you know?"

"Yeah, that's tough." Tony made his way outside, being careful to keep his distance. The kid didn't acknowledge him.

"Those guys are pretty good. Are they friends of yours?"

"I know 'em," the kid said without looking at Tony.

"Do you play ball with them?"

"Sometimes."

"A man of few words?" Tony asked.

The kid gave him a whatever look. *But he did look at me.*

"My name's Tony. This is where I work." As soon as he said it, he knew how stupid the statement was.

The teenager looked like he was about to say something, probably *duh*, but surprised Tony by replying, "Terrell."

"Nice to meet you, Terrell." *Okay, I'll give it a minute, then offer him a tour of the station.* But before he could, the overhead speaker came alive with a series of high-pitched tones, followed by the booming *ah-ooga* of the klaxon.

"Mon Area Fire. Station-300, Station-400, Battalion-1. Structure fire reported at 1166 Main Street, River Bend. Smoke issuing from a vacant storefront. Respond East Fire, Frequency-2. First alarm transfers in effect."

"Watch yourself," Tony warned Terrell as three garage doors rattled up on their tracks and firefighters scrambled for their rigs.

Joined by his driver-engineer, Big Pappy Papadopoulos, Tony jumped into his bunker pants and leather boots, pulled the Nomex hood over his head, donned his turnout coat, and climbed into the officer's seat of Engine-301 for his first response as a lieutenant with the Monongahela Area Fire Authority. Warren Jones and probationary firefighter Maddie

Foster were joined in the back of the enclosed cab by Benjamin Fitzpatrick.

Concurrently, Captain Dudek and the five other members of his truck crew jumped aboard Ladder-302 and pulled out of the station behind Battalion Chief Richard McMahon in his Chevy Trailblazer. Papadopoulos followed the ladder truck into a hard left onto Main Street.

"Everyone belted?" Tony asked as he scanned the crew.

Maddie flashed a thumbs-up. Warren rolled his eyes. Fitzpatrick looked out the window.

All right, then, Tony thought as the Mobile Data Terminal—or MDT—mounted between the front seats, lit up. He punched an icon to bring up a street map and a plot plan of the building in question. "Looks like it's six blocks to the east. The nearest hydrant is . . ." He studied the map.

"The closest hydrant is at Main and Jackson, one block from the structure," Fitzpatrick said with detectable snarkiness in his tone. "The call is at the old Chalmer's Beauty Salon. Been vacant for years."

"Thanks," Tony said.

"County, BC-1," McMahon radioed. "I'm on the scene with smoke showing from Side-A of a vacant two-story building with a vacant beauty salon on Division-1. No visible fire. Attached exposures on either side. I'll have Main Street Command."

"County copies, smoke showing from Side-A. Main Street Command established at 1428."

"Ladder-302 from Command," McMahon radioed. "Take position at the Alpha-Bravo corner. I want a search of Divisions-1 and 2, and raise your aerial to the roof. Engine-301, wrap the hydrant and stand by. Rescue-303, get to the roof and check the HVAC system. Station-400 apparatus, upon your approach, take a Level-1 staging position at Main and Charles."

A haze of black smoke hung over Main Street as Engine-301 approached Jackson. "That's our hydrant," Tony said. Papadopoulos slowed to a stop as Ladder-302 continued to the scene.

Tony turned to the crew. "You've got the hydrant, Maddie. Pull a section, wrap it, and stand by in case we're ordered to lay in."

"Got it, LT," Maddie said, but the look on her face betrayed the girl's anxiousness.

"You'll do fine. Just remember your training."

Maddie, her eyes wide, nodded rapidly.

"I'll jump out with her," Fitzpatrick said. "I'm the extra guy here."

"Good deal," Tony said. "If we lay in, Warren and I will take the initial attack line. Once you two catch up, grab the backup line."

Fitz scowled.

Did I say something to piss him off? Tony wondered.

"We're here," Pappy said as he braked the pumper to a halt.

"Go, Maddie," Tony said.

She opened the door to get out but was yanked back into her seat.

"Jesus Christ," Warren said. "Release your seat belt, you stupid probie."

Tony glared at Warren as Maddie unclipped the belt and climbed out of the cab. Fitzpatrick, in the middle seat, followed her.

Tony stuck his head out the window while Maddie, with help from Fitzpatrick, pulled a section of five-inch large-diameter hose—LDH—wrapped it around the hydrant, put a boot just behind the coupling, and waved her arm.

Awaiting further orders, and only a block from the action, Tony had a clear view of the scene. Captain Dudek's crew forced entry into the structure while Ladder-302's driver, Danny O'Reilly, positioned the aerial to the roof with such a smooth process of elevation, rotation, and extension that it brought to mind Rosie Roosevelt's work with the airport tower ladder. The duo from Rescue-303 climbed to the roof and disappeared over the parapet.

In less than five minutes, Dudek reported the fire extinguished, the HVAC system checked, and the entire occupancy searched. An impressive display of speed and coordination. *Maybe Captain Dudek exaggerated their shortcomings during our talk.*

Tony's crew secured the hydrant, repacked the big yellow supply line, and drove to the scene. A positive-pressure ventilation fan, or PPV, sat on the sidewalk in front of the open door to the abandoned salon. After returning Station-400's apparatus to their quarters, Battalion Chief McMahon invited Tony's crew inside.

The walls were charred, the ceiling blackened, and the seats and backrests of two salon chairs were completely burnt away. The floor showed a scorched trail along the walls, which led to the back door.

Captain Dudek explained that the fire had been out when they'd entered, and the truck crew had only to soak the chairs with their *water can,* the silver two-and-a-half-gallon water extinguisher they always carried. There hadn't been any extension to the second floor or either of the two exposures. "Not enough fuel in here to do much damage," he said. "The O_2 level must have dropped quickly and reduced it to a smolder. Whoever lit it wasn't on their game today."

"Hmm, kids, maybe?" McMahon asked.

"Maybe . . . or maybe not," Fitzpatrick said as he traced the burn pattern with his box light.

"You're the old hand around here, Fitz. What do you suspect?" McMahon asked.

"About five years ago—I'd have to check the old fire reports to be sure—we had a series of arsons in the communities south of the river, most of them in River Bend. Like this one, most didn't amount to much, but the arsonist got lucky in an old warehouse in Furnace one January night. Lots of storage of combustibles and no sprinkler system. The place burned to the ground."

"Nothing since?" Dudek asked.

"Nope, the arson activity lasted a couple of months, then stopped as quickly as it started."

"Okay, let's secure the scene and get back in service. I hope this is a one-off, but I'll pass along your info to the county fire marshal's office. They can take it from here."

McMahon stopped Tony at the door. "I was hoping to see you in action today. Get a feel for how you lead the troops." The chief narrowed his eyes. "No matter. You'll be in the thick of it soon enough, I suppose."

Tony was taken aback. Was McMahon questioning his skills? His experience? Tony could deal with that; he was confident in his abilities. But another thought nagged at him. Had word of his other issues made its way from Reynolds International to MAFA? If so, things could get complicated.

7

Sunday, September 14

Balanced on one knee, Tony held his camera in a vertical orientation and focused on three crushed beer cans in a weed-infested lot next to the Axion Automated Launderette. The slate-gray morning sky provided ideal mood lighting for the current subject of Tony's photography: the grittiness of the vacant lot contrasted with the cleanliness of the sidewalk in front of a business struggling to stay afloat. An island steadfast amidst the roil of an angry sea. Tony chuckled. *We're poetic this morning, aren't we, Anthony?*

But he had another purpose for this foray into the neighborhood. When he looked up from the lens, he spotted Terrell riding his bike. He swung the camera and took a series of shots as the young man stopped in front of Olivero's Market, chained the bike to a post on the sidewalk, and walked to the door. The kid favored his right leg.

Mrs. Olivero, who'd taken a liking to Tony, told him that Terrell delivered groceries every weekend, and that the limp stemmed from a form of hip dysplasia, a congenital condition.

"Good morning, Terrell," Tony called.

The kid eyed Tony but said nothing.

"It's a great day to be outside, don't you think?"

"You just happen to be here? I think you're getting in my business."

Tony stuffed the camera into his pack, stood, and held out his hands, palms up. "I mean you no harm, earthling. I come in peace."

Terrell shook his head. "You're one weird-ass white guy. Don't you have nothing else to do with your time?"

"As a matter of fact, I do. I'd like to invite you to the fire station once you're done with your deliveries. I'll give you the grand tour and introduce you to the crew."

"Then lock me up and use me for some crazy sex experiment."

"What can I say? You found me out. I'm off today, but I'll be at the station anytime after three o'clock, working on a few projects. Come and visit if you want. Or don't. It's up to you." With that, Tony hefted his backpack, slung it over his shoulder, and walked away. Was Terrell watching him, considering the offer? He hoped so.

***

"Lieutenant Moretti, if you're in the building, there's someone out front to see you."

Tony poked his head out from the back of Rescue-303, where he'd been familiarizing himself with the truck's specialized equipment. There was Terrell, looking through the glass panels of the garage doors. *All right!* He glanced at his watch—three fifteen. He hadn't waited long to show up. *Excellent.*

"I see you decided to join me," Tony said as he opened the front door. "Not worried about those sex experiments?"

"I can take care of myself if you try any shit."

"I'm sure you can." But with that limp, and as thin as he was, Tony had his doubts.

"You gonna show me around or what?"

"Yes, sir," Tony said and led Terrell into the garage bay, where they examined all four trucks and inspected the contents of every compartment. Terrell soaked it up, peppering Tony with questions. And he surprised Tony by dropping the street talk. *It's all an act. This kid is smart.*

Terrell was particularly interested in the thermal imaging cameras, mobile data terminals, and other high-tech gear, but he also wanted to try out some of the portable equipment. Tony obliged where he could, but when it came to items like the chainsaws and hydraulic spreaders, Terrell had to settle for a description, which clearly disappointed him.

"Let's go meet the crew," he said and put a hand on Terrell's shoulder.

Terrell shoved the hand away. "Get the fuck outta here with that stupid shit. Ain't no one said you could touch me."

"Okay, okay, my bad." *I'm such an idiot.*

"I don't need some white guy goin' all big brother on me."

Tony raised his palms in surrender. "Sorry. It won't happen again."

Terrell stood his ground but softened his expression.

Taking the change in facial features as apology accepted, Tony called the crew to the day room, introduced them, and invited Terrell to ask them anything he wanted.

A sharp and sassy kid, Terrell quickly won the crew over with his intelligent questions, his teenage sarcasm, and his softball shots at the firefighting profession. At one point he commented: "You get paid for sitting around all day, texting and watching idiots on TikTok? That's sad." After a few seconds of silence, he added, "I'm yankin' your chains, dummies." The day room erupted in laughter, except for Dontrell Carter.

"You come and see what we really do, little man, before you take shots at us," Dontrell said in his intimidating, gravelly voice.

"I just might do that, old man," Terrell said, garnering some "oohs" from the crew.

That was enough, and it was a good segue for Tony's real purpose. He motioned Terrell back to the bays and Engine-301, where he pulled his backpack from the officer's seat.

"Tell me if I'm wrong, but I thought you looked interested when you saw me taking photos on the street," Tony said.

"Maybe. I was wondering why you didn't just use your phone."

"There's a good reason, but first, were you serious when you told Dontrell you wouldn't mind seeing us in action?"

"I guess. So what?"

"Well, I have a proposal."

"Dude, you think I'm stupid. I know how this shit works."

Tony laughed. "Easy, Tiger. You're anything but stupid, and you haven't heard the proposal yet."

Terrell hesitated. "Aight. Go on and tell me, then. Gotta be something shady."

Tony had the pattern down. Terrell resorted to street talk as a defense mechanism when he felt threatened by a new situation. *I bet that hip has a lot to do with it.* He reached into his pack and pulled out a camera.

Terrell's eyes went wide. "Ooh, dope."

"Huh?"

Terrell rolled his eyes. "Just say what you wanna say."

"I propose that you become the unofficial department photographer." He let that sink in before continuing. "If you agree, you'll need a real camera, not some cell phone."

"Uh-huh," Terrell said without taking his eyes off the silver-and-black camera.

"You've seen my camera—it's a Canon EOS 5D. Think of this one as its little brother." He handed it to Terrell. "It's an EOS Rebel XT, a DSLR. That means digital single-lens reflex. It's an older Canon model, and it's equipped with a basic eighteen-to-fifty-five-millimeter zoom lens, but it's a quality piece and a good one to learn on."

"What's to learn?" Terrell asked as he looked through the viewfinder. "Just point and shoot, right?"

"Well, yes, it *can* operate on a fully automatic setting, but if you use it that way, the camera makes all the decisions for you. It focuses the scene, selects the shutter speed, and matches it with the aperture opening—"

"Aper what?"

"Ap-er-ture, the size of the lens opening. It determines how much light the camera lets in. But don't worry about that right now."

"Whatever," Terrell said, still holding the camera.

"If you agree to my proposal, there are two conditions."

"Here it comes. There ain't nothin' for nothin'."

Tony ignored the comment. "First, you agree to learn the advanced capabilities and functions of this camera. It's okay to learn on auto, but a good photographer uses *manual* settings to achieve the perfect shot. I'll be happy to teach you, right here, in the station."

Terrell turned the DSLR over in his hands, pushing buttons and spinning dials. "Yeah, and second?"

This was good, the kid was hooked. "Second, you have to agree to take care of this camera as if it was your own." Which Tony intended it to be if his plan worked out. "It comes with a padded bag and a lens cleaning kit."

"What's your game?" Terrell asked. "Why are you doing this for me?"

"I've been taking pictures ever since I can remember, and I think you have the curiosity and the smarts to be very good at it. And I suspect you'd like it. Who knows where it could lead you? My dad had gigs as a wedding photographer. Made some good money part-time. He trained me on an old Nikon. It wasn't digital, it didn't have any automatic settings, and you had to load it with real film, if you can imagine. He carried rolls with twenty-four or thirty-six exposures, so he had to be very selective with his shots."

"Film? Like last-century shit?"

"Yep." Tony aimed his index finger at the lens. "But with this, like your cell phone, you can snap away. The card inside holds thousands of photos. It'll take some work, but I bet you're up for the challenge. What do you say?"

Tony had expected more debate, or even a smart-ass refusal, but Terrell said, "All right, Lieutenant Morelli, I agree."

Tony smiled, almost patted the youth on the shoulder, but thought the better of it. "It's Moretti, but I think you know that. Call me Tony."

Now it was Terrell's turn to smile.

"So, when do we start . . . Tony?"

"As soon as you get an okay from your parents. I'm sure they're going to want to meet me, make sure I'm not that psycho sex maniac you were worried about."

"It's just my mom, but I'll ask." Terrell held the camera out to Tony.

No dad? It helped explain the defensiveness. "You do that, but keep the camera. Show it to your mom and let me know if she's okay with it."

"Thank you."

"You're welcome, and you know where to find me. I work every three days, so I won't be back until Tuesday."

"Every three days? That shit ain't right."

Tony shrugged. "It's a good job if you can get it."

Tony was uplifted by their growing trust, yet sorrow crept in as he watched Terrell limp into Olivero's.

8

Monday, September 15

Slumped at his cluttered desk, headset hanging loosely around his neck, Dylan ran a hand through his hair, his fingers brushing against more scalp than he cared to admit. "In a few years, I'll be a cue ball, just like Dad," he muttered. Disgusted, he let the next call slip to voicemail while his gaze drifted to the framed photograph on the wall. What had once been his mother's sewing room was now his makeshift office.

In the faded photo, his parents stood arm in arm in front of Suzie's Mid-Town Café, the quaint family-owned diner that had been a River Bend fixture for decades. Young and proud, they beamed with happiness.

For Dylan, the café—closed twelve years now—wasn't just a business; it was a childhood. He'd spent countless hours in the little restaurant, pitching in with small tasks in the kitchen or clearing tables in the dining room. He could almost hear the clinking of plates and the chatter of regulars who had nicknamed him "Little Dill."

As he'd grown, so had his role. After he'd graduated high school, his parents had involved him in every aspect of the business, grooming him to take over the restaurant one day. But those plans had been shattered by cold, hard reality.

The local economy, heavily dependent on manufacturing jobs, was devastated when steelmaking declined. Factories closed, people moved away, and the once bustling café slowly lost customers. The local politicians did nothing to stem the exodus.

His parents had hung on into the second decade of the twenty-first century, long after most of the town's small businesses had disappeared. When they'd finally shuttered their beloved café, they'd urged their twenty-one-year-old son to relocate south with them, citing better job prospects. That would have been the easy route to take, but he couldn't abandon a town that held so many memories.

The house they left him was a gift of stability, but it came with the challenge of forging his own path. Yet without higher education, his opportunities were limited. He parlayed his food service experience into stints at a couple of local restaurants, but with memories of Suzie's fresh in his mind, he couldn't stick with those positions for long.

During the next years, he'd drifted from job to job, trying his hand as a retail associate and an insurance salesman, and had even worked with a landscaping company before settling on a position as a customer service representative for a local bank. It was steady, with job security, benefits, and the flexibility of working from home. Yet it was far from satisfying.

As he lingered on the photograph, the phone rang. He adjusted the headset and answered it in his practiced, pleasant voice: "Thank you for calling Mon Valley Savings, this is Dylan. How may I assist you today?"

He closed his eyes as the customer droned on about irregularities in his checking account. The café had been his future, his legacy. How had it come to this? *Thirty-three, balding, and going nowhere.*

At four o'clock, he ditched the headset and signed out of the bank's virtual private network. *Time to do something worthwhile.*

***

As Dylan stepped out of the modest Cape Cod and walked to his car, he paused to gaze at the old Schwarz house. Once the home of his closest childhood friend, Dieter, the house was a shadow of its former self. The shutters, painted in bright colors by Mr. Schwarz, were now faded, hanging crookedly from the front windows. The beautiful flower beds that Mrs. Schwarz tended so lovingly had been swallowed by weeds.

A pang of sadness swept over him. The neighborhood that had been the scene of his happiest days—the baseball games, bike rides, and laughter— was almost unrecognizable. Run-down houses, cracked sidewalks, and empty lots where homes once stood. *Disgusting,* he thought as fond memories of Dieter dissolved into the grim reality of decay.

He drove his aging but dependable 2009 Saturn Vue—itself a relic of better times—across the city line to East Forge, where he parked in the lot of Valley Ministries. Tugging the black hoodie over his unbranded dark gray baseball cap, he stuck his hands in his pockets and made his way into the residential district. Today, his task was clear: find an abandoned house with secluded access and broken windows.

On Sumner Avenue, he studied a duplex, its pillars rotted and its second-floor porch in danger of collapse. A junk car, windows smashed and covered with graffiti, sat in the driveway, rusting away. The place was a possibility, but he wanted to explore further.

On Castle Street, he paused in front of a two-and-a-half-story colonial that must have been beautiful once but now stood as a burned-out hulk with its roof partially caved in. In his mind's eye, he pictured a handsome home with a lush green lawn dotted with evergreens. But the yard was an overgrown mess, littered with a discarded washing machine and a moldy mattress sprouting weeds. Another possibility.

Three blocks on, he found himself on a street lined with fifties-era one-story homes. He ambled past a ramshackle brick with a tattered American flag flapping above yard signs warning **Keep Out** and **Beware of Dog**. *Do they really think anyone would visit?*

Next door, a handmade **For Sale** sign sat atop an old commode. *Unbelievable.* The old neighbors would have been appalled.

But not everyone had given up. Midway down the block, a beige brick ranch with a cyclone fence surrounding a well-manicured lawn stood out. A statue of the Virgin Mary graced the front yard. Homeowners were trying to hold the line against the shabbiness all around them. *These are the people I'm fighting for.*

On Wilson Street, he came across an entire block reduced to one lone house surrounded by empty lots overgrown with wild grass and scattered with debris. He paused at a set of crumbling steps that must've led to a porch but now disappeared into nothing but weeds. It was hard to believe this emptiness was once the foundation of family life. Plenty of space to build new homes, but who'd want to?

These streets were once filled with the sights and sounds of everyday life. Passing cars, joggers on their morning routes, the buzz of lawnmowers, and children's laughter. Now, only the occasional barking dog or distant siren broke the silence. The few people he'd seen—a handful of elderly residents sitting on crumbling porches and a couple of guys about his age, walking with their heads down as if to avoid detection—seemed like ghosts. The shuttering of the steel mills gutted this community, driving out stable families, the ones he considered *the good stock*. Left behind were the elderly, the poor, and the criminal element.

At times, Dylan worried about walking these neighborhoods alone, but in this culturally mixed and neglected area, no one bothered with the guy in the old ratty jeans and hoodie. Just another nobody, a druggie looking for his next fix. Almost as if he were invisible.

Dylan's pulse quickened when a River Bend police cruiser crawled by, the officer inside casting a suspicious glance before continuing down the block. *Dammit! I shouldn't be out in the open like this.* Ducking into an alley, he headed for a more populated area.

Barely wide enough for a modern SUV, the alley was lined with crumbling one-car garages and choked with so much garbage that he pressed his sleeve to his nose to ward off the stench. In one garage, where the door had been replaced by two haphazardly hung pieces of particleboard and held in place by discarded tires, he glimpsed the rear quarter panel of an old black car, possibly from the 1970s.

The backyards along the alley were no better—collapsing fences, rusting appliances, weatherworn chairs, and toys abandoned to the elements. Without warning, a dog sprang to the top of a low wall, barking ferociously and snapping its jaws. Gripped by fear, Dylan bolted. The dog, probably restrained by a rope or chain, didn't follow.

Exiting the alley, he came across a small two-story house with shattered windows and a front door barely hanging off its hinges. The area was deserted. *This one will do nicely.*

***

Lights flashing and sirens wailing, a fire department SUV and a humongous ladder truck sped past Dylan as he stood back from the gathering crowd. *Six minutes. Damn.* A lot faster than he'd expected.

The ramshackle house was another shithole, and he could have lit it easily, he thought with a pang of regret. But no. This was an experiment to see how fast the fire department would respond to the report of a fire in River Bend.

He'd set two smoke pots in the front room before retreating to the backyard and hustling to phone 911. He walked closer to the action, where a small group of neighbors gathered on the sidewalk. He spotted an elderly black man standing at the edge of the crowd. "What's going on?" he asked.

"Heard the sirens and came out to see what the fuss was about," the man said. "Somebody musta started that fire." The man pointed at the house across the street, where a column of smoke issued from a broken picture window—a feature Dylan had noted during an earlier reconnaissance drive through the neighborhood. "Probably kids, or dopers."

"Wow, I hope no one's in there."

"That place been empty for years, but the city won't tear it down. Building inspector said it was still *habitable*." He shook his head. "Does that dump look habitable to you?"

"Well, no. I guess not."

While the ladder truck crew jumped out and made for the house, Dylan chanced crossing the street.

Hoooonk, hoooonk. Dylan's head snapped to the left at the blasting of the horn. Another fire truck slowly bearing down on him. He jumped back to the sidewalk and gathered his wits as the truck—one of those pumpers—laid a line of monster yellow hose to the house, big silver couplings clanging off the asphalt. *Oops, don't think you'll need all that hose, fellas.*

The old guy was right. The city should have torn the house down. Dylan had once made a point of attending River Bend city council meetings. He even spoke out at a couple, arguing that the vacant houses, and all the other empty buildings, were more than an eyesore. They were magnets for dopers, and they drove people away. Good people, like his parents. But the answers he got were always the same. "The funds aren't available. We'll try to put it in next year's budget. We have other priorities." Blah, blah, blah. All talk and no action. It was the same in all towns along the Mon.

The pumper crew pulled some hose out of a tray behind the cab, loaded it onto their shoulders, and made for the front door. *Pretty impressive. These guys aren't just fast. They're good.*

He could have sold his parents' house and fled to the suburbs, but he hadn't. He'd stuck around when all his friends and neighbors had bailed, and guess what? The region was finally showing signs of life, with start-up businesses popping up everywhere, like that new tech firm on Main Street. And new people were moving in. Young people, like himself, looking for affordable housing, were bringing life back to entire blocks. White, Black, Asian, Latino. It didn't matter to him. If they had skin in the game, he was all for it.

More importantly, Dylan wasn't sitting around waiting for others. He was actively supporting their efforts. Just like his mom had once done in her vegetable garden, he was doing some weeding so the new plants could thrive. Clearing some of the abandoned stock, he reasoned, gave residents reason to stay, to keep their homes and businesses in River Bend.

As he had expected, the activity at the house stopped abruptly. Firemen came out with their tools, and the guys with the hoses took their loads back to the pumper. They'd found the smoke pots.

The crowd dispersed, and Dylan realized he'd lingered too long. He crossed the street, turned the corner onto Elm, and was almost run over by a kid on an old, beat-up red bike.

"Sorry, mister," the kid said but didn't wait for a reply as he disappeared around the corner. Curious, Dylan retraced his steps and watched the kid lean the bike against a fence, unzip the saddlebag under his seat, and pull out a camera. He walked with a limp as he moved back and forth along the sidewalk, taking photos of the trucks, the firemen, and, Christ, the people on the sidewalk.

Dylan spun around and followed a group of teens until he dared look back. The kid was still there, but focused on the firemen. *Did he get a shot of me?* The idea passed quickly. *Nah, I'm just another guy in the crowd.*

9

Tuesday, September 16

"**L**ieutenant Moretti, you have a visitor at the front door . . . and she doesn't look happy."

The intercom broke Tony's concentration as he planned afternoon training. *Terrell again? Who else even knows me around here? And a woman?*

The figure he saw through the glass-paneled door—a thin black woman in her fifties, dressed in a brown pantsuit and a stern expression—puzzled him. He opened the door and invited her inside.

"Let's talk out here," she said in a no-nonsense tone. "It won't take long."

Hesitantly, Tony joined her on the sidewalk.

"I'll get to the point. I'm Terrell's mother, and I want to know what your intentions are for my son."

Unnerved, Tony said, "My intentions? Uh . . . I don't have any intentions. Terrell is a fine young man and I enjoy talking to him. And I'm pleased to meet you, Mrs. . . . .?"

"Cooper, and cut the crap. Middle-aged white guys don't pay any attention to black teenagers unless they're drug dealers, perverts, or do-gooders." She stepped back and looked Tony up and down. "You don't have the dopey look of a drug dealer, and I'm betting young boys aren't your thing, so it's number three, isn't it? A do-gooder."

Tony didn't know what to say.

"Let's get a few things straight," she said without waiting for confirmation. "First, my son *is*, as you say, a fine young man. He gets good grades, he has a part-time job, he's polite, and he's responsible. I intend to keep him on that path."

"Mrs. Cooper, I have no intention of—"

"Shush," she said with a raised palm. "Second, Terrell is an only child. The product of two working-class parents, one of whom died of pancreatic cancer when he was nine. Third, he has a stable family life in a good home, and fourth, he doesn't need a *big brother* or whoever the hell you think you are. Nor does he need presents from strangers, that's for damn sure." Lecture complete, she lifted the flap of her oversized purse, pulled out the Canon camera, and thrust it into Tony's chest.

Tony rocked back but maintained his composure. *The camera.* That was the real object of her anger. In the moment Tony realized he hadn't thought the situation through.

"Do you know he took this damn thing to a fire on Monday?"

"He did? No, but I—"

"In East Forge. Rode his damn bike there. After school, when he should have been doing his homework." Mrs. Cooper jabbed a finger at the camera. "Said you made him the fire department photographer."

Tony raised his hands in surrender. "Mrs. Cooper, I've handled this badly. I did inform Terrell he had to ask your permission to accept the camera, but I should have made myself known to you before I gave it to him. I meant no disrespect, and I'm very sorry."

Mrs. Cooper's facial features relaxed, but the stern look remained. Terrell was her only son, and she wasn't going to be placated so easily.

Tony took the camera, not that he had a choice. Yet the situation might still be salvageable. She was obviously a strong woman, proud of the way she'd raised her son, but maybe he could offer some benefit.

"I normally think things through, but in this case, I was taken by Terrell's interest in photography, one of my favorite hobbies. The camera is a spare. It's an old model and not worth very much."

Holding the camera up, he added, "Cell phone cameras are everywhere, but photography, real photography, is done with one of these. It has a countless array of settings. Change the exposure, adjust the amount of light into the lens, find the perfect setting for the photo you want to take. It's not easy, and it takes time and practice to master. The perfect challenge for an intelligent, inquisitive young man, would you agree?"

"Hmm," she said, "maybe." The beginnings of a smile formed at the edges of her mouth.

"I'm harmless, but I've never thought of myself as a do-gooder."

"Oh, you're a do-gooder all right. Plenty of those types around here. They swoop into town, try some antipoverty theory of theirs, and disappear."

"I'm not going anywhere. I plan to work here a long time, and I have an apartment right here in River Bend, a few blocks from Main Street."

The woman's anger dissipated, but the smile was replaced by suspicion. She said nothing for several seconds. "Here's the deal. You might be a really good man. I suspect you are, and I'm sorry I came on so strong, but I don't take chances where Terrell is concerned."

"Perfectly understandable," Tony said. Things were turning.

She paused and eyed the camera in Tony's hands. "He doesn't play organized sports and I've been hoping he'd find a hobby to keep him away from the wrong kind of people. God knows this town is loaded with them." Another pause. "If I permit my son to associate with you, and learn photography from you, there are conditions."

"Okay."

"You are to meet him *only* in daylight, and in public places. Not anywhere dangerous. Don't try to make some photo story about drug dealers or gang members. And he is *never* to go to your apartment. Do you understand me?"

Tony hadn't even thought of that one. "I understand. I'd say for now we meet right here at the station, where he'll always be welcome. We have a good bunch of firefighters, and he's already won them over. If we go outside, we'll stay on Main Street, and I'll be careful of shady characters."

"Shady characters?" She shook her head as if talking to a child. "There's a lot worse around here, and you'd better learn that for your own safety."

"Understood," Tony said, sticking to the safety of one-word answers.

Mrs. Cooper pursed her lips. "As for taking pictures at fires, I'll have to think about that one. He's a street-smart kid, but if I agree, it'll be in River Bend only, and you better make sure someone's looking out for him. If not a fireman, then a cop."

"Agreed," Tony said. "But I don't get how he knew there was a fire."

"Aha," she said. "You don't know my son. He put some app on his cell—a phone I only let him have so I can keep track of him. He told me it sends him an alert when there's an emergency."

"Wow, very impressive."

She held out her hand. "Give me the damn camera." The corners of her mouth curled into a smile, as if to indicate that she had accepted, albeit reluctantly, Tony's reasoning. "I suppose there are worse places to hang out than a fire station."

Tony hadn't realized how tense he'd been during the exchange, but now he relaxed as she walked away. A do-gooder? Maybe, but what the heck? He really liked Terrell and looked forward to teaching him photography. He and Lisa had never had kids, and he suspected he'd benefit as much from the experience as young Terrell would.

10

Monday, September 22

Tony sat on the bench in front of the sad little vegetable garden the firefighters maintained behind the station, lost in thought as the late-afternoon sun cast long shadows across the parking lot. Today marked his third week on the job, and after four uneventful shifts of learning the ropes and building connections with his engine crew—Warren was particularly problematic—he'd begun to wonder just how much action he was going to get with this new MAFA gig. His pondering was cut short by a series of high-pitched tones, punctuated by the earsplitting *ah-ooga* of the klaxon.

"Mon Area Fire, Station-300, Station-400, Battalion-1. Respond to a reported structure fire at 268 Cresson Street, River Bend. First alarm transfers are in effect."

Tony jumped to his feet and bolted for Engine-301, but his crew beat him to the pumper. "I know that block, it's near my duplex," he told them as he climbed into the officer's seat and slipped the straps of the seat-mounted self-contained breathing apparatus—SCBA—over his shoulders.

He activated the pumper's Mobile Data Terminal and pictured the area in his mind. Cresson Street ran parallel to Elliston Street, the site of his apartment. "Most of the houses are vacant." *Death traps for firefighters.*

"County, BC-1 responding to 268 Cresson Street," McMahon radioed from his Chevy Blazer chief's wagon.

"County, Station-300 apparatus responding to 268 Cresson Street,"

58

Captain Dudek radioed as Ladder-302 pulled out of the station.

Tony hit the foot pedal for the ear-piercing Federal-Q siren and yanked the halyard on the air horn twice as Big Pappy wheeled Engine-301 onto Main Street behind Ladder-302, with Rescue-303 trailing.

Immediately following Dudek's radio message, Lieutenant Timothy Brookin announced Station-400's response, while Engine-501 reported en route to Station-300 on their assigned transfer detail from Battalion-2's area north of the river.

"County received. Station-300 and 400 responding at 1631. Engine-501 transferring to Station-300. Be advised, we have several calls on this fire."

"County from BC-1." McMahon radioed. "I'm out at the scene. This is a two-and-a-half-story brick-and-frame residence. Fire showing from the second floor of Sides Alpha and Bravo. The house appears vacant. Ladder-302, take position on Side-A and stand by. Engine-301, catch the hydrant at the four-hundred block of Cresson and lay in."

The chief's report confirmed Tony's suspicions. A vacant house. No civilians at risk. A defensive fire. Trying to save vacant houses wasn't worth risking firefighter lives. *Fight it from the outside, protect exposures, and get everyone back safely.*

"All responding units from BC-1, neighbors are reporting that a family of four had been squatting in the house recently. They might still be inside."

The chief's report changed Tony's calculations. *Shit, people inside.* Heat inflamed his face and he pressed his hands to his knees as they began to shake. *This can't happen now. Keep it together.*

"Ladder-302, I want a primary search of the first and second floor if conditions are tenable. Engine-301, deploy an attack line into the front door. Engine-401, when you arrive, take a second attack line from Engine-301. Rescue-303, ladder the second-floor windows on both sides of the Alpha-Bravo corner. All other incoming units are to stage at the corner of Cresson and Lincoln and send your manpower to the scene."

Pappy swung Engine-301 onto Lincoln Avenue, its tires thumping across the uneven surface. The street retained its original brickwork from the early twentieth century, now faded to a weathered orange. The admirable attempt at preservation lent character, but the effort was incomplete. Potholes, trench cuts, and excavations from long-ago utility work were patched with unsightly asphalt. Decades of traffic had warped the street, creating dips and rises that tossed the heavy pumper around like a small boat on rough water.

Tony's hand shot to the grab rail as the truck jolted hard, sending a shock through the cabin. "Ease up, Pappy!"

The big man complied, and the bouncing diminished as he turned onto Cresson. "The city should've paved these damn streets years ago," he muttered.

"You're up, Maddie," Tony said as the pumper came to a stop just past the hydrant. "Warren, you and me into the front door."

Maddie, exhibiting newfound confidence and initiative, jumped down and pulled the first folds of the large-diameter supply line off the tailboard in under thirty seconds. Tony watched in his sideview mirror as she wrapped the hydrant, put a boot on the hose, and swung her box light up and down.

"She's ready, Pappy." Tony smiled. He'd worked with Maddie during the past two shifts, and it was paying off.

Tony pressed the button for the siren brake as they closed on the smoky scene, its wails replaced by the pumper's revving engine and the loud clangs of five-inch aluminum couplings hitting the pavement.

Pappy brought the rig to a stop while Tony snugged up his SCBA harness straps, donned his facepiece and helmet, and pulled his gloves from the dashboard. Once on the ground, he took two deep breaths to calm his nerves and slow his heart rate, but the shaking continued. *Get a grip. Maybe nobody's inside.*

The distinct, momentary chime of low-air alarms—nicknamed audi bells by firefighters—sounded, and electronic personal alert safety systems—a.k.a. PASS devices—chirped as Tony and Warren cranked the cylinder handwheels to activate their MSA G-1 self-contained breathing apparatus.

Tony passed the team's accountability tags to Pappy as Warren pulled the first seventy-five feet of the 150-foot inch-and-three-quarter crosslay, hoisted it onto his shoulder, and advanced five feet. Tony hefted the second stack and shouted, "Go." With the hose flaking off their shoulders, they advanced to the porch steps, dropped the remainder, and quickly arranged it in a rough S pattern.

"Charge the blue line," Tony radioed.

"Follow us in, Tony," Captain Dudek called from the front porch as his truck crew forced the door with a Halligan tool. A cloud of smoke rolled out and lapped the porch roof.

"Right behind you, Cap."

Tony pulled the second-stage regulator—which reduced the 4500 psi cylinder pressure to a breathable 100 psi—from his waistbelt holster and plugged it into the facepiece's docking port. Cool air washed over his face as he took a deep breath to activate the positive-pressure flow. All four LEDs of his heads-up display glowed steady green, confirming a full cylinder.

"Search teams one and two entering with five firefighters," Dudek radioed as smoke rolled over his head.

"Command copies," McMahon replied. "Be careful, Barney."

Should've waited for us, Cap, Tony thought.

Once the attack line firmed up, Warren pulled back on the bale of the nozzle, directed a two-second burst of water into the grass, pushed the bale shut, and climbed the porch steps.

"Attack-1 entering with two firefighters," Tony reported and switched his chest-mounted flashlight on.

"Command copies," McMahon replied. "Keep an eye on the truckies, Lieutenant. We'll get you a backup line in a minute."

Tony's anxiety subsided, and the trembling ceased as he directed his focus to the task at hand. Knock the fire on the first floor and protect the stairwell for the search teams.

A haze of dark brown smoke—probably a mixture of ordinary combustibles and plastics—hung low, about three feet above the floor. Tony dropped to his hands and knees and directed his box light into the room. He and Warren were five feet from the stairway, with a large open space, probably a living room, to the left and a smaller dining room to the right. Good position for now. "Let's stop here and wait for the search team's report." The wait wasn't long.

"Search-1, primary search of Division-1, Bravo side, is clear," Pet reported. "No victims or fire. Moderate smoke."

Captain Dudek reported for Search-2. "Primary search of the Delta side complete. No victims, but the kitchen is heavily involved. We've slid a pocket door closed to contain it. Attack-1, get in here."

Tony acknowledged the order while Warren, rising to a crouch, moved into the living room through a thickening cloud of smoke.

"Romeo has the door," Dudek said as the attack team approached.

Warren dropped to one knee and squeezed in beside Romeo while Tony grasped the line and crouched low behind them. "Open it."

Romeo slid the door into its slot in the wall. Thick black smoke billowed out, blinding the crew and enveloping them in a wave of intense heat.

"Hit it!" Tony ordered.

Warren yanked the bale, causing the hoseline to jump as one hundred pounds per square inch of nozzle pressure pushed the team back on their heels.

Tony shoved the line to the floor to tip the nozzle up while pressing his weight into Warren's back. "Straight stream, ceiling first, Z pattern."

"I know how to fight fire," Warren remarked as he spun the nozzle's rubber bumper to the right, creating a tight, nearly solid stream of water that ripped into the flames. As Tony leaned into him, Warren directed the stream at the upper-left corner, swept the nozzle to the right, then pulled it diagonally down to the left and swept right again. The fire darkened, but smoke production reduced visibility to zero and radiated heat assaulted the attack team.

"Again!" Tony ordered.

Warren repeated the Z attack pattern while both men ducked as low as they could to avoid the heat.

The sound of glass breaking cut through the noise of the rushing water. A dim light appeared in front of them.

"The window is vented," Tony said. "Push the smoke outside."

Warren aimed the nozzle at the window and spread the pattern to a narrow cone. The air cleared and the heat dissipated as the products of combustion were expelled from the room.

"Nice work," Dudek said as Warren used short bursts to extinguish the few remaining hot spots in the cabinetry. "Get your hoseline back to the front room and cover the stairway. My truckies will take it from here."

"What about Division-2?" Tony asked.

"Station-400's crew has a line up there now."

Seconds later, Lieutenant Brookin reported they'd extinguished the fire on the second floor.

Dudek returned to the front room. "You're relieved, Tony. Find rehab and get something to drink."

Tony complied, but other than some Gatorade, he didn't need rehab. He felt fine physically, and his mental state was much improved. Once the fire attack had begun, his mind had cleared and his anxiety eased. *That's the ticket—work hard and concentrate on the job.*

"What's wrong, big tough fireman?"

Tony spotted him immediately, standing behind the police tape with the camera in his hands. *Uh-oh.*

"You all worn out?" Terrell asked as he lifted the camera and snapped the shutter.

"Does your mother know you're here?" Tony asked as he walked over. "It'll be my hide if she doesn't."

"Aw, don't worry. She likes to act all tough."

"We both know it's more than an act."

Terrell shrugged. "After she yelled at me, she told me about her talk with you. Thought she was gonna make me give this back," he said as he held up the camera.

"We have an understanding." Tony cocked his head. "But it didn't include taking pictures at fire scenes, not yet anyway."

"Does now!"

"Really?"

"Well, only around here. Ten blocks either way from our house."

"That's good, but I'm supposed to have someone looking out for you, so I'll let the crew know."

"Whatever."

Tony held out his hand for the camera. "Let me see what you've got."

As he reviewed the photos, a warm feeling washed over him. Not for the first time, he wondered what kind of father he would have made.

***

Through the filthy second-floor window, Dylan followed the action across the street. The bedroom smelled of piss and who knew what else. Hypodermic needles littered the floor. After setting the fire, he'd used the back alleys to circle around the block, careful not to attract attention. He hadn't needed much effort to access this garbage dump; two kicks at a rotted back door and he was inside.

The firemen, as he'd expected from his little test run, had gotten to the house quickly. Even so, things were heating up, literally, and a crowd had already packed the sidewalk to watch the action.

Bright orange flames broke through a second-floor window and dark brown smoke was pouring out of the right side of the house, where he'd set the kitchen on fire. Much more satisfying than the beauty shop fiasco. This time, there'd been plenty of old furniture to pile up in the bedroom, and the wood paneling in the kitchen burned like a mother. Things were going according to plan, but he wanted—needed—a better view.

Using the sleeve of his hoodie, he rubbed the grime off the bottom right corner of the window, which only smeared the glass. He should have brought a bottle of water. He clucked his tongue to build up saliva, spit it onto his sleeve, and tried again. The glass cleared as he dried his viewport into a rough circle.

The firemen moved fast, dragging their hoses and carrying their ladders to the house. What were they doing? Let it burn. One less shooting gallery for the crackheads. *Shit! I can't believe they're going inside. Why would they risk their lives for an old piece-of-crap house that nobody's lived in for years?*

In what seemed like no time at all, the smoke turned white and then disappeared altogether. *What the hell?* Dylan slammed his palms against the dirty glass. The pane cracked, and he dropped to the filthy floor. Damn, that was stupid. He doubted anyone could've identified him, but they might have seen *someone*, and the cops would've come charging into the house. Worse, he could have cut his hands, maybe slashed his wrists. He waited five minutes before poking his head up. No one was looking. He relaxed. He was safe, but in the future, he'd need to control his temper.

Dylan had been sure the house would burn to the ground. He'd screwed up again, but the city would have to tear the place down. Good enough. Who'd called it in, anyway? He scanned the crowd. Plenty of neighborhood derelicts, but they didn't give a shit about anything but their next fix. He also spotted some old people. Had to be one of them.

The crowd started to thin as the firemen wrapped up their hoses. He was about to head for his car when something caught his attention. At the edge of the sidewalk, a fireman walked over to someone holding a camera. A skinny black teen. *Shit, that's the same kid!* The one on the bike who'd almost run into him at the smoke pot job. And there it was, lying on the lawn behind the kid—the same junky red bike.

Dylan's senses came alive with apprehension as the kid packed the camera in the saddlebag and pedaled away. *Did he get a picture of me?* No, that'd be a one-in-a-million chance.

***

"Nice work today, Tony," Lieutenant Brookin said as he entered the day room.

"Thanks, Tim. Same to you."

"Likes to tell everybody what to do," Warren mumbled.

"Huh?" Brookin asked.

"Nothing," Warren said and skulked away.

Tony bristled. He'd known he'd have to win over a skeptical crew, but Warren was becoming a major irritant.

The room quieted when Chief McMahon entered. He'd gathered the crews from Stations-300 and 400 for an after-action discussion, also known as a *hot wash*.

"I know it's late, and you're tired," he began, "but it's important we talk about this afternoon's operation while it's fresh in our minds. I've authorized overtime for those of you who were due to go home after the day shift."

"Thanks, Chief," Maddie said.

McMahon nodded. "I know you've been busy reservicing your equipment and probably haven't had time to eat, so I've ordered pizza for us."

Two classy moves. McMahon's stock continued to climb in Tony's estimation.

McMahon began by explaining his reasoning for the aggressive interior attack in a house that couldn't be salvaged. "I made the decision because civilians, a homeless family, might have been inside." After an examination of the tactical choices of the officers and the actions of the attack and search teams, the chief fielded some tough questions and answered candidly.

Tony was impressed. McMahon exhibited the qualities of an excellent leader. One who cared about his people, on and off the fireground.

Afterward, he assisted Captain Dudek with the details of the fire report. In all, four inch-and-three-quarter hoselines, each flowing 150 gallons per minute, had been deployed to the house from Engine-301, demonstrating efficient water management by the engine crews. Equally efficient, the truck crew's search and their timely ventilation of the kitchen windows had been textbook.

The entire operation was a credit to the organization, training, and leadership provided by the chiefs and company officers. For the first time in his brief tenure, Tony felt the pride of being part of and contributing to a top-notch team. Yet his initial reaction to the report of people in danger troubled him. *I've got to get past this.*

11

Sunday, September 28

"Smells amazing, Maddie," Tony remarked, inhaling the rich aroma of garlic and onions.

"Thanks, LT," Maddie said, flashing a smile as she layered pasta sheets with ricotta and mozzarella, a smudge of tomato sauce on her cheek.

"Any Italian roots buried in the Foster family?"

"My grandma. She's a Venturini."

"What do you know about that?"

"I'm trying out her special recipe."

"Bold move considering the food critics on this platoon. I'd be happy to lend a hand. My three-cheese lasagna is legendary at Reynolds International."

"We've got this, LT," Luke said as he strode into the kitchen, juggling vegetables and bagged lettuce. "I'm her assistant chef today."

"It's the rookie's turn to cook Sunday dinner," Maddie added. "How will we get any respect if we use a ringer?"

"She's right, LT," Luke said. "For better or worse, it's on us."

"Point taken, but if you need me . . ."

"We'll have County set the tones off," Maddie said.

Tony laughed. "I know when I'm not wanted."

Station-300's Day Room was typical of modern, open-concept fire station design. A tiled dining area with five square tables at the back of the room, a carpeted lounge with three rows of recliners, and a big-screen TV mounted on the front wall. A spacious kitchen, nestled into a nook adjacent to the dining area, boasted a commercial-grade oven and ventilation hood. With some time to kill, Tony approached a table where Romeo, Pet, and Corey pecked away on their laptops. "Mind if I join you?"

"Not at all," Pet said, kicking out an empty chair. "Just don't expect stimulating conversation."

"Noted," Tony said with a laugh. Since the day he'd heard the mention of Romeo pursuing Maddie, Tony had been watching for signs of contact between them, or evidence of sexual harassment, but in the month since that first shift, he hadn't observed anything that suggested a relationship of any sort. He decided to push the issue.

"Romeo, why aren't you in there with Maddie? Letting Luke horn in on your turf?"

Romeo arched an eyebrow. "What are you talking about, LT?"

"Remember my first day, when you introduced yourself at morning briefing and the crew got on you for chasing her?"

"Romeo?" Pet asked. "We were busting his chops. He's infamous for his taste in ladies."

"Not true," Romeo said. "I prefer older, more sophisticated types. Women of the world."

"Like the high school dropout with three kids?" Pet shot back.

"What about the girl who turned into your stalker after one date?" Corey asked.

"Or the woman whose husband came storming into the station looking for you?" Pet added.

"Are you two finished?" Romeo asked. "I think Maddie's boy toy is in the kitchen with her right now."

"Luke?" Tony asked.

Romeo smirked. "Don't look so surprised, LT. They're both barely out of diapers."

Tony spread his hands in mock apology. "I stand corrected." *So much for knowing the intricacies of my crew.* Mercifully, the intercom saved him from further discussion of firehouse romance.

"Lieutenant Moretti to the front door."

Mrs. Cooper again? Tony hoped not as he made his way to the garage. *But who else could it be?*

***

At the far end of the apparatus bay, he saw two familiar figures at the front door. *I'll be damned.*

"Look who's here," he said as he pushed the door open. "How could you two rubes find this place without the smell of cow manure to follow?"

"Very funny, city boy," Nikki Leach said as she reached out and pulled Tony into a tight embrace.

"Hold on now, not in front of the children," Tony said.

Nikki's companion, Robbie Stegler, stuck out his hand. "Hi, buddy . . . I mean Lieutenant Moretti."

Tony ignored the hand and gave his friend a bear hug that lifted Robbie to his toes. "I see firehouse cooking hasn't fattened you up yet."

"We've been trying," Nikki said. "He eats like a pig but never gains any weight."

"Ahh, the constitution of the young," Tony said and shot Nikki his best conspiratorial look. "Where's Phil? Embarrassed to bring your boyfriend along?"

Nikki blushed. The first time Tony had ever seen her with a red face. "No . . . he wanted to come, but the pull of a time-and-a-half callback at lieutenant's wages was too strong."

"I get it," Tony said. "Where's the ring? Did he pop the question yet?"

Nikki jabbed Tony's shoulder. "No! Shithead."

"We've got a pool going," Robbie said. "Guess the date Phil's going to propose. Want in on it?"

"Absolutely!" Tony said. "I'm betting he'll do it on Christmas Day."

"Stop it. You're both assholes." With a sly look, Nikki said, "I hope he asks me by Thanksgiving."

"I want to be the first to know," Tony said. "A text. No, a call, as soon as he gets off his knee."

"You know you will be," Nikki said. "We miss you at the airport."

"Same here," Tony said. "Anyway, you two are the perfect interruption to a boring afternoon. By the drool on your chins, I can see you want the grand tour."

"We sure do!" Robbie said. "But we're really here to see you."

"Right," Tony said with a laugh.

"We want to hear all about your exploits," Nikki said. "Imagine, a whole new group of firefighters to show what a screwup you are."

"Hah-hah. Come on in and try not to embarrass yourselves."

Robbie ate up every second of the tour. "I love the white cabs over the red bodies. Wish the airport could paint our crash trucks like that."

"This is what real fire trucks look like after they ripen," Tony said, alluding to the FAA-mandated yellowish green of the airport fire department's fleet.

Nikki, showing only mild interest, seemed to have other things on her mind. *Probably the impending engagement.*

The tour finished up in the day room, where his old friends shared stories of Tony at the airport with his new colleagues and joked about him fighting forest fires.

"You mean he actually fell off a ladder and landed on a pile of hose?" Luke asked.

"That's nothing," Robbie said. "You should've been there the time he passed out on the EMS call."

The B-Platoon crew howled, and Tony feigned indignation, but his spirit soared as his former colleagues commiserated about him. Fond memories of his time at Reynolds International Airport came flooding back.

"And then there was that time he—"

"They get the picture," Nikki said. "It's a beautiful day, let's go outside where we can talk."

"This is an awesome fire station," Robbie said as they stood in the back lot. "You even have a vegetable garden."

"And red bricks. Just the way you like it, right?"

"You remembered!"

"How could I forget? You'd really love our two refurbished stations.

Very traditional, two-story buildings with poles to slide down from upstairs bunkrooms."

"Cool, can we go see one of them today?"

"Maybe next visit," Nikki said. "I want to show this bumpkin what downtown Pittsburgh looks like before we hit the road. Work tomorrow."

The trio stood in the shade as the conversation ebbed, but Nikki's expression was one of concern.

"What's up, Nik? Why so solemn?"

"Have you seen Allie lately?"

"Allie? Sure, we text a lot."

"That's not what I mean, and you know it."

"Um, not since I moved my stuff out of the old apartment in Greencastle and headed west."

"Jesus, that was six months ago," Nikki said.

"What's going on, Tony?" Robbie asked. "She's a great girl."

Tony didn't want to go there. "It's hard to explain. It was such a hectic time. We just drifted apart, and we haven't really reconnected."

"Crap," Nikki said. "You guys know what you want, but you keep dancing around it. Are you going to wait until it's too late?"

"She's been busy managing airport operations, and I'm still getting settled into my new job. We are four hours apart, don't forget."

"From here?" Nikki asked. "You're full of it. We made the trip in two and a half hours, and we weren't speeding."

"You're right," Tony said. "Truth is, we're still dealing with a lot of conflicting emotions. It's been a rough road since . . ."

"I know, since the crash," Nikki said. "But that was over three years ago."

"Seems like yesterday."

"That's because nothing's happened since then to get your mind off that night."

"Maybe."

"Are you still having those nightmares?" Robbie asked.

"Nightmares? What do you mean?"

"Come on, buddy. Our bunk rooms were right next to each other and those walls are pretty thin. I heard you calling out. Lots of nights. You woke me plenty of times. It was always the same. You were trying to save someone but couldn't, right?"

"Yeah," Tony said in a barely audible voice. "I couldn't."

"Listen," Nikki said. "Robbie isn't the only one who knows what's going on with you. The whole station does, and they understand. Hell, everyone who worked the scene that night came away with some kind of psychological trauma. How could any human being not be affected by what we saw? It hit you harder because of the way you're wired."

Tony couldn't face her. He didn't want to deal with this now.

"Listen," Nikki said. "The fact is, we couldn't help a lot of those poor people. They were gone before we got there. You *know* it, but your brain won't let you *accept* it."

"I don't know about that," Tony said.

"Remembering how Allie got impaled and almost killed makes it worse, doesn't it? I know you blame yourself for that."

"Ease up on him, will ya, Nik?" Robbie said.

Nikki sighed. "Shit, Tony, I'm sorry. We came here to visit a dear friend, not to lecture you. Let me just say one more thing and I'll never bring the subject up again."

"Okay."

She placed a hand on his shoulder.

"You and Allie have been suffering with the same issues for three years. You've managed to keep the symptoms at bay, but they're still there. The counseling the airport provided helped a little, maybe. But I'm betting it was the way you faced your problems, *together*, that gave you both the strength to keep going. You've lost that support, and so has she. Her guts are probably churning the same way yours are."

Tony bit his lip and avoided her gaze.

"Reconnect with her. Soon. You love each other. You *need* each other."

"Thank you, my friend," Tony said. "You're right. I needed to hear it from someone who knows the situation." He met her eyes. "I'll try."

"All right, then," Nikki said.

"We're heading back in a few hours," Robbie said. "How about pulling a couple of the trucks outside?"

Nikki laughed. "A kid in a candy store."

"I'd be happy to," Tony said.

Nikki's words stung, but their importance hit him like a brick after he bade goodbye to his friends, when the corpse of the heavyset man in seat 14-F returned to torment him.

***

"We haven't talked in weeks, and I'm sure you didn't FaceTime me for this BS chitchat, so what's up?"

"Nothing." He'd hoped the conversation wouldn't go this way. "It's just that . . . seeing Nikki and Robbie made me miss you even more than I usually do."

Allie's eyes narrowed and her lips pressed into a thin line. He knew that expression from the months of rehab to the leg she'd almost lost at the crash, when he'd tried to coax her to do a few more squats, or jog a little bit farther.

"Is that your director of operations face? Bet it scares the hell out of your minions."

She cocked her head. The gesture reinforced the glare.

He could fool others, but not Allie. "I've had some . . . adjustment issues."

"Tell me something I don't know."

"A lot of issues, actually."

"What about the dreams?"

"They're back." *What's the use of this dance?* "With a vengeance. Every night."

"I thought so. And counseling?"

"I haven't found the right . . . situation."

Her features softened. "Oh, Tony, all this time and you've been bottling it up inside."

"The department has a tie-in with a good group," he said. "Lots of first responders."

"Uh-uh. We both tried the group thing after the crash. It didn't work.

73

We're too private to admit our feelings in a group setting. I was a mess until I got one-on-one therapy, remember?"

He did, but he couldn't bring himself to follow her example.

"I'm not going to let you get yourself killed. If you don't find someone who can help you—and soon—I will. And I'll hound your ass until you go."

"Yes, ma'am. I wouldn't dare question your wisdom or your determination."

"Smart boy."

Smart? Maybe, but would he follow through on his promise? That was the million-dollar question.

12

Wednesday, October 1

Tony sprang from the mattress as the klaxon blared in the hallway outside the lieutenant's bunk room and the lights surged to full intensity.

"Mon Area Fire, Station-300, Station-400, Battalion-1, respond. Automatic fire alarm. Wilson Village apartments, Building C, 3211 Front Street, West Forge. Two smoke detectors in alarm in the fourth-floor hallway."

Tony yanked up his uniform pants, ran out the door in his socks, jumped into his bunker pants and boots, tugged the suspenders tight, and donned his turnout coat. With a swift climb aboard Engine-301, he felt the rumble as Big Pappy fired up the engine. Warren and Maddie arrived after they'd settled into their seats.

"Pretty sad when the old guy beats you to the rig," Tony said.

Maddie blushed. Warren ignored the comment.

"Wilson Village is an ancient housing project," Big Pappy said as he pulled onto the pad and followed Ladder-302 onto Main Street.

Tony pulled up a plot plan on the MDT that showed five mid-rise apartment buildings arranged in a semicircle facing Front Street, the main drag in West Forge. "We have a hydrant right in front and the building has a standpipe system, but no sprinklers."

"The whole complex should have been torn down years ago," Pappy said.

Tony had toured the area on a familiarization ride and was struck by the abject poverty of the little town. The modest residences in his River Bend neighborhood were palatial by comparison.

He laid on the Federal-Q and sounded three blasts of the air horn at each intersection, but with the ladder truck in front of them and little traffic on South Shore Boulevard, the warnings were unnecessary. *All I'm doing is waking people up.*

Station-300 was first due, but the complex was situated on a hilltop, and once the apparatus entered West Forge, drivers had to navigate a network of winding, ascending streets. Speed slowed from thirty to twenty to fifteen and finally dropped below ten miles per hour.

"This is why I say following the ladder truck is bullshit," Big Pappy said. "Look at that big pig crawl up these hills. We'd be there already if we were leading the parade."

Tony couldn't disagree with the logic, at least in this instance, but that was a debate for another time.

"Mon Fire from County, we're getting numerous calls for fire and smoke on the fourth floor, with reports of possible trapped residents."

"BC-1 copies. I'm on the scene with fire showing on the Alpha side of Building C, Division-4. I'll have Wilson Village Command."

"Christ, it's three in the morning," Big Pappy said. "This isn't gonna be good."

Civilians in peril. Tony's throat tightened and his hands began to quiver. Would he be able to help them? *God, I hope they're all outside waving to us when we get there.*

By the time they hit the entrance to the housing plan, Tony's muscles were alive with the shakes. *Come on, man, keep yourself together. Your crew depends on you.*

"This is Wilson Village Command," McMahon radioed. "Building residents believe the fire is in apartment 408, and they aren't sure if the couple living there got out. No one has seen them."

People could be heard shouting in the background as the chief continued: "Ladder-302, initiate a search of the fire floor. Engine-301, there's a hydrant in front of the building. Hook into the standpipe and attack the fire."

Arriving on scene, Ladder-302 took position at the Alpha-Bravo corner of Building C while Big Pappy spotted the pumper at the Alpha-Delta corner, next to the hydrant.

Ignoring the growing anxiety, Tony hit the street amid panicked shouts from the onlookers as fire rolled out of two fourth-floor windows on Side-A.

Big Pappy pulled the preconnected fifteen-foot intake hose from the front bumper well and connected it to the hydrant while Maddie ran two three-inch lines to the building's standpipe Siamese connection.

Warren pulled the high-rise pack: one hundred feet of inch-and-three-quarter line with a nozzle and a gated wye from a high side compartment.

Tony clipped the portable thermal imaging camera to the retractable carabiner on his SCBA backplate, slung a box light over his head, and grabbed his A-tool, a seventeen-inch bar with a flat striking surface at one end and tapered forks at the other.

Warren led the way into the main lobby, where McMahon had established his command post.

"The truckies are on their way to Division-4," McMahon said. "Captain Dudek has Division-4 Operations. This building's got good firewalls, but who knows if they've been penetrated. Contain the fire to apartment 408. I'll get another attack line in action as soon as Engine-401 gets here. The stairwell is there." He pointed to the right of the lobby. "Get going."

"On our way, Chief," Tony said and handed his and Warren's accountability tags to McMahon. The shakes eased as he concentrated on his duties.

"Hold up! I'm coming with you."

From the stairwell, Tony saw Maddie sprinting through the lobby. "Over here!" he called. "Leave your tag with the chief and catch your breath. We'll meet you upstairs." *Not bad. I underestimated that girl.*

On the third-floor landing, Warren pulled the inch-and-three-quarter hose bundle from the pack and connected the gated wye—an adapter with a two-and-a-half-inch female inlet and two inch-and-three-quarter male discharges—to the standpipe connection. Tony spread the line across the steps. Warren spun the handwheel on the standpipe as Maddie arrived.

"Welcome to the party," Tony said. "Wait here. I'll tell you when to open the gate valve."

They carried the dry line to the fourth floor, where Warren lifted the hose and knelt at the fire door to the hallway.

"Open the gate valve, Maddie," Tony called.

As water filled the hoseline, Maddie rejoined the crew.

"Let's mask up."

Audi bells rang, PASS devices chirped, control modules lit up, and integrated voice amplifiers activated as the trio cranked their air cylinder handwheels.

The trio donned facepieces, slid Nomex hoods over their heads, cinched their helmets, and plugged second-stage regulators into facepiece docking ports.

Tony inhaled to activate the BA's airflow and eyed the LEDs of the heads-up display. Four green lights.

"Ready, LT," Maddie said.

"Ditto," Warren added.

"All right. Let's go." Tony ran an ungloved hand over the door while Warren and Maddie knelt behind him. "It's okay," he said and cracked it open.

He dropped low to the floor, raised the TIC, and peered down the hallway. The heat signature read ninety-seven degrees. *I thought it'd be a hell of a lot worse than this.*

"Attack-1 entering Division-4 with three firefighters," he radioed.

"Command copies. Attack-1 into the fourth floor with three."

"Attack-1 from Division-4 Operations," Captain Dudek radioed. "My search teams have cleared half of the floor. The fire is still confined to apartment 408, four doors down on your left. Get here ASAP, Lieutenant."

"You heard the man," Tony said and hit the button on his lapel mic. "Attack-1 copies. Moving to 408 now."

With Warren on the nozzle and Maddie backing him up, Tony followed as his crew moved quickly down the hallway. Shouts of "Fire Department, anybody in there?" sounded as the two search teams entered the units farther down the corridor. *God, I hope no one is.*

"This is the apartment we spotted coming in," Tony said when they reached 408. "So we know it's vented."

"We forced it already," Dudek shouted as he approached. "You can push it open."

"Thanks, Cap," Tony said and shoved it with the fork end of his A-tool.

Smoke spewed from the open doorway, enveloping the trio in superheated air that forced Warren and Maddie onto their heels. Tony leaned in to steady them as Warren pulled back on the bale. A tight stream of water, pressurized and flowing at 150 gallons per minute, shot into the apartment.

Crouched low, the attack team held their ground against the nearly intolerable heat as Warren used the standard Z pattern to sweep the area in front of him. The seven-eighths-inch solid-bore tip ripped into the flames but didn't afford much protection against the radiant heat.

Behind them, Tony lifted the TIC, but he didn't need the temperature reading to tell him the crew was taking a beating. He grabbed Maddie's shoulder. "It's too hot. Let's back up."

"Attack-1 from Command, status report."

Tony grabbed for his mic. "We're hitting the fire, but conditions inside the apartment are untenable."

"Command copies," McMahon replied. "Tower-502's crew is setting up PPV in the far stairwell. Are you ready for ventilation, Attack-1?"

"More than ready, Chief," Tony replied.

"500-Captain, vent it now," McMahon radioed.

"Stay low," Tony shouted. "The truckies are venting."

The cough and rumble of a gasoline engine sounded as the Tower-502's crew fired up their twenty-four-inch positive-pressure ventilation fan.

Seconds later, a powerful stream rushed into, over, and around the attack team as the forced air sought the only exhaust port available in the now-pressurized hallway—the shattered windows of apartment 408. The temperature dropped quickly and the heaviest of the smoke cleared as ventilation took effect.

"Move in!" Tony commanded.

Warren and Maddie used a knee-walking technique—forward legs up and pulling with back legs dragging behind and pushing—to pull themselves across the floor, sweeping the nozzle left, right, and diagonally as they advanced. Their technique extinguished the fire in the living room and kitchen in half a minute.

"You got it, Warren," Tony said. "Let's hit the hallway and get into the bedroom. Maddie, take the nozzle."

"Let me finish," Warren said.

Tony's anger flared. "Give her that nozzle, now!"

Warren huffed as he pushed the bale halfway forward to reduce flow and passed the nozzle to Maddie. The duo pivoted left toward the blazing hallway.

"Nice and high, Maddie," Tony said. "Knock it back."

Maddie opened the nozzle and swept the ceiling and upper walls rapidly. Moving forward, she stopped and directed two short bursts into a bathroom before moving to the open bedroom door. Flames filled the room.

"Z pattern, Maddie," Tony said.

Warren leaned in and pushed down on the line to help his partner tip the nozzle up, and Maddie responded with a series of rapid side-to-side sweeps, starting at the ceiling and finishing at the baseboard.

The fire died off, leaving a smoldering mattress and two blackened humps of what had recently been a dresser and chest of drawers. The bedclothes were burned away and the box spring had collapsed in on itself.

"Kick-ass work, probie," Warren said in a rare moment of praise.

"Nice job, Maddie," Tony said. "Give that mattress a soaking."

"Will do, LT."

Tony keyed his mic. "Command from Attack-1, the fire in apartment 408 is extinguished. We're completing a secondary search now."

"Command copies. Be advised, the missing residents have not been accounted for."

An icy fear ran through Tony's veins. *Oh, please no.*

"Hold on, Tony. We're coming in behind you."

Tony couldn't make out the amplified voice, but it didn't matter; the bedroom needed to be cleared. He circled to the window, where a few burnt photo frames and the stub of what must have been a nightstand lay in a heap beside the headboard. Turning sideways to squeeze into a narrow space between the wall and the bed, he directed his light to the floor.

That was when he saw it.

Blackened, skinless fingertips, jutting out from under the bed frame. *My God.* Not comprehending, he blinked rapidly to drive the horrific image away. He turned the bypass knob on his regulator to clear his visor, but his facepiece wasn't fogged; it was his mind refusing to acknowledge what he'd seen. His muscles tensed as a rising panic urged him to run from the obscene vision.

"Everything okay, LT?" It was Maddie, and the question brought him out of his fugue.

"I'm good," he lied and waved an arm over his head.

He dropped to one knee, bent low, and shined the light under the bed. Some of the supporting slats had burned away, but enough remained to hold the sagging box spring high enough for him to get a good look at the horrible sight.

A body. No, two bodies. A man and a woman. Intertwined. The man's arm, split open with exposed muscles and tendons, wrapped around the woman, her face contorted and unreadable. The light reflected off splotchy white blisters bursting from the couple's reddened skin.

What did they think at the end? How terrible was the pain? Tony's mind tried to tell him it was the smoke, not the heat, that had killed them. But he held no illusions. *I know what happened. They couldn't make it to the window and took refuge under the bed as a last resort.* No, it wasn't the smoke.

Nausea gripped him and he felt himself falling. His helmet smacked off the floor and dislodged his facepiece. Pressurized air hissed out from the broken seal. He lay there, head turned toward the sickening sight, until everything went black.

***

Tony opened his eyes. Where was he? The hallway? *How did I get here?* His helmet, facepiece, and breathing apparatus were gone. Strong arms reached out and hoisted him. He pushed against their efforts. "I have to get back to my crew."

"Easy, LT. Your crew is fine," a voice assured.

"We'll have you outside in no time," another said.

Tony's head cleared. He eyed his helpers. Romeo and Muscles, from the truck crew.

"Just help me up. I can walk on my own."

The pair escorted him down the stairs to a waiting EMS crew as the gravity of what had occurred struck him like an axe between the eyes.

Part II

Peaks and Valleys

13

Saturday, October 4

No matter how hard he massaged the spot, Tony couldn't get the knot out of his shoulder muscles. He'd taken the day shift off and spent the time unpacking boxes and rearranging his living space, trying to get his mind off the apartment fire.

The image of the dead couple, his panicked reactions, and the fear of judgment from his crew gnawed at him relentlessly. The incident was stark confirmation that his psychological problems were far from resolved, and busywork was the best tonic he could think of to get his head straight before reporting for work.

With an hour and a half until the 6:30 night shift, his stomach was empty. He didn't feel like cooking, but the leftovers from Mrs. Olivero's most recent care package, two containers filled with spicy six-bean chili, were long gone. He pulled a Tupperware container from the fridge and sniffed its contents. *Ugh.* The leftover chicken stir-fry smelled like dead rodent. He considered a wrapped package of lunchmeat, but he'd tossed all the moldy bread out yesterday. The only other edibles were a couple of bags of arugula and a half-empty quart of skim milk. He'd have to visit the market soon, or maybe have Terrell deliver. He chuckled. *If that doesn't violate Mrs. Cooper's rules.*

Desperate, he eyed the lone frozen dinner—spaghetti and meatballs. What had possessed him to buy this crap? "Oh, what the hell," he muttered before voicing an apology to his Italian forebears and popping the meal into the microwave. With no veggies or cheese on hand, he dumped the arugula in a bowl and doused it with raspberry vinaigrette. A bottle of Sattui Family Red, from his favorite Napa Valley winery, sat on the countertop, but the thought of pairing it with *pasta in plastic*, as he called it, was too much. Instead, he opted for a bottle of Sam Adams, sat at the dinette table, and let out a hearty "Bon appétit, Tony," to the empty apartment.

After a *delightful* meal, he plopped his tired ass onto the sofa and examined his decorating handiwork. Fresh latex paint, courtesy of his landlord, masked the smell of the frozen dinner. His furniture, the portion of it he'd gotten after the split with Lisa, meshed uncomfortably with the odds and ends he'd picked up at the Mon Furniture Warehouse.

Neat and eclectic, the apartment carried none of the feminine touches Lisa had so expertly applied to their three-bedroom house in Pittsburgh. The thought of his ex-wife triggered a brief sadness. After three years, memories of her still elicited an emotional response, but now it was more of a nostalgic feeling, rather than a longing. Allie had certainly helped that process along.

Two limited-edition art reproductions by the Civil War artist Don Troiani flanked the fake fireplace: *Lions of the Roundtop*, a depiction of Chamberlain's charge at Gettysburg, and *Burnside's Bridge*, detailing the costly crossing of the Antietam Creek. In prior times, he'd spent hours looking at those scenes and imagining the battles they depicted. But now he hung the Civil War prints as a matter of course, without taking any pleasure in them. He smiled when he recalled how Lisa had consigned them to storage during their brief time at the townhouse in Greencastle.

Triple bookcases spanned the wall opposite the kitchenette. Two were loaded with books on military history, while a few John le Carré and Stephen King novels fought for space among a hodgepodge of fictional titles on the third. His Denon stereo receiver, flanked by a pair of Bose speakers, stood on a cart next to the door to the balcony. Not perfect for acoustic quality, but it would do. An eight-by-ten of him and Allie, taken at the airport awards ceremony, graced the lone end table, while a Celestron telescope stood on a tripod next to the door to the balcony.

Behind him, a cheap painting of a nondescript Dutch village hung above the sofa. The remaining wall space held photos of his old crewmates in action, and his award for valor, presented by the CEO of Reynolds International. His old yellow fire helmet, signed in black Sharpie by every member of his former platoon at the airport, completed the modest collection.

He thought about playing some music, but the couple downstairs had a new baby boy, and he didn't want to wake him. He spent the next forty-five minutes in thought, stewing about the fire, before getting up and showering for work.

****

Lost in thought after slipping into the station almost unnoticed, Tony stared at the lieutenant's desktop, trying to wrap his head around the tragic scene in apartment 408. His version of events would be tacked to Captain Dudek's main fire report before crossing Battalion Chief McMahon's desk.

"I thought I'd find you here."

Tony lifted his gaze from the computer screen. "Hello, Barney. I'm finishing up my report from the fire. You want to check it before I attach it to yours?"

"Check it for what, grammar, spelling errors?" Dudek asked. "It's a routine report, Tony. Don't stress over it."

"Two deaths? The way I had to be carried out of there? I wouldn't call it routine."

"I'm talking about the decisions you made, and the actions of your crew in response to those decisions. What happened after that has no place in that report. It's medical information, protected by HIPAA. Nobody's business but yours."

"I doubt my colleagues see it that way."

Dudek closed the door and took a chair in front of Tony's desk.

"May I help you, Captain?"

"I was there, remember? You and your crew did everything right; textbook, in fact. Those are the facts for your report. Nothing more."

"But that poor couple."

"They were dead before we pulled up to the building. It's tragic, but there it is."

"I guess, but . . ."

"But nothing. You've seen death before. Horrific, terrible death. Things no one should see." Dudek paused. "I'm no shrink, but don't you think the things you saw at that airliner crash are the real reason you reacted like you did?"

Tony shrugged. *Of course they are, but I am getting better.*

"Listen, we hear a lot about how police officers keep all their problems in house, but firefighters are worse. At least the cops talk to each other. Most firefighters won't. They keep everything bottled up inside. It doesn't have to be that way. There are people in this department you can talk to. People who will listen and not judge. I'm one of them."

"Thanks, Barney. I hear what you're saying."

"You hear it, but do you comprehend it?"

"I do, and I'm working on it." *Work* was exactly what he needed. His demons had fled while he'd worked in the forest . . . at least until that last day. *If I work my ass off and focus on my job, I can get past this.*

Dudek started to say something but stopped. His features brightened. "Okay, Tony. You're an honest guy. A smart guy. I'll take you at your word. But please, remember you're not alone."

"I know, and I'll keep it in mind," he said, anxious to change the subject. "Tell me, why aren't you retired and enjoying life? You've put in more than a full career of firefighting, a distinguished one from what I hear. What's left to accomplish?"

Dudek maintained eye contact, but his expression turned.

Tony detected a sadness he'd not seen in the normally upbeat captain. "Sorry, it's none of my business."

Dudek looked away. "I retired from the Pittsburgh Bureau of Fire three years ago. I was fifty-four. Nancy, my wife, left her job the year before. We had great plans for the next thirty years. We'd travel to all the places we'd dreamed of when we were young. Great adventures awaited us, two people who were still pretty young."

"Sounds great," Tony said, but from the captain's countenance, he doubted things had worked out as planned.

"Yeah, doesn't it?" Dudek shifted his gaze to his hands. "Three months after I retired, and a month before our first international trip, she found a lump." Dudek lifted his head. Tears brimmed. "Four months later she was gone."

"Oh my God, I'm so sorry." *Damn, I should have suspected. He never talks about his personal life.*

Dudek pulled a Kleenex from his pocket and dabbed his eyes.

"Sorry, Barney, I shouldn't have pried into your personal life."

Dudek regained his composure and waved an arm. "It's okay. Helps to talk about it, sometimes. But listen, it ties into what I'm talking about. I got through it by leaning on family and friends, and you can too. Firefighting is a brotherhood, and we're here for you."

Tony spent the rest of the day feeling like a stupid jerk and thinking about Barney's suggestion. Help from his colleagues? No, not when he was so new to the job and yet to prove himself. He barely knew most of them, and he wasn't about to come off like a weakling, especially after being carted out of a fire and into a medic wagon.

Yes, Tony appreciated the captain's words, but he remained firm in his thinking. Work was the answer, and he would throw himself into it like never before.

14

Monday, October 6

Two blocks from his handiwork, Dylan pulled his hands from the front pocket of his hoodie and pressed them against his ears as a big ladder truck zoomed past. *Way too loud.* If those firemen weren't already deaf from those sirens, they would be someday.

Bystanders crammed the sidewalk, watching the action as the firemen arrived. He wanted to get a closer look, be right there in the front row, but that was stupid. Much better to wander into a crowd, where no one would notice the stranger in their midst.

Dylan checked his watch: 4:25. He'd started the fire in the vacant two-and-a-half-story rathole twenty minutes before, but the fun was just beginning. No, not fun, he scolded himself. *I'm doing this for a reason, not for entertainment.* But that was a lie, in this case, anyway.

He drifted closer to the street as the smoke got thicker. He'd done the job properly this time, way better than when he'd first tried his hand at *weeding.* He didn't consider it arson. *I'm providing a community service.*

His mind returned to those first attempts, almost half a decade ago. What an idiot he'd been. The fires he'd set back then either went out on their own or were quickly extinguished by that old River Bend Volunteer Fire Department. He'd given up in less than six months, figuring the cops were onto him.

A dozen years had passed since Suzie's Mid-Town Café had shut its doors and his folks had relocated to a retirement village in North Carolina, but after witnessing even more urban decline and inactivity from the politicians, he'd decided to try his hand at urban renewal once again.

Admittedly, he'd made some of the same old mistakes at the beauty shop and house fires he'd set recently, but he was learning fast and wouldn't give up so easily this time.

Dylan forced himself to study building construction, relying heavily on online resources. He'd learned that a house like that one featured balloon framing, an old-time technique where the studs extend from the foundation all the way to the roof rafters. A critical detail since balloon framing lacked the fire stops found in modern platform construction, where each floor is built separately. It was the reason he'd chosen that particular house, probably built around 1920. He used what he'd learned by setting the fire in the basement, knowing it would spread throughout the house quickly.

As if to confirm this construction peculiarity, flames burst from the top-floor dormer. Dylan smiled. *All it takes is a little research. And some smarts.*

The firemen—there must have been twenty on scene—scrambled to get ahead of the flames with their ladders and hoses, but Dylan knew it was useless. By now, the fire was moving through hidden void spaces and spreading to every floor. But they weren't going to stop this one like they had on Cresson Street. *This won't take long.*

And it didn't. Unlike the other house fires he'd set, this one spread to the roof before breaking out on the first floor. *Pretty cool.*

"Ain't no way that mother is going out."

The voice, close by, brought Dylan out of his trance.

"There's fire on every floor."

Dylan looked to his left. *No way! Not again.* But there he was, ten feet away, the black kid with the camera, chatting to an elderly man while he photographed the flames, now lapping from every window.

A cold chill ran up Dylan's spine. *Take it easy, man. You're too jumpy. It's just a kid. He didn't see you at the other two fires, and he doesn't see you now.*

But then the kid panned his camera to the right and shot the crowd, with Dylan in full view. *Son of a bitch!* He turned away, snugged up the hoodie, and pretended to watch an arriving fire truck before risking a quick look back. He let go of a pent-up breath. The kid had resumed watching the fire.

The whole house was engulfed, and it was time to get out of Dodge. He backed out of the crowd, walked to the corner, and made his escape.

Three blocks away, he relaxed. His heart rate slowed, and his breathing returned to normal, but one thing was certain. He'd have to be a lot more careful in the future, and keep his eye out for that annoying little shit.

15

Friday, October 10

"Keep going, I'll get it," Tony called to Maddie as the seventy-five-foot stack of inch-and-three-quarter hose slipped off her shoulder. A vision of his own failure in a hose advancement drill during his first shift at the airport came to mind as he bent to retrieve the fallen attack line. *That was me, three years ago.*

"Hurry, please," a woman's weak, anguished voice called. "Everything I own is inside."

Tony glanced at the hunched figure, her weathered face framed by long, scraggly gray hair that caught the late-afternoon sun.

Scooping what hose he could, he grunted, pulled the ungainly mess to his chest, and advanced across the lawn to the two-story frame dwelling. With its insulbrick siding, the old house in Buchanan was a carbon copy of his early childhood home in Meadville.

Maddie, rebounding from her setback, spread the flakes across the ground below the porch as smoke issued from the open front door.

Tony dropped to one knee on the cracked concrete steps and eyed the BA's control module—4,350 psi on both the analog gauge and the digital display. A full air cylinder.

He doffed his gloves, spread the Kevlar hairnet with both hands, and pulled the attached facepiece down, anchoring it with his chin. After cinching the temple and chin straps, he covered the docking port with his palm and inhaled. The visor was sucked in. Good seal. He forced a heavy breath. No sticking. The exhalation valve operated freely.

93

Captain Dudek appeared in the doorway with a set of *irons*, an axe strapped to a Halligan bar. "Tony, the fire's in the Charlie-Delta corner. Gotta be the kitchen. We tried to hit it with the water can, but we couldn't get close enough. It's a mess in there. Stuff stacked everywhere. Make a right when you go in. Search-1 is pulling back now, but they'll be right behind you. Search-2 is upstairs."

"Copy, Cap. We're on it," Tony said. "Let's go on air," he instructed before he plugged the regulator into his facepiece and listened for the confirming click as it snapped into place. "Attack-1 entering Division-1 with three," he radioed and tossed a box light over his helmet.

"Command copies," McMahon replied. "Entering with three. Be advised, I'm sending a backup crew to side Charlie. They won't hit the fire unless you call for them."

"Thanks, Chief," Tony replied. McMahon was too smart to allow hose streams from inside and outside to oppose each other. *But he must suspect something unusual.*

Tony activated the thermal imaging camera, switched his chest-mounted flashlight on, fed ten feet of hose to his team, and followed them inside. Surprised by the lack of heat despite the heavy smoke, he advanced behind Warren and Maddie at a crouch.

"Wait. You can't go that way," Pet called from behind. "The kitchen's straight ahead, but you've got to go around. Follow my light and try it that way," she added, indicating a spot to the right, near the Charlie wall. "It's tight in there."

Before moving, Tony raised the TIC, but the image was blocked by . . . something. *What the hell is that?* He reaimed the camera toward the ceiling. The heat signature flashed 170 degrees, with ominous convection currents visible on the infrared display. He had to find out what they were facing. "I'm taking the lead."

Tight was an understatement. It was a tunnel, Tony realized as he knee-walked into a corridor barely wider than his shoulders. Sweeping his light across the claustrophobic sides, he halted. Boxes on top of boxes, piled halfway to the ceiling. Unafraid, although logic indicated he should be, he resumed the advance.

Five feet in, he jerked to a halt. A dead end. Heat stung the back of his neck. He dropped to all fours and lifted the box light. An opening, diagonally to the left. *Christ, it's a damn maze.*

"I don't like this," Warren said. "We're not getting anywhere."

Tony considered. He should pull them out. But not yet. "Follow me. We're almost there."

Before he made the turn, the inside of his facepiece lit up bright orange as flames shot across the ceiling and searing pain erupted in his ears. "Rollover! Hit it! Straight stream!" he ordered.

Warren reacted instantly. Dropping to the floor and rolling onto his back, he sent a series of three-second bursts into the ceiling. The technique, known as *penciling*, was designed to extinguish a fire at ceiling level without disturbing the thermal balance. If he'd used a wide fog pattern, the heat would have dropped to the floor and cooked them like lobsters in a pot. Warren was good, his pain-in-the-ass attitude notwithstanding.

The fire darkened quickly, but the high-pressure stream jostled the boxes at the top edges of the stack.

"They're coming down!" Maddie warned.

"Back out," Tony ordered, but Warren, still on his back, couldn't get up in time as the boxes toppled.

"Cover up, Maddie!" Tony ordered as he draped himself over his vulnerable nozzleman.

"Nooo! Ahhh!" Maddie screamed.

"Omph." Tony's breath escaped in an involuntary rush as falling boxes crashed onto his back and helmet, dislodging his facepiece and driving him into Warren's chest. The cascade continued, pinning Tony's legs and plunging the space into darkness.

Personal Alert Safety System prealerts sounded and air hissed from Tony's facepiece as his SCBA tried to maintain positive pressure despite the broken seal. He snapped his eyes shut against the sting of wood smoke.

"Can't . . . breathe. Get off me," Warren said. But his pleas were in vain. Tony couldn't move.

Pet called to them. "Are you guys okay?"

"We're trapped," Maddie said in a voice audible only because of her voice amplifier.

Before Tony could report their situation, flashing strobe lights reflected off his visor and high-pitched, modulating tones filled the air as three PASS devices leapt into full alarm.

The radio erupted with Pet's frantic voice. "Mayday, Mayday. Firefighters down. Division-1, Side Delta."

Tony tried to follow the jumbled radio transmissions.

"Command from Search-1, they're buried under . . . and we're digging . . . but the fire is still . . ."

"Command to Attack-2, can you reach . . . fire from . . ."

Tony's mind whirled at the thought of Warren pinned and unable to breathe. Fortunately, his adrenaline spiked as well. He punched his arms through the debris to the carpeted floor. Groaning, he used every bit of strength to push himself up.

Freed of the compressing weight, Warren let out a series of fast, raspy breaths.

"Easy, buddy, they're coming," Tony said. His maneuvers caused his facepiece to dislodge further, and he began coughing from the acrid taste of charcoal. Braced in full plank position, he turned his head and jammed his facepiece into the wall of boxes to his right. Airflow from the hissing facepiece slowed. *Almost.* He slid his jaw back into the chin cup and the seal reseated.

"Are you okay, Maddie?" Tony shouted over the wailing PASS alarms.

"I think so, but I can't move," she said. Her voice was stronger now, seemingly devoid of fright.

"You're tough," Tony said. "Hang in there. We'll be out soon."

"I found one!" Pet said. "It's Maddie. Get these boxes off her."

"We're trying," another voice—Muscles—replied. "Come on, Luke, lift."

"That's it," Muscles said. "Pet, grab her legs while we hold this shit up."

"Got her," Pet said.

Relief washed over Tony, but his arms started to give under the weight of the boxes on his back.

"Tony and Warren, we're almost there," Pet called.

Tony grunted. "Okay."

Pet must have read the distress in his voice. "Just toss this crap out of the way," she said. "We've got to get them out of there."

Amid the frantic shouts and jostling of boxes, the smoke lifted and a flow of forced air cooled the space. "The fire's out," Pet said. "We're venting."

"'Bout . . . time," Warren said.

"There they are," Muscles said as Tony's arms gave out and he eased himself down onto Warren.

"Ooof. For Chrissake, not again," Warren said.

"Sorry," Tony said, disgusted with his inability to hold himself up longer.

"Come on, Luke, pull!" Muscles said.

"Wait," Pet said. "We shouldn't move them until we can check them out, put them in C-collars."

"I'm fine," Warren grumbled. "Get him the fuck off of me!"

"Do what he says," Tony added.

The truckies relented and pulled the three members of Attack-1 from the debris.

Chief McMahon rushed to meet them in the front yard. "Everybody okay?"

"We're good, Chief," Tony said. "Just got the wind knocked out of us."

"More than once," Warren said.

"Sorry we couldn't finish our job," Tony said. "Who put it out?"

"We did," said Fitz as he and two guys from Engine-401 shouldered bundles of hose from behind the house.

"We appreciate it," Tony said, ignoring Fitz's snarky tone.

Fitz narrowed his eyes. "Glad we could help save your asses."

Tony said nothing. The comment was deserved. *I should've backed us out.*

"That's enough," McMahon said. "Let's finish the overhaul, repack these lines, and get out of here."

***

Back at the station, Tony separated the outer shell, moisture barrier, and thermal lining of his turnout gear and dumped the smoky, sweat-drenched bundle into one of the extractors, heavy-duty washing machines designed to clean and thoroughly remove contaminants. Next, he sanitized his facepiece in the stainless steel utility sink. Lastly, he scrubbed the soot from the polycarbonate shell of his red lieutenant's helmet with soap and water. After drying it to a shine, he held it up. *Am I truly qualified to wear this? Or am I fooling myself?*

"Big responsibility, isn't it?"

Tony turned as Barney Dudek carried his own protective clothing into the gear room.

"How are you, Tony?"

"Physically? I'm okay. A few bumps. Nothing a few ibuprofen and a hot soak won't fix."

"And mentally?"

"Well, Barney, my pride's wounded a bit. The job went undone."

"Is that all?"

"I didn't have a panic attack, if that's what you mean."

"How about when you were trapped, and *your team* was trapped with you?"

Tony lowered his gaze. "I managed." *Trapped.* He didn't like the connotation. *But that's what we were. What I led the team into.*

"How bad was it?" Dudek asked.

"I was anxious for a few moments, but I kept myself together."

"I see. And your decision-making?"

"I can't blame the dumb call to keep advancing on any psychological issues. My head was clear."

"Good to hear," Dudek said in an unconvinced tone. "Have you found anyone to . . . talk to, as we discussed?"

"Not yet, but I'm looking."

"Uh-huh." Dudek ran a hand across his shiny dome. "Listen, Tony. You made a judgment call today, an aggressive one. We can debate the merits, but I'd have done the same. It's the way we're all wired."

"I'm not sure about that."

"Well, be sure. We're humans, not machines. We can't take in all the information, account for all the . . ."

"Variables?"

"Yes, the variables, but that's not what concerns me. I'm worried about how you might react if one of your crew gets hurt during a working incident. Would you be able to function? Make sound choices?"

"I haven't lost it yet," Tony replied a little too strongly.

"That's not what I asked. Would you freeze up?"

Tony lifted his gaze. "Well, Cap, I can't honestly say."

"I appreciate your honesty," Dudek said. A frown flickered across his face. "Something is screwing with your head, Tony, and we both know what that is. You need to find someone to help you get rid of your demons, and soon. I can't have you putting your crew, or anyone else, at risk. Do you understand what I'm saying?"

"I do, and I promise, I'm working on it." It wasn't a lie. In his own way, by working hard and improving his performance as a leader, he could overcome his troubles.

16

Monday, October 13

From his front-row seat between Captain Dudek and Chief McMahon, Tony imagined accusatory stares boring holes into his skull from the twenty-odd firefighters seated behind him in the training room.

Until recently, sessions like this, held within a week of the hot wash, were known as *critiques*, but to encourage crew members to participate in frank discussions, the process had been renamed *after-action reviews*. Yet despite the less-threatening euphemism, Tony expected a head-hunting expedition. *And it's my head they're hunting.*

Deputy Chief of Training and Administration Mason O'Connell stood at the podium, flanked by Chief Ramsey and Deputy Chief of Operations Rockwell "Rocky" DeFazio. *All the big guns are here.* Mounted on the wall to their left, a seventy-inch HDTV displayed an image of last Friday's house fire.

Deputy Chief O'Connell tapped his laser pointer three times, and the room quieted. "We all have things to do, so let's get to it. Chief Ramsey, would you like to lead us off?"

"Thank you, Mason." Ramsey welcomed the B-Shift crews from Stations-300 and 400 with his patented broad smile. "This department has been in business a little over a year, and we all know it's still a work in progress. We're still finding out about each other's strengths and weaknesses—learning to work together." He paused to scan the crowd. "Remember that after-action sessions like this one are tools for us to learn. A conversation among professionals. Free of judgment, yet brutally honest. It's all in the delivery. Knockout blows delivered with kid gloves, I like to say."

Tony took no comfort in the chief's words.

"We had a close call last Friday, and we're here today to discuss how to avoid a repeat."

"Thank you, Chief," O'Connell said as Ramsey took his seat. "Chief DeFazio and I have studied the reports and spoken at length with Deputy Chief McMahon and Captain Dudek. We have a pretty good idea of what happened." He aimed his laser pointer at the display, with the dot on the front door. "Here we have an unremarkable two-story frame dwelling with fire reported in the kitchen, which was located at the corner of Sides-C and D." He nodded to BC McMahon. "Ritchie, can you take us through the initial actions?"

McMahon stood, accepted the pointer from O'Connell, and pulled a note from his breast pocket. "I arrived on scene at 1619 and was immediately approached by a woman who stated the fire had started on the stove. I asked her if she lived alone and if anyone else was inside. She shook her head no but seemed confused. I escorted her to the sidewalk and performed a three-hundred-sixty-degree survey of the residence. Flames were showing on Side-C of the first floor, which I assumed to be the kitchen. Light smoke was issuing from the second-floor windows and the eaves. The smoke was grayish and wasn't pumping out under pressure, so I ruled out an impending backdraft."

McMahon changed the slide to a plot plan of the neighborhood. "I ordered Engine-301, approaching from the west, to lay in from a hydrant here." He aimed the red dot at the location and continued. "In the meantime, Ladder-302 arrived and took position on Side-A, leaving a space for Engine-301 at the Alpha-Delta corner. I ordered Engine-401 to drive directly to the scene and had Rescue-303 and Special Services-402 park their rigs and send their manpower to the command post."

McMahon switched back to the slide of the house. "Next, I directed Ladder-302's crew to throw ground ladders to the second-floor windows of Sides A and D, and to raise their aerial to the roof for possible ventilation. Since I couldn't get a definitive answer as to whether anyone else was in the house, I ordered Captain Dudek, with his truck crew, to search both floors." McMahon nodded to Dudek, who stood and faced the audience.

"I divided my truck crew into two teams and entered the structure via the front door," Dudek said. "I directed Search-1, consisting of Pellegrino and Petruska, to sweep Division-1, and sent Search-2, with Green and Bennett, up the stairs to Division-2. I took position between the front door and the staircase." Dudek paused. "Any questions so far?"

"Let's hold questions until later," Deputy Chief O'Connell said.

"Will do," Dudek said and continued. "Search-1 wasn't able to complete their assignment because access to the dining room and kitchen was blocked by high-stacked storage of what we later learned were boxes of books, magazines, and other household goods."

"Yeah, that crazy old bird was a real pack rat," Romeo said. The comment drew a sharp unspoken reproach from Chief Ramsey.

"Thanks, Captain," McMahon said, and picked up the description. "When Engine-301 pulled up, I directed its crew to advance a line to the front door so we could attack from the unburned side." He aimed the pointer at the front door. "Lieutenant Moretti's hose team entered the residence at approximately 1625. When firefighter Fitzpatrick arrived at the scene, I directed him to deploy an inch-and-three-quarter backup line to Side-C. The line was charged, but since it was a precautionary measure, Fitzpatrick wasn't to open up unless I ordered it. The main effort was to be conducted by Attack-1, inside the structure."

Here goes, Tony thought. Without waiting for a signal from McMahon, he stood and turned to his colleagues. "As I entered the front door with firefighters Jones and Foster, I noted a thick concentration of smoke, but only moderate heat. Captain Dudek, standing near the stairway, informed me that the fire was in the kitchen and that his truck crew had been unable to extinguish it with their water can. He also warned me that the path to the Charlie-Delta corner might be blocked. Shortly after, firefighter Petruska passed a similar warning."

"Pay attention," Ramsey said at the sound of comments from the back of the room.

"We moved quickly," Tony continued as sweat formed on his brow, "until we got to the stacked boxes. At that point, we dropped to our knees and continued forward, but more slowly. The temperature became noticeably hotter, but not untenable. We came to a dead end, but I found another passage open on our left. Before we could take it, fire rolled across the ceiling, directly above us. Warren—firefighter Jones—opened up with a straight stream and extinguished the flames with a few short bursts."

"Slow down, Lieutenant," O'Connell said.

Without realizing it, Tony had been racing through his report. *Calm down.* He took a slow breath, cleared his throat, and continued. "The sweeping action of the stream caused the boxes at the top of the stack to sway, and then fall. A domino effect followed, and we found ourselves immobilized beneath the weight of their contents." He went on to recount his efforts to get free, and the help they'd gotten from the truckies. The room was silent until he returned to his seat, then the murmuring resumed.

Tony bit his lip as Pet described how Ladder-302's crew dug the engine crew out of their predicament. *I should've pulled them out, and everyone knows it. What the hell was I thinking?*

Fitz added salt to the wound by relating how his hose team had saved the day by knocking in the kitchen door and dousing the flames. Pet's account was matter-of-fact, but Fitz told his story with unmistakable smugness and condescension. *Twist that knife a little more, won't you please?*

O'Connell quieted the muttering and opened the floor for comments and questions.

Tony expected Fitz to sound off, but it was Lieutenant Tim Brookin from Station-400 who led off. "Captain Dudek, what did your search teams find on Division-2? Were conditions similar to those on Division-1?"

"The same," Dudek replied. "Boxes, magazines, newspapers—a massive fuel load. If the fire had penetrated those stacks, we wouldn't have stopped it." The captain nodded at Brookin. "We owe you our thanks for knocking it down so quickly, Lieutenant."

From his seat, Brookin beamed.

Tony did not. *Thanks for nothing, Tim.*

Egan Coyle, a probie, also from Station-400, stood. "Chief McMahon, did you consider going defensive once the situation got worse?"

"No, I didn't," McMahon replied with a hint of umbrage. "We had a fire in the kitchen with no extension. Nothing unusual for us. Once things deteriorated, you ask? I take that to mean when Attack-1 encountered the maze of boxes, yes?"

"Um, yes, sir."

"I see. Once that occurred, we had a crew in need of assistance. I couldn't possibly go defensive, could I?"

"No, sir," Coyle said as a pink hue spread across his cheeks.

McMahon was a bit hard on the kid, but Tony was grateful for the way he phrased his answer: *In need of assistance.* But the tone he'd taken with the young probie had a dampening effect on the crowd and the questions died out. Hardly conducive to learning, and while it relieved him from answering questions about his decision-making, he wouldn't have minded fielding a few tough ones. Better to put any lingering doubts about his actions to rest than to let them fester in the minds of the crew.

O'Connell checked his watch and scanned the room. "I believe that's it. Our final report will be distributed by the end of the week. Thanks, everyone."

Fitz caught Tony as he headed for the office. "Do you have a minute?"

Today was Tony's Kelly day, and he had reports to enter before he left at 6:30, but he didn't mind the interruption. "Let's talk in the office. Barney's out on the pad with 302's crew."

Fitz closed the door and took a seat in front of Tony. "Listen, I'd never say anything in front of the crew or the chiefs, but . . ."

"But?" With his right hand, Tony gripped the fuzzy tennis ball he kept next to the keyboard.

"I've got to be honest with you."

"Please do," Tony said as he squeezed the ball. *Let's see what you've got to say, Mr. Fitzpatrick.*

"You're a good guy, I can see that."

Tony transferred the ball to his left hand and wrapped his fingers around it.

"But you're not qualified to be a lieutenant in this department. At your old airport, maybe, but not here."

The ball wouldn't compress any further. "Go on."

"You should never have taken Maddie and Warren into that situation, that maze of boxes. It was an empty house, for Chrissake."

Tony released the ball. "You're right."

Fitz looked stunned. "What?"

"I already came to that conclusion. It was a judgment call, and it was the wrong one." The chair squeaked as Tony leaned back. "I've learned from it and I won't repeat my mistake."

Fitz was clearly taken aback but recovered quickly. "Maybe not, but you're reckless. Do you even care about your own safety? And what about the safety of your crew?"

Tony's calm evaporated. His hands quivered as he released the ball.

Fitz put his arms on the desk and leaned forward. "What if I'm not there to save you next time?"

Tony shot up, sending the chair rolling into the file cabinet. "Save me? Who the fuck do you think you are?"

Fitz got to his feet and matched Tony's glare. "I'm someone with a hell of a lot more experience than you'll ever have, buddy. Someone who's telling you to go back to that fucking airport, where you belong."

Tony saw red. He aimed an index finger at the door. "Get the fuck out of here!"

Fitz, at least five inches shorter than Tony, stood his ground. In a conspiratorial tone, he asked, "What really happened in that house? Did you freeze up? Have one of your panic attacks? Pass out again, maybe?"

All focus gone, Tony snatched the tennis ball and sent it whizzing past Fitz's head. "Get out, now!"

Fitz walked to the door before pivoting. "You don't belong here. Resign before you get one of us killed."

Tony broke for the door and slammed it shut.

Twenty minutes later, his anger had cooled, but his stomach churned.

Filled with regret for his unprofessional behavior, he sat at his desk, stunned by how fast he'd reached a boil. An uncharacteristic outburst, it had to be tied to his complex emotional issues. His mental state was getting worse, despite the work he'd put in to shore it up.

17

Wednesday, October 15

Tony checked the time on his Fitbit as he watched the green soft-side bag complete a lazy loop around the baggage carousel for the umpteenth time. Twenty-five minutes since the plane landed. *Where the heck is he?* Every other passenger on the Harrisburg flight had fetched their luggage and gone. He pulled the phone from his back pocket and fired off a text message.

Are you coming or what?

His tritone text alert sounded.

C U in twenty

The reply confounded him. "Twenty more minutes?" he asked aloud.

"Or sooner, ya dope!"

Tony spun. The tall, thin figure with the bushy orange hair had arrived. "You ass. What did you do, stop for lunch?"

"Well, yeah. A man's gotta eat, and I wasn't about to pay for yours too," Evan O'Brien said with a laugh.

"Asshole," Tony said.

"Rookie," Evan replied. "It's good to see you, *Lieutenant* Moretti." He shook his head. "Who in their right mind made *you* an officer?"

Tony reached out and pulled his friend into a tight embrace.

"Okay, no PDA, please. I've got my dignity."

Tony wiped his eyes. "Or what's left of it. How you doing, buddy?"

"I'm tolerable. How about you?"

"Same."

"Glad to hear it," Evan said. "Is this the new terminal?"

"Yep. Pretty slick, isn't it?"

Evan surveyed the gleaming new landside terminal of the Pittsburgh International Airport. "Wow, this place makes Reynolds look like a third-world relic."

"Looking for a transfer?"

"You mean start at the bottom again? No, thanks. Besides, I'm no city boy."

Tony laughed. "I've got a Kelly shift tomorrow and I scored a couple of tickets to the Pitt–West Virginia basketball game, if you're interested."

"Hell yes! It's about time you did something for me."

"Yeah, yeah," Tony said as he clapped Evan on the shoulder. "After you saved me from myself so many times."

"All part of the mentoring process, Anthony," Evan said as he fetched his bag. "Shall we get out of here?"

"Sure, but who checks such a small piece of luggage?"

"What can I say? I'm an old-fashioned guy."

There had to be more to it, and his suspicion was confirmed as Evan winced when he lifted his carry-on-sized bag from the carousel. "That thing's been spinning around forever. If you'd put a name tag on it, I would have snagged it for you."

"Not a problem," Evan said while he massaged his left shoulder.

"Still rehabbing?"

"Yep, and they've still got me on light duty, mostly classroom work at the academy."

"There's no finer instructor in Central PA, that's for sure."

"I'm itching to get back to the real thing," Evan said.

"You'll get there," Tony said. "I'm in short-term parking." "Follow me."

Evan's tone made clear he didn't want to talk about his injuries, and Tony didn't push it. His friend had clearly not recovered from his brush with death at a mutual aid house fire almost four years before.

***

"Take a seat," Tony said as he carried the suitcase into the apartment. He'd grabbed it from the trunk, and Evan hadn't protested.

"Interesting place. Decorated in Civil War modern."

"Lisa got all the nice stuff."

"She deserved it," Evan said.

Tony laughed. "Still wearing it, I see," Tony said, indicating the chain around Evan's neck.

"This?" Evan asked, pulling a silver amulet from his shirt and holding it up. "Always."

"The Celtic protection talisman," Tony mused.

"Yes, sir. I should have worn it the night of that damned house fire. Maybe the roof wouldn't have collapsed on me."

"Maybe," Tony offered, remembering the night his mentor had almost died.

"You sure you don't mind me crashing here?"

"Not at all. I don't get many visitors. Nikki and Robbie drove back the same day they dropped by."

"Speaking of those fine firefighters, they relayed some disquieting information," Evan said.

"Come on, I'm sure Robbie didn't say *disquieting*. Maybe Nikki, but not Robbie."

"Don't sidestep the issue."

"Yes, Professor. Cut to the chase, why don't you?" The last thing he wanted to do was talk to Evan about his psychological issues.

"I hear all's not well with the lieutenant situation. I assume you're getting crap from the folks who preceded you here."

Tony breathed a sigh of relief. Evan's question was about work, a topic he was eager to discuss. "You assume correctly. The crap, as you so eloquently put it, is coming from a few experienced firefighters. It's no big deal."

"Let me guess. They don't think you have enough experience in structural firefighting or leadership to be their lieutenant."

"You nailed it. One former volunteer chief just plain resents me because I'm in a position of authority over him."

"Not surprising," Evan said.

"And? Where are your words of wisdom?"

"Oh, right. Here they are. Tough shit."

Tony waited for a humorous follow-up comment, but Evan's features held no mirth.

"You've been around the block, Tony, but no matter what you've done in the past, you're still the new guy. You had to expect some hazing, or did you think they'd hail the big hero?"

The comment stung. "Of course not, but I thought they'd get past their misgivings by now."

Evan eyed Tony with his patented *wise old owl* look. "Do you remember your first shift, when you fell off the ladder into that pile of hose?"

"How could I forget? It's burned into my memory along with the time I got rejected by Patti Lesner when I asked her to the eighth-grade Christmas dance."

"Weak jokes aside, did you ever think you'd get past either of those disasters, or the ones that followed? That you could regain your self-respect and that of your peers?"

"Nope."

"But you did. The whole platoon came around. Hell, in three months, even Ron Jarvis was singing your praises, and he hated your guts."

Tony nodded, but he wasn't convinced the two situations were comparable.

"Listen," Evan said as he leaned in. "You're qualified, and not just because you can rapidly assess a complex emergency scene and make great decisions, but because you're a leader. A *natural* leader who cares about his people. I know it, everyone at Reynolds International Airport knows it, and I bet the guy who's giving you the most trouble knows it too."

"Thanks, buddy. I needed to hear that." Evan could always put things into perspective.

"So now you have," Evan said. "And that's the last I want to hear about this topic. I came here to get away from my wife and kids for a couple days. I want to have some laughs with a good friend."

"That can be arranged," Tony said. "But can you run a comb through that mess of a red mop before we're seen together in public?"

***

"Hello, stranger." Allie's broad smile lit up Tony's laptop screen and instantly lifted his mood. "To what do I owe this honor?"

Tony chuckled. "Wanted to find out what my favorite airport operations director is up to."

"Oh, the usual. The annual FAA inspection is scheduled for the week of the twenty-seventh, so we're all scrambling to get ready."

"Scrambling? With you in charge? I'll bet the inspectors could show up today and the airport wouldn't get written up for a single discrepancy."

"We'll see," Allie said with a self-satisfied smile. "I thought you'd forgotten about me."

"Are you crazy? I think about you all the time."

Allie's smile faded. "Is that so?"

"Come on, you know how I feel."

"Tony, since you went on your Forest Service sojourn, I can count on five fingers the number of times we've FaceTimed, or phoned, for that matter. And the visits to see each other . . . oh, wait, there haven't been any."

"Sorry, Al. It's been a little . . ."

"Busy?" Allie huffed. "I wouldn't know anything about that."

Now it was Tony's turn to frown. "Evan's here," he said.

"Weak attempt to deflect, but yes, I know he is. I gave him permission to smack some sense into you while he's there."

"It's nice to see him. Lots of great memories, you know?"

"Along with plenty of bad ones, right?"

"Some."

"Is that why I see an empty bottle of Napa Valley red on the table?"

"Oops." Tony held the wine bottle up. "It's Russian River zin, if you must know."

"What a classy guy," Allie said. "Listen, the memories are normal, and you know Evan is going through the same thing you are, the same thing

I am. But you're the only one not doing anything about it." She rubbed her temples and said, "Do yourself a favor, Tony, and talk to him. Listen to what he says."

Tony noted the nervous energy in her eyes. "I can practically see you tapping that right foot like a woman possessed, am I right?"

"Tony?"

"Sorry. I was planning to talk to him tomorrow, but I needed a little shove."

"Finally!" The strain on her face dissolved. "I expect a full report tomorrow night, capeesh?"

"*Sì*, Signorina Robinson, I will obey."

"You better. Now catch me up on your new job. I'm dying to know if you're still the lovable screwup I fell for."

They talked for an hour as Tony related his experiences and his growing pains as a lieutenant. But while he mentioned the recurring dreams, he steered clear of the bouts of anger and the brain-muddling anxiety.

Why couldn't he open up to Allie, of all people? Whatever the reason, he knew one thing for sure—he missed her dearly.

18

Thursday, October 16

"We have lots of high-tech equipment," Tony said as he conducted B-Platoon's afternoon training with Evan O'Brien looking on from the back row.

He'd given Evan the use of his Cherokee and invited him to visit the station for lunch with Station-300's firefighters. The good-natured Irishman quickly won the crew over with his personality and wit.

Tony enjoyed teaching and had prepared a detailed lesson plan, but he was eager to get Evan's take on his classroom skills and had convinced his reluctant friend to hang around for the session.

"Technology is a great help to us, but sometimes we rely on it when the fundamental aspects of firefighting are more appropriate."

A hand shot up. Tamyra Miller, on loan from Station-400 and one of the four true firefighting newbies assigned to B-Shift, Battalion-1.

"How do we find the right balance, LT? I mean, we have all this stuff, but . . ."

"That's a great question," Tony said. "What's most important is our situational awareness. Where are you in the building? Where is your partner? Where are you in relation to the other crews? Have you found the fire? If so, where is it? How is it behaving?"

A few heads nodded, but not many. Tony's doubts rose. Were they buying it? *Do I have the legitimacy to teach this class?*

Warren, sitting in the front row, said, "Most of this new technology is bull. Who needs it?"

"I'd have to disagree with you," Tony said. "Technology has its place, especially in the tradition-bound fire service. It's enhanced our firefighting capabilities and safety. A thermal imaging camera, for example, helps us find the seat of the fire, or a victim, and it can warn us about changing conditions before we sense them through our protective envelope."

Bored looks from all but Tamyra, Maddie, and Luke, the eager beavers.

"Look at the strides made in our turnout gear. Would you want to be fighting fire in canvas overcoats and hip boots? Steel helmets? Demand-type SCBA that didn't provide positive air pressure?"

From his seat in the back row, Evan flashed Tony a look of concern.

"Next year we're going to invest in an electronic accountability system that will keep the IC informed of where we are at all times and speed help if someone's in trouble."

"Big waste of money," Corey Adamski said. "We keep track of our own."

"Yeah, forget that shit and bump our pay," Danny O'Reilly added.

"Don't have enough money, Danny?" Pet asked. "Quit letting Tracy drag you on cruises. You'd get the same buzz at your neighborhood bar." Peals of laughter filled the room.

Tony pushed forward and brought up a slide showing a two-story house with flames emanating from one of the first-floor windows. "Take a look at this scene and assume the floor is at least twenty-five percent involved."

"Big whoop," Corey said. "That's called a room and contents fire. We fight 'em all the time."

"Agreed," Tony said. "But let's look at it from the perspective of today's training, VES: Vent, Enter, Search. It's a method we've long employed in the fire service, and other than a TIC, it doesn't require fancy technology—just an axe and a short pike pole."

"What do you know about it?" Warren asked. "You've been a firefighter for what, three years and change?"

More laughter.

I'm losing them, and doing it in front of my mentor, Tony thought.

"An *airport* firefighter," Warren added. "If you can call that firefighting." This time, oohs arose from the crew.

More laughter.

"Wait a minute now, I resemble that remark," Evan interjected with a laugh of his own.

Tony felt the heat rise in his cheeks. He glanced at Evan, who was shaking his head as if to say *he's not worth it*.

Warren huffed. "Teach us all about it, Loo-ten-ant."

Tony slammed his fist on Warren's table. "I've had enough of your bullshit."

Warren slumped back and wiped splashed coffee from his face as the room went dead quiet.

"LT," Luke began.

"What?" Tony snapped.

"Your lip, it's bleeding."

Tony unclenched his jaws and tasted the sharp, coppery flavor of blood—he'd bitten his lip. "Take five," he said and hurried to the locker room. When he returned, the crew was seated and silent. In the back row, Evan swung his upraised palms forward.

"I apologize for my outburst," Tony said. He wiped sweat from his forehead as he willed his anger to cool. "Let's get back to it, shall we?"

All eyes were on him, except for Warren, who stared at the tabletop.

He paused a beat before advancing to the next slide. In the computer-generated image, the fire lapped out from every first-floor window. He aimed the laser pointer at a second-floor window, behind which a woman was visible, her hands pressed against the glass. "Here we have seventy-five percent involvement on Division-1, with a victim trapped on Division-2." He flipped the slide, and the woman disappeared. "Entry is going to be tricky, if not impossible. What do you do?"

"Go around the back and try to make entry with a hoseline?" Luke asked.

"No way," Danny said. "Even if you got in, them stairs gotta be blocked or on fire. You ain't getting to her that way."

"Yeah," Corey added. "She'd be dead by the time you screwed around with a hoseline."

Romeo chimed in. "Right, you need to get her out, fast."

Tony exhaled. Now they were engaged. "If that's the case, what *would* you do?"

"I'd throw a twenty-four-footer," Muscles said. "Then I'd take a set of irons and climb to that window."

"You'd be better off with a flathead axe and a closet hook," Pet said. "Smash the shit out of that window, sash and all."

"You're taking a risk," Tony said. "You'd be above the fire floor without a hoseline for protection."

"What else are truckies for?" Warren asked. Good-natured hoots and whistles followed the comment.

Tony's sweating abated. Evan smiled and shot a double thumbs-up. The focus had shifted from the new lieutenant's perceived deficiencies to the problem at hand. "Seriously, how would we get that woman out safely?"

"I'd just take an axe and the TIC," Muscles said.

"Ahh, there's our technology," Tony added. *Maybe I am getting through.*

Muscles continued. "While my partner followed me up, I'd punch out that window."

"You better lock into that ladder and duck after you swing," Big Pappy said. "Whatever heat and gas is built up is gonna blow out in your face."

"Duh," Muscles said with an eye roll worthy of Tony's ex. "I'd use the TIC for a quick look around the room. Then I'd sound the floor with my axe." He raised a hand. "Before you say anything, LT, I'd *gently* probe the floor first, in case the woman is lying in front of the window."

"Good," Tony said. "What's next? Someone else."

Maddie spoke up. "Climb down into that bedroom. If the woman isn't at the window, I'd get on my hands and knees and do a fast sweep of the room."

"What would you do about the bedroom door?" Tony asked.

"If it's still open, I'd check the conditions in the hall, then push it shut. If it's closed, ignore it. I've got to find the victim. Once I do, I'd drag her to the window and hand her to my partner. Then I'd get the hell out of there."

Tony watched as the crew turned to listen to her, surprise on more than a few faces. *Maddie is one smart firefighter.*

"Wouldn't you go back to that closed door and feel it for heat?" Luke asked. "Maybe poke your head out to check if the fire's reached the second floor?"

"I might," Maddie said. "Or I might not. It's my ass and I'll make the call." The comment drew some loud lip-smacking.

"That's VES, folks," Tony announced. "A technique we use when fire has cut off our access to an upper floor. A quick and dirty search of a room to extract a trapped civilian." The bored looks were gone. He'd won them over. *But I let my temper get the best of me.* "Any comments or questions?"

"I have one, LT," Luke said. "At the academy, we're taught to use *two* ladders for second-floor victim removal."

"That's right, but VES is only for extraordinary circumstances. This stuff is bang-bang." He snapped his fingers twice. "Grab a ladder, throw it, climb it, break and clear the glass, get inside, and get the hell out." He paused to let his comments sink in. "Or most likely, they'll die."

"Hang on," Tamyra said. "Why couldn't another team throw a ladder while you're—"

The squeal of high-pitched tones and the klaxon's *ah-ooga* interrupted the debate. "Mon Area Fire, carbon monoxide investigation, 784 Duffy Way, borough of Furnace."

"Great discussion, folks," Tony said. "We'll pick it up later."

"Hey, Tony," Evan called. "I've had enough fire station for one day. I'll catch you later."

"Understood," Tony said. "Pick me up at six thirty and we'll head straight to the game."

"You got it," Evan said.

Tony smiled, but his insides were torn by his burst of anger in the classroom, his second bout of anger in less than a week. First with Fitz, and today with Warren. *I've got to get this under control, and soon.*

19

Friday, October 17

“I thought you'd take me to some fancy place on Mt. Washington before I left,” Evan said. “Especially after the expensive breakfast I bought you this morning.”

Tony chuckled. “Pamela's Diner, expensive? Nah, you're just used to small-town prices. I didn't see you complaining while you were downing those crepes.”

Evan shrugged.

“And don't forget the nachos and beer I bought at the game last night.”

“Okay, okay,” Evan said. “Anyway, here we are again, sitting at a corner booth in a little bar and grill when you need advice.”

Tony chuckled. “Who said I need advice?” *But you're right, buddy, I do.*

“Okay, then, let's pound a few beers and shoot the shit.”

“Sounds like a plan.” While they polished off their burgers and fries, Tony related tales of his stint with the Forest Service and his first two months with MAFA while Evan brought Tony up to speed on recent happenings at the airport.

“Well, my friend, you certainly had a more eventful five months than I did,” Evan said.

“It's been a challenge.”

“You certainly flipped the crowd to your way of thinking after your little outburst yesterday.”

“You thought I'd lost them, didn't you?”

Evan pursed his lips. "Well, I . . ."

"It's okay. I thought so too."

"But the way you recovered, got them engaged." Evan shook his head and smiled. "Very impressive. You'd make a good firefighting instructor."

"I've thought about that. Maybe one day, when I have more time under my belt."

"Of course," Evan said as the waitress deposited two more beers on the table.

Tony couldn't let the moment pass. When might he see Evan again? "You know, if you want to offer a few words of wisdom, I won't stop you."

"Uh-huh," Evan said and took a swig of his Heineken. "I only saw one training session, so I don't know what I can say about the bigger picture."

"Come on. You have a sixth sense about these things," Tony said, lifting his Sam Adams.

"Tony, we've been talking about this stuff for three years. What do you want? A few tips about conducting a performance evaluation or taking a hoseline crew into a burning building? You're way past that. What could I possibly tell you that you don't already know?"

"Something . . . anything. This people management thing . . . it's new to me."

"That's because you've never stayed at one job long enough to get promoted to a supervisory position."

"Ouch."

"Truth hurts sometimes," Evan said and took a sip. "You signed up for it, didn't you?"

"You know I did."

Evan placed the bottle on the table. "There's no secret sauce that'll make this stuff easier, but you've got the skills. You're a natural leader. I've seen how people follow you. If there's something you don't know, you'll figure it out. Or you'll ask your captain. He seems like a sharp dude."

"He is. The guy knows everything, and he's easy to talk to."

"There you go. What more could you ask?"

Tony shifted position in his seat.

Evan seemed to search for words. "I think . . ."

"What?" *Come on, Evan, give me something I can use.*

"I believe the problem lies in the past."

"No!" Tony slapped his palm on the table and looked up at the ceiling. "It's not about—"

"Everything okay here, fellas?" the waitress asked as she approached the table. Other diners were looking in their direction. An elderly couple in the next booth appeared startled.

"Sorry, we're good," Evan said and waved her away.

Tony lowered the volume, if not the intensity, of his voice. "It isn't about the *damned crash*. It's about being accepted as a lieutenant in charge of a crew stocked with seasoned firefighters."

"Bullshit. Those are growing pains. Everyone in a new leadership position has them, and it doesn't matter how experienced your crew is. Six months from now, it'll be a memory."

Evan's words, as always, rang true. Tony wasn't worried about his job performance, not really. And he knew his issues with the crew were temporary, yet he couldn't bring himself to admit that his time in the forest hadn't banished his inner turmoil. "Okay, if that's true, what do you suggest?" But Tony knew what Evan was going to say.

"You're one of the smartest, and stubbornest, men I know. What do *you* think I'm going to suggest?"

"That I should get some therapy."

Evan nodded. "Give the man a cigar."

"I've been down that road."

"Double bullshit." Now it was Evan's voice that rose as he pointed a finger. "I wasn't with you that night, and I didn't participate in those group counseling sessions the airport provided, but don't try to pawn them off as some kind of in-depth therapy. Firefighters are loath to admit their vulnerabilities, especially in front of their colleagues. How many of our people opened up in those group sessions?"

"Not many."

"Of course not." Evan leaned forward and gripped Tony's shoulders. "Listen to me. You need serious counseling. The sooner the better."

"Spilling my guts to a stranger? That's not for me." *Can't I just admit it? It's Evan, for Chrissake.* "I'm working hard, and if I keep it up, I'll be fine."

"Isn't that what your Smokey the Bear stint was supposed to accomplish? Did it work?"

"It *was* working. I was almost there. No issues for weeks. Then I—"

"Then one of your coworkers almost got killed. Remind you of anything?"

It did, but Tony didn't say. Just as with the victims of the plane crash, the image of Evan pinned under those fallen rafters was never far from his mind.

"You've got a great situation here," Evan said. "Firefighting is what you love. You had a taste of it at the airport, but this is where you can really put your skills to work and make a difference. You're driven to it. But it doesn't jibe with the problems you're having." Evan sat back in his seat and scooped the beer mug. "You asked for my advice, and I gave it. Now it's up to you."

"Yeah, Evan, but intensive therapy? I'm not crazy. I'm telling you, I can—"

"I'm in it."

"What? Therapy?"

"Yes, therapy. Intense, in-depth, one-on-one, honest-to-Christ therapy."

Tony's mind whirled. Evan was a rock. If he needed help after all this time, then . . .

"As I said, I wasn't at the plane crash, but that roof collapse did a lot more than screw up my shoulder and give me pounding migraines that blur my vision."

Of course. *That's why he checked his bag.*

Evan pushed the half-eaten plate aside. "That experience made me question what kind of leader I was."

"You're the best leader I've—"

Evan raised his palms. "To have people in that attic when the fire was out, in a house we already knew was vacant." He shook his head slowly. "And it made me think about what would happen to my wife and kids if I were gone."

"Christ, I never knew. You never said."

"In that way, we're the same. An Irishman and an Italian, both too stubborn to talk to anyone about our problems, even if they're eating us alive." A frown flickered across his face. "My behavior was erratic. I took my frustrations out on Shannon and the kids. Yelling, withdrawing, being anything but a good husband and father."

Tony couldn't believe what he was hearing. He'd spent a lot of time with Evan after his injury. Helped him rehab. But, wow, this was a shock.

"Shannon is such a great partner. She supported me all the way. But it wasn't until I found her hiding in Mason's room, rocking back and forth on the edge of his bed and crying uncontrollably, that I realized what I was doing to my family. That's what shook me out of my denial."

Tony couldn't find words. *I'm such a jerk for not seeing it. Too wrapped up in myself.*

"Like you, I was skeptical of therapy, of baring my soul. Thought I had to work through it on my own." Evan glanced away. "And I was afraid."

"Of what?"

"Afraid it might not work."

"Did it?"

Evan's face brightened. "Yes, it did. Therapy brought me back to some semblance of normal, but it took time. At first, I met with my psychologist twice a week. After a while, it dropped to once a week. Now I check in every couple of months for a little chat. The guy's ex-Army. An infantryman who's seen a lot of shit in Iraq and Afghanistan. Good guy." Evan eyed Tony. "That's the kind of person you need. It's much easier to open up to someone like that."

Tony could see the wisdom in his friend's words.

Evan slumped back in his seat. "I think we've beaten this dead horse long enough, don't you? Let's get out of here before I'm late for my flight or you get banned for life from this crappy joint."

During the ride to the airport, the friends reminisced and made plans for another get-together, but neither returned to the subject of therapy. At the departure drop-off, Tony pulled Evan's bag from the back seat and stuck out his hand.

"Come here, you idiot," Evan said and held out his arms.

"Thought you didn't like PDA?"

"I'm making an exception," Evan said. "Take care of yourself."

Tony barely registered the rush hour traffic as he drove back to River Bend. He hadn't realized how much he had missed . . . and needed Evan's company and counsel. He wasn't going to waste his friend's advice.

20

Saturday, October 18

When Tony arrived at Albright Park, River Bend's largest patch of green space, he spotted Terrell snapping photos of a drone hovering high above the fountain. He figured the park was as good a place as any to satisfy Mrs. Cooper's requirements for meeting in a safe, public area, although the three homeless hovels tucked against the trees cautioned him not to take anything for granted.

"I'm impressed," Tony said as he swiped through the fire scene photos Terrell had downloaded from the camera to his cell phone. "You've taken lots of great action shots, and I think it's time to get a little more advanced, like zooming in on your human subjects."

"All right! Let's find some babes."

"Let's skip the babes for now. How about those three men playing chess on that picnic table in front of the fountain? Focus on their faces, their expressions."

"Whatever you say." Terrell aimed, zoomed in, took three shots, and handed the Canon to Tony.

"Not bad, but let's try to blur the background. Do you remember how?"

"Set the ISO speed real low?"

"No, that's how you blur the shot when your subject is moving."

"Why would I wanna do that?" Terrell said. "Who wants to look at a blurry picture?"

"Maybe you're taking photos at a football or basketball game and you're trying to emphasize the speed of the players. You can do that by blurring the action."

"If you say so."

"It's very artistic."

"Artistic," Terrell said and shot him a *poor, dumb old man* look.

"Remember, you're telling a story with your photos. Right now we're trying to blur the *background* of this shot, not the subjects. Why would we do that?"

"That's easy. So we notice the people."

"Right, we're taking a deep dive into their world."

"More artsy shit?"

Tony ignored the comment. "How would you adjust the settings?"

Terrell examined the camera's controls. "I'd change the setting with this little wheel on top—"

"The mode dial," Tony said.

"Right. The mode dial. I'd turn the wheel to AV, the aperture . . . whatever."

"Very good," Tony said. "It's called aperture priority. What does it do?"

"Um, it lets me change the f-stops."

"Right again. And why would you want to change the f-stops?"

"To let more or less light into the lens."

"Great. So if you're trying to blur the background, how would you set it?"

"I'd open it up wide. Let as much light in as possible," Terrell said, examining the lens. "The lower the number, the bigger the opening, so on one of your fancy lenses, I'd set it to 1.4 or 2.8, but this cheap-ass lens you gave me only goes down to 3.5, so that's it."

Tony laughed. "Very good! You were listening."

"Not really, but you went over this boring shit like five times."

"You're welcome," Tony said. "Do you remember *why* letting more light into the lens blurs the background?"

"'Cause if you let in more light, the, um . . . depth of field shrinks."

"Excellent!" *He's sharp, even though he pretends not to be.* "Well, go on, do it."

Terrell thumbed the dial to AV, adjusted the f-stops until 3.5 appeared in the LED display, focused on the chess players, and snapped three shots.

"Easy. Hold the camera steady and squeeze the shutter button slowly."

Terrell repeated the sequence, but in a more methodical fashion.

"Show me," Tony said.

Terrell brought the photos up on the display and held them up. "What do you think?"

"I can see the pores on their cheeks. You're gonna be one kick-ass photographer."

Terrell's radiant smile warmed Tony's soul.

"All right. Let's practice. Try to find some other things to focus on."

"Hopefully not any young children."

Tony and Terrell whirled in unison. A police officer, fiftyish and stocky with thick salt-and-pepper hair sticking out from under his blue uniform cap, stood two feet behind them.

"We got a call about a weird white guy hanging out in the park with a black teenager, taking photos of kids." The cop shook his head. "But I see it's just young Terrell Cooper and the new lieutenant from the fire department."

"Photos of kids my ass," Terrell said. "That's bullshit."

"Language, Terrell," the cop said. "I'd hate to have to tell your mom."

"Yes, sir, Officer Friendly," Terrell said and gave the cop a mock salute.

The guy knew Terrell, that was obvious. *But how the hell does he know me?*

The cop stuck out a hand. "Desmond Fitzpatrick, River Bend PD. And you're Tony . . ."

"Moretti," Tony said. *Fitzpatrick?*

"I'm no detective, but I can see you're confused. It's a small department, and we all know Terrell. Delivers groceries to my ex-mother-in-law. We watch out for him. His mother would have our heads if we didn't."

"I see," Tony said. He knew his puzzled look remained. "Are you by any chance related to—"

"To Ben? Yep, he's my little brother." He doffed his cap and pointed at the gray hair. "He's sixteen years younger, to be exact. Our mother had him when she was forty-five, long before it was fashionable to have children later in life. Probably an accident, but she'd never admit it. He was her baby." He winked. "By the way, I wasn't smart enough to be a fireman."

"Fire*fighter*," Terrell corrected.

"Geez, Terrell, you sound just like Ben," Officer Fitzpatrick said. "And if you're wondering, I go by Dez. Ben's the one who goes by Fitz. Of course, I refuse to call him that, just to drive him nuts."

"He told you about me?" Tony didn't hide his surprise.

"He tells me about everything. We were always close. Our dad was gone by the time he was twenty, and our mom passed when he was twenty-nine. We're both divorced, so it's me and him. Like a couple of old biddies, we talk almost every day."

Fitz was divorced? Interesting.

"He said there's some new hotshot in town."

"I'm no hotshot."

Dez turned to Terrell. "Go take some pictures, squirt. But don't go too far."

Terrell rolled his eyes but complied.

Dez took the unoccupied space on the bench. "He's giving you a hard time, isn't he?"

"Terrell? No, he's a good kid."

"I'm talking about Fitz."

"You could say that, but I expected some resistance to my hiring."

"Again, I'm no detective, but I can smell a lie when I hear one. And I know my brother. He's probably riding your ass every time he sees you. Picks even the smallest little mistakes apart till you feel like you can't do anything without screwing up. Am I right?"

Tony shrugged.

"Did the same to me when he was growing up. Every time I tried to act like a parental figure, he'd cut me to pieces, the little shit. He can be a hard man, but he's also a good man. Fitz put twenty years into the River Bend VFD, only to see it pulled out from under him."

"I know," Tony said.

"You can't know. I golf, bowl, hunt, fish, play cards with my buddies, travel, and even go to dinner with my ex once in a while. But Fitz, all his activities revolved around that volunteer fire department. Hell, he found most of his friends there. Now he's alone. He and Marie didn't have kids before they split. I tried to get him into other activities, but he wasn't interested. See what I'm saying?"

"I do," Tony said. "The fire department was his life."

"It was, and now it's gone. He works at home, talks to me, and takes a few volunteer shifts as a *firefighter*. He was a chief, for Chrissake. I worry about the guy."

What could Tony say? It was a side of Fitz he'd not considered.

"Listen, none of this is your fault, and I know he's treating you like shit, but maybe you can make a connection. It might help both of you."

"Does it seem like I need help?" Tony asked.

"Come on, Fitz told me a little about you, which is weird for him. Told me you're both college grads, about the same age, both divorced. See? Lots of things in common." He pointed to Terrell, who was photographing an impromptu coed soccer game. "Come on, you're hanging out with a kid."

"I suppose." Tony didn't like the implications, but Dez was right.

"The way he talks about you means he's got some admiration for who you are and what you've done. He told me about some of it."

Another surprise. "I hear you. Those are good points, but I need to think about it."

Dez smoothed his hair, put the cap back on, and stood. "That's all I can ask. It's nice meeting you, Tony. Make sure you watch out for our young friend over there. Mrs. Cooper is not a forgiving soul when it comes to Terrell."

Tony let out an amused laugh. "I'm well aware," he said, but it was the possibility of turning things around with Fitz that intrigued him.

21

Wednesday, October 22

A low-wattage bulb above the back door of Mid-Town Tattoo cast a weak glow in the trash-filled alley across from the shuttered Shoreline Cinema. Squinting, Dylan scanned for movement. Nothing. Not even a drunken bum or a stoned druggie.

He examined the cinema's emergency exit door, dented and bent along its outer edge. Someone had tried to break in. Kids, probably. From the rust on the frame, the attempt had been long ago, and unsuccessful. But it left a convenient gap for a crowbar, which he pulled, along with a stubby sledgehammer and a hand towel, from his backpack.

After working the thin end of the crowbar into the gap, he wrapped the towel around the curved end. Not a perfect striking surface, but it would have to do, and the towel would muffle the sound. With two sharp taps, the bar sank deeper. Holding it steady with his left hand, he swung the hammer with his right. The resulting *thunk*, as the tool bit deeply into the gap, was quieter than he'd expected. *Not that anyone's within five blocks of this place.*

Satisfied, he surveyed his surroundings one last time. Dropping the sledge, he leveraged the crowbar forward and pushed the bar toward the block wall. Metal groaned against metal as the door sprang open. He ducked inside and pulled the door shut behind him. It didn't latch, but no matter.

Pitch darkness enveloped him, and the reek of mildew assaulted his senses as he fumbled through the pack for his flashlight. The thought of inhaling mold deep into his lungs disgusted him. "Fuck me." The curse echoed through the theater, amplifying his frustration. He fought the urge to plunge back into the alley and away from this foul place, but he had work to do, and it wouldn't take long.

He set his light on one of the old cloth seats, casting a weak beam that illuminated the dusty aisle. Kneeling beside his pack, he retrieved three cans of lighter fluid and a butane lighter. *Damn.* He'd forgotten his gloves. But if he played his cards right, there'd be no trace of his fingerprints, or anything else for that matter.

Back in the day, he'd attended this theater often. He recalled the innocence of watching *101 Dalmatians* with his parents. And *The Blind Side*—he'd taken Robin, his high school sweetheart, to that one. He could almost feel the warmth of her hand and the way she'd leaned into him during the intensely emotional scenes.

He shook off the nostalgia. This place was just another decrepit eyesore in need of some weeding. *I'll make sure the city bulldozes it.*

Methodically, he zigzagged through the aisles, inundating four clusters of seats with the accelerant, careful not to oversaturate any single spot. Let the fire start small, in isolated pockets, and it would come together in one big-ass blaze. *Brilliant!*

Breathing through his mouth in a vain attempt to avoid the stench, he made his way up the inclined aisle and pushed through the swinging door to the main lobby. The front windows had been boarded up years ago, so he didn't fear discovery from the street.

With the last can of lighter fluid, he doused the concession stand counter and squirted the walls and felt-covered seat in the ticket booth. *Perfect.* Tossing the empty can aside, he pulled the butane lighter from his pocket. One flick of his finger and the concession burst into flames. He then set the felt-covered chair of the ticket booth ablaze.

Flashlight gripped in one hand, lighter in the other, he dashed back into the main theater, scurrying from one seat grouping to the next and ending up at the exit door from which he'd entered.

Unable to help himself, he paused, mesmerized by the glowing flames as they climbed the seat backs, casting dancing shadows across the walls.

Soon the cavernous space would fill with thick, acrid smoke. This was too easy, especially for someone with brains and a mission. *Someone like me.*

A loud popping sound from the lobby broke his trance. An explosion? Whatever it was, he knew it was time to go. He pushed the panic bar, but the door didn't budge. He tried again. It was stuck. His eyes watered and he began to cough as he took smoke into his lungs. *I've got to get out of here.*

Panicked, he backpedaled before charging forward. Pain ripped into his shoulder as he slammed into the stubborn door, forcing it open. Gasping for breath, he stumbled into the alley and managed a few shallow inhalations before collapsing to his knees in a fit of deep coughs. As he regained his feet, his vision swam and he dropped back to the pavement.

By the time his coughing subsided, a stream of smoke was wafting into the alley. Gingerly, he stood, slammed the door shut, and staggered away.

22

Wednesday, October 22

Tony's vision blurred, as if he were seeing double. He rubbed his eyes and glanced at the clock. Almost 11:30 p.m., and he hadn't finished entering the daily reports into the lieutenant's desktop. He and Dudek usually split the duties, but since the cap was off today, it was up to him. But his concentration was shot, and mistakes peppered his entries. Time to hit the sack. He'd set his alarm early and finish the reports before C-Platoon arrived.

The fire alert tones and the blaring klaxon nixed his plan.

"Please, not now," Tony implored the wall-mounted intercom.

"Mon Area Fire, Station-300, Battalion-1, respond to a smoke detector activation, Bartlett's Plumbing Supply, 1380 Main Street, River Bend."

Wearily, he rose and headed for the apparatus bay. The 1300 block of Main Street was a mere eight blocks east of the station. Maybe they'd clear quickly, and he'd be tucked into his bunk in half an hour. No chance Chief McMahon would get out of bed for this one. *So, Tony, for the first time, you're the man.*

Warren was the last one to jump aboard the pumper, again.

"Were you in a deep sleep or what?" Tony asked.

"It's just another bullshit alarm. I don't need to break my neck over it."

"You need to move like you give a shit," Tony said.

Warren looked away.

His act is getting old.

"County, Engine-301, Ladder-302, and Rescue-303 are responding to 1380 Main Street," Tony radioed as Big Pappy followed the ladder truck onto a deserted Main Street.

"County receives, responding at 2335. Be advised, we're getting a second auto alarm, this one from the Main Street tailor shop."

"Those two businesses are on either side of the old Shoreline Cinema," Big Pappy said. "I don't like the sound of that."

"I don't either," Tony said as he brought up the plot plan on the Mobile Data Terminal. The theater dominated the north side of the block, flanked by the aforementioned businesses. Smoke detectors alarming in both exposures. *Something's going on in that theater.* He studied the screen and spotted a hydrant one block east of the theater.

"Maybe it's a dumpster in the back alley," Pappy said.

"Maybe." But Tony wasn't so sure. Could one dumpster generate enough smoke to infiltrate both exposures? Better to be cautious. He keyed the headset. "Ladder-302, take position at the Alpha-Bravo corner and send crews into both businesses. Squad-303, check out the theater." He turned to the firefighters in back. "We're going to lay in. Maddie, you're on the hydrant."

"Copy, LT," Maddie said.

"Aww, come on," Warren said. "That's a lot of trouble for an auto alarm. Why don't we just stop at the plug and stand by till the truckies have a look?"

"You heard my order, dammit," Tony said, his voice sharp and raised several octaves.

Warren grumbled something as Big Pappy stopped at the hydrant.

Maddie got out, pulled a section of large-diameter hose, wrapped the hydrant, put a boot just behind the coupling, and waved her box light for the pumper to proceed with the lay.

With the LDH playing out behind them, Pappy pulled up just short of the theater just as the two search teams radioed they were entering the exposed businesses with their Knox Box keys.

"County from Engine 301," Tony radioed. "We're on the scene with nothing showing from the plumbing store or the tailor shop. A vacant multistory theater is situated between them. Station-300 Lieutenant has Main Street Command."

"County receives. Main Street Command established at 2341."

"Command from Search-1, we have a light haze of smoke inside Bartlett's. We're trying to find the source."

"Command, Search-2, we have the same in the tailor shop. Also investigating."

"Command receives," Tony radioed. A smell of smoke hit him as soon as he climbed down from the cab. Looking up, he spotted wisps of smoke emanating from the theater's facade. He turned to Pappy, who was pulling a section of LDH from the hosebed. "Get that supply line hooked up, fast!"

"Be ready in a minute," Pappy said.

"County from Main Street Command, it looks like the theater is involved. Respond Battalion-2 and alert the chiefs."

"Ready for water," Pappy called.

Tony looked toward the hydrant but couldn't discern Maddie's progress. "Hydrant from Command, charge the supply line."

No response.

"Maddie, did you copy?" Tony radioed.

"Charging now, LT."

Tony scrambled to the opposite side of the street for a better view of the theater and spotted an orange glow. *Dammit. It must be going good.* If so, there'd be no stopping it.

Moments later, his fears were confirmed when flames leapt into the air above the roof and the facade burst into flames.

Oh shit! "All units from Command, the fire has broken through the roof. The theater appears to be fully involved."

Tony scanned the two exposures. The tailor shop looked okay, but black smoke appeared above the plumbing supply store. Was its roof compromised? *I can't take the risk.* "Search teams from Command, evacuate to the street. All firefighters retreat to safe positions outside the collapse zone of the theater. Sound the evacuation alarm."

Big Pappy, standing on Engine-301's top-mounted pump panel, initiated a series of long blasts on the air horn. Danny, atop Ladder-302's rear-mounted turntable, followed suit.

"Command, Search-2 has evacuated the tailor shop. Relocating to the ladder truck."

Tony unclipped the lapel mic from his turnout coat and raised it to his ear, but he barely caught the transmission above the deafening blasts from the air horn. "Command copies. Search-2 out of the building." He waited five seconds. "Search-1, what's your status?" No reply. "Search-1, are you out of the building?" he asked as the density of the smoke above the plumbing supply store increased.

"This is Search-2. We'll get them, LT."

The transmission did nothing to lessen Tony's growing anxiety. The mic fell from his trembling hand. His focus clouded.

"Command, Search-1 is out of the structure."

Tony let out the breath he'd been holding but struggled to evaluate his options. *Think, man, think!*

He scooped the dangling mic. "Ladder-302, raise your aerial and stand by for water tower operations above the plumbing store's roof. Engine-301, play your deck gun off the Delta side of the theater. I want water on the roof of the tailor shop." Water applied from the outside had little chance of extinguishing the fire in the theater, but it might just save the exposures. "Engine-401, take a second hydrant and lay in. You'll feed Ladder-302."

"County from Main Street Command, fire crews have evacuated. We're shifting to defensive operations."

Three minutes after he'd given the order, Battalion Chief McMahon and Deputy Chief DeFazio arrived and approached Tony's makeshift sidewalk command post.

"What's the situation, Lieutenant?" DeFazio asked, his tone even, but unsympathetic.

"The theater is fully involved. I sent truck crews into the exposures but pulled them out when smoke appeared above the plumbing supply store. We're initiating defensive tactics."

Engine-301's revving engine signaled the operation of its deck gun, directed at the Delta wall of the theater.

DeFazio glanced that way before returning to Tony. "I can see that. So you intend to save those businesses by *pissing* on the walls and roof from the street?" he asked with not a little skepticism in his tone.

"Hold on, Rocky," McMahon said. "That's not fair."

DC DeFazio raised a hand to silence McMahon without taking his eyes off Tony. "If you were a little more *experienced*, the fire might be knocked down by now and protecting the exposures would be moot."

Tony tried to explain. "I didn't see any option, Chief. I wasn't willing to risk the lives of my people with no civilians at stake."

"This job is full of risks, Lieutenant. It's our job to take risks when necessary. Don't you think saving two thriving businesses, which this town desperately needs, is worth some risk?"

He met the chief's glare. *What the hell does he want me to say?*

As Tony struggled for words, McMahon came to his defense. "Lieutenant Moretti exercised his judgment for the safety of his crew, and I agree with his decision."

This time, DeFazio turned to McMahon and shook his head. Before he could utter a retort, loud cracks, accompanied by flying shards of glass, caused the trio to duck. Flames burst from the ticket booth and display window, lapping the underside of the old marquee.

"Well, it's too late to change tactics now." DeFazio keyed his mic. "County, MAFA Deputy-1 is assuming command of this scene. Activate our second alarm mutual aid resources and recall the off-duty personnel from A-Platoon to Station-300. We'll transport them from there as needed."

"County copies, DC-1 assuming Main Street Command at 0013. Second alarm mutual aid and overtime callbacks initiated."

"All right, Lieutenant, we'll take it from here," DeFazio said. "For the time being I want you to oversee the *watering* operation. If, by some miracle, we figure out a way to save the exposures, we'll let you know." As he turned to walk toward his vehicle, he motioned to McMahon. "Come on, Ritchie, we'll set up command at my rig. It's going to be a long night."

Tony watched them go, and as he started for the ladder truck, the marquee, enveloped in flames, collapsed onto the sidewalk. Moments later, an avalanche of bricks from the Bravo side of the theater crashed onto the roof of the plumbing supply store, enveloping him in a gray dust cloud. Chief DeFazio was right. It was going to be a long night.

***

From the back of a three-deep group of onlookers, Dylan cringed. The cops had pushed the crowd back one block to the west, but he still had a clear view of the theater. The wall collapse had pretty much destroyed the plumbing supply store. Not at all what he'd intended. His goal had been to rid the area of abandoned buildings, not destroy open businesses. *Dammit! I can be such a dumbass!* What would his parents think if they found out?

Breaking his new rules of caution, Dylan pushed his way through the throng of spectators, all the way to the police tape. As far as he could tell, the tailor shop was okay. He exhaled. That was something, at least, but it didn't excuse his carelessness. *The plumbing store might never reopen, and it's my fault.*

Watching the firemen try to protect the tailor shop, he lost track of time, even as the crowd began to disperse around him.

"Such a beautiful old building. What a shame."

Startled, Dylan spotted a woman standing behind and to his right. Without saying a word, he turned back to the fire. *Shit, I stayed too long.*

"I wonder how long it's been closed," the woman said as she edged next to him.

If he didn't respond, it would look suspicious. "Um, not sure. Haven't seen a movie there since I was in high school," he replied as the urge to get away overwhelmed his senses.

"Wow, long time, then," she said.

"Hah, yeah, I guess. Well, gotta go. Work tomorrow." He drew the hoodie tight around his face and melted into the thinning crowd.

"That lady saw me, clear as day," he muttered as he scrambled toward his car, His second stupid move of the night. He could picture the cops zeroing in, using tonight's slipup as a gift-wrapped clue. *Time to disappear from their radar screens before they track me down.*

***

Chief DeFazio declared the scene under control at 0540. The collapse on Side-B did not repeat itself on Side-D, but while the tailor shop remained standing, it was deemed unsafe until demolition of the theater could be completed, and even then, it might have to be torn down.

Tony remained on duty throughout the morning, assisting with salvage and overhaul operations long after C-Shift had assumed responsibility for the scene. As he sorted through the rubble, he replayed the night's events over and over. Were his decisions correct? What could he have done differently? Would another course of action have led to a different result?

As the sun rose over the smoking hulk of the theater and the devastated plumbing supply store, he came to a few conclusions. There was little doubt the flames had been deeply seated before the fire department's arrival and the chances that an aggressive interior attack would have knocked it down were slim. And what of his crew? Would the risks to them have been warranted? *Not on a bet.* Nodding to himself, he held firm to his strategy. Despite Chief DeFazio's criticism, the decision to go defensive was the right one, and Chief McMahon agreed.

Would there be recriminations? Possibly, but his case was strong, and he was prepared to take it all the way to Chief Ramsey if necessary. More concerning was his brief period of anxiety and loss of focus. It didn't matter at this fire, but in the future it surely would.

23

Friday, October 24

Dez planted himself in the seat next to Fitz. "Here ya go. Two orders of nachos—salsa for you, artery-clogging cheese for me." He dipped a chip and held it up as a string of melted cheese stuck to his chin.

"They're your arteries," Fitz said. "Don't come crying to me when you're dead at sixty."

"You know I'm a cop, right?" Dez repeated the demonstration with another cheesy chip. "It can end at any time, so I'm gonna enjoy it while I can, bro. How about these seats?" he asked, changing the subject. "Ten rows back from center ice. Do I have connections or what?"

"Pretty sweet," Fitz said. "I haven't been to a Penguin game in years."

"Least I could do after you scored those Steeler tickets for the home opener."

"They were on the ten-yard line in the nosebleed section."

"So what? I have a little more class than you do, little bro. I don't hold it against you."

Fitz landed a lightning left jab into his brother's shoulder.

"Ouch. Assault on a police officer. That'll get you thirty days."

"Quiet, you nitwit," Fitz said as the lights dimmed and the Pittsburgh Penguins skated onto the ice.

***

"What a game!" Dez said as he wheeled out of the PPG Arena parking garage and headed for the Parkway East. "There's nothing better than an overtime hockey game."

"If you say so," Fitz said without much enthusiasm. A Steeler fanatic to the core, he enjoyed most sports, but his true passion was pro football.

"You're a real piece of work, you know?"

"So I've heard," Fitz said. "So why didn't you tell me you foiled a robbery at Anderson's Liquor Store the other night? The crew at the station was talking about it. Said you chased some big guy down Main Street, tackled him, and wrestled a gun from his hand."

Dez shook his head and smiled.

"Well?" Fitz asked. "I want to hear about my big brother the hero."

"First of all, it was a skinny seventeen-year-old kid, and he was carrying two bottles of whiskey, not a gun."

"That's it?" Fitz immediately regretted the question. "But you chased him down. That's pretty impressive."

"With this fifty-three-year-old physique? Are you kidding?"

"Okay, what *did* you do, exactly?"

"The kid jumped into a Nissan Versa. Lady left it running while she ran into Olivero's."

"You ripped the door open and yanked him out?"

"Not exactly. He didn't count on the Versa having a manual transmission. Tried to shift without using the clutch. Car stalled out."

"Ha! The perfect Gen Z antitheft device," Fitz said. "I'm still impressed."

"I'll bet," Dez said. "Anyway, I ran into your buddy Tony the other day. He was in the park with young Terrell Cooper."

"Oh yeah?" *Where did this come from?*

"Seems to be a good guy. He was teaching the kid photography, of all things."

"That's nice."

"What do you think about him? He's your new lieutenant, right?"

Fitz tensed and turned to his brother. "What's this about? Why do you care what I think? Maybe I don't give a shit about the guy."

"Sure, sure. Maybe not, but—"

"Look out!" Fitz warned as a black Sonata cut them off.

Dez hit the brakes. "Asshole! I oughta get his plate."

"And what? I'm no cop, but I know you can't ID him, if it is a him."

"Whatever." Dez took a breath. "I was about to say that the guy, Tony, seems to think you've got it out for him. Any truth to that?"

Fitz looked out his window. The lights on Mt. Washington seemed particularly bright on this clear, cold evening.

"You know, bro, you could have had that job. From what I hear, you were a shoo-in. Oh, that's right, you didn't apply."

"Your point?" *I've listened to more than enough of this crap.*

"My point is twofold."

"Great. Can't wait to hear it."

"First, there are plenty of assholes you could be working for, and this Tony character doesn't seem so bad. Second, since you *didn't* apply for the job, I don't think you're in a position to bitch about him."

"Insightful," Fitz said in the snarkiest tone he could muster. But he couldn't deny Dez was right, at least partially.

"Hell, Ben, it sucks they closed your fire department and ruined your chance at being chief. But that wasn't Tony's fault."

"Are you done?"

"Done, but cut the guy some slack, would ya?"

"I'll think about it," Fitz said. In fact, although he wouldn't admit it to Dez, he'd already started to view Tony in a new light.

Traffic came to a near standstill as they approached the Squirrel Hill tunnels. They'd be stuck on the parkway for a while, and he didn't want to spend the time discussing Tony. "How 'bout we lob the ball into your court, big brother?"

Dez raised an index finger. "Go for it."

"What about this firebug? Have the combined resources of multiple law enforcement agencies made any progress in catching the bastard?"

"As a matter of fact, yes. I'm just a lowly sergeant from River Bend, but I've been in on a few discussions with the task force."

"Task force?"

"They're not calling it that, but they might as well. It's a joint effort between the county police, the state boys, the fire marshal's office, and a few of the local PDs."

"Wow," Fitz said. "I had no idea."

"And you still don't," Dez said and shot Fitz an unmistakable *this is between you and me* look.

Fitz smiled inwardly. "Copy that. Now spill it."

"Well, two potential witnesses came forward after the big theater fire."

"Oh yeah?"

"Yeah, seems a young couple—they live in that renovated warehouse up the street from the theater—saw a guy, Caucasian, maybe mid-thirties. He looked, in their words, a little too excited about what he was watching."

"Christ, is that all? That describes half the *firefighters* I know," Fitz said. "Wait a minute, they don't suspect a firefighter, do they?"

"No, but they haven't ruled anyone out. Will you listen?"

"Typical cop go-to," Fitz said as the car entered the eastbound tunnel. Over the years, a few bad apples had wormed their way into the local volunteer departments and started a few fires. Most wanted to be heroes. But that problem was way overblown by the media. Ninety-nine percent of the volunteers he'd known were in it for the right reasons.

"The guy wore a gray baseball cap under a black hoodie."

"So?"

"So, it was an unseasonably warm night, and the heat from the fire pushed most of the crowd way back. But this guy didn't move or pull the hood off. The two witnesses, I'll call them *the curious couple*, found it a little suspicious. They split up and observed the guy from two sides. The husband kept an eye on him from behind while the wife moved right up next to him."

"A real-life McMillan and Wife, huh?" Fitz said.

Dez gave him an exasperated look as they emerged from the tunnel and hit the accelerator. "Will ya shut up?"

"Sorry. Just keep your eyes on the road."

"The girl stood there for a few minutes, even walked in front of the guy once. She's pretty good-looking, according to the State boys. Had on a tight pair of yoga pants, but the guy didn't notice her."

"No?"

"Nope, and get this. The girl spoke to him. Asked something about how long the theater had been closed. She said the guy almost jumped out of his shoes. He darted his head around like he'd just realized the crowd had moved away."

"Did he speak?"

"Didn't have a choice. Not if he wanted to look innocent. He said the theater went out of business when he was in high school, but before the girl could ask him anything else, he mumbled something about getting home and shuffled away."

"Did they see where he went?"

"At this point, the husband took over and followed the guy up Main. He turned onto Aiken, but the guy glanced back and the husband thought it best not to pursue any further."

"And the upshot of all this?"

"Well, the guy's face was pretty much covered by the hoodie, but she described him as best she could to the state police sketch artist. Not much facial detail, but better than nothing."

"I'll grant you that."

"More important is what he said about going to the theater. So now we think he's a local, probably in his late thirties."

Fitz didn't think the info was nearly enough, but it was a start.

"A composite drawing is gonna be distributed to police agencies throughout the area."

"Why not put it on the news?"

"That might come next, but they don't want to tip the guy off. Since he's only interested in vacant old houses and shuttered businesses, they suspect he's trying some crazy urban renewal thing, maybe because of a grudge of some kind. That's the angle they're focusing on."

"All that sounds good," Fitz said, "but I hope they get him before his *urban renewal* effort hurts or kills somebody." *Because, brother dear, it's only a matter of time.*

24

Monday, November 3

"**B**C-2 is on the scene," Battalion Chief Vincent Costello reported. "I have smoke showing from Side-A, Division-3 of a six-story mixed commercial and residential structure. Full evacuation in progress. I'll have Cedar Street Command."

"He got there fast," Warren said from the back of the cab. "Must've had insomnia or something."

Or something. Tony was familiar with the phenomenon of being awake most of the night.

At 5:00 a.m., traffic on South Shore Boulevard was sparse along the two-mile route through the boroughs of Furnace, Buchanan, and Rocky Shore. With the vigilant Big Pappy at the wheel and the ladder truck clearing the way in front of them, Tony brought up the preplan on Engine-301's Mobile Data Terminal and studied the building's specs.

A converted warehouse along the northern bank of the Monongahela River in Mill Town, the structure was a key component of the area's redevelopment efforts. Built in 1912, the same year *Titanic* had met its fate, it housed retail shops and restaurants on the ground floor, offices and a business incubator on the second, an art school and community college classrooms on the third, and upscale apartments on floors four through six. The building had been retrofitted with a sprinkler system during the rehab. A dual set of train tracks between the building and the shoreline limited access to Side-C. *Bet it's not easy to sleep through those early-morning trains.*

Tony's headset buzzed with activity as Costello issued rapid-fire instructions to incoming units from all four MAFA stations. Tony had only met the battalion chief once, but the man had a reputation as an excellent tactician and leader. Well deserved, from the sound of it.

As Station-300's forces entered the heart of Mill Town's industrial district, Tony found little evidence of renewal. Rows of idle factories, topped by long-silent smokestacks, stood in various states of ruin. Dilapidated warehouses, their walls crumbling and windows overtaken by ivy, remained untouched by redevelopment. Empty tracts of land spread between these imposing structures, bearing witness to years of abandonment, neglect, and decay.

In a dispassionate voice, Costello ordered Engine-501 to lay in, Engine-601 to support the supply line, and Tower-502 to set up at the Alpha-Bravo corner. Engine-401, en route from Battalion-1, was directed to drop another supply line from a second hydrant.

Listening to the action, Tony felt the first twinges of anxiety as Costello sent attack and search teams into the structure. *Easy, boy.*

"Command, Ladder-302, Engine-301, and Rescue-303 approaching," Captain Dudek radioed as the three rigs made the left off River Boulevard and crossed the New Industry Bridge.

"Command copies," Costello replied. "Ladder-302, take position on Side-A at the Delta corner. Raise the aerial to Division-4 and give me a primary search. Engine-301 and Rescue-303, I want you to stand by at the Level-1 staging area in the Home Depot parking lot on Cedar Street and await further orders."

Tony caught sight of the warehouse as Big Pappy turned onto Cedar. "Christ, that's a big building."

"They're all big around here," Big Pappy said. "This one's built like a bomb shelter."

"There's not much smoke," Maddie added with a note of relief in her voice.

On cue, her optimism was confirmed. "Command from Division-3, the main body of the fire is out. It was confined to the art school. Sprinklers knocked it down."

Despite the background noise, Tony recognized the voice of Captain Alex Jenkins from Tower-502. "That was fast."

"Command copies, Captain. The fire on Division-3 has been extinguished," Costello acknowledged. "Engine-301 and Rescue-303, change of plans. Pull up as close as possible to the scene and send your manpower to the CP."

Big Pappy parked the pumper while Captain Jenkins continued his report. "The place is loaded with art supplies. Stuff stacked everywhere, and a lot of it is still smoldering. We've plugged the sprinkler heads and we're hooking a handline to the standpipe for overhaul. There's a whole pile of burnt easels, and we've got rags, canvas, solvents, paints, and who knows what else in here. We're digging into it now, but it's gonna be a while. And be advised, we've got a heavy smoke condition up here but no reverse exhaust from the HVAC system. Our meter is showing high levels of CO, so I'm keeping my people on air until we get some ventilation."

"Command copies. Be advised, we're cutting power to Divisions-2, 3, and 4 as a precaution. The building manager is trying to figure out why the HVAC system didn't switch to exhaust. In the meantime, try horizontal ventilation if you can."

"Division-3 copies that, Chief," Jenkins radioed. "These windows are insulated but not break-resistant."

"Do what you think best, Captain," Costello advised.

"Will do, Chief," Jenkins acknowledged. "Better keep everyone clear."

"Look out," Tony said as the crew exited the pumper. "It's about to rain broken glass."

"Yeah, gird your loins," Corey said as he and Dontrell joined the engine crew. "Oh, sorry, Maddie."

"Knock it off, Corey," Tony said. "Report to the command post with Dontrell."

"Where our highly specialized skills must be needed," Corey said as the two peeled off.

"Yeah, to unclog some toilets," Big Pappy said.

"Now, now, old man, you're just jealous," Corey added while Dontrell, as usual, stayed silent.

Tony ignored the banter. "Let's stay on the street until we get to the ladder truck. Cinch your helmet straps and keep your gloves on," he warned as they weaved through a crowd of disheveled and disoriented apartment dwellers. Rousted from their beds, they cleared the front of the building reluctantly as state police officers, who'd been covering Mill Town since its police force was disbanded six months prior, shepherded them across the street.

"Tony, over here!" Captain Dudek called from 302's rear-mounted pedestal as Danny O'Reilly maneuvered the aerial ladder to the closest fourth-floor balcony.

"You're gonna be truckies today," Dudek said as four of his crew ascended the bed section of the ladder. "Keep your equipment to a minimum. Forcible entry tools only—drop your high-rise pack. We've got twelve apartments to check on the fourth floor, and we'll probably be called to the fifth unless the chief gets more people up there."

"We're on it, Cap," Tony said.

"Since they cut power, it's gonna be dark in those apartments until the sun comes up, but we've got to move fast. Some of the residents might still be in their apartments, and the fourth floor might be loaded with toxic smoke from that art school—especially from paint and paint thinners. My guys will take the units on Side-D. You take Side-B, and we'll work toward each other."

Dudek ascended the first three rungs and paused. "Pappy, I want you at the controls." To his driver-engineer, he said, "Danny, get your BA and join Lieutenant Moretti's crew."

"That's bullshit," Big Pappy grumbled. "I can do anything that old fucker can do."

"I know you can," Tony said. "But you heard the order. The captain wants his best operator on the pedestal." The platitude wasn't enough to save Pappy from embarrassment, but what else could he say?

Not waiting for Danny, Tony led his crew up. Despite the lightened load, climbing an aerial ladder with seventy-five pounds of turnout gear, SCBA, and tools required a tremendous amount of energy. Meanwhile, the sound of breaking glass meant Jenkins's truck crew had ventilated the third floor.

"Command from Station-300 Captain," Dudek radioed. "Search-1 and Search-2 are entering Division-4 with five firefighters."

Panting from the grueling three-minute climb, Tony, Warren, and Maddie reached an arched window, its insulated glass cleared by the truck crew. The tip of the ladder, extended two feet past the frame, crunched onto the shards under their collective weight.

"Command from Station-300 Lieutenant," Tony radioed. "Search teams three and four entering Division-4."

Tony swung one leg over the rail, sounded the floor, and dropped into the front room of an apartment illuminated by the two spotlights mounted on the tip of the aerial ladder.

"Whoa," Warren said. "You got to have some big bucks to live here."

"We've got six units to search," Tony said. "Warren, sweep this unit, wait for Danny, and continue on the right side of the corridor."

"I can keep searching without Danny," Warren said.

"No, stay here until he joins you."

Warren responded with a curt, "Whatever you say."

Tony chose not to respond. "Maddie, you're with me."

With power cut off, the building's emergency lights bathed the hallway in a pale yellow hue that did little to illuminate the situation.

"It's unlocked, LT," Maddie said at the first apartment on the left and added, "This place is huge," as she entered through the ornate wood-paneled door.

Huge was an understatement. Tony had never seen such a spacious apartment, but it wasn't a bad thing. The open-concept design facilitated their search. Using their box lights and taking advantage of the first streamers of dawn filtering through the big front windows, they split up and completed their sweep in two minutes flat. Once in the hall, Tony pulled the door shut, dug a piece of thick white chalk from his pocket, and marked the door with a big X to show the unit had been searched.

The next door was locked, but with a quick jerk of her Halligan, Maddie had the door open in seconds. When they emerged, Danny and Warren were in the hallway. "Can we drop these BAs?" Warren asked. "There's hardly any smoke up here." It sounded like more of a demand than a question.

"Keep your breathing apparatus on," Tony replied. "We don't know what's in the air and we don't have a gas meter." From his days at the airport, Tony knew that even small concentrations of smoke might contain enough carbon monoxide or other toxins to damage the lungs. Warren mumbled something to Danny and the pair entered the first apartment on the left.

As the search teams moved farther into the Bravo side of Division-4, Tony spotted a figure walking toward them in a red helmet—Barney Dudek. Twenty feet away, the captain staggered, stuck a hand to the wall, and dropped onto one knee.

Boots thumped off the carpet as Tony and Maddie rushed forward. "What's wrong, Barney?" *Please don't let this be a heart attack.*

"I'm . . . okay. It's . . . okay," the captain said between heaving respirations. "A little nauseated. Just need to . . . catch my breath."

Tony eased the captain onto his butt and leaned him against the wall.

"What happened?" Romeo asked as he and Muscles emerged from the apartment they'd been searching.

"He collapsed," Maddie said. "He needs the medics."

"I'm okay. No medics!"

"Any chest pain, Cap?" Romeo asked.

"Christ, no. I'm winded, that's all." Dudek reached out to Tony and pulled himself up. "See, I'm good."

"What do you think, LT?" Romeo asked. All four search teams were now gathered around their captain.

"Don't ask *him!*" Dudek snapped. "I'm in charge here, and you guys have a primary search to finish. Get to it. I'm going to the balcony to get some fresh air. But I'll be back."

"Okay," Tony said. "You're the boss, but Romeo and Muscles are going with you."

"I don't need any help. I'm fine."

"Sorry, Cap," Tony said and keyed his mic. "Command from Division-4, we need the medics at Ladder-302's entry point to check a firefighter with shortness of breath."

"Dammit, Moretti. I don't need them."

"Maybe not, but they're going to check you out anyway." *You can be pissed at me, Barney, but I can't let you blow this off.*

Part III

The Heat is On

25

Saturday, November 8

Mitchell's Tavern in Rocky Shore wasn't the kind of place Fitz normally patronized, but Barney Dudek suggested it. The atmosphere featured subdued light from low-wattage bulbs mounted under three whining ceiling fans. It didn't help that the original copper ceiling panels had been repainted dark green.

An ornate wooden bar dominated the long, narrow space, with ten tables crammed together, seemingly an afterthought. Four men, all in their sixties or older, sat clustered together on round barstools that were bolted into the oak plank floor.

The shelves behind the bar held gin, scotch, bourbon, tequila, vodka, and all the other hard drinks the workingman supposedly craves. It harkened back to memories of Mon Valley industry in its heyday, when tens of thousands of steelworkers plied their trade and dropped in at any one of dozens of bars like this one to grab a quick bite, some whiskey, and chew the fat with their buddies.

Fitz opted for the furthest table in the back. The bartender, who looked like an out-of-place college kid working a part-time job, acknowledged him with a nod.

Fitz lifted a finger. "I'm waiting for someone."

Despite the dank interior, an impressive array of full-color, autographed photos of Steeler legends Terry Bradshaw, Joe Greene, and Franco Harris, along with former Pirate stars Willie Stargell and Roberto Clemente, lined the walls. A number thirteen Pitt jersey, signed by Danny

Marino, took pride of place above the doorway, while a black-and-gold *City of Champions* banner hung from the opposite wall. The collection ended in the early 1980s, long before Mario Lemieux and Jaromir Jagr's glory days with the Penguins of the 1990s.

"What do you think of the decor?"

Fascinated by the memorabilia, Fitz hadn't noticed Barney's arrival. The captain placed two mugs of beer on the table. "Iron City, it seemed appropriate."

"Of course! This place is great. It's like being transported back fifty years. I half expect to see Dean Martin come through the door."

"Fifty years ago, you might have. He was a Steubenville kid, you know. This place is one of the last remaining mill bars in the area. Steelworkers used to crowd them after their shifts."

"I figured," Fitz said. "If you think I'm going to buy you lunch just because you're old, forget it."

"Not because I'm old, because I'm leaving the department."

"Are you kidding me?" Fitz asked. "You just got here."

"Correction, Fitz, *everybody* except you just got here. The entire department is only a year old."

"Yeah, but still . . ."

"I came here as a favor to Lou Ramsey when he was setting up this operation and I've done what I needed to do." Dudek raised his beer in salute. "I was happily retired before I got his call, you know."

Fitz nodded. *Retired, yes, but happily?* Fitz knew how the captain had struggled after his wife had died. He was such an iconic figure that the rumors of alcoholism and depression had spread quickly through western Pennsylvania's fire service circles.

"I've had my career, a long one. MAFA has been a little icing on the cake. It's been challenging, and I've enjoyed it, but it's time."

"If you say so, but with your experience, you have a lot more to offer."

"I have a standing offer from the county fire academy. Adjunct instructor. I can teach any class I choose. That'll keep my hand in the game, but it won't be with other firefighters' lives on the line." Dudek bit his lip as he looked up at the ceiling. "I can't do it anymore—physically or mentally."

Fitz wanted to protest further, but what would come of it? Knowing when to call it quits was always a struggle for aging firefighters, but when they finally decided, it was best to wish them well and let them go.

"Who've you told so far?"

"The chief, and you."

"Thank you for that." It was no small gesture on Dudek's part, informing a volunteer before any of the career staff.

"Enough of this," Dudek said. "There's something else."

"Okay?"

"It's about Tony."

"Oh, come on, Barney, you too?" Tony was the last person Fitz wanted to talk about.

"Easy, boy," Dudek said. "I see the fire in your eyes, but I want you to listen to the old retiring captain for a minute. I won't preach."

Fitz waved a hand across the table. "Go on, then."

"I disagreed with the chief over hiring Tony. Like you, I thought he wasn't qualified, wasn't ready. But once he got here, I accepted him into my station and backed him one hundred percent. That was my job, what was required of me."

"I understand, but how does this relate to me?" Fitz asked. "I'm not his boss."

"Patience. I'm getting there in my roundabout way."

"Sorry."

"It was my job to support him, but he surprised me. I think he surprised you, too, but you can't bring yourself to admit it."

Fitz frowned but didn't disagree.

"He has a rare blend of intelligence, dedication, and courage that makes for a genuine fire officer." Dudek aimed a finger. "He has the same qualities as you, Fitz."

"If you say so."

"I do say so. Haven't you seen him in action?"

"I'll admit the guy has some skills."

"Some?" Dudek shot a doubtful look. "Do you think this department has another like him, besides yourself?"

"Maybe not, but the guy can be a real short-tempered jerk."

"Just like the rest of us, depending on the situation."

"Sure, but there's something else, deep inside him. I can't pin it down."

"You're right," Dudek said. "He's got some issues, but he's dealing with them."

Fitz relented. "You want me to cut him a break. That's what you're leading up to, isn't it?"

Dudek nodded slowly. "In part, yes."

"What else?" Fitz asked. "Just spit it out, Barney. We've known each other too long to play games."

"Tony's got talent, but as an officer, he's raw. Needs a little home cooking. Over the last couple months, I've tried to help him develop his leadership skills. We've talked about his performance as a lieutenant, and I've given him suggestions and more than a little constructive criticism. I think it's working."

"Okay, I'll agree with that assessment," Fitz said.

"Good. I hoped you might." Dudek pursed his lips. "Because I'm not going to be around here much longer, and I was hoping you would take over for me."

"Take over?" Fitz sat bolt upright. "Wait, no, hold on, Cap. You want me to *mentor* him?"

Dudek cocked his head. "Yep, that's the gist of it."

"No way. That's not my job. What about the deputy chief of training? Isn't that his responsibility? I'm not even an officer; I'm a *volunteer*, for Chrissake!"

Dudek didn't react to the outburst. "Those are four words I'd never thought I'd hear from you."

"Huh? Which words?" Yet he knew, because he'd never uttered them before.

"That's . . . not . . . my . . . job." Dudek folded his hands on the table.

"Shit, that's not what I meant. Hell, Barney, the guy's supposed to be qualified already."

"He is qualified. He needs seasoning."

"Oh, fuck your food metaphors."

"Listen," Dudek continued. "Everyone knows *you* should be an officer, probably a chief, but you didn't apply, remember?"

"I couldn't. I have a full-time job. A pretty good one."

Dudek raised an eyebrow. "Can you honestly say you enjoy accounting more than firefighting? You made a mistake not applying. Sure, you have a great job, but the fire service is what you love."

Fitz couldn't argue and didn't.

"All I'm asking is that you help the guy along a little. Unofficially. I know he's tried to mend fences with you."

"I don't know about that."

"Give the guy a break, will you? It's about fire protection in *your* community, after all. The town you and your father spent your lives serving."

"Hit me where it hurts, Barney. That's low." *You've been saving that one, you sly dog.*

"Desperate times . . ."

Fitz threw up his hands. "All right, all right. I'm not making any promises, but I'll give it a shot. It may not be my best shot, though."

"Of course it will. It's the only kind you know." Dudek nodded toward the bar. "Now buy me that lunch."

Fitz sat back, drained the last of his Iron City, and shook his head. The captain knew him too well. *I'll help Tony, but I don't have to like it . . . or him.*

26

Wednesday, November 12

Tony spotted the smoke from South Shore Boulevard while Ladder-302 was still a quarter mile from the reported house fire on the border of West Forge and Rocky Shore. He'd lost sight of Battalion Chief McMahon, who'd weaved through rush hour traffic in front of them. Lieutenant Brookin, responding in Engine-401, had just radioed that they were lying in.

A minute later, McMahon radioed a report. "County, BC-2. I'm on the scene with a working fire on Division-1 of a two-and-a-half-story frame dwelling. Exposures on both sides. I'll have Packer Street command."

"Ain't this a doozy on your first day as acting captain?" Danny O'Reilly asked.

"You said it, Danny. A real baptism by fire, but I couldn't ask for a better crew." Still, Tony knew empty words wouldn't cut it. *I've got to prove myself, show them I'm not a fraud.*

"County receives. Working fire on Division-1. Packer Street Command established at 1319."

"I know that neighborhood," Danny said. "Had a kitchen fire there last year. The ground is flat on one side of the street, but there's a steep slope on the other side. They ain't row houses, but they might as well be, the way they're crammed together. Can't be more than ten feet apart. Hope this one's on the flat side."

That would be nice, but Tony wasn't counting on it as he considered potential tactics. Absorbing and analyzing complex inputs and transforming them into solid tactics was his strong suit, but today he was switching to truck company operations, a different beast entirely. He ran the list through his head: forcible entry, search and rescue, ventilation, laddering, salvage and overhaul. With limited crew, he'd have to prioritize based on the situation. *Time to turn all that training into action.*

Tony gauged the area. Unlike in River Bend, the lack of any real progress toward renewal was painfully evident. The streets—riddled with potholes—were flanked by boarded-up businesses and empty homes. On the surrounding hills, imposing mansions from a bygone era had been carved into apartments. A nondenominational ministry in a former Lutheran church was the only active concern in sight.

Turning to his new crew, he surveyed the faces and nodded at each. Danny, Romeo, Muscles, and Luke. Minus Pet Petruska, who'd taken Tony's position on Engine-301, where she now served as acting lieutenant. Since the department's minimum authorized truck staffing was five, overtime hadn't been called to fill her slot. Tony didn't like it. This was no time to be down a firefighter.

"County from Packer Street Command, this house is . . . stand by."

"Sounds like he just ran a marathon," Danny said. "Bet he's climbing steps."

"County from Command." Another pause. "This house is on a hillside. I can't do a three-sixty, but . . ."

"I knew it," Danny said. "He's out of breath. Must be a million steps. We're gonna have a—"

"Hold on!" Tony said as he shot his left arm up. "We need to hear this."

"Looks like the main body of the fire is on Division-1 of Side-A," McMahon continued as his breathing eased. "There's another hill right behind the house. No alley. The only access is up two flights of steps from the street."

"County copies, fire on Division-1 of Side-A. Access from the street side only."

"Engine-401 from Command, you're going to need a three-inch leader line. The crosslays won't reach from the street."

"Engine-401 copies that, Chief," Lieutenant Brookin replied. "Will we be able to hit it with our deck gun?"

"Negative, Lieutenant. The hillside's blocking a direct shot into the Division-1 windows," McMahon said. "But you might be able to use it on the exposures. With this wind, they're both going to go up if we don't put water on them fast."

"Sounds like it might be a defensive fire," Tony said. His tense muscles relaxed. No civilians reported, thank God.

Station-300's apparatus neared the scene as Deputy Chief DeFazio arrived on scene. "County DC-1 is assuming Packer Street Command," he radioed and added, "Ritchie, take over Operations. I'll get everything organized on the street and get those hoselines up to you."

"Thanks, Rocky," McMahon replied, amusing Tony by eschewing standard radio call signs. *When the shit hits the fan . . .*

"Ladder-302 from Command, when you arrive . . . wait one."

"Uh-oh, this ain't gonna be good," Danny said.

"Command from Operations," McMahon radioed. "I see one . . . no, two faces in a window! Alpha side, Division-2. Looks like kids."

The shock to Tony's system was immediate. *Kids.*

"LT, we're here," Danny said.

Tony regained his composure as Danny wheeled the truck into position in front of the house. "Ladder-302 on scene," he radioed. His driver was right, this was going to be a real mother.

"302 from Command, get into the Division-2 window, fast!" DeFazio ordered.

"Hurry up, Tony," McMahon added. "Those kids won't last long." Tony had never heard either chief so distressed.

"On our way," Tony replied before jumping down from the cab. From the street, he squinted at the house through the glare of the low-angle sun. Smoke billowed from the picture window and overlapped the second floor. Cold early-November gusts gave him brief glances of the window, but he was too far to make out faces.

"Danny, let's short-jack the truck and extend the ladder to that middle Division-2 window."

"Ain't gonna work, LT. Look at them power lines."

"Shit," Tony said. The lines hung in the direct path of the aerial ladder.

Why the hell didn't I see that? It's my fricking job.

"Let's move, 302," McMahon shouted from atop the steps.

Heart pounding, Tony fixed his attention on getting into the house. Two sets of steps, zigzagging up the hillside. The first flight had maybe thirty steps and ran up to a knoll about twenty feet below the house. From there, the stairs cut diagonally to the front porch.

DeFazio rushed over to meet him. "What's the plan, Lieutenant?"

Tony held up a hand. Sirens, radio chatter, the shouts of bystanders, and the din of revving engines did nothing to break his concentration as he mulled over the options.

From the knoll it was another twenty-five feet to the window. The angle would be about . . . *That'll work!* He turned to Muscles. "Take the thirty-five-footer up those steps and plant it on the lawn. We'll be able to reach the window from there. I'll grab the tools and meet you at the top."

"On it, LT," Muscles said and took off for the back of the ladder truck.

"That'll work," DeFazio said. "We're running the hoselines up now."

Tony clipped the thermal imaging camera to his backplate, grabbed an axe and short pike pole, and hit the steps.

At the top of the first flight, he glanced at the ladder truck. The crew had already slid the thirty-five-foot ladder from the bed and were carrying it toward the steps. The knoll was about ten feet deep and covered with dead grass. Not perfect, but it would do.

Halfway up the second set of steps, Tony dropped to one knee as a heat wave washed over him. The Division-1 windows disgorged a cascade of flames, making entry impossible. If those kids had any chance, it would be via ladder, and in the next few minutes. He prayed their bedroom door was closed as he donned his facepiece.

"We're coming, LT!" Muscles shouted as the truck crew ascended the steps with the three-section, 140-pound beast on their shoulders. *Just get that ladder up to me and I'll take it from there.*

The truck crew planted the feet of the ladder into the hard earth of the knoll. Luke anchored the bed section by jumping onto the bottom rung while Muscles and Romeo, with arms outstretched and hands on the side rails, *walked* the ladder to a vertical position. Luke grasped the halyard and, with a hand-over-hand motion, raised the two fly sections.

"Four more rungs," Tony ordered.

Luke followed instructions and then, in unison, the three firefighters lowered the tip of the thirty-five-footer to the window.

"That's good," Tony said. He handed the pike pole to Muscles, docked his regulator, and hopped onto the bottom rung. "Follow me up."

"You gotta wait till the engine crew gets some water on that fire, LT," Romeo said. "The ladder's too close."

Tony ignored the warning as he gripped the axe in his left hand, the ladder rail in his right, and climbed. The sturdy fire service ladder bucked under his weight as he scrambled upward, the cumbersome turnout gear hindering his speed. Halfway up, flames shot through the rungs and searing heat penetrated his protective envelope. Pushing through the pain, he gritted his teeth and focused on the window above. *Almost there.*

At the top of the ladder, two young boys stared at him in sheer terror, their small hands pressed to the glass.

"Get away from the window!" He banged the frame with the side of the axe to emphasize his instructions. The boys looked at each other and dropped out of sight.

Tony couldn't be sure the kids were out of the way, but there was little choice, and no time. Foregoing the prescribed ladder lock, he raised the axe. Glass cracked and smoke belched from the opening as the adze end met the upper pane. He hauled back and smashed the middle sash before running the axe across the edges of the window to clear the opening. He couldn't see the kids. *I've got to get them—now.*

"The fire's on us," Muscles warned. "We can't stay here."

"Gimme the pike pole and back down," Tony ordered. "Command, Search-1 entering with one." With that, he slithered over the top of the sill, poked the floor gently with the handle of the pike pole, and dropped inside.

Momentarily disoriented but shaking it off quickly, he hooked the pike pole to the windowsill to mark his egress position and listened. The exterior noise had dropped away, but he couldn't hear the kids. Smoke continued to enter the room. He lifted the TIC. The temperature was 110—survivable for the boys if the smoke didn't get them first. He scanned left to right. *There!* A motionless form at the back corner silhouetted on the screen.

Axe in one hand and TIC in the other, he raised himself to a crouch and found the boys, wriggling and crying, one huddled on top of the other. *Thank God!* He shoved the door shut, dropped the axe, hooked an arm around each child, and stumbled blindly toward the window.

"LT, over here!" Muscles shouted.

Moving toward the voice, Tony reached the window and handed the smallest boy up.

"I've got him," Muscles said. "I'll pass him down to Luke."

"Hurry," Tony said and cradled the older boy. *He won't last in this smoke.* Pulling off his helmet, he reset the regulator and doffed his facepiece. Gently, he pressed the visor to the youngster's face and opened the bypass valve. Air hissed. "Breathe, little one. Breathe."

"I'm back, LT. Give him to me."

Tony handed the boy to Muscles. "Get him to the medics. I'm right behind you."

"The engine crew has water on the fire floor," Muscles added before disappearing with the child.

The two kids were safe, but his mind raced with questions. Were there more children? Wasting no time, he replaced his facepiece and helmet, dropped to his knees, and reversed his original search pattern. He pulled off a glove and ran the back of his hand over the door. Hot, but not untenable. He cracked it open.

"Hey, LT, are you okay?" This time it was Luke's voice. "I'm coming in."

"Stay there!" he ordered. "I'm going to check the hallway."

"Don't do it, LT. The fire's not out. The engine crew's not even inside yet."

Tony entered the smoke-filled hallway. Ten feet to the right, he found another door. Easing it open, he edged inside and shut it behind him.

"Search-1 from Command, report PAR."

Shit. Did DeFazio know he was alone? "Command, Search-1 is okay with a PAR of one. I'm checking the second bedroom on the Alpha-Delta side."

"Get out of there, Moretti," DeFazio ordered. "There's a crew waiting for you on the ladder."

Ignoring the command, and the pain shooting through his ears, he swept a hand along the wall while probing with the axe handle. The heat intensified with each passing second. No one under the bed. No one hiding in the closet. Search complete. Time to get back to the ladder. He cracked the door and—whoosh!—a wave of blistering air slammed into him as flames erupted through the breach.

Tony dropped to his side and shoved the door shut with his feet. He got to his knees, crawled toward the window, and rounded the bed as a cacophony of air horns blared. Evacuation signal. The damn place must have flashed. He was in serious trouble, yet he wasn't frightened. *I should be shitting my pants.*

"Moretti, where are you?" This time it was Chief McMahon on the radio. "We've had a flashover on the first floor. Evacuate immediately."

Huddling at the corner of the bed, Tony fumbled in his right bunker pants pocket until he found the carabiner. He yanked it out, wrapped the attached escape rope around the metal bed frame, and clipped the ends together.

"Moretti, evacuate now!"

Tony pushed himself to his knees, the heat inside his turnout gear becoming unbearable. *I'm coming, Chief.* He rammed the axe head through the window, sending glass shards and pieces of sash flying. Hot gases found the opening. The room cooled.

Voices called to him from below. "LT, wait! We're moving the ladder."

Tony eyed the crew, scurrying like children from a hornet's nest as they rushed to the thirty-five-footer. *No time.* He ran the axe around the frame, let it fall to the carpet, and stood. Hoping he'd gotten all the big pieces, he threw a leg over the sill, gripped the rope with both hands, and launched himself out the window.

Ten feet below, he held on tight as his feet crashed into the siding. Flames roared overhead. The door must have failed. Holding the rope at his waist with one hand and behind his back with the other, he rappelled to the ground in two measured jumps, pushing himself off after each contact with the wall. A crowd met him on the grass.

"That was a close one, LT," Luke said.

"Thank you, Mr. Obvious," Muscles said. "What got into you, LT?"

"Yeah, LT, Rocky's gonna have your ass," Romeo added.

"I'll deal with the deputy chief later," Tony said. He was safe. He'd put himself in a bad situation and gotten himself out of it. He should have been elated, or pissed off and questioning his sanity, but he felt nothing. Even the shakes were gone.

***

Busy commanding the fire attack, DeFazio didn't notice Tony as he descended the steps, but McMahon grabbed him and pointed to the street. "See that medic wagon? Get down to it now and get yourself checked out."

"Copy, Chief," he said, happy to escape further scrutiny from his superiors.

He lay low until the crews returned to the station, where McMahon and DeFazio took turns chewing his ass.

Tony tried to explain that the hallway was tenable and he thought others might be trapped, but the chiefs weren't buying it, so Tony took his medicine without further comment.

After DeFazio left for headquarters, McMahon came up and put a hand on Tony's shoulder. "You were extremely lucky today, Lieutenant."

Tony made no reply.

McMahon eyed him gravely. "You need help, son, and soon."

The chief was right. He now realized hard work alone wasn't the answer. Time to take action before it was too late.

27

Friday, November 14

Tony yawned, exhausted and in need of a nap. He hadn't slept much since the house fire, the relentless pain in his ears keeping him awake despite repeated applications of aloe vera cream. So, it was a choice of which streaming program to watch tonight. Action? Sci-fi? British murder mystery? His Prime, Netflix, Paramount, and Apple TV watch lists were packed, but after ten minutes of flipping through the potentials, he pulled on a sweatshirt, liberated two beers from the fridge, and settled into a comfy wicker chair on the second-floor porch.

Indian summer in Western PA. The night air was warm, the beers were cold, and save for the almost nostalgic calls of the lady who'd been calling Joey home for dinner—*Doesn't every kid have a cell phone?*—the neighborhood was quiet. He briefly considered using his telescope to scan the night sky, but the light pollution and full moon made him abandon the idea. His mind drifted back to the two boys in the window as he drained the second beer.

The family had hailed him as a hero, but he felt anything but. It wasn't the save that troubled him but what followed, how reckless he'd been *after* the two boys were safe. What had he been thinking? His actions could have gotten him killed, or at the very least suspended by DeFazio, but the only result was a suggestion from McMahon to get help. *What's happened to me?* Not for the first time, he questioned his fitness to lead a crew.

The door buzzer jolted him from his alcohol-induced lamentations.

He checked his watch: 6:35 p.m. *What now?* Other than Evan, his only visitors in the last two months had been a couple of pizza delivery guys and a woman running for city council.

The buzzer sounded again. *Who the hell is that?* He shuffled inside, dropped the empty bottles on the coffee table, and pushed the intercom button. "Can I help you?"

"It's Ben Fitzpatrick. Can I come up?"

Fitz? The last person Tony had expected. His finger hovered over the door button.

The intercom crackled again. "I come in peace."

This should be good. Tony hit the buzzer and walked out to the landing.

"Pretty warm out tonight," Fitz said as the door swung shut behind him. The uncarpeted stairway creaked with his every step. Tony stood aside and motioned Fitz in. "Have a seat."

Fitz chose the sofa, forcing Tony to the uncomfortable wingback chair. They eyed each other in awkward silence until his surprise guest spoke up.

"What's up with your ears?" Fitz asked.

"Don't ask," Tony said.

Fitz seemed puzzled but didn't press it. "I heard about your exploits at the East Forge fire. Pretty impressive."

"Just doing my job," Tony said without a trace of satisfaction in his voice.

"That's not what your crew said. They're impressed."

Tony stared at the empty beer bottles. Impressed? *More like wondering if their lieutenant is crazy.*

Fitz scanned the room. "Anyway, my brother mentioned he'd met you."

"I did. Nice guy."

"So he thinks. Did he tell you what an asshole I was?"

"Um . . . no, but he did say you were very passionate about the department and the community."

"Bull. I know my brother. Fact is, I *can* be an asshole."

"He was looking out for Terrell," Tony said, not knowing how to respond to Fitz's admission.

"Yes, young Terrell. His mother has half the population keeping an eye on him. I'll bet she asked Dez to check on you."

"Of course! I *suspected* our little meeting in the park was more than happenstance. Everybody seems to think I'm a pedo."

"Are you?" Fitz said with a straight face that took Tony by surprise. He let the question hang before cracking a wide smile. "Sorry, couldn't resist. I think what you're doing with the kid is great. We need more of that around here. I volunteer with the Mon Valley Cares literacy program."

Another surprise. "Nice." *Maybe I haven't given this guy a fair shot.*

"I do what I can," Fitz said with a shrug. "But getting back to the reason for my visit, I'd like to change the direction of our relationship before it gets any worse."

As if it could, Tony mused. "I'm all for that, but can I ask what made you change your mind?"

"Well, it's been gradual. I'm a stubborn bastard. Bet Dez told you that too."

Tony smiled.

"From the day you showed up, I had you pegged as an unqualified, inexperienced officer wannabe. Somebody trying to get ahead and using MAFA as a stepping stone to something bigger, like you did at that airport of yours."

"That's not what I did at the airport and it's not why I took this job," Tony shot back. *This guy doesn't know squat about me.*

Fitz held up his hands. "Sorry, that came out wrong. I've been wrong about a lot of things when it comes to you, and I shouldn't have given you so much shit. Maybe it's too late for an apology, but I'm offering one anyway."

Tony wasn't sure if he was ready to accept it, but a little exploration of the issue wouldn't hurt. "Tell me more."

"I realized I was focusing on all your little missteps to build a case in my mind against you. Feeding my confirmation bias, if you know what I mean."

"I do," Tony said, surprised by Fitz's admission. "I'm afraid I've done the same when it comes to you."

"Can't blame you for that," Fitz replied. "Anyway, I'm making a conscious effort to give you the benefit of my doubt. It turns out you do a hell of a lot more right than you do wrong."

"I appreciate that. But why now? What tipped the scales?"

"Fair question." Fitz paused. "Captain Dudek."

Tony raised his eyebrows. Another unexpected development.

"I had all the evidence I needed to admit you were a big asset to the department, but . . ."

"But?"

"Um . . ." Fitz seemed to search for words. "It's like when you're online and waiting for a site to connect and watching the little loading icon? It keeps spinning and spinning. It can't quite get there until you hit refresh."

"The captain was your refresh button?"

"Yes." Fitz leaned halfway across the table. "He ran down your list of attributes, things I already knew but suppressed, and bingo! Can you believe it?"

"I can, actually," Tony said. "Something similar happened to me, about three years ago. Just like that, my preconceived notions of where my career was headed and what I wanted to do with my life crystallized."

"Wow, an epiphany."

"Not exactly, but close. Sometimes it takes a third party to lay it out for you." Or a wife in a failing marriage, Tony didn't add. "That's when I realized my aspirations had been wrong, but by then I'd wasted fifteen years." He shook his head. "You're lucky, Fitz. I bet you knew firefighting was it from the get-go."

"I did, but what did I do with that knowledge? I became an accountant."

"Why didn't you pursue firefighting as a career?" Tony asked.

"Almost did. I took firefighter civil service tests in Arlington and Fairfax Counties in Virginia. I scored high on both, enough to be offered the jobs, but both times I turned the offers down."

"I can guess why," Tony said.

Fitz eyed him curiously.

"You had too much invested in this area, right? Family, the fire department, friends, maybe a wife."

"She came later, but you're right. I grew up in this town, and I wanted to stay here. But there weren't many opportunities to become a career firefighter in western Pennsylvania back then, and the City of Pittsburgh still had a residency requirement, so I became an accountant. It's a good gig, but . . ."

"But it's not your passion." The words came out so easily, yet not so long ago, Tony would have scoffed at such a nebulous notion.

"Right."

"I'd say you made the right decision."

"You think? Look where it's gotten me. My passion has been farmed out to the paid guys."

Tony said nothing. He couldn't refute Fitz's words, and anything he did say would trivialize this man's dilemma. He didn't want to do that.

"Enough about me," Fitz said to Tony's relief. "We're here to talk about a new start." He eyed the empty bottles of Sam Adams. "Got any more of those?"

"Yes, Mr. Fitzgerald, I believe I do."

28

Thursday, November 20

The Mon Valley Wellness Center, housed in a modern three-story office building in the heart of Mill Town, looked completely out of place amidst its shabby surroundings. Arriving twenty minutes early for his nine o'clock appointment, Tony found a parallel parking space less than a block away.

Jimbo, Nikki, Evan, Captain Dudek, and Chief McMahon had all given him their not-so-subtle advice, but it was his love for Allie, the added stress of the unsolicited promotion to acting station captain, and his near-suicidal actions at the recent house fire that finally broke his resistance to seeking professional help.

Despite the nearby parking spot, Tony walked past the building three times, until, at 8:55, he stopped and faced the gleaming double glass entry doors. *Now or never.* Gathering his resolve but wishing he was here for his physical, not mental, health, he entered the lobby and took the elevator to the third floor.

The door opened onto a reception area, where a burly security guard sat behind thick glass. The place had an institutional, and not very welcoming, air. *Guess they can't be too careful, especially with crazies like me.* He smiled at the thought.

"May I help you?" The guard, no doubt noticing Tony's inappropriate grin, gave him a dubious look.

"Ah, yeah. Tony Moretti. I have a ten o'clock appointment with Dr. Harrison."

The guard checked his computer screen. "Photo ID and insurance information."

Tony pushed his insurance card and driver's license through the slot in the glass.

The guard scanned the insurance card and held the license up to compare the photo with Tony's face. Apparently satisfied, he returned the documents.

Tony took a seat. The movie *One Flew Over the Cuckoo's Nest* came to mind.

The door next to the guard station buzzed and a smiling girl in her early twenties emerged and escorted him to an open door with a gold plate that read:

David J. Harrison, PhD

"Anthony, welcome," a short, chubby fortysomething said as he came out from behind his desk and grasped Tony's hand.

"Thanks, but I prefer Tony, if you don't mind."

"Tony it is. I'm David Harrison. Let's sit."

Dr. Harrison led him to a seat at a small round table where two padded office chairs faced each other. Other than an odd three-headed wood carving atop the table, the office was rather sparse.

"Ah, you were expecting me to sit in a black leather chair in front of a high stack of books while you reclined on a matching sofa, yes?"

"Well, I . . ."

"A common misconception from too many TV depictions, and besides, I'm a therapist, not a psychiatrist." Harrison broke out into a warm smile that put Tony at ease. After five minutes of small talk, the doctor got down to business.

Harrison donned a pair of reading glasses and leafed through the papers on his desk. "I've studied the information you submitted, and I must say, this is one of the most comprehensive and detailed self-assessments I've ever received. You're certainly starting off on the right foot."

"Thank you. This is a big step for me, and there's no sense going through this process if I'm not going to be honest with you." What he didn't say was that he had poured himself into the document for almost a week: writing, editing, and revising. The exercise had been therapeutic, and he'd left nothing out.

Harrison tipped his head forward and peered over his glasses. "From what I gather, you began to experience symptoms shortly after the terrible Leisure Air crash three and a half years ago. Am I correct?"

"You are."

Harrison flipped a page. "You're currently experiencing irritability, nightmares, and loss of sleep, but the most debilitating issue, according to what you've written, is severe anxiety that affects your ability to concentrate. It seems to be especially troublesome when human suffering has occurred or is imminent."

"The anxiety overwhelms me at times," Tony said. "When it happens, my hands shake and my mind turns to unfocused mush. The symptoms usually pass, but I can't trust myself to make good decisions during the critical early minutes of an emergency situation." He took a breath before continuing. "I'm afraid I'm going to get someone hurt . . . or killed."

"Understandable. Your symptoms are classic signs of post-traumatic stress disorder." Harrison removed his glasses and met Tony's glance. "That's what you have, Tony, PTSD, and the first step is admitting it to yourself. A lot of people can't, especially first responders and members of the military. Because of their professions, they believe they have some special armor against it, but they're wrong. It's the mind, not the musculature, and all humans are susceptible, no matter what they do for a living. PTSD can result from a single traumatic event, and you've been subject to several."

Tony shifted in his chair. He'd known what it was all along, of course, as had his friends and colleagues, but hearing it from a professional psychologist hit him squarely between the eyes.

"It's important for you to accept these facts"—Harrison didn't say *diagnosis*—"for us to move forward and agree on a course of treatment. Are you willing to do that?"

Tony hesitated before answering. "I do. I've been rationalizing my symptoms for a long time, but I won't anymore."

"Good. That's progress." Harrison flipped to the last page. "But what I don't see here is any mention of your personal life. Your relationships with family and friends."

"Well," Tony said, "I've kind of disconnected. I call my folks—they're up in Meadville—about once a week, but I haven't visited them in a while. I do have some old college buddies in the area, but I've been away from Pittsburgh for three years and I haven't reached out to them since I got back."

"I see. Is there anyone special in your life? A romantic relationship, perhaps?"

"I have someone I'm very much in love with, but I've distanced myself from her, and I don't know what to do about it. I don't want to lose her."

"Of course you don't. Estrangement from loved ones is very common in situations like yours, but it's not healthy. Your world outside of work is critical to your progress. It's a foundation and a support structure. We'll be talking about those relationships soon." Harrison put a finger on his chin. "Thanksgiving is a week from today. Might I suggest a trip to Meadville?"

"Step one in the process, Doc? That's doable, but it seems I need to work on *every* aspect of my life." *How is this ever going to work?*

"Don't be disheartened. We'll get there. One step at a time, as they say." Harrison picked up a pen and jotted a note. "Before we discuss a course of action, do you have any questions for me?"

"A few. What is the treatment for . . . PTSD?" *There, I said it out loud.* "And when can I expect to see results?"

"Excellent questions. The treatment I recommend is known as cognitive processing therapy, commonly called CPT. It's an evidence-based therapy—meaning it's proven effective through rigorous research and practice." Harrison paused as if waiting for a follow-up question, but with his master's degree, Tony was familiar with evidence-based studies.

"CPT fosters an understanding of how the exposure to traumatic events affects your thoughts, feelings, and behaviors. The course of treatment lasts three months, divided into a dozen one-hour sessions. By the midway point, say the end of December, you should see results."

"Three months? I was expecting a year, at least."

Harrison smiled. "Another misconception. Hollywood stars might stay in counseling for years, but our focus here is to get you back to your previous lifestyle and level of functioning as soon as possible, not milk you for money."

The comment surprised but pleased Tony. He had to get past this—and soon—if he was going to continue to lead fire crews during critical situations and salvage his relationship with Allie.

"PTSD is often caused by the thoughts you harbor about the traumatic events you've witnessed, and by *avoidance*. The typical individual uses avoidance as a defense mechanism to push the trauma out of his or her mind. It's an acceptable coping strategy in the short term, but if it lingers, it becomes debilitating."

Tony leaned in toward Harrison, hanging on the doctor's every word.

"During CPT, we'll expose your trauma by having you write about it in what we call impact statements—you'll fill one out weekly—and discussing what you've written with me.

"We'll talk about the parts of your life that have been affected, including your health, your job, and your relationships. Then we'll list the triggers that lead to your symptoms. Finally, we'll work on the skills you need to regain your previous level of functioning, getting you back to normal so you can return to life as you knew it before the traumatic events occurred."

"Makes sense," Tony said. "Confront it and move on."

"That's the idea," Harrison confirmed.

"I was afraid you were going to put me on medication."

"Antidepressants and anxiety medications are available, but I wouldn't recommend them in your case. We've got to keep you clear-headed for the important work you do."

Tony leaned back in his chair and grinned as his doubts gave way to optimism.

"Don't get too excited just yet," Harrison warned. "It will require a lot of work on your part, and there's no guarantee that three months will do it. But if you stick to the plan and put in the work, I'm confident you'll see positive results."

Harrison laid out the game plan for the next twelve weeks, emphasizing Tony's responsibilities: developing a reliable support structure, journaling, exercise, and healthy eating. He also cited positive results from others he'd worked with. But Tony didn't need any motivation. He was hooked. *This might just work.*

Elated by Harrison's proposal and its promise of psychological rehabilitation, Tony pulled out his phone. "Hello, Mrs. Cooper? Would you allow Terrell to go on a little photographic expedition after school?"

***

"Over there, he's the perfect subject," Tony said, pointing to a middle-aged man with a long gray beard sitting on a milk crate. With his elbows on his knees and his hands propping up his chin, the man, old beyond his years, stared into space.

"Work with the colors. Show the contrast between his navy-blue coat and the dark red bricks, but don't let in too much light. Tell a story."

Terrell adjusted the camera's settings, framed the shot, and snapped five quick photos.

The man turned toward them but offered no change in his blank expression.

In the fenced-in playground of the River Bend Community Center, shouts of "give me the ball" mixed with the sound of basketballs bouncing off the asphalt. A little farther ahead, the savory scent of beef filled the air. A young black vendor grilled ribs and chicken at a makeshift barbecue stand. Tony couldn't help but admire the man's entrepreneurial spirit, even as the mouthwatering aroma left him craving a taste.

On the next block, they spotted a group of teenagers hovering at the edge of an alley. Heeding Mrs. Cooper's warning, Tony placed a hand on Terrell's shoulder. "Not them."

"Duh. You think I'm stupid?" Terrell asked. "Man, why we gotta be doin' this when it's twenty degrees out?"

"You're exaggerating." Tony gestured to the scrolling LED display

176

above the entrance of the Mon Valley Savings Bank. "Look, it's thirty-seven. Are you telling me you're strictly a warm-weather photographer?"

"My hip hurts. We been at this long enough."

"I suppose we have. I guess that's enough for today." *I should be more aware of his physical limitations.*

After a three-block walk to the station, they made themselves comfortable in the unoccupied reading room, where Tony inserted the CD card from the Canon Rebel XT into his laptop and pulled up Terrell's recent photos. "Nice shots. You've developed quite the eye for composition and use of light."

"Thanks, it's pretty cool to mess with all those settings."

"You're getting very good at it," Tony said. "Let's take a look at your fire scene photos."

"Check the folder marked *Big Ass Blazes*, see it?"

"Big-ass blazes? Really?" Tony asked as he opened the file. Flames licking the sides of houses, smoke pouring from roofs, firefighters throwing ladders and advancing hoselines, onlookers with wide-eyed expressions. "Impressive action shots. Way to zoom in on the action. You've come a long way since the days you let the automatic setting do all the work."

Terrell beamed.

"Uh-oh, I think you got a little too close to the action in this series."

"Don't worry, I heard about it from the firemen—*firefighters*, I mean." Terrell eyed Tony suspiciously. "You put them onto me, didn't you?"

"Guilty," Tony said. "I was afraid you'd get a little too exuberant when I wasn't around, so they're my *keep Tony out of trouble with Mrs. Cooper* team."

"Whatever," Terrell said with a roll of his eyes.

As Tony continued to scan Terrell's work, a shadowy figure, standing just beyond a line of police tape, caught his attention. *I've seen him before.*

"What's up?" Terrell asked.

"Hang on," Tony said and scrolled through Terrell's first fire scene photos, taken before he'd learned to zoom in on his subject matter. Although most were taken as wide-angle shots, their two-megabyte sizes lent themselves well to enlargement.

He selected four photos, put them in a new folder, and cropped them. Then, turning to the more recent images, he selected four more and did the same. It was definitely the same guy. He sported faded jeans in some shots, sweatpants in others, but he consistently wore a black hoodie tucked around his face—even in the pictures taken in warm weather. The gray bill of a baseball cap poked out in every picture.

"Do you recognize this guy?" Tony asked.

Terrell examined the photos. "Seen him a couple times, I think. Why?"

"Just curious," Tony said.

Maybe it was nothing, but the guy was showing up at fire scenes all over town. Tony cropped the photos and saved them to his laptop.

"Come on, let's get you home before your mom puts out an APB."

29

Tuesday, December 9

Tony, always one to guard his privacy, spoke softly into his iPhone. "It's slow here today. The chiefs are out at some leadership course at the fire academy. We just wrapped up training. Bleeding control. Not nearly as thorough as the classes Iggy used to teach at the airport, but we don't have many EMS types here. What about you? How does such a busy career woman have time to call a lowly fireman?"

"Fire*fighter*," Allie corrected. "You ragged me for saying fire*man* about a thousand times."

"Touché."

"Ellis Kim is holding down the fort in Operations this afternoon. He's the senior manager these days and he's doing a great job. But never mind my world. If you have so much free time, why haven't you FaceTimed, or called, or even texted until now? It's been two weeks since we talked, but that was a group call while you were visiting your parents for Thanksgiving. I love them, but our conversation wasn't exactly private."

"Oh, you know, one thing after another."

"Bullshit." The expletive came out so sharply that Tony pulled the phone away from his ear. "I'm beginning to think you've given up on us."

If you only knew, Allie. I think about you all day, every day. Tony cursed himself for not saying so out loud. He wished Dr. Harrison was there to prod him.

"Well?"

"You're never far from my thoughts."

"That's encouraging," Allie said in a voice laced with skepticism. "We need to have a serious conversation, and soon."

"Agreed. I'm off duty this Saturday. Let's talk then."

"I was thinking more of an in-person visit. You know, where we can actually talk to each other face-to-face."

"Ahh, I'd love to, but it's not really a good time right now." He wanted to see her more than anything, but not in his current state. "How about we hook up in a couple of weeks?"

"Couple of weeks, huh?" She remained silent for several seconds. "Okay, I guess I have no choice." With that, the line went dead.

They'd had a few spats since he'd moved away, but she'd never hung up on him before. Tony mulled over her words. If she was mad, why had she agreed to his timeline so quickly? Something was cooking in that sly brain of hers, but the klaxon saved him from contemplating what it might be.

"Mon Area fire, Station-300, Station-500, Battalion-1, Battalion-2, respond to a vehicle accident with fire on the Steelworkers Memorial Bridge."

Not exactly the distraction I wanted, but it'll do. He shoved the phone into his back pocket and dashed for the ladder truck. Two stations and two battalion chiefs for a vehicle on fire? Odd.

"Mon Area from County. Incoming reports describe a collision between a tractor-trailer and a gasoline tanker. At least one is on fire. We're bringing up the PennDOT traffic cameras now."

Tony visualized the scene. *Possible flammable liquid fire.* "Rescue crew," he shouted. "Take the foam truck."

"Dontrell's firing it up now, LT," Corey called as Foam-304's diesel engine coughed and sputtered to life in a cloud of white exhaust.

"Okay, Danny, Engine-301 will respond first on this one. Follow them. We'll hang back in 302."

Tony spotted the black cloud as soon as Danny wheeled right onto Main Street. *Damn.*

"Responding Mon Area units from County. There's a thick column of smoke on the PennDOT camera at the northern bridge approach. We can't make out the tanker, but it looks like civilians are abandoning their vehicles on the bridge."

Civilians . . . and gasoline. The thought spiked Tony's senses.

With the pumper and foam truck clearing the way, Station-300's vehicles covered the half-mile east to Bridge Street in three minutes flat. During that time, Chief Ramsey, Deputy Chief DeFazio, and Battalion Chiefs Costello and McMahon called in from the fire academy, but they were responding from the North Hills, at least twenty-five minutes away.

"Christ, look at that mother burn," Danny said as they neared the southern approach ramp to the Steelworkers Memorial Bridge.

"I was hoping for a milk tanker," Romeo said from the back of the crew cab. No one laughed.

Tony examined the map on the MDT. "Engine-301, you're coming up on a hydrant on your right. Hook up to it and send your manpower forward."

"301 copies," Pet replied.

"Foam-304, lay a supply line from Engine-301. Stop within deck gun range of that tanker, but no closer. You've got fire attack." Tony considered his manpower needs. They'd be isolated from Station-500's resources on the other end of the bridge. "County, respond Engine-401 and Squad-403 to this location."

Complying with Tony's instructions, Engine-301 stopped at the hydrant while the foam truck stopped beside it, dropped a supply line, and drove onto the bridge.

"Beach us along the curb, Danny, behind 301," Tony said as he got his first clear view of the scene. "County from 300-Lieutenant, we're on the scene of a fully involved tanker fire on the Steelworkers Memorial Bridge. The tanker is sitting alongside a box-type tractor-trailer. I see three abandoned vehicles, but no civilians." *Where are the truck drivers?* "It looks like the tanker is spilling its load onto the bridge. Stand by for a further report. I'll have Bridge Street Command."

Tony raised his binoculars. The green and white tanker, from Ebbet's Petroleum, had apparently sideswiped the scorched tractor-trailer. He couldn't make out the tanker's hazardous materials placard, but from his airport training and experience, there was no mistaking the distinctive black smoke of a petroleum fire. *Must be gasoline. At least five thousand gallons.*

"County from Bridge Street Command, this is definitely a gasoline tanker. Contact the airport authority and have them respond with a crash truck from the Allegheny County Airport. Also alert the fire station at Pittsburgh International and have them start their foam tanker and a second crash truck. We're initiating our attack with Foam-304."

Even though the Allegheny County Airport, a satellite to Pittsburgh International, was situated in nearby West Mifflin, it would take at least fifteen minutes, best case, for its crash truck to arrive, and Pittsburgh International's resources were more than half an hour away. MAFA was on its own for a while, but Foam-304 carried five hundred gallons of AFFF—Aqueous Film-Forming Foam—and he was confident they could keep the situation in check in the meantime. *With a little luck, we might even extinguish it.*

"County, 500-Captain and Station-500 units are on the scene at the northern end of the Steelworker's Bridge."

Tony didn't recognize the voice. "That's not Alex Jenkins."

"No, it's Tom Decker," Danny said, "C-Platoon Captain. Must be on a switch with Alex."

"Oh, right, Decker," Tony said. "Only met him once."

"You ain't missing nothing."

"I confirm the report from 300-Lieutenant," Decker radioed. "The tanker is side by side with the tractor-trailer. I've got a wall of abandoned vehicles blocking my access." After a pause, he added, "I'm assuming Bridge Street Command and designating 300-Lieutenant as Southern Bridge Operations supervisor."

"Dimwit," Danny said. "He just said he can't do nothing from there. Should've left you in command."

Tony didn't care about the demotion, but it wasn't tactically sound. Station-300's equipment was less than half a football field from the tanker, while Decker's crews were twice that distance, and with blocked access. Observers, basically. But the captain was the senior officer on scene. No matter. The fight would be carried out on the southern side of the bridge, regardless of who commanded it.

"County, Bridge Street Command," Decker radioed. "Contact the

Airport Authority and cancel the request for assistance."

"No, no, no!" Tony blurted. He took a breath before keying the mic. "Command from Southern Bridge Ops—based on the potential of this fire, I recommend we keep the airport resources coming."

"We don't need them," Decker radioed. "You're an airport guy and you have a foam truck, so get to work and extinguish this fire."

Tony fumed but didn't reply.

"Did you copy, Moretti?"

Besides the breach of radio protocol, Decker's transmission was a personal affront. *Fine. It doesn't change what we'll do.* Tony uttered a terse "Copy" before ripping off his headset and hurling it into the windshield. "Danny, give Pappy a hand with the pumper hookup. Muscles, Romeo, Luke, you're with me."

Despite a stiff westerly breeze, pungent fumes permeated the air as Tony's crew from the ladder truck, along with Pet, Warren, and Maddie from the pumper, strode onto the bridge, where Dontrell stood at the side-mounted pump panel of Foam-403, with Corey positioned at the deck gun atop the rig.

"We're hooked up and ready for water, LT," Dontrell said.

Tony hit his lapel mic. "Engine-301, charge the supply line."

"It's getting worse," Pet called.

Tony stepped forward to survey the situation. The scorched tractor-trailer was now ablaze from end to end. *Hurry up, folks.*

Impatient for action, he shifted his gaze to Foam-304, where Dontrell examined his gauges as the five-inch supply line slowly firmed up. "Ready to flow foam, LT."

"Open it up," Tony ordered.

Dontrell slid the chrome discharge lever to the right, and a thick stream of Aqueous Film-Forming Foam erupted from the deck gun. Corey aimed it directly into the gasoline-fed flames.

"Sweep it across the tanker, Corey. Let it *roll* down into the flames." Vivid memories of using the same technique on that cold February night at the airport came rushing back as he gave the order. *Only that's not an airplane with people in it.*

"Command from Southern Bridge Ops, we're flowing foam now."

"Need a hand, Tony?"

Tony pivoted and spotted Lieutenant Brookin from Station-400.

"We just got here," Brookin said. "What's the situation?"

"Both trucks are on fire, but the tanker is my main concern. It's dumping a lot of product onto the bridge deck, but I'm hoping we can smother the flames before they cause structural damage."

"Yeah," Brookin said. "A tsunami of gasoline, released all at once? That would suck, big-time."

"Big-time," Tony agreed. "I requested foam and crash trucks from the Airport Authority, but Captain Decker countermanded me."

"Yeah, I heard," Brookin said. "How'd we luck out with Decker? He's such a dick."

"Don't know, but there it is. We should see some results in the next few minutes, but for now, you should take over Ops from me. You're senior."

"No way," Brookin said, holding up his hands. "You're an acting captain, and besides, flammable liquid fires are your thing, not mine. Just tell me what you need."

"Okay, then. How about taking my crew and deploying the two crosslays from Foam-304? We're going to need maneuverable handlines if this thing turns to shit."

"My man, don't you think we're already there?" Brookin asked as he swept the antenna of his portable radio across the scene. "Hold your crew here, Tony. I'll use my guys. They need a little action."

Yes, they were in deep shit, and it all came down to the numbers. Foam-304 carried five hundred gallons of AFFF, and its deck gun was discharging one thousand gallons per minute, proportioned at three gallons of foam to ninety-seven gallons of water—the standard three percent mixture for hydrocarbon fires. At that rate, they were using thirty gallons of foam every minute. This meant their foam supply would last less than twenty minutes, and five of those had already elapsed. Tony didn't like the result of his calculations, but the math didn't lie. *We've got fifteen minutes, max.*

Without enough foam for a decisive knockdown, a lengthy battle of attrition was out of the question. He could reduce the flow to 750 gpm, but doing so would allow the gas-fed flames to overpower the AFFF blanket. Stalemate. Foam-304, by itself, wouldn't cut it. And what about the structural damage being done to the fifty-year-old bridge? *We need that damn crash truck.*

"Southern Bridge Ops from Command," Captain Decker radioed. "What's your status?"

Tony keyed the mic. "We're holding the fire in check, but we haven't been able to extinguish it."

"I can see that," Decker snapped. "I've got eight abandoned vehicles on fire on this side of the bridge. I'm ordering Engine-501 to open up with the two-inch tip on their deck gun. We'll flood this thing with a thousand gallons per minute."

"Negative, Command!" Tony replied. "You'll dilute the foam blanket."

"You're pissing in the wind, Moretti. I'll show you how it's done."

Tony pushed the mic button, but a hand grabbed his arm and pulled it away.

"Don't do it," Pet said.

Tony released the button. "That arrogant bastard."

Pet shrugged, a *nothing you can do* look on her face.

In front of them, Lieutenant Brookin's handline crews, each fielding a nozzle operator and two backup firefighters, had stretched their hoselines to within seventy-five feet of the burning tanker. Too close for what was about to happen.

Tony's anxiety level skyrocketed, but he kept his wits. "400-Lieutenant, pull your lines back immediately." He wasn't going to leave them in harm's way while Decker screwed around. "Go hurry them up, Pet."

While she rushed toward the hose teams, Tony called to Dontrell. "Be ready to abandon your position in a hurry."

Dontrell pulled the headset away from his ears, a puzzled look on his face. "If you say so, LT."

"I do, but no matter what, keep the foam flowing. Jump on top of the rig if you have to."

"Jesus!" Corey shouted. "Get those guys out of there!"

"Cover them!" Tony shouted as a wave of water, gasoline, and chunks of the foam bore down on the exposed firefighters.

The two hose teams retreated, never taking their eyes off the blaze. The crew on the left dropped their inch-and-three-quarter line and darted to the rear. The other team followed suit, but the nozzle operator stopped, took a step forward, and yanked back on the bale.

The man lost his balance and fell hard onto his backside, losing his grip on the hose. His backups, unprepared for the sudden change in direction, jerked to a halt. Lieutenant Brookin sprinted to the fallen man as the hose, like an enraged king cobra, sprang off the ground, spraying water wildly as it corkscrewed through the air.

"No, get back, for God's sake!" Tony screamed as he ran toward the imperiled crew. Suddenly, his neck jerked forward as something heavy slammed into his helmet, sending him crashing to the concrete. Dazed and gasping for air, he got to his feet and watched the unfolding disaster.

The hellish mixture rolled into Brookin and his people, whose backs were bent low as they scurried away. Piercing screams. Shouted orders. Radio transmissions. *My God, is this really happening?*

Enveloped in flames, the crew disappeared under a smothering white blanket as Corey redirected the foam truck's deck gun. But as he swept the foam stream over the struggling hose team, the gasoline-infused mixture gained momentum.

And then it was over. A second streak of white flew overhead, ricocheting off the bridge deck where it met the onrushing flame front. Working in unison, the two large-caliber streams smothered the diminished flames in a thick blanket that spread across the width of the bridge.

Tony's vision cleared, but as he started forward again, powerful hands held him back. "Let go! I've got to help them, get them out of there."

"It's okay, LT. Pet's on it," Muscles said as he held fast to Tony's shoulder. "She told Decker to shut down his deck gun. Should've heard how she slammed him over the radio."

Tony looked up at the streams. "Where did the second one come from?"

"It's from the airport crash truck," Muscles said. "Got here just in time."

"But it was canceled."

"I uncancelled it." Chief Ramsey, in his white helmet and turnout clothing, came up beside Tony. "As soon as I heard Captain Decker's order, I called the chief at the airport and got the crash truck moving again. I've assumed command." The chief removed his sunglasses. "Nice work here, Lieutenant."

Brookin and two of his people were on their feet, covered in foam but seemingly okay. *Thank God.* The nozzleman, however, was a different story.

The distinct smell of burnt flesh and hair hung in the air as medics carried the man toward the ambulance. Even with an oxygen mask covering his mouth and nose, Tony recognized him—Scott Peterson, the senior firefighter from Engine-401.

Tony's pulse quickened and his body began to tremble. Gripped with nausea, he doubled over and retched.

Ramsey grabbed him. "Are you okay, Tony?"

No! I won't succumb. Forcing thoughts of the injured firefighter away, he stood erect. "All good, Chief. Just a little nauseous from the fumes."

Ramsey eyed him dubiously. "Maybe, but I want you checked out."

"Will do, Chief."

But instead of visiting the medics, Tony took a seat on the tailboard of the foam truck and tried to deconstruct the events of the past hour.

30

Saturday, December 13

The buzzer jolted Tony from his wine-induced nap. The Iwo Jima documentary he'd been watching on the History Channel had apparently ended. He checked his watch: 5:32 p.m. He'd been asleep for almost two hours.

The buzzer sounded again. *Who now?* Woozy, he angled the blinds downward, but as usual, the overgrown pine tree blocked his view of the front door. He thought about peeking over the porch wall, but oh, what the hell. He punched the talk button. "Yes?"

"My, my. Sounds like *someone* is in a bad mood."

The voice jolted him. "Allie? Is that you?"

"Who else would it be?"

I knew it. She had no intention of waiting two weeks. He hit the buzzer, stepped onto the landing, and there she was.

Tony's heart swelled as he rushed to meet her halfway up the steps. Embracing her tightly, he savored the softness of her delicate curves and the sweet, familiar scent of her perfume. *It's been much too long.*

"Easy, big fella. Don't break me."

Inside the apartment, she gave him the once-over. "You look like shit."

"Geez, Allie, I'm home. What am I supposed to look like?"

"Like a human being. A T-shirt without sauce stains would be a start." She reached up and ruffled his hair. "Shower lately, Moretti?"

"We had an alarm overnight and I couldn't get back to sleep. Been reading ever since."

"Uh-huh." She squeezed his upper arms. "Well, you still have muscle definition, so you must be working out, but by the looks of that belly, you've either stopped running or you're drinking so much you can't burn off the calories."

The comment hit him where it hurt, but she wasn't wrong. "I lift weights at the station, but I've kind of let the running lapse."

"I see." Allie pointed at the half-empty wine bottle on the coffee table. "Well, if you think I'm going to bed with a guy who's three sheets to the wind, you can forget it."

Tony laughed. "Who said anything about—"

"Oh, come off it. I saw the look on your face the moment you saw me. When's the last time you got laid?"

"Other than in my dreams? You know exactly when. The night before I left for the Forest Service job."

"What, you couldn't find any good-looking skinny black chicks in the woods?"

Her tone was playful, but the edge in her voice masked an underlying anger. He needed to head off the coming explosion. "You're looking good."

"Yeah, right," she said and took a seat on the sofa.

Tony plopped onto the coffee table in front of her.

"I'm glad you came." And he was.

She huffed. "Not sure I buy that. Thought I might have to turn around and head back home."

"Allie. Come on now."

"What?" She sat up and leaned forward. "Every time I suggest we get together you come up with some lame-ass excuse. That doesn't exactly fill me with confidence. Do you want this romance—if we're still calling it that—to continue or not?"

"You know I do." He and Dr. Harrison had yet to probe his relationship with Allie, but after looking into her beautiful brown eyes for several seconds, he expressed his true feelings. "I love you, and I want to spend the rest of my life with you."

Allie slumped back into the sofa, all traces of anger gone. "What am I going to do with you?" She shook her head. "Do you have anything to eat in this place, or do you live exclusively on a liquid diet?"

"You don't want to know."

"All right, then, you're taking me out to dinner, so clean yourself up."

***

Tony chose Mulligan's, a cozy bar and restaurant across the river in Union Center, where he asked for a back corner booth.

"I saw that tanker fire you texted me about," Allie said. "It was all over the news." She eyed him closely. "Pretty rough, huh?"

"The fire wasn't the issue. We'd just about had it knocked, when . . ."

"When some dumbass captain got spooked and pushed the fire into your crew, something you didn't see fit to actually phone me about."

That part had been carefully omitted by MAFA's public information officer. "I didn't want to call you with that kind of stuff."

"Why, because of what I've been through? I'm not a fragile flower, you know. I can handle bad news."

"Noted for future reference," he said by way of apology. "How'd you find out about those details, anyway?"

"I called the station and asked for your boss. I was told he'd retired, and you were taking his place." She hesitated. "Something else you failed to tell me about."

Tony shrugged. "It's temporary."

"Anyway, the guy at the station put me onto the chief's admin."

"Iris."

"Yes, Iris. Nice lady. She said she was worried about you. Said the chief was too."

"They're blowing things out of proportion."

"Are they?" She gave him a stern but empathetic look, her *tough love* face. "The captain doesn't think so."

"You talked to Barney? What the hell, Allie?"

"Sorry," she said without looking like she meant it. "Nikki called and told me what she'd heard, but I had to find out what really happened."

"I get it." *Another mess of my own doing.*

"Captain Dudek was reluctant to talk, but I got him to loosen up. He began by mentioning your mood swings. Angry one day. Withdrawn the next. Shaky at fire scenes."

Tony squirmed in his seat.

"Then he told me all about the tanker fire and what happened to your crew. What an awful situation. You're blaming yourself, aren't you?"

"A little, I guess."

"A lot, I'm sure," she said. "And then he hit me with another surprise. A fire where you found an old couple dead in their apartment. I can't fathom what that did to you."

"Part of the job," he mumbled.

"Maybe, but I can only imagine how it affected you."

"I'd have to be a machine for it not to."

Her eyes narrowed. "But the captain saved the worst for last. That house fire last month, when you saved the kids. You *did* tell me about that one, but you sugarcoated it, said you scooped them from the window. The captain told me what really happened. You dove into a fully involved house fire and wouldn't come out, even after the kids were safe. Why would you do that?"

Tony's stomach churned, but he couldn't upset her further.

"Well?"

"I'm in therapy."

Allie's mouth dropped open at the sudden revelation.

"Don't look so surprised. You threatened me, remember?"

"That's all it took? Who are you kidding?"

"Not you. I wouldn't even try," Tony said without a hint of emotion. "You surprised me with your visit, that's all. I was going to tell you, soon."

"I'll bet, but let's set that aside for the moment. Give me the details."

"Wow. Not even a little foreplay?"

"Tony?"

"Okay, okay. I'm seeing a psychologist, one-on-one. He's a great guy, a PhD. The program is three months long—twelve sessions—and the success rate is very high."

Relief washed over her face, as if she'd jettisoned a great burden. "That's great! What does he specialize in?"

Tony hesitated. "He treats people who've seen the kinds of things you and I have. Soldiers, emergency responders, people suffering from post-traumatic stress disorder."

"Finally." Allie smiled. "That's the first time in three years I've heard you say those words. I'm very proud of you, you big stubborn ass."

He felt an immense sense of relief.

She searched his eyes. "What caused you to find a professional after all this time?"

Tony settled into the chair. "Lots of reasons. The anger you mentioned, the nightmares, my inability to keep my head clear at fire scenes." He paused, his voice softening as he held her gaze. "But the most important factor was you. My symptoms were tearing us apart, and I couldn't let that happen. It'll take some time, but I'm going to get back to my old self."

Allie bit her lower lip. "You're a real pain, Anthony Moretti."

"I'm . . . complex. It's one of my many endearing qualities."

31

Sunday, December 14

"You gonna get out of bed or what?"

The voice woke Tony from his latest nightmare. The girl in coach whose slack-jawed face sprang up at him when he'd inadvertently grabbed her long brown hair. But in the dream, she was alive and pleading. "Please, help me. I'm getting married in May."

"Hello. Earth to Tony." Allie stood at the bedroom door, holding a cup of coffee and a bag. "I borrowed the Cherokee. Hope you don't mind. I had to drive all over creation to find a half-decent coffee shop."

Tony sat up and glanced at the clock—8:23. "Good morning, Ms. Robinson."

"This caffeine's to get your sorry ass moving." She held up the bag. "Two scones, not to be eaten until *after* the run."

"Run?"

"R-U-N. You remember how to run, don't you?"

"Yeah, but . . ."

"I'm not taking any crap this morning, especially after you roped me into dinner tonight with some family I don't know from Adam."

Tony laughed. "You'll like them."

"I better. Now get dressed and I'll meet you outside. I want to run a warm-up mile."

Despite Allie's suggestion that they jog to the starting point, Tony opted to drive to the Three Rivers Heritage Trail, where early-morning fog from the Monongahela coated the riverbank. From somewhere in the mist, a tugboat's horn echoed across the water.

"Wow, this is beautiful," Allie said. "It'll be like running in the clouds."

"Did you know that the Monongahela is one of the few rivers in the US that flows from south to north? It comes up from West Virginia."

"Fascinating, but quit stalling," she said and began jogging.

"I'm with you," Tony said, but soon he fell behind.

"Man, this is just like our first run around the airport. Do I have to whip you into shape all over again?"

"I'm going to get back at it," he said through huffing breaths.

"You better," she said. "Now come on, we've got more work to do."

They ran three miles, and while he continued to lose ground, he didn't quit.

"There's hope for you yet," she said when he caught up with her at their starting point. "You've earned your reward, and maybe a little bonus."

Back at the apartment, they showered, scarfed up the scones, and made love with an urgency and passion that Tony hadn't experienced in a long time. The dark cloud that so often accompanied him of late disappeared, at least for now. Allie had a way of making him leave his troubles behind, and once again, he wondered why he'd held her at a distance for so long.

***

"Come on," Tony called. "We're going to be late." Dressed in a forest-green button-down shirt and a pair of black Dockers for dinner at the Coopers, he was anxious to get going.

"I'm ready," she said, emerging from the bedroom wearing a sleeveless silky blue blouse and tight gray pencil skirt that fell to midthigh.

Tony whistled. "Could that skirt be any shorter? I did say there'd be a teenage boy at dinner, didn't I?"

"Oh, shut up," she said and smacked his arm. "Would you rather I wear an old pair of jeans? I packed this skirt for *you*, by the way. I didn't expect you'd take me visiting."

As they prepared to leave, his eyes caught the scar on her right thigh, a jagged, silvery reminder of the night she had thrown herself into the chaos of the crash of Leisure Air 741. It told a story of bravery and pain, a testament to her resilience.

"Are you sure we're not imposing?" Allie asked. "It's such short notice."

"Don't worry, we've been invited, and I dared not turn Mrs. Cooper down."

Ten minutes later, they stood on the porch of the neat two-story brick residence.

"Hey, man," Terrell said, answering the door before Tony finished knocking. "Whoa!" he said as he eyed Allie. "You didn't tell me your girl was a sister. And a hot one, too."

"Terrell!" Mrs. Cooper admonished as she came to the door. "Come on in, folks, and don't mind my son. He's forgotten his manners." The look she gave her offspring made him lower his head and fall silent. "Teenagers," she added. "Between the hormones and what he hears from his friends in school, I don't know what I'm going to do with him."

"Oh, no, Mrs. Cooper," Allie said. "It's all right. I have friends with teenagers. I understand."

Mrs. Cooper smiled at her new guest. "You must be Allie. I've heard a *whole* lot about you."

"You have?" The surprise on Allie's face made Tony wish he had a hole to jump into. *I'm in for it now.*

Mrs. Cooper, sharp as a tack, raised her eyebrows. "Allie. That's a beautiful name," she said, as if to rescue Tony from his predicament.

"It's short for Althea. My middle name is Grace. Both of my grandmoms."

"Why, that's so sweet. What a nice tribute."

"Don't stand there, Terrell, take their coats," Mrs. Cooper said.

When Allie removed hers, Terrell's face brightened at the sight of her long, slim legs.

"Something smells amazing," Tony said, trying to give Terrell some cover. "I'm famished."

"Give me one second," Mrs. Cooper said.

Tastefully decorated and cozy, the front room of the Cooper household featured a cream-colored sofa and love seat, complemented by a navy-blue La-Z-Boy recliner.

"My dad's," Terrell said. "I crash in it sometimes when I think about him."

"I get it," Tony said. *Poor kid.*

"It's ready." Mrs. Cooper ushered her guests into the dining room, slipping Tony a sly smile that he couldn't help but return.

"Oh my God," Allie said. "I know this."

"Braised, smothered pork and black-eyed peas," Mrs. Cooper said. "An old family recipe."

"Yes! My grandma Gracie used to make this for us. I haven't had it since I was a little girl."

Mrs. Cooper beamed. "I hope it measures up to your grandma Gracie's cooking."

While they enjoyed the tasty home-cooked meal, Tony and Allie filled the Coopers in on the history of their relationship and how it had evolved and changed over the past three years. Red wine loosened their tongues, and the conversation flowed freely. Uncharacteristically quiet, Terrell's eyes glazed over more than once, although he continued to sneak lecherous glances at Allie, delighting Tony to no end.

Mrs. Cooper served pecan pie for dessert, and Tony scarfed down two pieces.

"What a delicious meal, Mrs. Cooper," Allie said. "Thank you so much."

"Yes, it was fantastic," Tony added. "I ate way too much."

"I'm glad you enjoyed it. I don't have many opportunities to cook a traditional meal these days. Terrell lives on hamburgers and macaroni and cheese."

Terrell rolled his eyes.

Mrs. Cooper held the wine bottle up. "A little more, anyone?"

"None for me," Allie said.

"I've had too much already," Tony said.

"Of course. Terrell, could you please get our guests something else to drink?"

"Aight, I'm down with that. Whatcha dudes want?"

Mrs. Cooper shot her son a look that could melt ice. "I know the pressures of fitting in at school, and I tolerate that kind of talk when you're around your friends, but in this house, you'll speak like a polite and educated young man."

"Yes, Mama," Terrell said, his gaze dropping to his plate. After a deep breath, he offered a bright smile. "May I get you a glass of water or perhaps a soda, Ms. Robinson? How about you, Mr. Moretti?"

Allie burst out laughing. The whole table joined in.

"Boys," Mrs. Cooper said before changing the subject. "How long are you in town, Allie?"

"I'm heading back tomorrow."

"Oh, that's too bad. By that smile on Tony's face, I can see what your visit has done for him."

"Really?" Allie said. "And I thought he was having a grand old time without me."

"Him?" Mrs. Cooper asked. "He's so mopey his face practically drags across the floor."

"Is that so?" Allie asked with a sideways glance at Tony.

"Excuse me," Tony interjected. "I might have something to say about this."

"Save your breath," Mrs. Cooper said. "Have another glass of wine while I embarrass you in front of this lovely thing."

"Do it, Mama!" Terrell said. "I wanna see the big fireman sweat."

"Fire*fighter*," Tony said. But the droplets had already formed on his brow.

A puzzled expression crossed Mrs. Cooper's features. "Forgive me, but watching you two, listening to your story, I can't help but wonder why you're not together."

"Simple," Tony said. "It's our jobs."

Allie folded her arms and looked away.

"Hmm, I don't think Althea agrees."

"She doesn't," Allie said.

Mrs. Cooper raised a finger to her chin. "Okay, then, tell me why you two live hundreds of miles apart? It must be more than your work. You can always get another job, but love, that's something you can't find so easily. If you have it, why let it slip away?"

Allie cranked a thumb at Tony. "Ask my partner here, because I can't figure it out."

Tony's heart sank. "We've, ah, got some issues to work through."

"We?" Allie asked.

"Me," Tony corrected but didn't elaborate. He wasn't about to discuss his ongoing therapy, and Mrs. Cooper didn't push it. After thanking her for her hospitality, they drove back to Tony's apartment in complete silence.

***

By nine o'clock, the wine had worn off. Allie was putting the finishing touches on a colorful green, orange, and black afghan while Tony pretended to watch some lame movie about zombies.

"I can't believe you brought your knitting along for such a short trip," Tony said, hoping to steer clear of any more discussions about relationships or psychological problems.

Allie wasn't having it. She set the afghan down, picked up the remote, and switched the TV off.

"I'm sorry I went behind your back to your old boss."

"Not a big deal," Tony said.

"It is, but I had to find out what was going on with you. I've been going crazy with worry ever since you packed up and went west to play Smokey the Bear. Hell, Tony, you haven't been back to see me since."

"I wanted to, but . . ."

"But you're still dealing with the same shit. I know. I didn't experience the horrors you did at the crash, but I saw plenty, and I'm still dealing with it, too."

"I know you are, and I'm sorry for avoiding you. I didn't plan it that way."

"What aren't you telling me?"

Tony took a deep breath. "After three months with the Forest Service, I thought I'd worked it—the PTSD—out of my system. I still had nightmares, but everything else was fine."

"And?"

"It was my last day, the big fire I told you about. There was a little more to it."

"Yes?"

"The fire trapped us. We had to deploy our escape shelters."

"Good Lord."

"One of the guys, Jimmy . . . Jimbo, a good friend. He almost didn't make it. He was hurt. We got him into his shelter, but the fire caught us."

Allie's face twisted from concern to horror. Her right foot began its habitual stress-induced tapping.

Pointing at her face, he said, "That's why I didn't tell you."

She dropped her hand. "I want to hear the rest."

"I got into my shelter okay, but I knew Jimbo was in trouble. He called to me, but I couldn't help him. That's when it all came rushing back. The crash, those people in the plane, watching you slide down that hill . . ." Tony's hands were shaking now. The panicky feeling was back.

"What could you have done?" Allie asked. "If you'd tried to help him, you wouldn't be here with me now."

"I know. But I almost jumped out of that shelter. I didn't care what might happen to me. I couldn't let another person die."

"Oh, Tony, I should have been here for you sooner."

"No, this isn't on you. I'm the one who avoided getting help. Thought if I worked through it, it would go away."

"It doesn't go away."

"I know. I've tried the same thing here, with the same results."

"Do you know the worst, most frightening thing your captain told me?"

Tony didn't. *Take your pick.*

"He said you had no fear, no matter how bad the situation. Didn't care what might happen to you." Allie wiped a tear from her cheek. "As if your life meant nothing."

Tony lowered his head. *Maybe it didn't then, but it does now.*

"Is that why you've distanced yourself from me?"

"Maybe. I honestly don't know."

She gathered herself and leaned forward. "Three years, Tony. The crash, your divorce, my rehab. We struggled, together. During all that time we waited, took things slow, built something together. Something natural, a bond."

Tony looked deeply into the eyes of the girl he loved. "Sometimes that bond is all that keeps me going."

She dabbed at her eyes. "The more you push me away, the less I believe it."

He moved to the sofa and put an arm around her. "I never meant to push you away," he said in a tone laced with emotion. "I can't lose you. You're everything to me."

"Don't you think I feel the same?" She smiled and put a hand on his cheek. "Mrs. Cooper was right. We should be together."

"But how can we be?"

She put a finger to his lips. "Hush. We're going to figure this out. You've taken the first step by getting yourself into therapy."

Their lips met, and in that moment, Tony's love for her washed over him. For the first time in months, his dark visions of the future melted away.

32

Monday, January 5

"County from BC-1," Chief McMahon radioed. "I'm out at the scene of a three-story taxpayer—Valley Cooperative Thrift on Division-1 with two floors of apartments above. There's an SUV halfway into the display window and light smoke showing, probably from the engine compartment. Attached exposures are Schneider's Bakery on Side-B and a vacant hardware store on Side-D. I'll have Commerce Street Command."

"County copies. Vehicle into the building with light smoke showing. Commerce Street Command established at 1124."

From the cab of Ladder-302, Tony visualized the scene. The term *taxpayer* was the fire service nomenclature for the typical two- or three-story occupancy with a business on the first floor and residential units above. Most were built in the first half of the twentieth century and featured masonry walls and flat frame roofs covered with several layers of tar paper.

He slid his headset band to the back of his neck and punched the address into the Mobile Data Terminal. The Valley Cooperative Thrift Store, 3698 Commerce Street, Borough of Rocky Shore. Another business district experiencing hard times.

"County from Commerce Street Command, the SUV sheared off the gas line and it's leaking under pressure. The thrift store manager reports her employees are out of the building. County PD is evacuating the immediate area. Get the gas company here now." After a pause, McMahon added, "Engine-401, lay in."

"And I thought this was gonna be a milk run," Danny said.

"County from Command. The gas line just ignited."

"That place is packed with stuff that'll burn like a mother," Danny said.

"Agreed, a gas line on fire is a blowtorch. Pray it's an outdoor leak." Tony's hope was dashed less than a minute later.

"County from Command, I've got smoke showing from the thrift store and flames visible inside. Speed up the gas company."

"We're on the line with them now, Chief. ETA ten minutes."

"We don't have ten minutes," McMahon replied. "Division-1 will be fully involved by then. Get me the second alarm."

"Holy shit, I can see the smoke," Danny said.

Three blocks from the scene, Tony saw it too—grayish clouds billowing into a clear January sky.

"Engine-401 from Command," McMahon radioed, "I want you to blitz the fire on Division-1 with your deck gun."

Tony checked his sideview mirror for the trailing apparatus and hit the toggle for the radio. "Command, Ladder-302, Engine-301, and Rescue-303 approaching."

"Ladder-302 from Command, pull in behind Engine-401 at the Alpha-Delta corner. Raise your aerial to Division-3 and initiate a search of both floors. Engine-301, pump the supply line and send your crew to me. Rescue-303, beach your rig and bring up some tools to get this gas shut off."

"Ladder-302 copies." Tony turned to the crew. "We'll set the outriggers and split into two search teams. Me and Romeo, Muscles and Luke."

"302 from Command, I've got people at a window on Division-3 and, Christ, they just broke it out. Get that aerial ladder up!"

Horrified screams came across the open mic.

"Wait! No! Don't jump, we're coming!" McMahon implored, his voice frantic.

Tony and Danny shared an uneasy glance.

Bright orange flames rolled out of the shattered display window as McMahon, standing on the sidewalk, waved Ladder-302 into position in the middle of Commerce Street. On the ground in front of them, two members of Engine-401's crew were hooking their five-inch supply line to the main intake on the pump panel. Atop the pumper, a third firefighter swung the deck gun toward the thrift store.

As Tony hit the ground and huddled with his troops, Corey Adamski dashed over.

"The gas company's already here," Corey said. "They don't need us. We'll handle your outrigger plates."

"That'll work." Tony glanced up and tried to spot the trapped occupants as distraught voices from the crowd implored the firefighters to hurry. Division-3 was still obscured, and now the flames were lapping at the windows of Division-2. *We've got to be fast, but not stupid.*

Alarmed shouts from the crowd faded beneath Ladder-302's revving engine as Danny, at the pedestal control box, extended all four outriggers. Tony climbed the tailboard, following Muscles, Romeo, and Luke onto the crowded platform.

"I can't see the windows, LT," Danny said.

"Use your best guess, but don't put the tip too close to the building until we're up there. They need to know we're coming, but I don't want them to jump for the ladder."

As Danny lowered the outriggers onto the plates, water splattered off the bricks above the display window. The firefighter manning the deck gun lowered his aim, and the heavy stream streaked into the thrift store.

"They're hitting it with tank water," Luke observed. "Their supply line isn't charged yet."

Tony saw the reason why. Beside Engine-401, two firefighters struggled to couple the quarter-turn fitting of the LDH to the pumper's matching intake connection.

"Water's coming!" Muscles said.

Tony hadn't heard the pump operator give the order to charge the hydrant, but it was filling fast. Too fast. The hose bucked and slid across the pavement as pressurized water shot through its five-inch liner.

The crew on the pedestal called out in unison to their colleagues: "Look out!"

Tony keyed his mic. "Shut the hydrant!"

It was too late.

The hose thrashed wildly as a torrent of water burst from the unconnected fitting. The aluminum fitting shattered a gauge on the side-mounted pump panel and ricocheted into the backs of both fleeing firefighters, knocking them to the ground. The firefighter in the lead got to his knees, but the trailing man lay prostrate and motionless.

"Shut that damned hydrant!" McMahon shouted into his radio.

Meanwhile, the pump operator juked left and right, trying to get to his stricken friends, the out-of-control hose blocking his path.

Corey bolted into the fray, dragging the downed man backward. Dontrell hefted the other firefighter to his feet and pulled him out of danger.

Moments later, the bucking hose settled to the pavement and water flow slowed to a trickle. The operator scurried to his pump panel and pushed a T-handle to shut the deck gun.

A pair of medics rushed up to the injured men. McMahon joined them. Tony shot a glance their way but immediately returned his focus to the matter at hand. "Double-check your gear and get ready to climb."

With McMahon, the incident commander, out of position, Tony keyed his mic. "Engine-301 from 300-Lieutenant, take over for Engine-401's crew. Get that supply line hooked up and the deck gun back in operation."

"Copy that, LT," Pet replied. "We're coming up now."

Tony spotted Dontrell. "Take Corey and join up with the engine crew."

"Copy that," Dontrell replied.

As flames lapped up the side of the building, a wind gust cleared the smoke from the third floor. The shattered window was empty. *Damn, where'd they go?*

A cold sweat broke out across Tony's forehead, but when he examined his hands, they were perfectly still. *Thanks, Doc Harrison.* He climbed aboard the ladder truck's pedestal as Danny simultaneously extended the ladder and rotated it toward the building. "Lower it to the sill of that broken window."

"Can do, boss," Danny said.

"We'll start our search on Division-3 and move to Division-2 if conditions permit," Tony shouted over the roar of the engine. He pointed to the vacant window. "The two residents we saw a few minutes ago must still be inside."

"We'll find 'em," Muscles said. The others nodded their assent as Danny eased the ladder a few inches above the sill.

"The ladder's set," Danny said. "Sixty-five-degree climbing angle. Rungs are aligned."

"Nice work, Danny," Tony said. "Luke, Muscles, get moving. You're designated Search-1." As they began climbing, he added, "Romeo and I are Search-2."

"Search-1, Delta side, copy," Muscles replied. "No heroics this time, okay, LT?"

Tony laughed. "No heroics. I don't have a death wish." And he meant it. His sessions with Dr. Harrison had awakened a strong sense of self-preservation.

In full turnout gear, with their breathing apparatus snugged to their backs, four closely spaced firefighters, with Luke in the lead, carried box lights, Halligans, axes, extinguishers, and thermal imaging cameras up the ladder.

Like the others, Tony kept one hand on the ladder rail and eyed each rung for footing. A misstep could slip a leg between the rubber-covered rungs, halting everyone's progress and risking injury to a firefighter.

The angle of the ladder protected the ascending teams from direct flame contact but did little to shield them from the intense radiated heat. The situation became untenable as they climbed above Division-2 and were engulfed by smoke.

"Oh shit, that's hot," Luke said and started coughing.

"Keep your mouth shut and move your ass," Muscles said.

"Stop!" Tony called. "Go on air." He pulled his regulator from his waist belt, docked it to his facepiece, and took a deep breath of clean air. "Let's go, Luke."

The young firefighter sped his pace, and despite the conditions, both teams reached the third floor in less than one minute. At the tip of the ladder, Luke scrambled over the windowsill, dropped his irons, and tumbled inside headfirst. A second later, he popped up and announced, "The floor's solid."

"Too bad if it wasn't, you knucklehead," Muscles said as he followed Luke inside—feetfirst.

Tony tilted his head and keyed the lapel mic. "Command, search teams entering Division-3 with four."

"Copy that," McMahon responded. "Utilities are off and we're hitting the fire now, but the flames have extended to Division-2. Find those civilians and get out."

"Will do, Chief." Tony swung a leg over the sill and glanced down. The smoke had thinned, the deck gun was back in operation, and two hose teams were moving to the front of the building. *Nice work, Pet!*

Tony pulled the thermal imaging camera from the SCBA backplate, activated his chest-mounted flashlight, and made his way between a bed and a chest of drawers. From his preplan examination, he knew each floor contained a spacious residential unit with two bedrooms on Side-D and a kitchen and living room on Side-B. "Search-1, take the bedrooms, they're on the right. Romeo and I will go left to the kitchen and living room."

Tony shut the bedroom door and entered the dark hallway. Conditions were tenable, with moderate heat and no signs of fire, but they could change quickly.

Muscles, bent low and trailing Luke as they moved toward the Delta side of the apartment, called out. "Fire Department! Can anyone hear me?" There was no answer.

Bent over and moving fast, Tony turned left behind Romeo. "Fire Department. Call out if you hear me." Still nothing.

"Where the hell are they?" Romeo asked.

It was a good question. If the residents had remained at the window, they'd have been rescued by now.

"Sweep the kitchen and meet me across the hall," Tony instructed. In the background, Muscles and Luke announced their primary search of the bedrooms was complete.

Tony searched the perimeter and center of the living room before moving to the apartment door, the main entrance from the stairwell. Wisps of smoke issued from the bottom sill. Not good. He removed a glove and ran his hand over the wooden frame, which was hot to the touch. *Dammit!*

"No victims, LT," Muscles said as the others met up with Tony at the door.

"Good work, now listen up. The two civilians must have tried to escape downstairs. The floor plan is identical to this one. We know there's fire in at least one bedroom and no help coming from the hose teams." Tony examined his men. Through their facepiece visors, he detected no fear or hesitation, only determination. "We have to try," he said as the four green LEDs in his facepiece were replaced by two yellow ones. He raised the BA's control module—2230 psi. Half the air in his forty-five-minute cylinder remained, but the level would drop quickly as he exerted himself.

"Come on, LT," Muscles said. "Let's find 'em and get the hell out of here."

"I'm with you," Tony said. "Romeo, get ready to open the door. Luke, wedge it so we don't get locked out."

"Command from Search-1, the Division-3 apartment is clear. Search teams are moving to Division-2."

"Command copies, Lieutenant. Be advised we have at least two rooms off on the Delta side. Use extreme caution."

"No shit," Muscles remarked.

"Open it, Romeo," Tony ordered.

Romeo turned the knob, slid the lever on the spring-loaded deadbolt, and cracked the door. Dark smoke entered the living room as he shoved it fully open and moved onto the landing on his hands and knees. "No fire in the stairwell," he reported.

Tony followed Romeo onto the landing while Luke pulled a wooden wedge from his pocket and inserted it below the middle hinge to prevent the door from closing completely.

Muscles pulled a heavy-duty rubber strap from the crown of his helmet and looped it around both knobs and across the bolt. "Just being sure, Luke."

Luke's box light sliced through the smoke, illuminating their descent. Each step resounded with a metallic clang as Muscles dragged the water extinguisher down. On the second-floor landing, the smoke was lighter, but the heat level was noticeably worse.

Tony assessed the situation. Had the hose teams made progress on the blaze? Was it still burning and about to burst into the stairwell? "Command, search teams are entering Division-2 from the Bravo stairwell. What's the status of the fire attack?"

"Division-2 from Command, we've knocked down the bulk of the fire on Division-1, but we haven't been able to access Division-2 from the ground, and we don't dare hit it from the outside with victims unaccounted for."

"Shit, this is gonna be a bitch," Romeo said, summing up Tony's thoughts perfectly.

"You think they're still alive?" Luke asked.

"We're about to find out," Tony said. "Check the door."

Romeo removed a glove and slid it over the steel frame. "Hot . . . real hot."

Tony expected as much. "Get ready with the can, Muscles." *As if two and a half gallons of water is going to do anything if the whole floor is lit up.*

"We'll take right, Search-2, stay left. Everybody, keep low." He patted Romeo's shoulder. "Do it."

As before, Romeo cracked the door, but this time the four firefighters were met by waves of heat, while heavy smoke rolled over their heads.

Muscles practically dove through, swapping positions with Luke. Romeo followed, with Tony on his heels. *Once more unto the breach . . .*

Four firefighters, cocooned in their protective envelopes, entered a world of superheated darkness where light didn't penetrate and the most modern and costly turnout gear afforded only limited protection.

Deprived of his sense of smell and sight, Tony relied on technology, touch, and audio clues. Entering the living room, he scanned it with the thermal imager. Nothing. On his hands and knees, he searched the center.

No victims on, under, beside, or behind the sofa or chairs. As he felt his way toward Romeo, he bumped an end table and something hit him in the back.

"You okay, LT?"

"Yeah, just ruined someone's lamp. The center of the room is clear."

"The perimeter is clear," Romeo added.

"Moving into the hall," Tony announced. Still on his knees, he craned his neck and scanned the corridor with the TIC, which told him what he couldn't see through the smoke. Bright white streaks radiated down from the ceiling. The digital temperature display indicated 420 degrees . . . and climbing. His throbbing ears confirmed the danger.

"Search teams from Command, report PAR."

"Search-1 has PAR of two," Tony responded.

"Search-2 has PAR of two," Muscles added.

"Command copies. What's your status, Lieutenant?"

"Command, be advised, the living areas are clear. We're moving toward the bedrooms, but we've got rapidly deteriorating conditions in the hallway."

"Search teams from Command, exit Division-2 immediately," McMahon ordered. "The hose crews are working their way into the stairwell now."

Tony didn't respond. *We can't leave yet.* Someone's air cylinder bumped into his left side, knocking him into the wall.

"We gotta get out of here," Muscles said. "If they're in those bedrooms, they're dead."

"Lieutenant Moretti from Command, did you copy me? Get out of there, now."

Tony took a deep breath—the air from his cylinder was warm—and righted himself. "Get Romeo and Luke to the stairwell. I'm going to check one more room."

"Like hell," Muscles said. "We're not leaving without you."

Tony lowered the TIC and grabbed Muscles' shoulder. "The bathroom! We can make it. Come on."

Like infantrymen under machine-gun fire, both men dropped to their bellies and slithered forward. The LEDs in Tony's facepiece flashed red, and his quarter service bell began ringing. The pain in his ears spread to his cheeks as heat penetrated his Nomex hood. "Fire Department. Can you hear me?" Still nothing. *Dammit!*

Blue flames penetrated the smoke as a column of fire rolled over their heads. "Get down!" Tony shouted.

"I got it," Muscles said. Rolling onto his back, he aimed the nozzle of the water extinguisher at the ceiling and squeezed the handles. A tight stream tore into the flames, ricocheting off the ceiling as he worked the stream from right to left. The flames disappeared.

The extinguisher had done its job, but the stream upset the thermal balance. Heat from the ceiling plunged to the floor. Tony groaned.

"Get out of there," Romeo called from behind them as another low-air alarm bell sounded.

Tony feared a flashover, a deadly phenomenon where a rapid rise in heat creates a sudden, near-simultaneous ignition of combustible materials in an enclosed space. As if to confirm his suspicion, his BA's integrated thermal alarm wailed in a series of ascending high-pitched tones, indicating he'd been exposed to at least 350 degrees for five minutes.

"We can't take much more of this," Muscles said.

With no refuge from the heat, Tony got to his knees, tuning out the clamor of the warning bells, the electronic tones, and McMahon's voice on the radio. Was the bathroom on the right or the left? *Think!* The living room was roomier than the kitchen, so it had to be on the . . . "Muscles, the next door on your side."

"On it," Muscles said, already moving, with his Halligan scraping across the uncarpeted hallway. "Got it."

Operating solely by touch, Tony followed Muscles, who'd pushed the door inward.

"It's a fucking closet," Muscles shouted.

What? That made no sense. "Then it's got to be the next one," Tony said. "I'm going for it."

Tony stuck his left hand to the wall and crawled forward. *Come on, come on.* An indentation—the door. "I found it!" He reached up, turned the knob, and pushed. The door moved slightly. He pushed again. It opened a little more but sprang shut. "Shit!"

Muscles edged Tony to the right. "Are they in there?"

"Yeah, must be a body against the door. I'll take high."

Waves of heat distorting the air, Tony rose to a crouch, braced his shoulder against the door, and pushed. "Aaaaargh," he groaned as his fatigued quad muscles impelled him forward. With Muscles pushing from below, the door moved just enough for entry.

Tony tumbled into the bathroom, landing beside a motionless figure at the door. In the instant before smoke obscured his view, he spotted a woman's head hanging over the side of the bathtub.

He rolled the prone figure—a big guy—away from the door, allowing Muscles to open it fully. "Take this one. I'll get the one in the tub."

Tony got himself low, hooked his hands under the woman's armpits, and, using his butt for leverage, heaved. God, she was heavy. The woman, as obese as her husband, flopped onto the floor. The impact sent him sprawling. His air cylinder slammed into the toilet bowl with a shattering crack while his helmet smacked the tank, sending a loud reverberation through the space. Stunned, he gripped the edge of the sink and pulled himself up.

"Christ, LT, what was that racket?" Muscles asked as he pitched in to help evacuate the unconscious woman. "Was that your head?"

Tony barely registered the questions.

"Come on," Muscles said. "Romeo and Luke have the guy."

No words were exchanged as Tony and Muscles, side by side and grasping the woman's armpits, dragged her into the hallway.

Despite his fatigue and lightheadedness, Tony's effort didn't slacken, and the pain in his ears was forgotten. As his low-air alarm bell clanged its warning, his vision blurred. *Just a little farther.* He stumbled and lost his hold on the woman. *I can make it.* Though his limbs protested, he re-gripped her arm.

With one last pull, his body collided with the panic bar as he and Muscles crashed through the door with the woman in tow. He dropped to one knee, removed his facepiece and helmet, ran a hand through his sweaty hair, and began to laugh.

"You okay, LT?" Romeo asked.

"Never better," he replied as the scene got fuzzy. "Guess that takes care of tonight's workout." Laughing again, he felt himself falling backward. Voices . . . then nothing.

***

A face hovered. Hands appeared . . . lifting his head and offering a bottle of water. "Welcome back, LT," Muscles said.

Tony drained half the lukewarm liquid and eased his head back onto something soft.

"It's our hoods, LT, we didn't have anything else to use for a pillow."

"Nice work, LT." The voice was Romeo's, standing beside Luke on the stairs.

"You're the man, LT," Luke added.

"How long was I . . .?"

"Out?" Muscles asked. "Only a few seconds, but you've been in a fog for the last five minutes. Not bad considering that crack you took to your head." Muscles narrowed his eyes. "Didn't you promise me no heroics today?"

Tony offered a weak shrug. The smoke was gone and an inch-and-three-quarter hoseline snaked into the door to the hallway. The hose jerked up and dropped to the floor.

"Engine pukes," Muscles said. "Just don't know how to open and close a nozzle slowly."

Tony smiled as cool air washed overhead. "PPV?"

"Yep," Romeo said. "They finally knocked the fire on Division-1 and cleared the stairwell. They're mopping up this floor now. They kept the fire out of the exposures, but the bakery has some smoke damage."

"Maybe we'll get to keep the goodies," Luke said. "They're just going to throw them out."

Muscles shot the youngster the kind of look a parent gives to a petulant child.

"Good thing the stairs were still intact," Romeo said, "Or they would've had to take the victims down from that third-floor window."

Victims. Tony's senses came fully alert. "Did they make it?"

"Looks like they'll live. Tower-502's crew just took 'em downstairs on portable stretchers. The guy was worse off. Barely any pulse. The woman was breathing okay and regained consciousness while they were carrying her down."

"All that happened in five minutes?"

"When the *Mafia's* bravest get in gear, we don't mess around," Luke said and raised a hand for a high five.

"Shut up, you nitwit," Muscles said, ignoring the gesture. "When we get back to the station, we're gonna talk about how you entered the building."

Luke's smile faded.

Tony took another swig of water and poured the rest over his face as the radio crackled.

"Command from Attack-1, the fire on Division-2 is out."

"I copy that, Attack-1," McMahon replied. "County, Commerce Street Command. This fire has been extinguished. The scene is under control, but we'll be here a while. Keep our mutual aid transfers in place."

"County copies. Fire under control at 1308. We'll advise mutual aid to remain in place."

Tony reached a hand to Muscles, who hoisted him to his feet. "All right, my friends. Our work is done. What say we get the hell out of here?"

Shortly after exiting the structure, McMahon beckoned Tony over. *Here comes another ass chewing.*

"How are you, Lieutenant? I understand you hit your head and lost consciousness."

"I'm good, Chief. Just a little bump on the head."

"I doubt that," McMahon said as he eyed Tony closely. "You disobeyed my order to evacuate. It's becoming a pattern with you."

"Sorry, Chief. I knew the victims were close."

McMahon waved him off. "I should suspend you, but you saved the lives of two residents. That's twice in the last two months. A real coup for our young fire department."

"It was my crew. Without them—"

McMahon raised a hand. "I know, it was a collective effort, but you were the catalyst. You have your rough edges, and God knows you take too many chances, but your ability to think on your feet and take decisive action is a rare commodity, and I'm glad you're a part of my team." The chief stuck out his hand. "Congratulations, Lieutenant Moretti."

***

Citing the blow to Tony's head and his brief loss of consciousness, McMahon directed the paramedics to transport Tony to the University of Pittsburgh Medical Center in McKeesport.

After a CT scan failed to detect a brain injury, the ER doctor consulted with a staff neurologist, who explained that the symptoms of a concussion might not manifest until days or weeks after an injury. He told Tony to be on guard for headaches, confusion, or loss of memory and urged him to schedule an MRI as soon as possible. Tony assured the doctor he would follow his instructions, and after three hours of observation, he was released with the stipulation that someone drive him home.

He dressed, pulled out his phone, and considered. His crew was still on duty, but they'd be busy reservicing the equipment. He scrolled through his contact list until he reached Fitzgerald. Had he been at the scene? He didn't think so, and it was worth a try. Fifteen minutes later, as Tony sat in a wheelchair with his discharge instructions in one hand and a bottle of ibuprofen in the other, Fitz entered the double glass doors to the emergency department.

"What have you done this time?" Fitz asked, a concerned look on his face.

"What can I say?" Tony replied. "Trouble seems to follow me wherever I go."

"Uh-huh. You sure it isn't clumsiness? I hear you used that hard Italian head of yours to destroy a perfectly good urinal."

"It was a *toilet*, and I used my helmet. My brain is still intact."

"Thank the Lord for small miracles," Fitz said, and executed a slow and exaggerated sign of the cross.

"Hah hah hah. Where the heck were you anyway? Never thought you'd miss *the . . . big . . . one.*"

"Financial seminar at our main office in Oxford Center. Saw the text but couldn't leave. They pay my bills, you know."

Maybe not for long, Tony thought but didn't say. It was a topic for another day.

"I hear you did all right. You're gonna be a bona fide officer someday."

"High praise, but can you get me out of here?"

"Your apartment?"

"Nope, my car's at the station."

"His car might be at the station, but he's not going to drive it anywhere for twenty-four hours."

Tony wheeled the chair sideways. A nurse eyed him with a stern look. "Trying to tempt fate twice in one day?"

"Benjamin Fitzpatrick, meet Jennifer Ratched, RN."

"I . . . aah . . . Ratched?" Fitz asked, stumbling over his words like a schoolboy as he eyed the red-haired beauty.

"It's Kelly, Jennifer Kelly," she said, a bright red flush spreading across her peachy complexion.

"I stand corrected," Tony said. As he got to his feet, the room began to spin.

Fitz grabbed Tony's arms. "Whoa, buddy, take it easy."

Tony's vision cleared. "I'm okay."

"So you think," Nurse Kelly said. "Are you going to go home, or do I have to keep you here until morning?"

"Yes, ma'am, I'll go home."

In the car, he couldn't resist teasing his chauffeur. "Jen is pretty cute, don't you think?"

"Who?"

"Don't give me that, I saw how you looked at her."

"I suppose, but I don't know a thing about her."

"You know her name and where she works. Two Irish thirtysomethings. What else do you need?"

"What I don't need is a matchmaker."

"Could've fooled me," Tony mumbled.

"What was that?"

"Nothing, my friend. Nothing at all."

33

Thursday, January 8

"We have mechanics, you know," Pet said. "In fact, you're violating their union contract right now."

Fitz, lying on his back on a crawler, switched the shop light off and poked his head out from under Engine-301 and noted the disapproving look on Pet's face.

"Top of the morning to you, too, Pet."

"This isn't your volunteer fire department anymore."

"Don't blow a gasket. I'm not trying to fix anything, I just wanted to pinpoint the source of this pump leak. You know, so I can pass the details along to those mechanics."

"Right. That's why your toolbox is on the floor next to you. In case they don't bring their own. Makes sense."

"Busted," he said. "What can I say? I'm used to finding *and* fixing problems. I can't get used to this new reality." Which was an understatement. He abhorred the new system.

"Your secret is safe with me, and anyway, I don't give a shit." Pet gave the crawler a kick. "Get up and put your shirt back on. The chief's looking for you."

Fitz rolled himself out, stood, and wiped his hands on a rag. "Me? What for?"

"Didn't say. But I'd get my ass upstairs to his office, fast. He didn't look happy."

"Damn, what did I do now?"

"What do you care?" Pet asked. "How much cash will you lose if he cans you? A few hundred bucks a month?"

"It's not the money," Fitz said.

"Think of the free time you'll have for your other hobbies."

"Firefighting, Acting Lieutenant Petruska, is my passion. Besides, I don't have any hobbies."

"Then be respectful, and maybe he'll let you stay on as our mascot."

"You're a riot, Pet," he said with a laugh. But he didn't feel joyful as he climbed the steps to MAFA headquarters.

Iris, standing at the coffeemaker, greeted him. "Go right in. He's waiting for you."

"That's what I'm afraid of."

"There he is," Ramsey said. "Come in, Fitz. Grab a seat."

Iris followed close behind, cradling a steaming mug. "Black and bitter, just as you like it," she said as she set the mug in front of Fitz.

A low chuckle rumbled from the doorway. "Yeah, cream and sugar are for rookies."

Fitz twisted in his chair to find Tony Moretti, flanked by Lieutenant Sam Condon from A-Platoon—vice president of IAFF Local 5631. *Uh-oh.* The pair took seats on either side of Fitz. Their faces betrayed no emotion. *They're being very coy if this is a firing squad.*

Ramsey began. "Fitz, we've called you here to talk about an error in judgment we made last year when we offered you the opportunity as a paid-on-call volunteer."

Fitz's heart sank. *This is it.* The career guys, or maybe their union, wanted him out. "But, Chief, I thought the program was working."

Ramsey waved him off. "This error was a major one, but we're going to correct it now, if you let us."

If I let them? How, by resigning?

"We allowed you to volunteer as a *firefighter* on this platoon, and that was wrong."

Where was this going? Fitz had no clue.

"We should have offered you the chance to serve in a *career* capacity."

Okay, they're not going to get rid of me. "Thanks, Chief, but I had the same opportunity to work here as anyone else and I chose not to apply. That's on me, not you."

"I disagree. It *is* on me. I should have offered you a captain's slot."

Fitz stared at the chief.

"Look, we know you're a talented accountant with a great job," Ramsey said. "Why would you leave it for a rookie firefighter's salary and an entry-level job?"

"Chief, wow, I never—"

"Hear me out. As you know, this is a unionized fire department, but we're not civil service. That means we can hire based on our own guidelines, which, as you know, include an aptitude test, a comprehensive medical exam, a rigorous physical agility test, and a résumé.

"And we can promote based on an oral interview, without taking seniority into account. The IAFF agreed to those terms when we presented them with the opportunity to add a hundred new firefighters to their rolls. That's why Lieutenant Condon is here."

Fitz turned to Condon, who smiled but said nothing.

"We're going to sweeten the offer by crediting some of your time as a River Bend volunteer," Ramsey said. "Fifteen years, in fact. You'll start at the top of the pay scale."

"Chief, I'm flattered, but I'm not sure a paid job as a firefighter is the best thing for me."

"Not as a firefighter, dummy," Tony interjected. "As the captain of B-Platoon."

Captain? Fitz couldn't believe what he was hearing. A million things ran through his mind. *Can I quit my job? I'm thirty-seven. Is it too late to do this?* And there was something else. "But that means I'd jump over Lieutenant Moretti, who's been acting captain since Barney retired."

"Lieutenant Moretti came to me with the idea," Ramsey said.

Fitz looked at his new friend, who sported a shit-eating grin.

"You think I want to be captain?" Tony asked. "I'm barely keeping my head above water as a lieutenant."

"Thanks, Tony," was all Fitz could muster as his emotions welled up.

"Firefighter Fitzpatrick, I'm formally offering you the captain's slot vacated by Barney Dudek." Ramsey paused and, when Fitz didn't reply, added, "I can see you're conflicted. We hit you with this out of the blue and I understand completely if you'd like some time to think it over."

"I'll take it!" The words left his lips before he thought any further about the implications. An opportunity like this wouldn't come around again. He could always do the accounting gig on the side. *I've wanted to set up my own business, anyway.*

Now it was Ramsey's turn to look stunned. "All right, then. We need to work out the details, and I'm sure you'll want to give notice to your current employer, so let's set a target date about three weeks out." Ramsey examined the departmental schedule posted on the wall beside his desk. "How about Monday, January 26? That's the first day of the next B-Platoon pay period."

Fitz stood. "That's perfect, Chief. I won't disappoint you."

"I know you won't," Ramsey said.

Fitz shook hands with Ramsey and Condon, then turned to Tony and wrapped him in an embrace that nearly lifted the big man off his feet.

"I think we've made him happy," Ramsey said. "By the way, I hope Firefighter Petruska carried out a believable ruse."

"Oh yes. She had me convinced this was my last day."

In fact, it was a new beginning, and Fitz was going to make the most of it.

***

"**D**id you call me into your office to scream at me again and throw your tennis ball at my head?" Fitz asked with a mischievous glint in his eye.

Tony suppressed a laugh. "Not unless you give me cause. I can only imagine the revenge you'd take when you become my boss in a few weeks."

"Hmm . . . a lieutenant on latrine duty for a month." Fitz grinned. "Now that would be one for the MAFA history books."

Tony let out a theatrical sigh. "Have a seat, soon-to-be Captain Fitzgerald, and for God's sake, brush those cookie crumbs off that lip duster. How many mustache hairs do you ingest when you eat?"

"Probably fewer than the spiders that crawl into your mouth at night."

"Disgusting," Tony said in mock revulsion.

"Seriously, Tony. I can't thank you enough for what you've done for me."

"It wasn't just me. There are a lot of people in your corner."

"Bullshit, it was you."

"I did what I could. You deserve it," Tony said, thrilled that Fitz had accepted Ramsey's offer. "But I called you here to show you something."

"Oh?"

"As you know, the arsonist is back at it. A vacant house on the east end of town three days before Christmas—that was a C-Platoon shift. Then A-Platoon caught another one in Furnace on New Year's Day. Guy must not have any family or social life."

"Yeah, Dez is in on a police task force trying to catch the guy. They think he's a loner."

"Interesting," Tony said, surprised at the revelation. "Any leads?"

"Dez is pretty tight-lipped about it, but he mentioned the police might have a couple of photos of the suspect. Unfortunately, nothing clear enough to ID the scumbag. It's all hush-hush for now."

"I see." Tony opened the top drawer and pulled out a manila envelope. "Take a look at these." He handed Fitz the eight five-by-seven photos he'd printed of the man in the black hoodie.

Fitz flipped through the photos. "Where'd you get these?"

"From Terrell's fire scene shots. I cropped and enlarged the guy. He's been present at three fires, at least."

"This is good stuff," Fitz said as he ran through the photos again. "Wow, the guy's looking directly at the camera in this one."

"Can you get them to Dez and his . . . task force?" Tony asked. "Tell him Terrell can ID the guy, if necessary."

"You bet. He's working the sergeant's desk today. I'll take them there right now. This might be the break they need."

Satisfied, Tony nodded. *Good work, Terrell, good work.*

34

Tuesday, January 20

Dressed in thermal underwear, black sweatpants, hoodie, knit cap, and gloves, Dylan hunkered beside an old trash bin as he scanned for signs of life behind the former Gilbertson Tire Center. God, it was cold.

As he aged, he understood the pull of warmer climates. His parents lived in North Carolina, but he suspected their move was more of an escape from the memories of the restaurant they'd been forced to close than a happy sojourn into the sun. Casualties of the region's decline and the failure of local officials to do anything about it.

No movement, no sound. The parking lot behind the vacant tire center was still. He'd encountered a matted, shivering mutt and two feral cats during his three-block trek through the trash-infested alleyways, but little else. The dopers and their scumbag dealers wouldn't be out on a night like this.

Spooked by his encounter with that woman at the theater fire in October, he'd lain low for two months, but his weeding called to him again. By Christmas, he'd set an abandoned house ablaze, and another had followed on New Year's Day. It was now time for a much bigger target.

He'd scouted the abandoned tire center three days ago and identified the rear door as his best chance for an unseen entry. With an alley in the back and vacant lots on either side, he had no fear of fire spreading to an occupied business, like the theater fire had.

Concrete blocks framed the door, but a slender gap winked between it and the rusty frame. He retrieved his short crowbar and jammed it into the breach, prying it wider with a grunt of effort. From his pack, he retrieved a specialized putty knife and slid its curved blade between the frame and the door. With a downward swipe, he dislodged the bolt with a satisfying clink. The door groaned open, releasing a metallic screech as he edged himself into the inky darkness within.

The stale air assaulted him, thick with the musty scent of mildew and the reek of rubber. *Tires . . . perfect!*

He fumbled for the flashlight, switched it on, and looked around. Unlike what he'd found in the abandoned beauty salon, this place was a treasure trove of things to burn. He panned the light over boxes, fifty-five-gallon drums of who knew what, miscellaneous junk, and tires.

Tires everywhere! Stacked in the corners and strewn across the floor. Along the back wall, two metal storage racks were loaded with more tires. The racks stretched to the underside of the roof, which, he noted, was made of corrugated metal.

This area, set apart from the main service floor, was only half of the cavernous building, but it would do nicely. No need to explore further. Everything he needed was right here. Tires were a bitch to ignite, but he was determined, and after placing the flashlight on a wall-mounted shelf to light his way, he set to work.

The minutes slipped away as Dylan erected pyramids of rubber. Sweat dripped from his brow as he wrestled the massive truck tires into place, flipping them onto their sides and tossing smaller ones on top. By the time his arms gave out, each mound reached the second tier of stacked storage. Good enough.

Working quickly in the eerie glow, he snatched a can of lighter fluid, climbed the edge of the first rack, and, with one hand gripping the truss-like structure, sprayed the volatile liquid across the stacked tires. He jumped down, grabbed another can, and repeated the process on the second rack. With the last can of fluid, he doused the two base piles. Was it enough? He wasn't sure, but he'd done all he could to set the stage for a fiery spectacle.

Retrieving the flashlight, he pulled a butane lighter from the backpack and touched it to the first pile. Flames enveloped the mound and two of the four shelves above it. "All right!" he voiced with satisfaction. Time to finish the job before the smoke and heat forced him outside.

At a crouch, he scooted to the opposite rack, sparked the lighter, and stopped. "Shit." The flames in the first rack were petering out. "Damn it to hell!" He'd been afraid of this possibility. The lighter fluid couldn't sustain the flames long enough to heat the rubber into a self-sustaining blaze. And he'd emptied all three cans. *Now what do I do?*

So much effort and nothing to show for it. He'd worked up a sweat, and now his soaked clothing wrapped him like an icebox. Maybe he should have made an exception to his no-gasoline rule. Could he try again tomorrow night? Too risky. But maybe . . .

Panning the light across the room, he eyed the fifty-five-gallon drums. All three were painted black, with no identifying markings. They could be empty, or filled with nothing more volatile than antifreeze. *But I'm gonna check before I write this night off as a total waste of time.*

Cold metal bit into his hands as he gripped the top of the first barrel, straining to tip it over. It barely budged, but the sloshing sound inside told him it was nearly full. The container had a screw-on cap, but he couldn't turn it.

He pulled his gloves from the hoodie's pocket and moved to the second barrel. This time, the cap yielded. Breathing through his mouth to block out the smell of burnt rubber, he unscrewed it, bent to the opening, and took a whiff. "Diesel!"

Unsure and shivering violently, he forced himself to think. He'd read about diesel fuel. It wasn't easy to light, but if you got it going, it burned hot. Would it work on tires? Was there enough? Could he get it to the high rack storage?

With nothing to lose, he retrieved the short crowbar and swung it into the bottom of the first drum. The blow didn't penetrate the metal, but it made a dent. He hit it again. The spot deepened. "Come on, you bastard!" With a final, forceful strike, the crowbar punctured the drum, sending liquid splashing over his shoes. "Yes!" Working the tool in a circular motion, he enlarged the gash until diesel fuel poured out freely.

Dylan forgot the cold as he swung the crowbar like a madman on steroids, pummeling the other containers until they spilled their contents. Energized by adrenaline, he grabbed a scattered tire and rolled it to the pool of liquid. With a swift flip, he used it like a squeegee, pushing the fuel to the base of the two pyramids. Discarding the tire, he scooped the fuel with his gloved hands, lobbing it across the singed rubber. Soon his clothes were soaked, but he didn't care.

Fumes filled the storage area, and Dylan swallowed hard to push away the queasy feeling at the back of his throat. Retreating to the doorway, he cracked the rusted panel open and peered outside. His eyes, well adjusted to the dark, detected no movement, but now it was raining. He edged his body through the door, took a deep breath of crisp night air, and vomited.

Leaning back against the block wall, he wriggled out of his sodden pack and rubbed his temples. The contents of his stomach covered the ground, and his clothes reeked of diesel, but the nausea had passed. He gathered himself, took several deep breaths, and reentered the tire center. The beam of his flashlight reflected off the fuel-covered floor.

Dylan always carried two lighters, and now he merged both flames as he willed the diesel to catch. Nothing happened for almost a minute, but then a small circle of fire blossomed at his feet. He kept his fingers on the triggers, watching the flames as they grew and spread deeper into the storage area.

He backed up to the doorway as fire caught the piles at the base of each rack. The wait was torturous, but soon particles of burnt rubber coated his tongue and the inside of his nose. *This fire isn't going out.*

Cold and exhausted, and with the rain adding to his misery, he was nevertheless thrilled by his accomplishment. After one last satisfied glimpse at the growing flames, he hoisted the pack, slammed the door shut, and melted into the night.

35

Tuesday, January 20

"County, BC-1 is on the scene of the old Gilbertson Tire Center, 4311 Industrial Way," Chief McMahon radioed. "Heavy smoke showing from Side-A. No exposures. I'll have Command."

"County receives, working fire. Gilbertson Tire, River Bend. Command established at 0119."

Tony eyed the dashboard indicator in Ladder-302's cab as the thumping wipers battled to keep the relentless drizzle at bay. The outside temperature was twenty-nine degrees, threatening to transform South Shore Boulevard into a skating rink.

According to the preplan on the MDT, the vacant Gilbertson Tire Center featured a one-hundred-by-eighty-foot service bay, separated from a thirty-by-eighty-foot tire storage area by a block wall. An uninsulated bar joist roof ran the length of both sections, while a frame roof covered a one-story attached wing housing a showroom and offices.

"The platoon did a walk-through of that place last summer," Danny said. "Been closed for years, but there's old tires everywhere."

"Yeah, it's noted on the last fire prevention inspection," Tony agreed as he studied the display. "Tires stacked and scattered in the storage area, plus a couple of old delivery trucks in the service bays. No sprinkler system, of course, or the fire would be out by now."

"Utilities gotta be shut off in there, and I ain't betting on spontaneous combustion."

"Me either," Tony agreed. "A vacant structure on fire at one thirty in the morning? Has to be the arsonist."

"The cops need to catch that asshole."

"And soon," Tony added as he toggled the radio switch. "Command, Station-300 apparatus approaching."

"Command copies," McMahon replied. "Position Ladder-302 at the Alpha-Bravo corner. Engine-301, lay in. Engine-401, follow them in and pump the hydrant. Engine-501 and Tower-502, when you arrive, take position on Side-C and stand by."

As Ladder-302 rumbled past the battalion chief's wagon, Tony's ears perked up to a sudden whump, and his head snapped sideways in time to see the showroom window burst outward, raining glass fragments onto the asphalt. Flames licked the brickwork while heavy black smoke poured from the gaping hole.

Chief McMahon, silhouetted by flames, rushed to the cab as Danny braked to a halt. "Tony, I'm putting you in charge of Operations," McMahon said as water dripped from the brim of his helmet. "Knock that fire down and get access to the service bays."

"Got it, Chief."

"Keep me apprised while I get things organized and call for reinforcements," McMahon added.

As Tony jumped down from his seat, he plunged into a pothole, his right foot twisting as it landed. A sharp, searing pain radiated through his ankle, causing him to wince and stumble. "Damn it!"

"Easy, LT," Muscles said, grabbing Tony by the arm.

"Thanks," he said and scanned the building. Other than the main entrance to the blazing showroom, he could see no other man-sized access point. "I want you to cut a hole in that overhead garage door so we can check the conditions inside. Take the rescue crew with you, but leave two firefighters with the truck in case we need them on the roof."

"Copy that, LT," Muscles replied. "What a night for this shit."

Tony hit the transmit button on his lapel mic. "Engine-301, from Operations, I want a blitz attack through the showroom window with your Stinger."

"Engine-301 copies," Pet replied. "But we can hit the fire quicker with the deck gun."

"Negative," Tony radioed. "You need to hit it from the ground." With the optimal angle, the Stinger's powerful water stream would cut through the flames, creating a giant sprinkler-like effect as thousands of droplets ricocheted off the ceiling and saturated the space. The deck gun, mounted atop the pumper, couldn't achieve the same outcome since the crew would have to aim it downward. *Okay, smart boy, Time to see if theory matches reality.*

Pet exited Engine-301's cab and barked orders. Warren, in full turnout gear and SCBA, dashed to the hosebed and hefted the preconnected Stinger—a portable master stream device with a ground base, stream shaper, and four stacked solid-bore tips—from the tailboard.

Fitz, working his last shift as a paid-on-call volunteer, pulled a section of the color coded blue, lightweight three-inch line onto his shoulder. His presence had averted the need to transfer a body to the engine and leave the truck crew shorthanded.

Fitz, you couldn't have picked a more opportune shift to ride with us.

Moving with purpose, Warren planted the Stinger, spread the feet of its base section, and spun the handwheel to angle the nozzle tip upward.

Fitz flaked out the remaining hose and took backup position behind Warren.

"Use the two-inch tip," Tony barked. "I want a thousand gallons per minute on that fire."

Warren complied by unscrewing the top three stacked tips, leaving the two-inch orifice exposed.

Maddie, who'd wrapped and charged the hydrant with practiced efficiency, teamed up with Pet to deploy an inch-and-three-quarter attack line behind the master stream crew. The entire operation had taken less than two minutes.

"Charge the blue line," Fitz radioed.

Big Pappy, standing ready at Engine-301's pump panel controls, charged the master stream carefully. The sheer force of such a torrent could be lethal, and the anchor might not hold, risking the heavy device skidding across the slick asphalt or lifting off the ground.

Once Pappy dialed up to the predetermined nozzle pressure of 80 psi, the Stinger cut through the flames as if passing through clear air, bouncing off the ceiling in an earsplitting machine-gun staccato. The fire darkened in thirty seconds. A few spot fires remained, probably the tires, but the main body was out.

"Yes, that's the way it's done, Warren!" Tony bellowed. "Engine-301, shut the blitz line." Ankle throbbing and drenched with icy water, he beamed with pride. His crew had performed flawlessly. Pet, an officer in all but title, stood out—surpassed in skill only by Fitz. The stars were aligned tonight. "Command from Operations, we've extinguished the fire in the showroom."

"I see it from here, Lieutenant. Nice work," McMahon replied. "Be advised, Engine-501 and Tower-502 are on the scene with Captain Jenkins on Side-C. He's reporting smoke from the roof and is raising the aerial to get a better look. Station-600's troops are arriving now. I'll send them to you."

"Ops copies. We're mopping up the showroom and moving to the service bays now."

"Great call on the blitz line, LT," Pet said. "Want us to hit the hot spots?"

"That's affirmative. Just do it from *outside* the window. It won't take much for that ceiling to come down."

"I'm cautious to a fault," Pet said. Maddie took the nozzle, and they began hosing down the smoldering remains of the showroom fire.

The din of carbide blades cutting into steel resonated across the parking lot. Tony turned toward the crew, who were working feverishly to create an entry in the roll-up door.

Fitz, his handlebar mustache coated with ice, called to Tony. "Don't think that blitz attack order means you know what you're doing, Mr. Operations Section Chief. I would have done it better."

"Hah! Of course you would've, and twice as fast, but we're not done yet." Tony pointed to the garage. "They're going to need heavy stream backup once they cut that access point."

"You got it, boss," Fitz said. "Come on, Warren, we're moving this show to the garage. Disconnect the Stinger and I'll drain the line."

Engine-601's newly arrived personnel stepped in for Pet and Maddie, freeing them to rejoin the rest of Tony's waterlogged firefighters at the garage door. Sparks flew as the twin K-12 saws bit into the corrugated steel, creating a shower of fiery fragments.

"Look at that light show," Pet remarked.

"We're in," Muscles shouted as he and Corey killed the K-12s and an eerie silence descended over the scene.

Tony scrutinized the rectangular cut. Five feet high and three feet wide, with two small pieces of metal left intact at the bottom to hold the panel in place.

"Good work, men," Tony said. "Let's see what we've got. Open it up slowly."

Muscles and Luke stepped forward and widened the gap on either side of the cut with their Halligan tools. Corey and Dontrell moved in next, pike poles in hand. With a synchronized pull, the metal pieces snapped off and the door crashed to the pavement. As the four firefighters dragged the door aside, thin tendrils of smoke curled up from the top of the cut.

"There's barely any smoke," Luke said. "The fire must be out. We did it!"

"Don't bet on it, probie," Pet said. "It's hiding from us, but it's still cooking in there, somewhere."

Tony shared her concern as he keyed the mic. "Command from Operations, we have access to the service bays."

"Command copies. Use extreme caution, Lieutenant."

Tony dropped to his knees and shined his box light into the darkened bay. He discerned four delivery trucks and a high layer of smoke, but no visible fire. *Something's not right.*

He hit the mic again. "Tower-502 from Operations, what do you see from your vantage point?"

"Operations from 500-Captain," Jenkins replied. "We're looking down at the roof now. It's tough to make out through this rain and fog, but there's definitely smoke, maybe from the HVAC vents or maybe the insulation layers."

"Ops copies." *What the hell is going on inside?* "Muscles, get down here with the TIC. Let's see what we've got. Check the joists first."

Muscles aimed the thermal imaging camera at the underside of the roof. "Take a look at this," he said and handed the TIC to Tony. "Directly above us, it's a hundred and fifty degrees. But it gets hotter as you scan toward the rear. It's over five hundred degrees at the back of the bays."

Tony eyed the display. Bright white heat signatures jabbed out from the intersection of the roof and the top of the block wall. "I see it. Something's going on behind the bays in that tire storage room."

"Christ, you're right," Muscles said. "The fire must've gotten into the tires."

"That's a good bet, but whatever it is, those joists are heating up fast." Tony handed the TIC to Muscles and keyed his mic. "Command from Operations, the temperature is spiking along the underside of the service bay roof. We think there's a fire in the storage room, maybe tires or flammable liquids. I'm pulling everyone back."

Jenkins broke in before McMahon could reply. "Command from 500-Captain, the smoke just got heavy back here, mostly along the parapet. There's definitely fire under this roof." After a pause, he added, "I don't like this, Chief."

"Command copies," McMahon acknowledged. "Moretti, get everyone out of the collapse zone, now."

Tony, already moving, yanked Muscles' shoulder. "Everybody back! Leave the equipment."

Discarded tools clattered to the ground as firefighters scrambled away from the building. Amid the chaos, Tony spotted Fitz, hauling the Stinger and its attached hose to the hole in the garage door.

"Fitz! Get back here!"

"One second, LT. I'm gonna plant this thing so we can cool the joists," he shouted as he dropped the Stinger into place.

"Leave it! Get out of there now!" Tony's cries were joined by shouts from the crew, imploring Fitz to retreat.

Ignoring their pleas, Fitz spun the Stinger's tip up as the air filled with a series of cracks, pops, and the rumble of bricks giving way. "Tell Big

Pappy to charge the line," he shouted, making a break for the street.

Tony's heart pounded as he watched the tire center's wall bulge out. The parapet fell first, followed instantly by the entire front wall. Fitz reached out a hand, his eyes wide with terror as thousands of bricks buried him in a thunderous, earth-shaking collapse.

36

Saturday, January 24

Six pallbearers in full dress uniform, including Captain Dudek, whose tears belied the stoic expression on his face, carried the casket from the Romanesque Catholic cathedral and lifted it to the empty hosebed of Engine-301, which had been scrubbed, polished, and draped in black bunting. Tony, along with every member of B-Platoon, stood at attention and saluted as they passed.

Mourners, civilians interspersed with ranks of uniformed firefighters, police, and EMS personnel from all over the Pittsburgh metropolitan area, pressed closely together on the church's sprawling lawn and overflowed the sidewalks.

Tony caught sight of Jennifer Kelly, the nurse Fitz had met in the emergency room two weeks earlier. Had they dated yet? He shook his head, imagining what might have been.

Overhead, an immense American flag, suspended between the fully extended arms of Ladder-302 and Tower-502, flapped defiantly in the chilly breeze as the procession got underway. With Chief Ramsey and his deputies leading the way and Engine-301 close behind, emergency vehicles formed an unbroken line almost a mile along Main Street.

Mourners gathered along the route from the church to the Steelworkers Memorial Bridge and picked up the vigil on the other side. The solemn two-mile journey continued through Union Center and wound up the southern-facing slopes of Washington Heights, where the little cemetery awaited the fallen hero.

Such was the respect Mon Valley residents held not only for Fitz but also for his father, Daniel Fitzgerald. Two men who'd dedicated their lives to the service of their community. Tony guessed Fitz's parents would have swelled with pride at the sight.

The drive passed in a blur. Riding in the front seat of Battalion Chief McMahon's SUV, directly behind the flag-draped casket atop Engine-301, Tony sat in silence, his emotions a mixture of sadness, regret, and disbelief.

Try as he might, he couldn't wrap his head around the events of four days ago. The guy who had given him such a hard time in September and October, who'd since become a trusted friend, was gone. One minute, they'd been joking about promotions, and the next, Fitz was buried under an avalanche of bricks and crumbled mortar.

Every firefighter on the scene that night, Tony foremost among them, worked frantically with tools and gloved hands to dig through the rubble. Paramedics stood ready to render lifesaving aid and a Life Flight helicopter waited in a makeshift landing zone to fly him to a trauma center, but Fitz was beyond help.

Among the first to uncover the body, Tony knew the sight of his friend's bloodied, lifeless face would be seared into his memory forever, along with the image of Fitz running toward him with his arm outstretched as the walls of the tire center collapsed.

Fitz was laid to rest next to his parents in a plot overlooking the Mon River, with a clear view of his beloved River Bend. Audible sobs from the gathered mourners mixed with strains of "Amazing Grace," played by a traditional Scottish bagpiper in full Highland dress.

Tony, devastated but keeping it together, looked on in silence. *I didn't know you long, but I'll honor your memory, buddy. Please keep watch over us.*

***

Immediately after the cemetery service, friends held a wake in Fitz's memory at the Hibernian Club banquet hall in Mill Town. Tony stopped in as a measure of respect, but he didn't stay long. He wasn't in the mood for a party, no matter how well intentioned. Besides, how could he celebrate a life he knew so little about? Instead, he turned to a familiar form of self-therapy, solitary outdoor exertion.

When he'd lived in central Pennsylvania, Allie had worked him into the best shape of his life by running his ass off on the trail abutting the airport perimeter road. But during times of crisis or tragedy, when he'd needed to bring clarity to his life situation and ponder his next moves, the roadways of the nearby Gettysburg National Battlefield had been his choice. Gettysburg wasn't an option today, and since his running shape had deteriorated since those airport days, he opted for an extended bike ride.

Returning to the apartment, he wrapped his sprained ankle, dug his cold-weather gear from a box in the closet, pumped the tires of his Cannondale CX to 45 psi, and carried it down the steps to the Cherokee. Fifteen minutes later, he arrived at the McKeesport trailhead of the Greater Allegheny Passage—or GAP—which stretched from downtown Pittsburgh to Washington, D.C.

After taking a swig of Gatorade, he donned his riding gloves and sunglasses, secured a helmet over his knit cap, and pedaled northwest on a route that took him through the once-bustling Monongahela Valley.

Crossing the Mon on a repurposed railroad bridge, Tony noticed the traffic below, where a long, square-bowed towboat carved waves through the water, its chugging engines driving six open-hopper coal barges upstream. To one side of the barge, a nimble pleasure boat—a rare sight this time of year—slid gracefully past, music emanating from its enclosed cabin. A unique river symphony.

Tony had anticipated years of friendship and collaboration with Fitz as his captain, but now he needed the strength to move past this personal and professional setback.

How would Fitz's death, on the heels of Barney Dudek's retirement, affect B-Platoon? Fitz would have been the perfect man for the captain's job, and everybody knew it. Now, the responsibility of keeping the platoon united and functioning was up to Tony. *And I refuse to let them down.*

Tony entered a zone as he slid past the former mill towns of West Mifflin and Duquesne on his left, and the gently lapping waves of the Mon on his right. Up ahead, the Steel Curtain roller coaster of Kennywood Amusement Park came into view through the lifeless trees. He focused on the ride's brightly painted superstructure—a special formulation from PPG known as Steelers Yellow—and took stock of his psychological state.

Not long ago, his PTSD would have taken over, leaving him unable to function. Yet today, though deeply saddened, he felt a surprising sense of calm. Was he growing numb to tragedy and suffering, or was this simply the natural evolution of a seasoned first responder? He couldn't say for certain, but his mind was uncluttered, and he knew this loss wouldn't break him. The hard work he'd invested in therapy was paying off.

Continuing northeast, the smell of rotten eggs wafted into his nostrils at the same time he spotted the hulking structures of US Steel's Edgar Thomson Works, situated on the opposite bank. Built over a hundred years before, the massive complex was the last major steel mill in the Pittsburgh region. Produced by hydrogen sulfide, the distinctive odor was a byproduct of the steelmaking process, reminding him of his youth in Meadville, and his grandfather's stories of working at Sharon Steel in the 1960s and '70s.

Leonard Moretti had been Tony's rock—the strongest individual he had ever known. He'd instilled the importance of overcoming obstacles independently, without relying on others. But his death, as a withered, diseased old man, had pierced the superhero persona that a young boy had assembled around the man he called Grandpap.

A question lingered: Would the mental armor Tony had forged in therapy withstand his next traumatic event? He was sure it would. Harrison's treatment had equipped him with the tools to understand and manage his PTSD. While the doctor warned him to expect occasional episodes, Tony felt a newfound sense of resilience, confident his coping skills would see him through whatever came next.

Against the low-angle winter sun, he pedaled under the shadows of twelve towering smokestacks of the former Eliza Furnace. Preserved within a mixed commercial and residential development known as the Waterfront, the red brick chimneys were all that remained of US Steel's vast Homestead Works, another node in a Pittsburgh network that had produced more iron and steel during World War Two than all the Axis countries combined.

Those smokestacks stood as stark reminders that nothing, no matter how substantial, was permanent. Buildings were torn down. People were replaced. Everything changed. *God knows I've changed.*

The trail continued into a heavily wooded section where his tires crunched the brown fallen leaves until the sound was masked by a CSX freight train chugging along behind the tree line. Relying on the bike's midrange gears on this flat stretch of trail, Tony lost himself in thought, reorienting his contemplations to the state of his personal relationships. There, too, the arrow was pointing up.

Tony's efforts to reconnect with his parents—initiated on Thanksgiving—continued on Christmas Eve when he'd arrived in Meadville with a rap at their door and an armful of gifts. During the subsequent reunion, filled with laughter and a few tears, his mom had plied him with food while his dad peppered him with questions about his job. His sister, her husband, and their two kids had added to the merriment on Christmas Day, and as memories of a happy childhood flooded back, he'd lost himself in the company of those he held most dear. He'd even tracked down a couple of old high school buddies for some burgers and beer. But while he savored the trip home, the situation with Allie, in need of serious TLC, was never far from his mind.

The couple had previously agreed to spend New Year's together at Allie's apartment in Mercersburg, so on the twenty-ninth, after bidding his folks goodbye, he'd hit the road for south central Pennsylvania.

Over the next four days, Tony and Allie had bared their souls, sharing their deepest thoughts and feelings, forging a deeper connection than ever before. Despite how distant Tony had been, her unwavering faith in him shone brightly. But while she'd given him plenty of time and space to move beyond his personal struggles, it was clear she wouldn't wait forever.

Feeling a renewed sense of love and determination, Tony was ready to take their relationship to the next level. Together, with Allie's support and encouragement, they had finally mapped out an exciting and promising future, filled with shared dreams, mutual support, and endless possibilities.

In what seemed like no time at all but must have been at least fifteen minutes, Tony glanced up at the forty-two-story Cathedral of Learning on the campus of the University of Pittsburgh, his alma mater. Affectionately referred to as "Cathy" by students, Tony had spent countless hours in the building's classrooms, or in study sessions amid its gothic architecture.

Past the goal posts rising above the practice fields of the UPMC Rooney Sports Complex, a biting wind sliced through his layered clothing as he pedaled onto the historic Hot Metal Bridge, another repurposed industrial relic.

Once across, Tony veered left for the final stretch, catching sunlight glinting off the windows of the US Steel Tower—his first place of employment after college. Once the tallest building between New York and Chicago, and a sixty-four-story symbol of the nation's steelmaking prowess, the structure stood supreme among an impressive collection of high-rise buildings in a central business district known as the Golden Triangle.

How far he'd come since those days. For a twenty-two-year-old kid from northwest Pennsylvania, working in downtown Pittsburgh had been an exhilarating experience. Yet he was never meant for a nine-to-five office job, and his true calling lay not in business but in public service, a lesson that had taken him far too long to accept.

The last leg of the trail straddled the east and westbound lanes of I-376—the Parkway East. With the din of traffic drumming in his ears and the reek of exhaust fumes stinging his nostrils, he pedaled under the Birmingham, Tenth Street, and Liberty Bridges before coasting down a ramp to the riverside and his destination—Point State Park and the Confluence, where the Monongahela and Allegheny Rivers met to form the Ohio.

Laying the bike on the dried grass, he took a seat on the steps above the fountain, which had been drained for the winter. A frigid, swirling breeze enveloped him, but after his hard ride, the cold air felt good.

There he sat, rubbing his aching ankle and considering the events that had led him to this point in his life. By the time his mind quieted, his face was numb. He hadn't solved any urgent problems or experienced any epiphanies, but that was okay. He'd reached a point where he no longer needed to reinvent himself.

Nor did he need to contemplate his next actions. His course was set. He was determined to complete his PTSD treatment, cement his relationship with Allie, and excel as a fire officer. The old doubts were gone, and he was now on the right path for himself, his firefighters, and the woman he loved.

Thus, it was a confident and determined Anthony Moretti who drained the rest of the Gatorade and mounted his bike for the return trip.

Part IV

Fortitude's Gauntlet

37

Monday, January 26

In an act of compassion and understanding, Chief Ramsey had given B-Platoon the day off last Friday, covering their twenty-four-hour shift with overtime and allowing Station-300's firefighters time to prepare for Saturday's funeral. Today marked the platoon's first day back since the tire center fire. It was to have been Fitz's first shift as captain.

Tony touched his ID to the card reader, and his heart sank at the realization that Fitz would never walk through this door again.

He'd considered taking a few more shifts off—his sprained ankle would provide a legitimate excuse—but most of the crew had known Fitz far longer than he, and they were his priority. After a moment's hesitation, he straightened his shoulders, punched in his code, and went inside.

As he carried his bag through the apparatus bay, the silent emptiness of the station pressed down on him, adding to the ache in his chest. The usual preshift mingling of firefighters, the jokes, the laughter, the feigned insults, the cell phone conversations—all were conspicuously absent. Two A-Platoon firefighters nodded on their way to the door but said nothing. After relieving the outgoing officers, he sank into his desk chair, booted up the station software, and examined the duty roster.

Ladder-302 was short one firefighter due to Barney's retirement and Pet's transfer to Engine-301, but the remaining ten were all present. He'd expected a few to take the day off, especially those who'd been close friends with Fitz. The full house said a lot about the platoon's cohesiveness—a tight-knit fraternity.

His eyes rested on the desktop display, but his mind drifted back to the fire. The falling bricks, Fitz reaching out his hand.

"Good morning, LT. I've got the first shift in the alarm room."

Tony glanced at the figure in the doorway. "Morning, Luke. Thank you."

He reviewed A-Platoon's report from the previous shift—a few inspections, an EMS assist, and two automatic alarms at the rectory of St. Mary's Church, triggered by bugs in their new fire detection system. With a sigh, he hit the intercom button connecting the station to MAFA's upstairs headquarters.

"Is that you, Tony?" a pleasant but subdued voice asked.

"It is, Iris. Are you holding up okay?"

"Oh, you know . . ." she said, her voice trailing off.

"Yeah," Tony said. "You knew him a long time."

"Uh-huh," she whispered, her voice catching.

"If there's anything I can do . . ."

"No, it's okay. Just take care of the crew, and yourself."

"I will." Her heartfelt comment hit him hard, and he struggled to keep his own voice steady. "We've got eleven on duty, including myself. No call-offs."

"Doesn't surprise me," she said.

"I guess it shouldn't have surprised me, either. Does the chief want to see me today?"

"He hasn't said, but I'm sure he'll touch base at some point. It's 6:55, get your tuchus to morning briefing."

"Yes, ma'am. Hang in there, Iris."

***

The classroom was quiet. Ten firefighters, seated in the front three rows, sat upright. No newspapers, no iPads, no cell phones. *Are they sad? Angry? Both?* He studied the faces but discerned no obvious emotion.

Tony was not a rah-rah, rally-the-troops kind of man, but he needed to address the elephant in the room. "Good morning. I appreciate you all being here today."

A smattering of muted responses issued from the crew.

"We lost a good man. A man who dedicated his entire adult life to the local communities, on both sides of the river." Tony paused. *Good God, this isn't what they need to hear right now.*

"After so many years with the River Bend Volunteer Fire Department, Fitz was about to take over this platoon, and I was looking forward to that day." Searching for the right words, he glanced down at his clipboard, but the list of scheduled departmental activities held no insight.

"Leaders like Fitz can never be replaced." A few heads bowed. "I didn't know him as well, or as long, as many of you, but during the last month, we became friends. I will miss him." There wasn't much Tony could add. "I'll stay in my current role as acting captain until a replacement is selected. I'm certainly no Fitz, nor Barney Dudek for that matter, but I promise I'll do my best for all of you. It's going to be difficult, but we have a job to do. Truck assignments are posted, so let's get to it." After a pause, he added, "If you need anything, or just want to talk, I'm here."

When the crew remained in their seats, Tony didn't know what to think.

Big Pappy stood. "LT, we got together yesterday and talked."

"Okay," Tony said, anxious to hear the details.

"When you . . . when you were hired, we had our doubts. We didn't think an airport guy, especially one with only a couple years under his belt, would be able to run this shift."

"Please, go on," Tony said.

Pappy softened his tone. "What I'm trying to say is, you proved us wrong."

Tony was dumbfounded, and he knew his features showed it.

"We don't know who the next captain will be, but as far as we're concerned, the chief will have a hard time finding anyone as good as you."

With the exception of Warren, who averted his gaze, heads bobbed enthusiastically. Comments of "yeah" and "that's right" rang out.

"Thank you," Tony said, his voice thick with emotion as a comforting warmth spread through him. "I can't put into words how much your support means to me. We'll get through this . . . together."

As they filed out, each firefighter stopped and shook his hand. Tony was touched beyond words. He'd found a place in the fire service, among a brotherhood of individuals he'd come to respect and, yes, to love. That thought sustained him all day, as he knew it would going forward.

38

Friday, January 30

Lying on the musty sofa, Dylan stared blankly at the millipede skittering across the basement floor. He hadn't slept more than two or three hours a night since the fire, every waking moment a fog of fear and regret.

A burst of agitated voices from the police scanner app jolted him from his stupor. River Bend cops. He sat up, snatched the iPhone from the coffee table, and cranked the volume. His tense muscles relaxed. A bar fight—at 11:30 a.m. *No surprise for this town.*

For the past ten days, Dylan had been glued to local, county, and state police frequencies. Traffic stops, suspicious persons, domestic disputes, burglaries, and drug busts. Nothing to suggest they were onto him, but the cops weren't dumb. They were probably avoiding radio chatter about the investigation, figuring the killer arsonist was listening.

"Killer arsonist," he said aloud. The name local media had given him. *That's what I am. A man is dead because of me.* He pulled his knees to his chest, as he always did when something bad happened, and looked around the basement of the house he'd lived in since birth.

Cobwebs, dust, and forgotten junk. Once this basement had been his playroom, a shy little boy's world of make-believe. With a box full of toy soldiers, he'd set up and acted out great battles. Later, the space became a teenage loner's escape from the world above, where heavy metal tunes blared from the cheap stereo and rattled the walls. Now, it was just a place to hole up, a purgatory where he awaited his fate.

At noon, he grabbed the remote and switched on the news. The police were hunting a suspect captured on camera at multiple fires. Even though that tidbit had broken three days ago, it still sent shivers down his spine. Did they really have photos of him? His face? No way. If they did, local TV would be all over it, and flyers would be plastered on telephone poles. Public appeals to identify the suspect, cops going door to door—it would be a circus. He switched off the TV and hurled the remote at the screen.

Was he about to be arrested? The cops must have *something*, or they wouldn't have mentioned a photo. Maybe it was blurry, or taken from too far away to ID his face. Not knowing was driving him nuts. The report mentioned photos from multiple fire scenes. How was that possible? He'd been so careful to avoid security cameras and blend in with crowds. He doubted the woman at the theater fire had gotten a shot of him. *It must've been that damned kid on the bike.*

In the past week and a half, Dylan had ventured out only once—a late-night fifteen-mile trip to the Giant Eagle in Jeanette, where he figured no one would recognize him. He needed to restock his food supplies, but after hustling through the canned goods aisle, he couldn't get home fast enough. In his mind, every eye in the store was watching him. Every cop on the street was ready to pull him over. He had to get away. But where would he go? Without much sleep, he couldn't think straight.

Dylan's stomach churned. *How had it come to this?* He'd never meant to hurt anyone. Never even considered the possibility. He wanted to help the community, rid it of crack houses and empty businesses. Make some room for new construction. Help get the town going again, like when his mom and dad had run their restaurant.

What a nightmare. Rising from the sofa, he clutched his stomach and took the stairs two at a time, barely making it to the bathroom before puking the contents of last night's dinner into the commode. He rocked back, slumping against the tub, his sobs blending with cries of "Oh God, no. No, no, no."

39

Thursday, February 5

“So this is it?” Tony asked as Dr. Harrison ushered him to the familiar round table with its odd wooden carving.

“If you mean our twelfth and last *regular* session, yes. But the end? That’s hard to say.”

“Very cryptic, Doc.”

Harrison shrugged. “How are things?”

“Not bad. Still trying to make sense of it. Such a tragedy.” But, no, that wasn’t right. It was a crime, dammit. And what for? What would anyone have to gain by burning down an old tire center? Tony balled his hands into fists. *I’d love to get my hands on the bastard.*

“We may never be able to make sense of it,” Harrison said.

Tony didn’t want to consider that possibility. Instead, he picked up the three-headed statuette.

“What does this thing mean, anyway?”

“I wondered when you’d ask. What do you think it means?”

Tony nodded toward Harrison’s bookshelves. “Based on your affection for Freud, I’d say it represents his theory of the three parts of human personality, the id, the ego, and the superego.”

“You’re a smart guy, Tony,” Harrison said.

Tony flashed a self-congratulatory smile, which was instantly wiped away once the doctor added: “But in this case you’re wrong. It’s actually an Abusua Unity Centerpiece, symbolizing the importance of peace, strength, and harmony to achieve common goals.”

"Uh-huh." The symbolism, and its relation to his present situation, wasn't lost on Tony.

"Abusua is the Ghanaian word for family. The piece you're holding is actually quite expensive, so don't drop it."

Tony set the statuette down gently. "Peace, strength, and harmony. Worthy goals. Is that the direction you're steering me?"

"In fact, it is. Do you disagree with those goals?"

Tony didn't. He craved them, especially the thought of *inner* peace.

"I'll take your silence for assent." Harrison offered a gentle smile. "By this point in your therapy, you know how crucial it is to open up about the trauma you've endured in order to further your progress. To achieve what this carving symbolizes."

Tony did open up, as he always had with Harrison, explaining what Fitz's death had done to his psyche. "I'm very sad about what happened, but . . ."

"Yes?"

"This is going to sound selfish."

"Go on."

"I've come so far over the last three months. I'm worried that Fitz's death is going to set me back."

"It won't."

"Oh?" The doc rarely disagreed so sharply.

"Over the course of PTSD treatment, it's common for the sufferer not to notice how much resilience they've developed." Harrison walked to his file cabinet and retrieved a manila folder from the top drawer. Back at his desk, he pulled a sheaf of papers from the folder. "These are the impact statements you submitted for our first eleven sessions. You've just witnessed another devastating event, but if you dig deep into what you've written, you'll note the differences in your reactions. Let's review, shall we?"

Tony folded his arms on the table and leaned forward. "I'm all ears, Doc."

Harrison donned his glasses and, for the next ten minutes, read excerpts.

For Tony, the notes were sobering.

"Now let's take a look at where you are now." Harrison put the papers down and doffed the glasses. "Your nightmares have eased, and unless you've been holding out on me, the angry outbursts have stopped."

"I haven't held back, but I'm so angry right now I could . . ."

Harrison cupped his hands protectively over the carving.

Tony smiled. "You're a real cutup, Doc."

"I try. But to be clear, the anger you're feeling now is a perfectly normal reaction to what happened to your friend. Not comparable to the unwarranted temper flare-ups you described in your early narratives."

"That's true," Tony said. *This time it's justified.*

"Another encouraging sign is that you're getting outside and exercising again."

Tony was. Biking mostly, with a little running mixed in.

Harrison flipped a page. "In your last three statements, you haven't noted a single incident of shaking or sweating. Yet you describe situations that would normally have triggered you." Harrison pushed the glasses to the tip of his nose and eyed Tony. "Did you forget to note those symptoms?"

"Well . . . no," Tony said as he replayed the last few weeks in his mind. "I guess I didn't mention them because they've been so minor, or rather, nonexistent."

"Most important," Harrison continued, "you're no longer racked by the most debilitating effects of your PTSD: the severe anxiety and loss of concentration that impeded your decision-making abilities and prevented you from functioning in your job as a fire officer."

More truth. Even after the wall collapse, Tony had kept a clear head.

"Finally, you've rebuilt your support structure by connecting with people outside of work. Your parents, some old friends . . . Allie."

Her name sent a jolt up his spine. *God, Allie, how I wish you were here with me.*

"And maybe the most important connection for you right now, while you're dealing with this tragedy, is your relationship with young Terrell."

"Terrell? How do you figure? He's just a kid."

"Yes, a kid you've taken under your wing, and one who's benefited you in ways you probably don't realize."

"I suppose . . ."

"Listen, I'm not saying you're where you want to be, and we both know you've got some work ahead of you. Your sleeping patterns are erratic, and I can't gauge if you've stopped taking undue risks with your safety, and that concerns me no end."

"I have."

Harrison shot a suspicious glance. "Possibly."

"Truly, Doc. I have a lot to live for."

The doctor leaned back in his chair. "I'm glad to hear you say that."

"I'd been blind to the fact for a long time."

"Not uncommon in cases of post-traumatic stress." Harrison eyed Tony closely. "You've come a long way in a short time, and now you're ready to work without a net."

"I know I am, Doc. I feel strong. But where do I go from here?"

"Well, if you're agreeable, I'd like to continue to meet with you in person. Say, once a month."

"I'd like that."

"Excellent," Harrison said and checked his watch. "It's been quite a journey, but I'm afraid we're out of time. My secretary will set up a session in March, but in the meantime, I want you to call me if you need to talk."

"Will do," Tony said, but he didn't think he'd be making that call.

40

Friday, February 13 – 3:52pm

"Are you going to shoot the ball or dance with it, LT?" Muscles taunted as he jostled with Luke for rebound position under the basket.

"I'm picking my shot," Tony said, dribbling along the backcourt. After three and a half weeks of icing, elevating, and popping ibuprofen, his sprained right ankle was still taped but sturdy enough for some intense physical activity.

"Can't help himself," Terrell said. "Big slow white guys ain't got game."

"We'll see about that," Tony said and took the shot from outside the perimeter.

The basketball clanged off the metal backboard and ricocheted to Terrell, who set himself and drained a shot from the top of the key. "What I said."

"Don't you have homework?" Tony asked as he dried the sweat from his face with the sleeve of his sweatshirt. *I'm the only guy who sweats when it's forty degrees.* "And you can wipe that smile off your face, young man. The game's not over yet."

"You think?" Luke asked as he sank a shot from the corner. "Remind me to pick another partner next time we play two-on-two."

"Come on, it was the sun," Tony said as Muscles juked him and drove in for an easy layup.

"Case closed," Luke said.

"Game over," Muscles declared as a sequence of high-pitched tones echoed from the outside speaker and the klaxon blared.

"Uh-oh, they're dumping the whole district," Luke said.

"Stations-300, 400, 500, 600, Battalion-1, Battalion-2, respond. Water View Towers, 1000 Terrace Avenue, Hillcrest Acres. We have multiple reports of a working fire on the eighth floor, south wing, apartment 805. Evacuation in progress. Time is 1554."

"Isn't that a senior citizens' high-rise?" Luke asked.

"It is. Let's go," Tony said as the apparatus bay doors clanged up on their tracks.

"Man, good thing I brought my camera," Terrell said.

"Don't even think about it," Tony warned. "You can stay here, or go home, but you're not following us. It's five miles away."

"But—"

"Did you hear me?" Tony's words were sharper than he'd intended.

"Yeah, I hear you," Terrell said and looked down at the pavement. "I'll go home."

Tony wanted to reinforce the message, but there was no time.

****

Dylan shot up from the sofa at the message on the County Police frequency. "Mon Area Fire is responding to a reported fire on the eighth floor of the Water View Towers, 1000 Terrace Avenue, Hillcrest Acres."

"My God!" Dylan's grandmother had been a resident at Water View when he was a kid. The smell came back to him—antiseptic and musty. The place was a dump, a warehouse for discarded old people waiting to die. "They're gonna think I started it," he fretted to the empty basement.

The panic he'd felt since the tire center fire ratcheted up several notches. He *had* to go there. Had to do *something*. Make up for his terrible mistake. *Show them I'm not a bad person, not a murderer.*

Hillcrest Acres was miles away, on the north side of the river, so he had to get moving. Snatching his hoodie and baseball cap, he hustled up the steps and, for the first time in three weeks, left the house in broad daylight.

41

Friday, February 13 – 3:55pm

With multiple scenarios racing through his mind, Tony donned his gear, climbed into the officer's seat of Ladder-302, and checked his backseat crew. Romeo, Muscles, and Luke. All but the latter highly experienced—although even young Luke was gaining skills and confidence with every incident. "Seat belts."

He hit the siren pedal and sounded three blasts of the air horn as Danny wheeled the big ladder truck onto Main Street. After the turn onto South Shore Boulevard, he confirmed Engine-301 and Rescue-303 were in tow before firing up the Mobile Data Terminal.

Located at the northeastern corner of MAFA's district, Water View Towers, a 1960s-era apartment building, overlooked the Monongahela River. According to the preplan, its twelve floors were designed around a central core, or lobby. Spanning four wings extending south, east, north, and west, the twelve-story building housed three hundred and eighty-four apartments. Each floor housed thirty-two units, with eight apartments per wing.

The layout included two primary stairwells positioned at the northeast and southwest corners of each lobby, diagonally across from the building's two elevators. Additionally, four relatively narrow secondary stairwells marked the outermost end of each wing. Apartment 805, nestled in the south wing, faced west.

The main structural components were brick and block, with each unit compartmentalized to prevent fire spread. However, according to the details on the preplan, each apartment—and the stairwells—relied on double layers of drywall for fire resistance, rather than the solid masonry separations that typified the buildings of the era. The building featured standpipe connections in the two core stairwells, but it predated local codes requiring sprinkler systems, and no retrofit had ever been undertaken. *In a high-rise for senior citizens—inexcusable*, Tony thought.

The likely response routes meant that apparatus from Battalion-2—Station-600, followed by Station-500—would reach the scene first. Battalion-1's equipment, crossing the river at the New Industry Bridge, would arrive last, led by Station-400. With a ten-to-fifteen-minute drive ahead of them in midafternoon traffic, Tony's crews from Station-300 would bring up the rear. By then the supply lines would be laid and fire operations underway.

"They better save us a spot," Danny said.

Tony agreed. "You read my mind, Mr. O'Reilly."

***

Oblivious to his—or anyone else's—safety, Dylan kept his foot on the accelerator and his hand on the horn as he weaved in and out of traffic on South Shore Boulevard. He had to get there and . . . do what exactly? The scene would be crawling with cops, and if they spotted him, it'd be all over. *Doesn't matter, I've got to try.*

He swerved right and sped past a delivery truck hogging the left lane, cutting off a ridiculously large SUV in the process. The driver laid on his horn. Dylan checked the mirror. The guy was five feet from his tail, shooting him the bird and shouting.

The scanner app on his cell phone, tuned to the fire frequency, chirped with a steady stream of transmissions. His mind, wrapped up in the drive, couldn't process much of it, but from the increasing radio chatter, the fire was getting worse.

Traffic in Buchanan slowed his progress—why did such a tiny town need four traffic signals? "No! Go through it," he shouted as a car in front of him slowed for a yellow light. Not waiting, he veered onto the berm, drove over the remains of a tire, and ran the light as the cell phone flew from the seat.

His heart was beating so fast that it was hard to catch his breath. If he was going to pull this off, he needed to think, but he was too hyped up. As the congestion eased, he let up on the accelerator. He'd be of no use if he crashed the car or got stopped by a cop. After several deep breaths, a simple plan crystallized in his mind.

42

Friday, February 13 – 4:01pm

With the powerful Federal Q-Siren wailing, Tony scanned the road ahead, calling out intersections and traffic hazards—mostly civilians driving like idiots—as they sped east on South Shore Boulevard. Approaching the turn to the New Industry Bridge, he yanked the air horn halyard to clear stacked traffic in the left turn lane.

Battalion Chief-2, Vincent Costello, radioed he was on the scene, set up Water View Command, and gave an initial report that mimicked the county dispatcher's initial announcement, adding that the fire, while still limited to the south wing, had broken containment and spread to at least two more apartments.

"So much for a room and contents fire," Danny said. "Them walls are probably Swiss cheese."

Tony agreed. Drywall separations were often penetrated with water pipes, electrical conduits, and HVAC ducts, but whether they'd been properly sealed and fireproofed was anybody's guess.

Five minutes after Costello's arrival, Chief Ramsey announced he'd reached the scene and assumed Water View Command. He ordered Engine-601 to lay a supply line from the east and directed Engine-501, responding from the same direction, to stop and support the hydrant.

Radio traffic was heavy, yet disciplined and methodical. Tony cranked the volume in his headset as Ramsey directed 502 to elevate their tower to the seventh floor of the south wing as soon as they arrived.

"That ain't a good sign," Danny said.

Before Tony could agree, the chief ordered Engine-401 to lay in from the east and Engine-301 to support the hydrant.

Danny whistled. "Two hydrants? Both being pumped? That don't happen much."

"Let's hope it's just a precaution," Tony said. But knowing Ramsey, it was likely more serious than that.

"I know one thing," Danny said. "Big Pappy ain't gonna be happy sitting on that plug."

Tony agreed, but his mind was preoccupied with the implications of ordering two five-inch supply lines into operation. Each line could deliver up to two thousand gallons per minute to the scene. *If it's that bad, how are we going to evacuate the elderly residents?* He tensed up at the thought, but the familiar storm—anxiety, tremors, and panic—failed to emerge.

***

The police cordon forced Dylan to park two blocks from the apartment building. He dashed along an alley, splashed through a soggy vacant lot, cut between two houses, and emerged directly across the street from the apartment tower. He pulled the baseball cap low over his brow, flipped the hoodie up, and stuck his hands in his pockets. Struggling to control his labored breaths, he slipped into the throng of onlookers as flames leapt from three windows on the eighth floor. *Wow, this is a bad one.*

On the ground, the scene was a cluster. Firemen scrambling with their hoses and tools, paramedics rushing to help elderly residents who were exiting the front doors, and cops trying to keep the whole mess under control. And the noise—wailing sirens, shouted orders, revving engines. He relaxed. *Nobody will spot me in this mess.*

Police tape fluttered between signs and telephone poles, barring spectators from the sidewalk opposite the front of the building. No problem—he'd never intended to enter that way. At the corner, he cut behind a Port Authority bus that had just pulled up to the curb. Shielded from view, he skirted the building's left side.

The back wing of the building lacked street access, surrounded instead by a weed-choked lawn dotted with picnic tables and benches. Melted snow had turned the ground into a muddy mess. He trudged through, his tennis shoes sucking into the muck with every step.

Drawing closer, he hugged the wall, sidling past an unmarked flat-paneled steel door—clearly an exit only—and peered around the corner. Groups of residents trickled out of double glass doors, guided to the PAT bus by a lone cop and a couple of medics.

As he weighed his options, a metallic screech made him whirl around. A man in a white uniform—likely a nurse or staff member—emerged from the unmarked door with three elderly women in tow.

"I've got it," Dylan said, rushing to grab the open door.

"Thanks, I need to get back inside," the man said, pointing the women toward the bus.

Dylan held the door and glanced around while the staff member reentered. No one paid him any attention. *Perfect.* He counted to ten to put some distance between himself and the employee and ducked inside.

43

Friday, February 13 – 4:09pm

Tony toggled the mic switch. "Water View Command, Ladder-302 approaching."

"Ladder-302 from Command, we've got a spot for you at the Alpha-Delta corner," Ramsey advised.

A massed gathering of red and blue lights lit the way as Danny maneuvered the unwieldy ladder truck between parked cars on the left and the snaking supply line on the right. Standing in the street, Battalion Chief McMahon waved his flashlight toward the designated parking position.

"Get ready to elevate the ladder for an upper-floor search," Tony said as he opened the door to exit the cab. "I'll get some instructions."

He eyed the plume of smoke curling above the structure, quickly assessing the positioning of the apparatus. Tower-502 stood at the Alpha-Bravo corner, its basket elevated to a seventh-floor window. Engines 401 and 601 were parked nose to nose in front of the building, flanked by Ladder-302. With Rescue-303 and Special Services-503 also in play, every major piece of MAFA's fleet was now committed to the operation.

Tony exchanged a brief nod with Engine-401's pump operator, who was focused on charging a pair of three-inch leader lines to the standpipe Siamese connection on the Side-A wall. Then, as the south wing's west side came into view, his breath caught. *My God!*

Flames engulfed three-quarters of the eighth floor's west-facing apartments. Below, on the lawn, firefighters scrambled, hauling their equipment to the main entrance lobby at the southwest corner as elderly residents streamed out.

Tony arrived at the command post at the same time as Captain Tom Decker, who'd recently returned from suspension for his actions at the tanker fire. Decker shot Tony an unfriendly glance.

Incompetent prick, Tony thought and turned his attention to the assembled officers.

Chief Ramsey, joined by Deputy Chiefs DeFazio and O'Connell, stood behind a six-foot table with a command board and several radios. DeFazio wore a reflective vest labeled OPERATIONS SECTION CHIEF, while O'Connell's vest designated him as SAFETY OFFICER. The Hillcrest Borough manager, acting as the public information officer, and the apartment building's superintendent, serving as the liaison officer, joined them at the CP. The head of building maintenance and one of his electricians stood by as technical specialists.

"Battalion Chief Costello is supervising the fire attack on Division-8," Ramsey explained. "Captain Jenkins is also up there, sweeping the apartments with 502's truck crew."

"Do we know the extent of the fire?" Tony asked.

"At least four of the eight apartments are fully involved, maybe all of them by now, and that fire door won't hold forever. I'm moving Level-1 staging to Division-6, and I've sent Lieutenant Brookin up there to take charge." Ramsey turned to McMahon. "Ritchie, I want you to assist Chief Costello with the fire attack on Division-8."

"Will do," McMahon replied.

Ramsey traced a finger across his command board and let out a sigh. "Keep it in check, Ritchie. I'll get additional manpower and high-rise packs upstairs as soon as we can."

The chief raised his portable and cranked the volume knob. Radio traffic had increased markedly as personnel and equipment, including a rapid intervention team, responded from nearby communities. "County from Water View Command, move all mutual aid apparatus to a tactical channel."

"County receives. All incoming mutual aid units to Water View Towers, respond on East Fire, Frequency-3."

Turning to Decker, Ramsey said, "Tom, there's a vacant lot two blocks away, on Lutton Street. Set up a Level-2 staging area and coordinate with mutual aid on East Fire, Frequency-3."

"What the hell?" Decker mumbled.

Ramsey flashed an irritated look. "What was that, Captain?"

"Nothing, sir."

Tony suppressed a smile as Decker's face turned red.

"What are your orders for my truck crew, Chief?" Tony asked.

"I want you to evacuate any residents still on Division-9," Ramsey said. "I'll round up another search team to assist you, but get moving."

The radio crackled. "Command from Division-8, we've got smoke in the east wing. Repeat, smoke entering the east wing."

"Shit," Decker said. "If that fire breaks out . . ."

"I know the implications, Captain," Ramsey said.

So did Tony. If the fire spread to the other wings, there'd be hell to pay. *How many residents might be trapped up there?*

***

Through groups of descending residents, many holding on to each other for support, Dylan climbed the stairwell. He paused to allow two elderly couples, their steps slow and tentative, to pass him in the tight space. *Where the hell is the staff?* Three steps below the second-floor landing, a wizened old man stumbled and lost his grip on the railing.

"Andrew, no!" his companion called.

Dylan grabbed the man by the armpits and passed him to a tall, rugged-looking sixtysomething before resuming his ascent.

Voices echoed from below. *Firemen? Cops?* Edging his way past the evacuees, he darted to the third-floor landing and ducked into the north wing. The hallway was empty, with no residents or staff in sight. He could claim he was looking for a relative, but he'd rather avoid detection altogether. With his ear to the door, he waited until the voices faded before cracking it open and resuming his climb.

Doubts clouded his thoughts. Would he be able to reach the fire floor? And if he did, what was he going to do when he got there? His plan was short on specifics, but to redeem himself, he'd have to take chances.

44

Friday, February 13 – 4:17pm

Tony made his way from the command post to the ladder truck while a steady stream of residents and staff exited the lobby from the southwest stairs. Just like passengers evacuating an airplane, it was human nature to exit the way they entered—the most familiar route. Due to the growing congestion, Ramsey redirected the ascending firefighters to the northeast stairwell at the rear of the building. Tony opted to climb the ladder truck.

He tasked Danny with raising the 302's aerial to the seventh floor of the east wing, but by extending the four-section ladder to its 105-foot limit, he was only able to reach the outermost apartment unit of the sixth floor, where he positioned the tip just short of a picture window.

"That's got to be the living room," Tony said. "Break it for us."

Danny gave him a look. "You sure, LT?"

"I know it's against policy," Tony said as he surveyed the area between the truck and the building for firefighters and residents. "We need to get inside, not waste time clearing that glass with hand tools. The ground around us is clear. Take it out."

"You got it." Using the deft touch Tony had come to expect from his driver-operator, Danny eased the ladder's tip into the window. It shattered with a crack, sending large pieces cascading harmlessly onto the east lawn.

Tony clipped the TIC to the retractable carabiner on his backplate, gripped his officer's A-tool, and threw a box light over his shoulder.

"Let's do it," he said and led his three companions upward.

Muscles followed with a set of irons, Luke carried the water can, and Romeo brought up the rear with a second set of irons. With gear and SCBA, each man toted at least seventy pounds. Despite their encumbrances, the crew completed the laborious climb in less than two minutes. At the top, Tony cleared the remaining shards from the windowsill with his A-tool and squeezed the mic button. "Command from 300-Lieutenant, four firefighters entering Division-6 in the east wing. We'll take the stairs to nine."

"Copy, Lieutenant," Ramsey radioed. "Be advised, Captain Jenkins's crew cleared their search of Division-8, and they're holding position behind the fire door in the lobby while the engine crews get their lines in operation. So far, the fire is still contained to the south wing."

"300-Lieutenant received." Tony hooked his right leg over the top rung and sounded the floor with his boot. "It's solid," he said and lowered himself into the apartment.

***

When he reached the fifth floor of the north wing stairwell, Dylan paused to catch his breath. Since assisting the little group on the third floor, he hadn't encountered a single soul. But now, faint chattering and footsteps sounded from above. *Has to be firemen.* He dared go no farther. Without more information, he wouldn't be able to help anyone.

Reentering the north wing, he tried three of the west-facing apartment doors before finding the fourth unlocked. "Anybody in here?" he asked. When no one replied, he knelt in front of the living room window and slid the curtains aside.

As he feared, the back of the building buzzed with activity. Firemen, burdened by heavy tools and packs of hose slung over their shoulders, formed a line as they marched into the lobby. The residents he'd seen on the soggy lawn were gone, the picnic tables transformed into cluttered workstations covered with equipment. Though he didn't see any cops, he sensed they were down there somewhere, hidden in the chaos. And wait . . . *What?* A black teenager in a heavy coat and a ski cap, with a camera around his neck. It couldn't be. But it was. The kid. *How the hell did he get here?*

Dylan didn't think the teen could get into the building, even if he was dumb enough to try. Probably going to snap his stupid pictures from outside. *Doesn't matter, but it's definitely time for plan B.*

He slipped out of the apartment and cracked the door to the fifth-floor lobby, his breath hitching. Silence greeted him—an empty space. But luck had a nasty habit of running out. Someone was bound to spot him. Then the firemen would toss him out and the infuriating kid would ID him for the cops.

His mind raced. Should he try a quick escape while he still had time? No, fleeing wasn't an option. He steeled himself, dashed across the lobby, entered the door marked

Southwest Lobby Stairs

and resumed his climb.

45

Friday, February 13 – 4:24pm

"Hold here a minute," Tony said as the search team reached Division-8, the fire floor. He removed a glove and ran his hand over the metal fire door. No heat. He edged the door open and looked into the corridor. The lights still shone. *But for how much longer?* Chief Ramsey had declared the floor cleared, but after the report of smoke in the east wing, he needed to check for signs of fire. He detected none. "Let's keep moving."

On the ninth floor, there was nothing more than a faint scent of smoke. Satisfied, he thumbed the radio button. "Search teams entering the east wing on Division-9."

"Acknowledged, Lieutenant," Ramsey replied. "You're designated Search-1. Clear those units fast and head to the south wing. We're rounding up another search team now."

Tony's mounting apprehension rang like an alarm bell, but he pushed it aside. "No need for masks yet," he said. "Muscles, Luke, take the even-numbered units, Romeo and I have the odd numbers. We'll mark the doors as we go."

As the team split up, Muscles called out: "Fire Department, we're here to evacuate you." There were no replies.

Unlike hotel rooms, the apartments at Water View Towers had doors that did not lock automatically when closed, and the teams were able to access seven of the eight apartments without forcing entry. Since the apartments were still illuminated and free of smoke, the crew moved rapidly toward the building's core, drawing a big white X on each door with their chalk.

"This one's locked," Romeo said at apartment 911.

Tony moved up and pounded the door. "Fire Department! We're coming in." Not waiting for a reply, he took Romeo's Halligan and placed the adze end an inch below the deadbolt.

Romeo hammered the flat head of his axe against the matching surface of the Halligan, wedging it into the space between the door and the jamb.

"That's it," Tony said and pushed the Halligan toward the wall. The wood of the jamb splintered as the door sprang open. Romeo joined him in a rapid search that found no one.

"Can't believe the residents got themselves out," Romeo said. "A lot of them must be immobile."

Tony agreed. He'd expected trapped occupants and let out a sigh of relief as he bent to his lapel mic. "Command from Division-9, Search-1, the east wing is clear."

"I smell smoke," Muscles said.

"So do I," Luke added.

Smoke. Tony's nose registered the faint odor. *The easy part of the job is over—now comes the challenge.* He activated the mic. "Command from Division-9, Search-1, we're entering the south wing now."

"Command copies Division-9. Be advised, you'll have active fire directly below you, so make it quick. Keep me apprised of—"

The chief's transmission was interrupted by a loud beep. "Emergency traffic! Emergency traffic." The voice was strained and almost breathless, but Tony recognized McMahon's voice immediately. "Command from Division-8, the fire has spread to the . . . lobby and we're pulling . . .back to the west wing and . . . regrouping. Need additional crews . . . up here . . . now."

"Command copies, Ritchie. Fresh hose teams are coming up the northwest stairs now."

"Holy shit," Romeo said. "Never heard him so frazzled."

"Can it," Tony said. "Go on air," he added as he removed his helmet and donned his facepiece.

Audi bells clanged, regulators hissed air, and electronic PASS devices chirped as four sets of self-contained breathing apparatus powered up.

A glance at his crew told Tony they were ready. "Let's move."

***

Dylan dodged other people for just one flight on the southwest stairs. On the sixth floor, voices—definitely firemen—rose up from below. *I didn't think they were using these stairs.* Hell, he'd been too optimistic. He exited the stairwell and made a quick left into the west wing.

With his ear pressed against the metal door, he heard voices, but from the sound of their boots and the racket from their tools, firemen were going *down* the steps. Why would that be? Were they done searching? Was the fire out?

A thud against the door sent him lunging for the nearest apartment. Unlocked. He slipped inside as firemen flooded the hallway, voices and radios chattering away.

The floor fell silent, but Dylan waited an agonizing couple of minutes before daring a peek. The coast was clear. *What the hell?* Then it hit him— they'd taken the smaller stairway at the end of the west wing hall. No matter. He'd wasted enough time.

The smell of smoke engulfed him as he reentered the southwest stairwell, but what stopped him cold was the figure sitting two steps above the landing, head against the wall—the black kid.

46

Friday, February 13 – 4:33pm

I n the ninth-floor lobby, the team was met by a wall of concentrated smoke and rising heat. Tony's pulse quickened as he weaved his way around two chairs and knocked over a small table before reaching the south wing fire door.

"Quick searches, forget about chalking the doors," Tony ordered. "Romeo and I will take the odd side again. Let's go."

The crew burst through the door, bending low as a wave of radiated heat tore into them. At least the smoke was much lighter than in the lobby. Muscle's amplified shouts reverberated down the hall. "Fire Department! We're here to get you out." Silence answered back.

Romeo grabbed the handle of apartment 901. "It's locked."

Tony positioned himself beside his partner, and they repeated their practiced forcible entry procedure. Inside, the oppressive heat eased. "Take the bedrooms, Romeo," Tony said as he swept the living room and kitchen. They completed their methodical search in less than a minute.

Before returning to the door, Tony ripped the curtains aside. *Uh-oh.* Dense smoke spiraled menacingly up the building's exterior, and the window's lower edge was seared and blackened.

"That's not good, LT," Romeo said.

"Next unit," Tony said, giving no hint as to his own misgivings.

Tony ran through potential egress scenarios while he and Romeo searched apartment 903. The team had two escape routes—the lobby's primary stairwells or the smaller one at the end of the wing.

Back in the hallway, his radio squawked. "Division-9, Search-1 from Command, be advised, the fire has broken through the windows of the east-facing apartments and is lapping up toward you. Autoexposure is a real possibility. Acknowledge and report PAR and progress."

Tony held his reply until he glimpsed Muscles and Luke in the hallway ahead. "Division-9, Search-1 acknowledges. Potential autoexposure from eight. We have a PAR of four."

"Command copies. I've got another team headed for Division-9 to search the north and west wings." Ramsey paused before adding: "Complete your search of the south wing and get off that floor ASAP, Lieutenant."

With a two-and-a-half-gallon water extinguisher as their only defense, Tony had no intention of lingering. The search teams pressed on, urgency propelling their every move as the inferno closed in.

"Jesus!" Romeo said as he entered apartment 905.

Tony recoiled at the sight. Soot stained half the expansive picture window while fiery tendrils swirled and clawed at the glass, producing a rhythmic tapping akin to fingernails drumming on a metal table. *That's the crackling sound I heard.* Autoexposure in action.

"I can't believe it's not broken."

"It won't hold for long," Tony said. "One more unit and we're out of here."

Conditions were marginally better in 907, the apartment adjacent to the south wing stairwell, but every window was scorched black from top to bottom. Tony breathed a sigh of relief as they exited the apartment. It was short-lived.

Muscles met them at the door. "We've got a problem, LT."

∗∗∗

Dylan couldn't believe his eyes. The ski cap and winter coat were gone, but it was the kid all right. How the hell had he climbed six floors so fast? *I wasted too much time hiding.* The urge to duck back into the hall and get the hell away overwhelmed him. He pulled the door to the lobby, but something caused him to stop and look back at the one person who could positively identify him.

The kid's eyes narrowed. "It's you."

A million excuses ran through Dylan's mind. He was a good man. He never meant to hurt anyone. He was only trying to help the community. *Hell, what's the point?* "Yeah, it's me."

"Thought so," the kid said and winced as he rubbed at his hip. The stupid camera that had caused so much trouble hung by its strap, resting on his belly. Instead of fear, his eyes reflected pain—a lot of it.

"You gonna toss me down the steps? Get rid of the witness?"

Despite the situation, Dylan smiled for the first time since the tire center fire. "What's your name?"

"Why, so you can track down my family and kill them too?"

"Whoa. Nobody's gonna kill anybody. You watch way too much TV."

"Video games," the kid corrected with not an iota of apprehension in his voice. "Why should I believe you? You're already a murderer."

"I never meant for anyone to . . ." Dylan bit his lower lip. No point trying to justify what he'd done. "Are you hurt?"

"Been hurt all my life."

That explained the limp Dylan had noticed at the house where he'd set the smoke pots. The kid must have aggravated his condition on the way up. "How'd you get to this building? I don't think you live around here."

"Uber."

"Uber?" Dylan smiled again. "And you walked up six floors with a—"

"Jacked-up hip. Yeah, I did. What of it?"

The kid was tough, but there was no time to argue with him. "I'm Dylan."

The teen held his gaze. "Terrell."

"So, you *Ubered* over to a burning building to do what, take a few photos?"

"None of your damn business." The kid sneered. "What are *you* doing here? You set the fire, didn't you? Wanted to see how many people you could kill."

"Hell no!" Dylan took a step toward Terrell, and despite his bravado, the kid pushed himself up to the next step, fear in his eyes. *What am I doing?*

He backed off and held out his hands. "Listen, I never meant to hurt anyone, but I don't blame you for thinking that's bullshit. I did not start this fire. I heard about it on my scanner and rushed here to see if I could help. Make up for . . . you know." Dylan's throat tightened. "I'm not gonna hurt you, or anyone. You *can* believe that."

The kid's face was filled with doubt, but he seemed to relax a little. "Okay, say it's true. You wanna help people to make up for your crimes. I'm here to take pictures. But we're both stuck on these stairs. What do we do now?"

To that question, Dylan had no answer. "Can you walk?"

"I ain't no cripple," the kid said but quickly changed his tune. "Man, I don't know."

"Try."

Terrell tried to stand but crumpled back to the stairs and rubbed furiously at the offending body part. "Bullshit hip. Let me get all the way up here and screwed me."

Dylan removed the baseball cap and wiped the sweat from his brow. "Okay, we're on six. We know the fire is on eight. The firemen have got to be up there." He ran a hand through his matted hair. "One floor. That's our best shot. We've got to go up."

"No way I'm getting up two more floors."

"You can do it. I'll help you."

"Why don't we just go into that hallway and call for help? Phone's gotta be working in those apartments."

"They're not. I already tried." The lie came easily.

"You ain't thinking. We can break a window and yell if we have to."

"That won't work either. Those windows are tempered. We'll never break them." Another lie, but Dylan had no intention of waving his arms out some window so the cops could spot him. "I'm telling you, going up is our best bet."

"I'm not liking this idea," Terrell said, but he seemed resigned.

"Come on," Dylan said and reached an arm under the teen's shoulder. The kid didn't flinch as he was hoisted to his feet, but a whimper betrayed his pain.

"Okay, I'll try."

"Good, we're going to get out of here," Dylan said, bearing the brunt of Terrell's weight as he eased him up the stairs.

47

Friday, February 13 – 4:41pm

Behind Muscles, two heads peered out from the open door of apartment 906, terrified looks on their faces.

"Keep them there," Tony barked before following them inside and shutting the door.

"They've been waiting for someone to come and get them," Muscles explained.

Tony reset his regulator, popped it out of his facepiece, and eyed the little group. Four women and two men, their hair colored in shades of gray and silver. Not one of them looked younger than seventy-five.

A small, wiry woman spoke up, her voice unexpectedly strong. "My name's Mariam," she said and held an arm out toward the others. "This is Lizzy, Oscar, Janice, Deborah, and George. I called Kevin, the security guard at the front desk, twenty minutes ago. He told us to wait here and he'd send someone up." Her expression twisted into disgust. "Stupid bastard."

"Forget about him," Tony reassured her, voice steady despite his rising misgivings. "You'll be safe with us."

"I certainly hope so," Mariam said, wrapping an arm around Lizzy. "She's very afraid. George and Janice are okay, but Deborah has trouble walking and Oscar is a little confused."

These people need to see my face. Tony removed his helmet, pulled the facepiece over his head, and surveyed the residents. Lizzy, obese and near hysterics. Deborah, frail and struggling to stand. Oscar, a short, thin man, looking bewildered. George and Janice—the youngest and most robust of the bunch—seemed, as Mariam said, okay.

Taking stock of the situation, he ran through the options. None of these people was spry, but if he could get them through the smoky lobby to the northwest core stairs, they'd be out of harm's way and could descend.

"Listen up, folks," he said in a firm but reassuring tone, "we're getting out of here. Muscles, take position at the lobby door. We'll get them moving your way."

"On it," Muscles said.

"Can we take one of the lobby elevators?" George asked, a note of worry in his voice.

"Sorry, sir," Tony said. "They're not operating."

George frowned at the news but said nothing.

"You've seen the smoke in the hallway, but it's not bad," Tony said. "It's worse in the lobby, but it's passable and will be a quick walk. We'll help those who need assistance." *Which might be everyone.*

Mariam's eyes flickered with doubt, but Tony was relieved when she didn't question his strategy. *The last thing I need is a mutiny.*

Tony gestured toward Romeo. "This firefighter's name is Randy. He'll lead you."

"Are we going to be okay?" Lizzy asked, her voice quivering.

"You are." Tony grabbed his lapel mic. "Command from Division-9, Search-1, we've located six residents in the south wing. We're going to evacuate them through the lobby."

"Command copies," Ramsey answered. "Make it quick."

"Will do, Chief," Tony replied, knowing full well there'd be nothing quick about it.

Tony reaffixed his helmet and facepiece. "Luke, stay in the rear and keep them moving." He skirted the group and reentered the hallway. At the lobby door, he knelt beside Muscles. "Crack it."

Smoke surged in. "It's gotten a lot worse," Muscles said.

Tony peered into the lobby, surprised by the rapid change. Thick smoke, combined with a dull ache in his ever-sensitive ears, indicated a rapidly growing fire on the floor below. He pulled the fire door shut. *We're in a nose dive here.*

"No way are we getting them through this," Muscles said.

"I know it," Tony said and called to Romeo, who'd entered the corridor with the residents. "Change of plan. Get them turned around. We'll use the wing stairs." It would be tight, but they'd manage.

"Hey, wait," Romeo shouted. "Get back here!"

A man—Oscar—approached the door to apartment 905, the unit directly above the fire's origin. Smoke pushed out from the door's threshold as if propelled by a fan, enveloping the man's lower legs.

"My wife's pictures . . . her ring," Oscar cried as he reached for the doorknob. "I can't let them burn up."

"No!" Tony shouted while Romeo rushed for the man. "Don't open that door!"

***

"I gotta sit for a minute," Terrell said.

The pair had finally reached the eighth floor, where they found smoke filtering through the edges of the lobby door.

Dylan wiped his sweaty face. *Where the hell are the firemen?*

"What do we do now, genius?" Terrell asked as Dylan eased him onto the steps. "It's crazy hot in here."

"Hang on." Dylan tried to remember what he'd learned about the building layout from his crisscrossing climb. "I guess we'll go with your plan."

"Yeah? 'Bout time," Terrell said with a heavy dose of sarcasm.

"We know where the fire is, so all we've got to do is go through the lobby and take another route. It's okay in the other wings."

"You hope," Terrell said, exhaustion and pain written all over his face.

The kid was right, Dylan had no idea if the fire had spread to the other wings, but he didn't acknowledge that uncomfortable fact. "We also know the fire started on this floor, so we've got to climb to nine."

"No, man," Terrell said as he massaged the painful hip. "I can't do it." Tears appeared in the kid's eyes.

Nearing exhaustion himself, Dylan couldn't imagine carrying the kid up another flight. "All right. Maybe the fire hasn't reached the lobby," he said, even though the smoke and heat told him otherwise. He moved to the door, paused, and gripped the handle. "Motherfucker!" He jerked his hand away as scorching pain surged through his palm and raced up his arm.

"Shit, shit, shit," Terrell said.

Dylan eyed him. Tears were streaming down the kid's face. He pushed the pain away. *Maybe I can head upstairs and get help.*

"I know what you're thinking. You're gonna leave me."

Dylan climbed two steps, stopped, and met Terrell's frightened stare. "No, I'm not. But there's no help here. We've gotta go upstairs," he said as he returned to Terrell and helped him to his feet.

48

Friday, February 13 – 4:52pm

Tony's warning was lost in a whoosh of air and a thunderclap as Oscar pulled his apartment door open. His eyes registered what happened next, but his mind couldn't comprehend the sight as the door blew outward in a flash of fire and smoke, flinging the man across the hall like a rag doll.

The blast knocked the assembled residents off their feet and slammed Tony into the wall. Oscar lay sprawled on his back, his pants and shirt on fire. Romeo was slumped against the wall, head drooped on his chest, arms hanging limply at his sides.

"Division-9, Search-1, from Command. What the hell happened? A window just blew out."

Tony grabbed the water can from Luke. "Get them back inside!" he shouted as he and Muscles rushed toward the flames.

"Division-9, do you copy?"

Clutching the extinguisher by its handle, Tony squeezed the trigger and swept the water stream over Oscar's burning clothes.

Muscles grabbed Romeo by the boots and dragged him clear of the flames as the unconscious firefighter's PASS alarm blared incessantly.

Tony dropped the water can and hooked his arms under Oscar's armpits, pulling him up the hall and following Muscles into the apartment.

"Command, from Division-9," Tony radioed. "We had a backdraft in one apartment. We're taking refuge in another unit. I've got one firefighter and one civilian down. Stand by."

Tony's gaze locked on Oscar, sprawled on the sofa. His face was an angry cherry red, his eyebrows gone. Patches of raw, blistering flesh were visible through the charred tatters of his shirt. The reek of burnt flesh and singed hair filled the room.

Deborah staggered toward Oscar. "Oh my God!"

Tony caught her as she fell and eased her to the floor, where she sat, sobbing. The other residents stood around their prone friend, eyes wide with shock and disbelief.

On his knees, Muscles conducted a quick head-to-toe assessment of Romeo, whose eyes were open. "He's coming out of it."

Romeo turned his head toward Tony and mumbled something incoherent.

"His breathing is ragged, but his pulse is okay," Muscles said. "From what I can tell through his turnout gear, nothing's broken. I think he's just stunned."

Or he might have a concussion, Tony suspected, but Oscar's condition was much worse.

Tony cracked the door open and was met with floor-to-ceiling smoke. He didn't need the thermal imager to know it had gotten much hotter since the explosion. *Give us a fucking break, already.* He pulled the door shut. Everyone was staring at him.

"What's it look like, LT?" Luke asked.

Tony searched for reassuring words but found none. They were in real trouble now.

"Lieutenant Moretti from Command," Ramsey radioed. "What's your status? Can you evacuate?"

As the desperate little group looked on, Tony's hands grew shaky, his focus slipping at the sudden resurgence of his PTSD symptoms.

"What's going on up there, Moretti?" Ramsey radioed.

I'm beyond this. Slow down and think! Recalling Dr. Harrison's advice, he steeled his nerves and concentrated. The apartment was free of the effects of the fire, but that wouldn't be the case for long. His hands steadied and his mind cleared as he devised a contingency plan.

"Command from Division-9, Search-1, the south wing stairwell is blocked by fire in the lobby. We're going to try an alternate exit." *If we can pull it off.*

"Command copies. Chief McMahon is moving the attack lines from Division-8 to your location. Sit tight until they arrive. And keep me advised."

"Will do, Chief." But Tony had no intention of staying put. McMahon could take ten minutes to redeploy his hose teams and even longer to get water on the fire.

"We can't stay here, LT," Muscles said.

"We're not going to."

Lizzy began to sob. "The fire is so close."

Mariam gripped her friend's shoulders and eased her to the sofa.

Janice joined the chorus of despair. "We're going to die."

Mariam threw Tony a glance that asked for confirmation of Janice's grim assessment.

Tony shook his head emphatically. "We're not going to die."

"Luke, grab a couple of blankets from the bedroom. Let's protect Oscar as best we can when we move him."

"What's the plan, LT?" Muscles asked.

In his mind's eye, Tony pictured the floor plan. "South wing, west-facing apartments, stairwell," he said under his breath.

"West what?" Muscles asked.

"The odd side!" Tony said and shot his arm toward the door. "The first apartment on this side, 902, is adjacent to one of the elevator shafts. But across the hall, apartment 901 butts up against the southwest lobby stairs."

Muscles considered. "Yeah, but like I said, there's no way we can take these people—"

Tony held up his hand. "No, not through the lobby. Through the *wall.*"

"Wall?" Romeo asked, his faculties apparently back in business.

"Yes, the wall, and there's no time to argue. I'll take Romeo. Muscles, you carry Oscar. Luke, hustle everybody else as fast as you can. We're getting out of here."

✳✳✳

Dylan, shouldering most of Terrell's weight, managed to climb six steps before his breath hitched. Exhaustion closing in fast, he needed a moment to rest. The kid was trying to tough it out, but his moans couldn't disguise the pain he was in. Less than one more floor and they'd be on nine, where they'd finally be safe.

"Wait. Put me down. It hurts too bad."

"Come on, Terrell, we're almost out of here."

"It hurts. I can't take no more."

"You can. Even if I have to carry—"

Dylan shot an arm to the wall as the stairwell rocked. He tried to steady himself, but his knees buckled and he lost his grip on Terrell.

"Aaaahhh," Terrell called as he tumbled down, arms and legs flailing.

Dylan watched in horror as the kid's body smacked into the wall and dropped face down onto the eighth-floor landing with a sickening thud, arms and legs sprawled.

"Son of a bitch!" He reached Terrell in two bounding steps and knelt beside him.

Terrell pushed himself up. Blood oozed from a nasty gash above his left eye. The camera, still strapped around his neck, lay under him. "Ooohh shit, man, what was that?"

"Don't know, but I think we're okay in here."

"Says you," Terrell said, but with a lot less sass than before.

"You're a tough little bastard," Dylan said, surprised the kid hadn't been knocked out cold. "Looks like your arms are okay. Let's get you up and try your legs."

Terrell groaned as Dylan eased him into a sitting position before hoisting him to his feet.

"Ooh." Terrell's legs gave out and he sagged into Dylan's arms. "My foot."

"Which one?"

"Right foot. Damn!"

Dylan helped Terrell to the landing and gently squeezed the kid's ankle.

"Ow!"

"Sorry, it's sprained or broken. Either way, you're not putting any more weight on it." Dylan was grateful it wasn't a broken leg, but why did it have to be the foot on the kid's good side?

Terrell said nothing, but the tears were back, and the gash continued to bleed.

Dylan wiped the blood with his sleeve before it could reach the kid's eye and then pressed firmly to stem the flow. "It's not going to stop me from getting you out of here."

From the look of defeat on Terrell's face, he wasn't buying it.

Dylan had meant what he'd said. His half-assed plan to rescue elderly residents was a bust, but Terrell was his one chance, not to make up for what he'd done, but to do *something* good before he faced the consequences. "Ready to try again?"

"I . . . guess so."

"Hold your right foot up and see if you can bear some weight on your left leg."

"I'll try."

"Give me this," Dylan said and pulled the camera strap off Terrell's neck.

"No! I need it."

"Take it easy, I've got it," Dylan said as he looped the strap over his head. "Your camera doesn't look any worse than you do."

A smile crossed Terrell's face. "A friend gave it to me. He taught me how to use it, too."

The smile was a good sign. The kid had something left in him.

"Let's get out of here so you can tell him all about this screwed-up mess."

The weight on Dylan's shoulder eased as Terrell, grunting with pain, put weight on his left side. "Gotta show him these shots."

The thought of this unnamed friend seemed to infuse Terrell with new energy. *I hope to hell it's enough, because I don't have much left.*

49

Friday, February 13 – 5:03pm

"Command from Division-9, Search-1," Tony radioed. "We're moving the residents to apartment 901, adjacent to the southwest lobby stairs."

"Command copies. Chief McMahon's crews should be there soon."

Apartment 901 was only two doors away, but moving the elderly residents wouldn't be easy. Tony explained how they'd make the trip in two groups, the first with Romeo and Oscar. Over a few protestations, he helped Romeo to his feet while Muscles hefted an unconscious Oscar over his shoulder.

Crouching low and with a firm hold on Romeo, Tony led the way. Despite their chest-mounted lights, the smoke was a suffocating blanket that reduced visibility to mere inches.

He'd planned a dash, but Romeo, woozy and unsteady, stumbled to his knees. The sudden stop caused Muscles to collide with them in the inky haze. Oscar stirred, moaning as he woke and begging to be put down.

Tony pulled Romeo to his feet. "Keep moving," he urged. Running his free hand blindly along the wall, he found the door. "We're here!" he said as he turned the knob and entered the apartment.

The lights were still on, but the window he'd examined during his earlier search was now scorched black from top to bottom. *It won't hold much longer.* He guided Romeo to a chair near the door before helping Muscles place the writhing Oscar on the sofa.

"LT, the window," Muscles said.

"I know. We don't have much time. I'm going for the others," he said, and reentered the hallway.

"Thank God, LT," Luke said when Tony came through the door. "I thought something happened to you guys."

"Everything's okay," Tony said. "We've got to move."

Five residents, lined up in single file and holding dripping washcloths, eyed him warily.

"Listen up," Tony said. "It's smoky and hot, but it's breathable, there's no fire, and it's a short walk—a quick right into the hall and a left into the last apartment before the lobby."

The three women whispered among themselves while George addressed Tony. "If it's safe, why are you still breathing through your air tank?"

"To help you if anything goes wrong."

"Goes wrong?" Janice asked. "Maybe we should wait for help."

"There's no time to debate," Tony said, his firm tone augmented by the voice amplifier. "We're going, *now*."

The residents—all but Mariam—shrank back.

"Can you lead your friends, Mariam?" Tony asked, hoping to get her on his side. "I'm sure they'll follow you."

"I can do that," Mariam stated calmly.

That was good enough for Tony. "I'll lead, and Luke will follow behind. We won't let anyone get lost. Keep your faces covered and try to keep a hand on the person in front of you."

Tony cracked the door and glanced left toward the end of the wing. Pinpoints of flame darted in and out of view. *It'll be on us any minute.* He reached back for Mariam's hand. "Here we go. Move fast and stay low if you can." He doubted they'd be able to follow the advice, but the little train of refugees moved toward their goal with more dispatch than seemed possible, given their physical limitations.

Save for some coughing and that unsettling crackling noise, the hallway was quiet. In less than a minute, he'd ushered Mariam inside apartment 901. The needles jabbing his ears through the Nomex hood warned him that the heat level was rising fast. Once again, flashover was a real possibility, but this time, they had no water to prevent it.

Once Luke and George were inside, Tony pulled the door shut and undocked his regulator. The group gathered in the middle of the room, staring at the blackened window.

Senses overloaded, Tony strove to visualize the lobby layout. *The stairwell should be . . . there!*

"Get Oscar into the bedroom on the right," he ordered while helping Romeo to his feet. "Everybody else, follow them."

Oscar let out an agonized cry as Muscles and Luke carried him away by his arms and legs. The others watched, frozen in place until a resounding crack signaled the shattering of the picture window.

***

"One more floor, we can do it," Dylan said, but he wasn't so sure. Terrell was in serious pain and could barely move his legs. The smoke was minimal, but the suffocating heat of the fire floor was bad. It could all go to hell at any minute, and he was exhausted from carrying the youth he regarded as *his* responsibility.

Terrell's silence, and the hopeless expression on his face, wasn't encouraging. *Don't give up, kid.*

Dylan's legs wobbled despite gripping the railing for support, and he struggled to keep the kid standing. *I can do this. Just a little farther.*

"No more," Terrell pleaded as they reached the halfway point where the steps made their 180-degree turn. Dylan didn't argue; his muscles were jelly. With the ninth floor only ten steps above, he set the kid down and collapsed onto his ass, disgusted. *Christ, couldn't I do this one thing?*

50

Friday, February 13 – 5:11pm

Chaos reigned as residents' screams mingled with the urgent shouts of firefighters while smoke and flames rolled into the apartment. Tony rushed forward and seized Lizzy and Deborah by their shoulders. "Move it!" he ordered, shoving them toward the bedroom. Romeo, back on his feet, yanked George along beside him.

Tony did a quick headcount before slamming the door shut, sealing off the flames but trapping the group in the uncertain safety of the bedroom. The stakes had just skyrocketed, and if his understanding of the building's floor plan was wrong, it would take a miracle to survive.

"Oh my God, the fire," Lizzy shrieked.

Tony saw it. Smoke, pushing its way under the door. He hit his mic button. "Mayday, Mayday. Division-9, Search-1."

A high-pitched tone cut through the radio chatter. "County communications to all units operating at Water View Towers, clear the air. Division-9, Search-1 from County, go ahead with your Mayday transmission."

"Four firefighters and six residents, isolated in apartment 901 in the south wing. We've taken refuge in a bedroom, but the fire is right outside the door."

"Division-9 from Command, I copy. Do you have any avenues to evacuate?"

"Working on that now," Tony replied, "but the south wing hallway is fully involved and we're cut off from the lobby."

"You trapped us," George said through a fit of coughing.

"We're never getting out of here," Mariam muttered.

Tony removed his facepiece, ensuring they could see the fierce determination in his eyes. "We *are* getting out of here," he declared. The conviction in his voice seemed to allay their terror, but Mariam's dire prediction might easily come true.

"Division-9 from Attack." It was McMahon. "Hang on, Lieutenant. My hose teams are going into action now. We'll get to you."

Hanging on isn't an option. Tony lifted his A-tool and—crack—slammed it into the mirror mounted on the dresser along the back wall.

Lizzy screamed. The others shrank back.

"What gives, LT?" Luke asked.

"The southwest lobby stairwell is right behind this wall," he explained. "If I remember the preplans correctly, the fire separation is made of drywall, not masonry. We can cut through."

"I pray your memory is clear, LT," Muscles said, shoving his broad frame between the wall and the heavy dresser. "Luke, grab the other end!"

Luke didn't need to be told twice. Together, the two truckies heaved the dresser to the opposite corner of the room.

"Command from Division-9," Tony radioed. "We're going to attempt to breach the wall to the stairwell." Not waiting for a reply, he marked the area by punching holes in a semicircular outline with the point of the tool.

"We'll take it from there," Muscles said as he raised his Halligan and drove the fork end into the drywall. "Shit, it should have cut through." He spun the bar, reared back, and slammed the adze end into the small cut he'd made. The tool bounced off the wall without penetrating. "What the hell?"

"There's probably a double layer on each side of the studs," Tony said. "Punching through won't work. We have to *cut* through it."

Muscles dropped the Halligan, pulled off his facepiece, and retrieved his axe. Luke did the same. Positioned four feet apart, they started chopping.

Smoke infiltrated the room along all four sides of the door frame, and a dark haze began to form. *The flames won't be far behind*, Tony knew. "Romeo, use a blanket or some clothes and stuff them under that door."

"Division-9 from Command, report status."

"Command from nine, we're cutting into the wall now, but the bedroom door isn't going to hold for long. We could use some assistance."

"Lieutenant Moretti from Command, we have an idea to buy you some time."

"I'm all ears, Chief," Tony replied. *And it better be good.*

"Tower-502 is set up and ready for master stream operations," Ramsey reported. "We'd like to discharge several quick bursts into the window of apartment 901 to darken down the fire."

Tony looked to Muscles, who nodded. "Let's try it, Chief," he radioed. "Short bursts only. It was a risk. Water discharging from a master stream nozzle at five hundred gallons per minute could easily push the blaze into the bedroom and roast everyone alive." *This better work, because we're out of options.*

"Don't worry, Lieutenant, I'll make sure of it. I'm giving the order now."

***

"There it is again," Dylan said as he and Terrell rested on the steps between the eighth and ninth floors. He'd heard noises during their climb but hadn't been able to make them out.

"What is it?" Terrell asked, lifting his head from the steps.

"Quiet." Dylan pressed his ear to the wall. The sounds were distinct. A kind of thumping? No, pounding.

"I hear it," Terrell said. "Firemen?"

"I don't know. Maybe somebody trying to signal for help."

"That don't make any sense. Pounding a wall won't get them rescued."

Maybe not, Dylan supposed, but the pounding was definitely coming from above, and it was getting louder.

51

Friday, February 13 – 5:21pm

Tony's heart pounded as he monitored the three critical elements of the situation: the residents, the breaching operation, and the bedroom door. The situation was dire, and he took no solace in what he saw.

On the bed, Oscar lay semiconscious, his breathing harsh and irregular. His companions sat huddled at the foot of the bed, breathing through washcloths, their eyes wide with fear. Muscles and Luke, drenched with sweat, hacked furiously at the drywall barrier.

The lone glimmer of hope came from the water tower operation. It had slowed the fire's advance, as evidenced by the reduced level of heat and smoke entering the bedroom and the water seeping under the door. But since the application had, of necessity, been short and indirect, the reprieve wouldn't last.

"I'm through!" Muscles said. "You're right, LT, double layers on both sides of the studs." He pulled a strip of black fiberglass insulation from the hole and held it up. "With this shit in the middle."

Tony knelt and peered into the small opening while Muscles continued to work the edges. *Yes!* A fully illuminated open space revealed itself. "That's it. The stairwell."

"I see it too," Luke said. "There's some smoke in there, but it's not bad."

"I'll take over for you, Muscles."

"No way," Muscles replied. "Luke, you take a blow while I help the LT."

"Let me in there," Romeo said.

Tony eyed him.

"Really, LT, I'm good to go. I sealed the door as best I could, but it's still coming in." He nodded at the residents. "The floor's soaked, but they can breathe better now."

"All right. Our turn." Tony took the axe from Muscles while Luke passed his to Romeo. "Keep an eye on Oscar and make sure everyone's ready to go."

Tony clenched the axe, raising it above his shoulder before swinging it down with a grunt. It bit into the drywall, but the dual layer didn't give like typical wallboard, and the blade didn't penetrate far. Lifting the axe higher, he exhaled forcefully and swung again. The results were the same. "Damn."

"This shit is thick," Romeo said.

"That won't work," Muscles said. "You gotta take out one layer at a time."

Following the advice, Tony shortened his backswing and chopped with more measured strokes as his facepiece, hanging by its neck strap, swung wildly from side to side. It worked, but the effort to penetrate both layers took its toll.

Time became a blur. His turnout gear couldn't purge the heat generated by his exertions, and his swings began to lose force. Nerves frayed and nearing exhaustion, he fought to keep his apprehension in check as the sounds of moaning, coughing, and retching spoke to the misery of the frightened residents behind him. Yet thoughts of saving these people, of living another day, spurred him on.

When they finally completed their cuts, a roughly three-foot-by-three-foot hole to the stairwell appeared, obstructed by a lone vertical stud. Tony grabbed a Halligan and smashed it into the base of the stud, dislodging it from the floor. Once the two-by-four came loose, he tore it off and tossed it aside.

"I'll check," Romeo said and poked his head into the opening. "We're even with the landing. Great call, LT!"

Tony rocked back on his butt as relief washed over him. He'd been right, but they weren't out of danger yet. "Muscles, get in there. Luke will pass the residents through to you. Romeo and I will take care of Oscar."

He got to his feet as Muscles shimmied into the breach. Salvation was at hand, but it was going to be close.

***

The pounding stopped, replaced by shouting voices and a rain of white flakes. *What the . . . ?*

"Ow," Terrell called as something bounced off his head.

Dylan picked it up. "Drywall," he said as chunks of the white material peppered the steps. "It's got to be the firemen. Come on, we gotta get up there."

"I can't move, and I don't think you can carry me no more."

Dylan got to his feet. "I'll go."

"No," Terrell said, making a weak attempt to grab Dylan's leg. "Don't . . . leave."

"I have to. You're okay here. I'll be right back with help."

Terrell released his grip. His head slumped against the wall.

Dylan hesitated, ears straining to make sense of the sounds. Definitely voices. He craned his neck and squinted into the gap between the upper and lower flights. Then he saw it—a black shape poking over the landing. *What is that?* The answer struck him like a bolt of lightning. A fireman's helmet! Without thinking, he grabbed Terrell's camera and banged it against the railing. "Help! We need help down here!"

52

Friday, February 13 – 5:32pm

"Division-9, Search-1 from Command, status report."

Tony, in the process of helping Romeo lift Oscar from the floor, ignored Chief Ramsey's call. *No time.*

"Command from Division-9, Muscles responded. "We've breached the wall and we're evacuating the residents into the stairwell now."

"Thanks, Muscles," Tony called as he and Romeo, backs bent low to the floor, half carried and half dragged the whimpering Oscar to the opening.

"Be advised," Ramsey added, "Chief McMahon's team is still working their way to your location, but the fire has broken through to the lobby. They're trying to keep it from penetrating the southwest stairs while you escape."

What else already?

"LT," Muscles called. "We've got two people on the steps below us. I tried to get them to climb, but they say they can't."

That's what. "Tell them to sit tight." *One thing at a time.*

Ramsey continued: "The floors above you have been cleared of residents, but Division-10 might be compromised. Division-11 is your best bet. I have a fresh search team headed there to meet you."

That's the capper.

"If we lose the stairwell, we're done," Romeo said.

"We'll be out by then," Tony said as he crawled through the opening. When he emerged, five residents were already climbing, albeit slowly, with Luke in the lead.

"Hey up there," a man's voice from below called. "What are you waiting for?"

Tony turned to Muscles and Romeo. "Get Oscar up to eleven. I'll check the situation downstairs."

"Do you guys hear me?" the man shouted, his voice tinged with anger. "I got an injured kid with me. He can't walk and I can't carry him anymore. We need help."

"Hold on, I'm coming down now," Tony called.

"I don't like leaving you, LT," Muscles said, hesitating.

"Get going, I'll radio if I need help."

Tony hustled down, but when he turned the corner to the bottom flight, he froze. "Terrell?" He blinked in disbelief. It *was* him, sitting on the steps with his back against the wall and blood on his face. A civilian stood over him.

"'Sup, Tony," Terrell said in a faint voice, raising his hand in acknowledgment.

"He took a header," the civilian said. "Cut his head and hurt his ankle. He can't put any weight on his right leg."

Tony took stock of the man, who wore a baseball cap and a black hoodie. A familiar camera hung against his chest. The face sparked a hint of recognition, but from where? "Are you staff?"

"No, the name's Dylan, and I'm just trying to help." He nodded at Terrell. "I found him a few floors down. His hip hurts real bad from climbing the stairs. I pretty much carried him up here, looking for you guys."

"Thank you for that," Tony said. "Any idea how he got here?"

The guy turned to Terrell. "Tell him."

Terrell raised his head. "Uber."

"Uber? Are you serious? I told you not to follow us."

Terrell pointed at the camera. "Pictures, like you taught me." A smile lit the corners of his mouth.

Tony bent to his friend. "We'll discuss it later. Right now, we've got to get you out of here. He wrapped an arm around Terrell and hoisted him to his feet."

"Easy," Terrell said, his voice laced with pain. "Wait, my camera."

"I'll take it," Tony said.

Dylan handed the camera over. "He's a hurting puppy."

"A real piece of work is what he is."

"But he's got spunk."

"Too much for his own good," Tony said. "Not sure why you two were going up instead of down, but now we've got no choice. We need to get to the eleventh floor. I'll take care of Terrell. Think you can make it by yourself, Dylan?"

"I'll give it a shot."

"Good deal," Tony said. "Let's go, Terrell."

***

Dylan followed, but at a distance, watching as the fireman carried Terrell around the corner and disappeared onto the upper flight.

The climb was much easier without the kid, but he let the pair get ahead of him. As he reached the ninth floor, biting smoke from the hole the firemen had cut clawed at his nostrils and stung his eyes, causing him to blink rapidly and gasp for air.

"Are you still with us, Dylan?" the fireman called.

"Yeah," he answered but backed down the steps to cooler, clearer air, where he ditched the hoodie and sat. "Just need a couple minutes."

"You don't have a couple minutes, and don't even think about trying that lobby door. Keep climbing and I'll come back for you."

Dylan had no intention of burning himself on another hot door handle, but the guy was right. The fire was close, and the ninth floor wasn't an option. *But what if I . . .*

"Do you hear me, Dylan?" The voice grew distant. The guy, weighed down with all that fireman's gear, and with Terrell's weight to boot, was climbing fast.

"Yeah, I'm right behind you," Dylan replied but didn't move. He was bushed and needed a minute to figure out his next move.

Having saved the kid, there was no point trying to help anyone else. Staying meant almost certain capture, but if he escaped, he might never be caught. He'd avoided detection so far and could do it again if he was clever. If it wasn't already dark outside, it would be soon. Even if the cops did nab him, the kid and the fireman could vouch for his actions. It was a no-brainer.

His plan was simple: wait for the fireman to carry the kid a little higher, then climb to the tenth floor, slip into an empty hallway, and disappear. *Time to boogie.*

53

Tony's knees crackled like dry leaves, and his thigh muscles burned with every step. Skinny as he was, Terrell had to weigh at least 110, and Tony was bearing most of the load.

"How are you?" Tony asked.

"Uhh . . . o-kay, but my . . . head." Terrell's voice was strained and weak, but Tony was glad to hear him speak at all. The teen hadn't uttered a word since they'd left the ninth-floor landing.

"If you hadn't decided to face-plant on the stairs . . ."

Terrell raised his head. "You ain't . . . funny."

"*Aren't* funny. What would your mom say about your grammar?"

"Can we stop?"

"Sure, we'll sit for a minute," Tony said. He needed a break too but knew the signs: rising heat, acrid smells, and the taste of burning electrical insulation. The fire was closing in on them. "We're almost there."

"Where's Dylan?"

"He's coming."

"He's the one, you know."

Terrell was babbling. "He's what?"

"The guy that set all those fires . . . the firebug."

"What are you talking about?"

"You know, the guy who killed your friend at that tire store."

Tony's stomach dropped. "He told you this?"

"Yeah, aah, after I recognized him."

"Wait, he's the one in the black hoodie? From your photos?"

"Yep, that's him."

"Of course!" Tony said. *No wonder the bastard looked familiar.*

"Said he didn't mean to hurt no one, though."

"That's what he said, is it?" Tony asked, his words dripping with disgust. "Did he say he started *this* fire?"

"No. Said he came here to help. Try to make up for what he did."

Tony's fatigue disappeared in a flood of rage-fueled adrenaline. He grabbed the railing, pulled Terrell to his feet, and resumed the climb at double his previous clip.

"Fire Department. Anybody down there?"

Tony looked up. "Yeah! Down here. I've got a victim."

The sound of clomping boots was followed by the welcome sight of two familiar faces from Station-400: Lieutenant Brookin and firefighter Scott Peterson—the guy who had gotten caught in the flames at the tanker fire. "Hello, Tim," Tony said. *And it's about time.*

"I'll bet," Brookin said. "Sorry we're so late. We climbed from the sixth floor, but we had a crazy detour up to eleven."

"I thought you were the staging guru."

"I was, but when you called for help, the chief figured he'd better round up a couple engine boys to rescue the truckies."

"I'm not complaining. Do you have a way out?"

"Yeah, the tenth-floor lobby is a no-go, but eleven is clear, for now anyway. We're having a mother of a time with this fire."

"Don't I know it."

"Your crew is up there now with the people they evacuated," Brookin added. "I had two C-Platoon guys tagging along with us. I left them up there to help Muscles and the gang." Brookin nodded at Terrell. "How 'bout we take this young man off your hands?"

Tony considered. He would rather do it himself, but he had someone else to deal with. "He hit his head and hurt his ankle, so take it easy."

"We'll take care of him," Brookin said as he and Peterson took position on either side.

"See you soon," Tony whispered, allowing the two firefighters to assume the teen's weight.

"We'll take him to the northeast stairs and then down to six," Brookin said. "That's where the medics are set up. Anybody else downstairs?"

"Just one, an adult male. He's coming up from nine."

"Want me to stay and help you with him? Scott can get the boy upstairs."

"No," Tony said with a little too much emphasis. "This boy . . . Terrell, needs help *now*. The other guy's not hurt, just needs a little assistance. I can handle him."

"If you say so, but we'll be back to help as soon as we can."

"Thanks," Tony said, "but I won't need any." He wanted to confront Dylan alone. *He'll be lucky if I don't toss his ass down the stairs.*

***

Dylan stood and retraced his steps to the ninth floor. Things had gotten much worse in the five minutes he'd waited for that fireman to get out of range.

A heat wave, like when you opened an oven door, washed into him as he neared the landing. Smoke, darker and thicker than before, stung his eyes.

For a second, he considered going back down, but he dismissed the thought. *I'm dead if I don't get out of here.* If he could reach the tenth floor, he'd be in the clear.

Gathering his courage, Dylan took a deep breath. *Now or never.* He ducked low, raised a hand to shield his face, and dashed up the steps.

Heat seared his exposed skin as his feet hit the landing. *It's too late.* His assessment seemed to be confirmed when the world exploded around him.

54

Friday, February 13 – 5:53pm

Tony dug his boot heels into the rubberized stair treads as a wall of smoke enveloped him. Teetering at the foot of the upper flight, he reached for the railing, missed, and slammed into the wall. He regained his balance, yanked the regulator from his belt, and shoved it into the facepiece, drawing a gulp of clean air.

Hands groping in the darkness, he lowered himself to the steps. With his elbows pulled in and his arms stretched out under him, he duck-walked around the stairwell's turn, and as the wave of smoke cleared, he glimpsed Dylan pinned against the wall on the ninth-floor landing. Flames spouted from the wall breach, inches from his body. "Get down!"

Dylan rolled onto his belly and pulled himself down the steps. His jeans were on fire. "Help me!"

Tony sprang to his feet. Flames reflected off his visor and pain shot through his ears as he plunged into the fiery scene, grasped Dylan's shoulders, and dragged him down the steps.

"Aaaahhh, I'm burning up!"

Tony eased Dylan's head to the steps and smothered the burning jeans with his gloves.

"Oh man, oh man, it hurts," Dylan said, his words intermingled with choking coughs.

"I know it does, but I'm going to get you out of here," Tony vowed, but his promise became desperate as a sudden wave of heat erupted from below and a new column of smoke spiraled upward. *Christ, we're trapped between two fires.*

Tony draped himself over Dylan and hit his lapel mic. "Mayday! Mayday!"

"County to all units operating at Water View Towers, clear the air for a Mayday transmission."

"This is 300-Lieutenant. I'm with an injured civilian in the southwest stairwell, between Divisions-8 and 9. We've got fire above and below us."

"300-Lieutenant from Command, can you—"

McMahon cut off Ramsey's transmission. "Moretti, we're working our way into the Division-9 lobby. Hang on."

"Copy," Tony replied. *We can't wait.*

"Leave me here, save yourself," Dylan said through fits of coughing. "I've done . . . things."

Tony let the admission pass, thoughts of punishing this man forgotten as he figured a way to save both of them.

Dylan's coughs morphed into retching, and he threw up on the steps.

Tony pulled off a glove, turned Dylan's head to the side, and cleared the vomitus from his mouth.

Heat and smoke swallowed the stairwell, but Tony continued to shield the unprotected man with his body as he groped for a solution. *Up or down? We can't stay here.*

"300-Lieutenant from Command, what's your status?"

"This is 300-Lieutenant. This position is untenable. I'm taking the victim up to eleven."

"I copy that, Tony," Ramsey radioed. "Good luck."

Tony didn't acknowledge, but he'd need all the luck the gods would grant him in the next few minutes.

$$55$$

Friday, February 13 – 6:01pm

Thick with smoke and searing heat, the stairwell was a crucible, a battleground with an unyielding adversary. But Tony's resolve was fierce. He wouldn't let the fire win. Not today. Not as it had on that last day in the Oregon forest.

"Oh God, it hurts," Dylan blubbered, his voice cracking through fits of coughs.

Arms and legs shaking from exhaustion, Tony held plank position, eyes boring into the man who caused Fitz's death.

Dylan convulsed, his coughs violent and wet.

Carefully, Tony lowered himself to his elbows and violated a sacrosanct safety protocol. Despite the yellow LEDs shining in his heads-up display, he slid a finger under the rubber seal of his facepiece. Fresh air rushed out, mingling with the smoke as the SCBA attempted to compensate for the broken seal. Tilting his head, he guided the stream directly into Dylan's face.

"Deep breaths," he urged and watched as the man's cries of pain broke into ragged, desperate gasps. "We're not done yet."

Tony removed his finger, allowing the seal to reseat. "We've got to go up."

Dylan's gaze fixed on the stairs. "Into that? You're insane."

"If we don't go now, we won't make it out."

"No, man. You go. I don't deserve to get out."

Tony clenched his jaw, ignoring the plea.

"You don't know who I am . . . what I've done," Dylan whispered, shame adding to the agony painted across his face.

"I know who you are *and* what you've done, and I'm not leaving you here."

Dylan's eyes went wide. "You . . . know?"

"Yeah, I do," Tony said, voice filled with controlled anger. The memory of Fitz's death stirred his fury. *I should leave the murdering bastard to his fate. But what would that make me?* "It's live or die."

Dylan shrank back. "My life, it's over. Let me die."

The LEDs flashed red, and the low-air alarm bell began to clang. "There's no fucking time for this." With every muscle screaming in protest, he grabbed hold of Dylan's arms, squatted, and pulled him into a firefighter's carry.

"No . . . my legs, wait, you can't—"

"Shut up. We're going." He clamped an arm around Dylan's thighs, grasped the railing, and pulled himself to his feet.

With anger-fueled adrenaline coursing through his veins, Tony pivoted sideways to keep Dylan's torso facing the wall and stormed onto the landing.

"Stop! I can't take it."

The flames were behind them, but the oppressive heat only increased as the products of combustion rose relentlessly in the confined space. *It's like climbing inside a damn chimney.*

"300-Lieutenant from Command, report."

Tony's boot caught on a step as he made the turn to the upper flight. His balance wavered, but he pressed on. *If I fall now, it's over.*

His legs trembled as he reached the tenth floor. Smoke pushed out from the fire door. No escape there. He had to keep climbing.

Every step sent pain shooting up his injured ankle. His thigh and calf muscles burned, his lower back spasmed, and the arm holding Dylan went numb. Twenty steps. *I can do it.*

"One . . . two . . . three," he counted with each labored step as he gulped the remaining air from his breathing apparatus. His mind returned to that last day with the Forest Service, when the crew lay helpless in their little aluminized shelters. *Not this time, dammit! I control my fate today.*

"Nine . . . ten." *Come on . . . come on.* He hit the turn to the upper flight, struggling to breathe.

"Lieutenant Moretti from Command, do you read me?"

Suddenly, the low-air alarm bell stopped ringing. Less than 200 psi remained in the cylinder.

Ramsey's voice cut through the din. "Tony, report!"

Tapping reserves of strength forged during his summer in the west, he staggered on. "Fifteen, sixteen . . . arrrgh."

The visor sucked to his face. *I'm out of air!*

Holding his breath, he switched to a silent count. *Eighteen, nineteen.*

Lungs ready to burst, he dropped to one knee, yanked the regulator free, and inhaled the hot, smoky air. They'd reached the eleventh floor.

He eased Dylan onto the landing and flopped against the wall as the fire door burst open. A red-helmeted figure stared down at him through the haze.

"Command from Lieutenant Brookin on Division-11, we've got them."

Tony removed his helmet and tossed the facepiece aside. "Nice to see you, Tim."

"See, Tony, I told you I'd come back."

***

For the second time in his short MAFA career, Tony found himself in the back of a medic wagon.

The EMT, who didn't look old enough to vote, read Tony's vitals. "BP 174 over 76, pulse 64. No other obvious injuries. Did you hit your head? Your buddies asked me to check."

"Yeah, for signs of a brain," Pet said as she climbed into the ambulance. "Two emergency calls for help at one fire. We're going to start calling you Mayday Moretti."

"Very funny, and I'm not a patient. I didn't need checking."

"But McMahon ordered you here, right? He knows your tricks."

The EMT removed the blood pressure cuff. "He's good to go."

"Finally," Tony said. "Where's Terrell?"

"Follow me."

Pet led him to an ambulance parked in front of the ladder truck.

"How is he?"

"Ask him yourself." She pointed to the open back doors.

Tony hurried over and poked his head inside. Terrell, lying faceup on a gurney, winced as a young female paramedic dressed the wound on his forehead. "Hi, buddy, how ya doing?"

Terrell raised his head. "I'm . . . all right."

"What, no smart remark? You must be in bad shape."

"Ain't nothin' wrong with me. Don't be throwin' shade, now."

"Ah, that's better." Turning to the medic, he asked, "Will the patient live?"

"Other than this cut on his forehead and some bruises, he's okay, but I'm concerned about the blow to his head."

Terrell shot Tony a sly smile. "This is Emily. She's checking me out . . . *real* good."

Tony shook his head. "Same old Terrell. Sounds like you're just fine to me."

Like a switch, Terrell lost his smile and dropped his head to the pillow. "Mama's gonna have my head for this."

"Not just yours. I'm the one who got you started with photography."

Pet chimed in. "One of the River Bend cops already called her. I heard he got an earful."

"I have no doubt," Tony said. "Shoot the messenger."

"We need to get him to the hospital," Emily said.

"Of course. Where are you taking him?"

"UPMC McKeesport."

"Thanks," Tony said and leaned over the gurney. "I'll call your mom and tell her where you're headed. As soon as I get permission to leave the scene, I'll be there too. Maybe I can run some interference for you."

"Good luck with that," Terrell said.

"Come on," Pet said as Tony closed the doors to the medic wagon. "They want you at the command post."

Tony sighed. "Lead me to my execution, Acting Lieutenant Petruska."

"Drama queen."

"What about Dylan, the arsonist?" Tony asked.

"So you're on a first-name basis with him, huh?"

"We met."

"The county boys hauled his ass away about five minutes ago. They're bringing him back to River Bend, and you can bet Dez Fitzpatrick will be waiting for him."

"I'm sure." But Tony knew any satisfaction Dez got from the arrest would pale in comparison to the heartache of losing Fitz.

"Tony, get over here," Chief Ramsey said as they approached the CP.

Ignoring his protesting leg muscles and the pain shooting across his lower back, Tony squared his shoulders and quickened his pace.

"You did some amazing work today," Ramsey said. "Not one person lost their life."

"Thanks, Chief, but it was my team."

"Yes, yes, kudos for everyone," Ramsey said. "They're the ones who told me about your exploits. Couldn't say enough. You've certainly won them over."

Despite the cold, warmth spread across Tony's face. "How about the residents? One of them—Oscar—had some bad burns."

"He's probably got a long road ahead of him in the burn unit, but the medics think his injuries are survivable. The others are being treated for smoke inhalation, but they should be okay. One of them, MaryAnn, I think . . ."

"Mariam," Tony corrected.

"Right, Mariam. She made a point of telling the medics how *Lieutenant Tony* saved them when they thought they were all going to die." Ramsey smiled broadly. "You're building quite a fan club."

"What can I say, Chief?"

Ramsey clasped Tony's shoulder. "Lieutenant, you possess a rare blend of physicality and mental acuity. Hiring you into a leadership role was one of the best decisions I've made."

The entire command team came forward to congratulate him.

Tony, humbled by the praise, ensured all of his firefighters were okay before asking McMahon to return the crew to quarters. With the battalion chief's permission, he hitched a ride on one of the departing ambulances to check on Terrell.

En route to the hospital, Tony reflected on the challenges of the day with a deep sense of accomplishment and an intense pride in the performance of his firefighters. Every obstacle they faced had been met with unwavering determination and seamless teamwork, exemplifying the true spirit of their profession. All things considered, it had been an extraordinary day at the office.

Epilogue

The Water View Towers fire capped a remarkable year for the fledgling Monongahela Area Fire Authority, proving the promised benefits of the consolidation to a once-skeptical public. Despite the immense challenges posed by a rapidly spreading high-rise fire and the complexity of evacuating elderly residents with physical limitations, there were no fatalities. Chief Ramsey, lauded by the media and local officials, graciously redirected the praise to his valiant firefighters.

***

Dylan Ross, transported to the River Bend police station by county police, was interviewed by detectives in the presence of a public defender. Against advice, he offered a full confession for starting the fires, insisting that he'd never intended to harm anyone and was only trying to improve community conditions. He was then transferred to the Allegheny County jail.

At his formal arraignment on February 14, he faced charges of six counts of arson and one count of first-degree murder. He pled guilty and, in exchange for a reduced charge of second-degree murder, waived his right to a preliminary hearing. Request for bail denied, he was sent back to jail to await sentencing.

***

Dez Fitzpatrick took the death of his brother hard. A bachelor with few remaining family ties in the area, he considered taking early retirement and leaving the Mon Valley but ultimately decided to stay and continue his family's legacy of community service.

To honor Fitz's memory, Dez enlisted the help of Tony, Barney Dudek, and Chief Ramsey to organize an annual first responders' 5K. Despite his aversion to exercise, he pushed through and completed the inaugural run through River Bend in a respectable 38:42, a touching tribute to his brother's dedication and sacrifice.

***

Terrell required eleven stitches to close the gash on his forehead and was diagnosed with a mild concussion from his fall in the apartment building stairwell. With Tony's help, he recovered quickly and continued to hone his photography skills.

Mrs. Cooper, gradually loosening the reins on her only son, allowed him to visit Tony's apartment. To everyone's astonishment, she agreed when Chief Ramsey proposed that Terrell join the department as a junior explorer and become the official departmental photographer. Under strict instructions to remain alongside the designated safety officer and outside of burning buildings, he embraced this new role with enthusiasm, ready to capture his firefighter friends in action.

***

With the support of his deputies and the union, Chief Ramsey elevated Tony to the permanent rank of captain, entrusting him with the leadership of Station-300's B-Platoon. Hesitant to accept, the reluctant lieutenant acceded after every member of B-Platoon—except Warren—threw their support behind him.

***

Tony had been waiting for the right time to pop the question to Allie, and an invitation to the Cooper household for his birthday on March 28 offered the perfect opportunity.

Once again, Terrell met them at the door, but this time his anticipatory smile evaporated when Allie removed her coat to reveal a blue-and-black long-sleeved chiffon maxi dress that flowed elegantly around her.

Tony couldn't suppress a smile. *Sorry, kid.*

"Happy birthday, Tony!" Mrs. Cooper said as she welcomed them inside. "Allie, it's so wonderful to see you again."

"He's taking me to the symphony at Heinz Hall tonight—Beethoven's *Eroica.*" She chuckled. "It's so not him."

"What?" Tony asked. "I'm expanding my horizons."

Mrs. Cooper laughed. "Isn't that lovely?"

The aroma of home-cooked food filled the air as they settled in for another of Mrs. Cooper's delicious meals. Despite Allie's conservative dress, Terrell couldn't keep his eyes off her, sneaking peeks every chance he got.

After dinner, they lingered at the table, their conversation light and full of laughter, much of it at Tony's expense.

Allie's eyes sparkled as she chatted with Mrs. Cooper. Tony's heart swelled with love. *This is it.*

"Thank you for the amazing dinner, Mrs. Cooper," he said. "You always outdo yourself."

She waved a hand dismissively. "It's the least I could do for the man who saved my son's life." Her eyes shimmered with tears. "I don't know what I'd do without my Terrell."

"Oh, Mama," Terrell muttered as his mother dabbed her eyes.

Tony, unsure of what to say, offered, "I would never let anything happen to him. Terrell means a lot to me." He feared the evening would be spoiled with sadness, but Allie swooped in to save the day.

"I say it's time for a celebration," she said. "Terrell's fine, Tony's in a better place, and we're all here together."

Mrs. Cooper brightened. "Well said, dear. Forgive my old woman's foolishness. Terrell, why don't you fetch the cake?"

"Mrs. Cooper, you really didn't have to."

Allie poked Tony playfully. "Especially with this belly of his."

"Hey now!" Tony said, holding up his hands in mock defense.

Eyes lit up when Terrell returned with a beautifully decorated cake adorned with four flickering candles.

"It's from Schneider's," Mrs. Cooper said. "One of their famous butter creams. You saved that bakery, didn't you?"

"No, my crew was in the building next door, above the thrift store," Tony said.

"You're too modest," Mrs. Cooper said.

"It's the plumbing store he burned down," Terrell said.

"Mind your manners," Mrs. Cooper admonished. "The four candles represent our new friendship."

"Make a wish," Allie said.

Tony pressed his sweaty hands to his pants and closed his eyes, wishing with all his heart. *Please let her say yes.*

"What did you wish for?" Allie asked.

"Well," he began, "I guess I should let you in on it." He pulled a small velvet box from his pocket and dropped to one knee beside Allie. Hands trembling and heart thudding, he opened the box to reveal a dazzling diamond ring.

Allie's hands flew to her face. "Oh my God!"

"Althea Robinson," he said, voice filled with emotion, "from the moment you came into my life, everything changed. You've shown me what it means to love and be loved, you've stood by me during the worst times, and I can't imagine another day without you. Will you marry me?"

Allie's mouth dropped open, and silence filled the room as they awaited her reply.

Tony held his breath. *She's going to say no.*

"Yes!" she exclaimed. "Yes, yes, yes!"

Relief surged through him as he slipped the ring onto her finger. They rose together, and he pulled her into his arms.

"This is just wonderful," Mrs. Cooper said.

"You slayed it, dog!" Terrell exclaimed but caught sight of his mother's glare and tried again. "What a beautiful proposal, Mr. Moretti."

Mrs. Cooper shook her head, a faint smile playing on her lips. "Here's to friends, family, and good times."

After more toasts, hugs, tears, and laughter, Tony checked his watch. "We should get going if we don't want to be late for Beethoven. Thanks for everything, Mrs. Cooper."

"It was my pleasure. Thank *you* for sharing this special moment with us."

"It wouldn't have been the same without you," Allie said, hugging Mrs. Cooper tightly.

"Looking at you two, I just know you have a wonderful lifetime ahead."

Allie sighed. "Even if we *are* living three hours apart."

Mrs. Cooper patted Allie's hand. "Distance means so little when you're in love. You'll figure it out."

Taking hold of Allie's hand, Tony added, "That we will, Mrs. C, that we will."

Acknowledgements

After publishing *Out of the Fire*, I was eager to continue Tony Moretti's story and explore his evolving career in the fire service. As his skills and experience grew, I sought to challenge him further by placing him in a new, more demanding environment. The historic industrial towns of the Monongahela Valley, with their rich character and unwavering resilience, provided the perfect backdrop. I hope my readers agree.

I wrote *The Fire Inside* to entertain those who enjoy action-packed fiction paired with a deep dive into the psyche of the main characters. Beyond that, I aimed to shine a light on small town first responders whose stories are rarely told, offering a realistic portrayal of the physical and emotional challenges they face. I didn't plan on beginning Tony's latest adventure with a wildland firefighting scene, but I thought it appropriate to give a nod to the men and women who ply their incredibly demanding trade in the forestlands of the west.

The two-year journey of writing this book was demanding, but immensely rewarding. I'm deeply grateful to the incredible people who supported and inspired me throughout the process.

First and foremost, my heartfelt thanks to Karen, my lovely bride of forty years. A talented creator in her own right, she spends her time knitting and crocheting vibrant afghan blankets that she donates to those in need and crafting beautiful needlepoint artwork that brightens nearly every room in our home. Karen has always been my biggest booster, especially in times of frustration or doubt. My books wouldn't exist without her support.

I am also deeply appreciative of the public safety professionals who lent me their expertise. Tim Holmes and Shawn O'Brien, fire service leaders and longtime friends, reviewed the firefighting technology and procedures depicted in the story. Dave Volk, another close friend and former colleague, provided detailed insight into the MSA G-1 self-contained breathing apparatus, a key firefighting tool depicted in this book. Doug Garretson, a legend in Pennsylvania's Emergency Medical Services community, also contributed his extensive knowledge to enhance the narrative.

I firmly believe in the value of Beta Readers, and I was lucky to secure the services of three talented individuals from my local Mindful Writers group: Larry Ivkovich, Sharon Wenger, and David George. These generous people dedicated their time to read a 90,000-word manuscript, offering detailed and constructive feedback. Their care and skill helped me refine the characters, dialogue, and setting, elevating the book beyond what I could have achieved alone.

Professional help is vital to ensure a polished product, and I send many thanks to my cover designer, Jerry Todd, my copy editor, Amanda Oruha, my proofreader, Eliza Dee, and my book interior designer, Marina Anderson. Their skills brought the finishing touches to my second novel, and I'm thrilled to have worked with them. My special gratitude goes to Keira Colella, whose beautifully rendered map of the MAFA fire district brought the geography of this novel to life.

Last but certainly not least, a shout out to my amazing readers. I thank you from the bottom of my heart, and hope you've enjoyed the story!

Author's Notes

The Monongahela Area Fire Authority and its eleven communities are fictional creations, but the other towns mentioned in this book are real and form part of the industrial fabric of Western Pennsylvania. Their story is one of perseverance, marked by a rich cultural heritage and the enduring spirit of the Pittsburgh region. I believe in the continued revitalization of these iconic towns. To learn more about efforts to support this region, visit the Mon Valley Initiative—a dedicated organization focused on rebuilding community infrastructure and connecting employers with job seekers: www.monvalleyinitiative.com.

***

Post-Traumatic Stress Disorder is a serious issue in the first responder community. Thoughtful, caring individuals can't help but be affected by the emotionally challenging and often heartbreaking events they witness. If someone you know is suffering from PTSD, therapeutic treatment and support groups are available. Information can be found at the National Center for PTSD (www.ptsd.va.gov), or the National Alliance on Mental Illness (www.nami.org).

***

Following the release of *Out of the Fire,* many readers expressed interest in a guide to the specialized terminology. To that end, I've included a glossary of fire service terms used in this book. I hope you found it helpful. If you're interested in photos of firefighting apparatus and equipment, check out the Gallery section of my website.

***

According to the National Fire Protection Association, volunteer fire departments make up 82% of all fire departments in the U.S., providing protection to nearly one-third of the population. The shortage of these selfless individuals is a pressing concern. As a case in point, Pennsylvania boasted 350,000 volunteers in the 1970s. Today, that number has dwindled to fewer than 35,000. If your community relies on volunteers, why not stop at the fire station and find out how you might contribute? Whether you're ready for the exciting and rewarding challenge of firefighting, or prefer to assist with business operations or fundraising, there's always a need for individuals willing to support these vital organizations.

***

I hope you enjoyed this book. Please consider leaving a review (no matter how long or short) on your favorite platform. Reviews help potential readers discover new books, and I'd really appreciate it! If you'd like further information, please visit my website at bacolella.com.

Thank you for reading The Fire Inside!

Organization of the Monongahela Area Fire Authority

Battalion-1 (South of the Monongahela River)
- Station 300 (River Bend)
  - Engine-301
  - Ladder-302
  - Rescue-303
  - Foam-304
  - Battalion Chief-1

- Station 400 (Buchanan)
  - Engine-401
  - Reserve Engine-402
  - Squad-403

Battalion-2 (North of the Monongahela River)
- Station 500 (Union Center)
  - Engine-501
  - Tower-502
  - Special Services-503
  - Battalion Chief-2

- Station 600 (Mill Town)
  - Engine-601
  - Reserve Engine-602
  - Squad-603

Monongahela River
River Bend
MAFA HQ
Station 300
Fu...
Battalio...
West Forge
East Forge
MAFA
District Map

Wasington Heights
Battalion-2
Union Center
Penn's Grove
Station 500
Mill Town
Hillcrest Acres
Station 600
Station 400
Buchanan
New Industry Bridge
Rocky Shore
map by Heinz

Glossary of Fire Service Terms

A-tool (Officer's Tool): A 17" bar with a flat striking surface at one end and tapered forks at the other.

Aerial Ladder Truck (Ladder-302 in this novel): A multi-section, hydraulically operated ladder that can be extended to a variety of lengths, often reaching 100 feet or more. They are used for ventilation (opening windows and making way for smoke to escape), rescue (lifting people from windows or roofs), and extinguishing fires at higher levels. Ladder trucks also carry ground ladders of varying length, as well as numerous firefighting tools.

Aerial Tower Ladder Truck (Tower-502 in this novel): An aerial ladder equipped with a basket or platform at the top of the ladder.

AFFF (Aqueous Film-Forming Foam): A type of firefighting foam used to suppress flammable liquid fires. It is designed to create a protective film on the surface of burning liquids, preventing oxygen from reaching the fire and extinguishing it.

Attack Line: Hoselines with interior diameters ranging from 1-1/2 to 2-1/2 inches that are advanced from pumpers and used to extinguish fires. In this novel the attack lines are 1-3/4" and flow 175 gallons per minute.

Auto Exposure: The spread of flames from one floor to the floor above along the exterior of a building, often due to the upward movement of hot gases and smoke from a lower-level fire.

Backdraft: An explosion that occurs when air is introduced into a confined, oxygen-depleted environment, causing rapid combustion of accumulated gases.

Bale: The handle that controls the flow of water from a nozzle. When the bale is pulled back, the nozzle opens. Pushing the bale forward shuts off the water.

Box Light: Handheld, lantern-style flashlight with a powerful, focused beam for smoky environments.

Can: A 2-1/2 gallon, pressurized water fire extinguisher used on ordinary combustible materials.

CO (Carbon Monoxide): A colorless, odorless, and tasteless toxic gas resulting from the incomplete combustion of carbon-containing fuels like natural gas, gasoline, or wood.

CP (Command Post): The designated location on the fireground from which the incident commander (IC) directs operations.

Crosslay (aka Preconnect): Firefighting hose (attack line) permanently connected to a pumper, typically arranged in bundles or stacks for easy deployment to the fire. Lengths of 150, 175, or 200 feet are common.

Defensive Operations: Fire attack from the exterior (e.g. applying water through windows). Used when offensive operations are deemed unsafe or inappropriate.

Division: With structure fires involving multiple floors, the word Division is inserted for the level being designated. Division 1 being the first floor, Division 2 the second, etc.

Exposure: A structure at risk of fire spread from an adjacent structure.

Engine (aka Pumper): A firefighting apparatus used to transport firefighters, water, and equipment to fire scenes and to pump water from a source such as a fire hydrant and deliver it to the fire. Pumpers carry 500 or more gallons of water in an internal tank, as well as hose lines, ladders, and other tools needed for firefighting and rescue.

Facepiece: See SCBA.

Federal-Q Siren: A powerful electro-mechanical siren made by Federal Signal and known for its distinct, high decibel, long-distance warning sound.

Flashover: The rapid, simultaneous ignition of all combustible materials within a room or space due to intense heat buildup.

Halligan Tool: A multipurpose tool for prying, twisting, punching, or striking. It consists of a claw (or fork), a blade (wedge or adze), and a tapered pick, which is especially useful in quickly breaching many types of locked doors.

IC (Incident Commander): The officer in charge of the overall operation of an emergency scene.

Irons: The "irons" consist of two tools that go hand in hand. The flat head axe and the Halligan bar, which are partially interlocked and held together with a strap for ease of carrying.

Knee-Walking: A method of moving forward on one knee, while using the other leg to "sound" the floor by placing one foot ahead to test for weakness or hazards.

Knox Box: A small, wall-mounted safe that holds building keys for emergency services use.

Master Stream Device: A high-flow firefighting nozzle used to deliver large volumes of water—typically 350 to 1,000 gallons per minute—to suppress fires. These devices are not intended for handheld operation due to their powerful water output and nozzle reaction force. In this book, the Stinger, Deck Gun, and Water Tower are all examples of master stream devices.

MDT (Mobile Data Terminal): Similar to a laptop, an MDT is a real-time link to the central dispatch agency, providing critical information about an emergency incident to responding units. An MDT can display the best routes to the scene, maps of the area, hydrant locations, building pre-plans, and hazardous materials information.

Nomex Hood: Fire resistant hood with full head and neck protection.

Offensive Operations: Interior fire attack (e.g. bringing hoselines into a structure to extinguish the seat of the fire).

Outriggers (and Base Plates): Outriggers are hydraulic legs that extend outward from a ladder truck to provide stability when the aerial is extended. Base plates are positioned under the outrigger legs to distribute the weight and prevent sinking.

Overhaul: The process of searching for hidden fire extension, soon after the fire is extinguished.

PAR (Personal Accountability Report): A request—typically from the IC—to confirm that all personnel assigned to a specific group (e.g. search or attack team) are accounted for.

PASS (Personal Alert Safety System): See SCBA.

PPV (Positive Pressure Ventilation): A technique used to remove smoke, heat, and other combustion products from a structure by using a fan to create higher pressure inside, forcing contaminated air out through an opening. In this novel, PPV fans are gas powered.

PenDot: The Pennsylvania Department of Transportation.

Preconnect: See Crosslay.

Primary Search: A rapid search for victims conducted during or prior to fire attack.

Salvage: The preservation of a building and contents from fire, smoke, or water damage.

Secondary Search: A meticulous search for victims who may have been missed during the primary search.

Siamese: A siamese valve combines multiple water sources into a single outlet (e.g. Two 3" hoselines feeding a building's standpipe system and attached at a wall-mounted siamese).

Short-Jacking: A situation where outriggers are partially extended on the non-working side of an aerial truck. Used when limited space, or obstructions, prevent full extension.

Rescue Truck (Heavy): A specialized vehicle and crew equipped for highly technical and hazardous rescues, often including vehicle extrication, structural collapse rescue, and rope rescue. They handle situations requiring heavy lifting, cutting, and specialized equipment not typically found on standard fire apparatus, such as hydraulic rescue tools (e.g. the Jaws of Life), winches, hi-lift jacks, and cutting torches. In this novel, Rescue-303 is the department's heavy rescue truck.

SCBA (Self-Contained Breathing Apparatus, or "BA"): Firefighters in this book use the MSA (Mine Safety Appliances) Model G-1 SCBA. Its main components are as follows:
- Carrier and Harness Assembly: Backplate, Cylinder Band, Shoulder Straps, and Waist Belt (with regulator keeper).

- Air Cylinder: Contains compressed air. Each cylinder in this book has an operating pressure of 4,500psi, with a rated service life of 45 minutes.
- 1st Stage Regulator: Reduces cylinder pressure to an intermediate level, which is in turn further reduced further by the 2nd Stage Regulator.
- 2nd Stage Regulator: Connects to the facepiece and maintains a positive airflow while reducing air pressure to a breathable level.
- Facepiece: A tight-fitting, full face mask that protects the face, mouth, and nose from heat, smoke, flames, and debris. The MSA G-1 facepiece includes a Heads-Up-Display (HUD) indicating cylinder pressure and alarm status.
- Control Module: The interface between the SCBA and the PASS Device. Positioned over the right shoulder strap, it features an analog gauge and an LED display to provide numeric cylinder pressure.
- Low Pressure Warning Bell (aka Audi-Bell): Sounds when approximately 35% of the SCBA's rated service life remains.
- PASS (Personal Alert Safety System): A device to signal distress or the need for immediate assistance. PASS devices monitor the body's movement and automatically trigger an alarm if the firefighter remains motionless for a set period (e.g., 30 seconds). In this novel, PASS devices are integrated into the MSA-G1 SCBA.
- Voice Amplifier: Housed in a speaker module on the left shoulder strap, it amplifies and clarifies speech from the facepiece.

Sides of a Building (as defined by the Incident Command System): The geographic designations of a building, beginning with the front of the building (Side-A), and working around the structure in a clockwise manner.
- Side-A (Alpha): The front of the building.
- Side-B (Bravo): The left side of the building.
- Side-C (Charlie): The back of the building.
- Side-D (Delta): The right side of the building.

Squad: Definitions vary, but for the purposes of this novel, a Squad is an SUV type vehicle used to transport personnel and equipment.

Special Services vehicle: Definitions vary, but for the purposes of this novel, Special Services 503 includes roof-mounted and portable lighting equipment, an air compressor for refilling SCBA at the scene, hazardous materials response gear, and an electrical generator.

Staging Area: A designated location where vehicles, personnel, and equipment are assembled and held awaiting assignment.
- Level 1 Staging: Typically located a block away from the scene. This positioning prevents congestion at the scene and allows the incident commander to assess the situation before deploying additional resources.
- Level 2 Staging: Used for larger or more complex incidents. Units report to a designated staging area further from the scene, where a staging officer organizes and ensures efficient deployment of personnel and equipment.

Standpipe: A network of pipes and hose connections installed throughout a building to provide water for firefighting. Standpipe systems allow firefighters to access water at different levels of a structure without needing to drag hoses up stairs.

Stinger: A portable master stream device manufactured by Elkhart Brass. It provides high water flow for firefighting operations. In this book it is used on the ground in portable mode and fed by 3" hose.

Supply Line: Hoselines used to transport water from a hydrant or other water source to a fire department pumper. In this book 5" large diameter supply line is used.

Supporting / Pumping a Hydrant: A procedure where a "supply" pumper is placed at the hydrant or other water source to assist the flow of water to the "attack" pumper at the scene by boosting pressure to maximize the volume of water available.

TIC (Thermal Imaging Camera): A handheld instrument that captures infrared radiation emitted by objects and converts it into a visible image. It detects heat, not light, allowing it to visualize temperature differences in a scene. A TIC allows firefighters to see through smoke, darkness, and other low-visibility conditions to help locate victims, identify fire hotspots, and improve situational awareness.

Truckies: Nickname for firefighters operating from a ladder truck or tower ladder.

VES (Vent, Enter, Search): A firefighting tactic used to quickly locate and rescue victims in a burning structure. VES is used when traditional entry points are blocked or when a quick rescue is needed before full suppression efforts begin.

Voice Amplifier: See SCBA.

Vollie: A term—sometimes derogatory—used to describe volunteer firefighters.

Water Tower Operation: Using a ladder truck or tower ladder in conjunction with a master stream device to deliver water to elevated areas of a structure for fire suppression.

Wye: A valve—usually controlled by two levers—used to divide one water source into two or more outlets (e.g. A 3" hoseline connected to a wye and divided into two 1-3/4" attack lines).

About the Author

Brian Colella, a lifelong resident of Western Pennsylvania, holds a PhD in Public and International Affairs from the University of Pittsburgh. Drawing on thirty-five years of firefighting experience, he writes fast-paced action tales that celebrate everyday heroes—ordinary people who rise to confront extraordinary challenges.

An avid runner, history buff, amateur photographer, classic rock fan, and 2nd generation Camaro enthusiast, he and his wife Karen can often be found exploring Pittsburgh's many parks, coffee shops, libraries, and bookstores.

Website: www.bacolella.com

Facebook: www.facebook.com/bacolellawrites

Instagram: www.instagram.com/b.a.colella.author

Linkedin: https://www.linkedin.com/in/brian-a-colella-phd-88404839